RULE OF TWELVE

BOOK 3

I0650617

REGENERATION

BRADLEY ALLEN

Published in Ireland 2024.

Published by TPAssist LIMITED.

Copyright © 2024 TPAssist LIMITED.

ISBN 978-1-9162074-8-6

[1]

TPAssist LIMITED
14 Penrose Wharf
Cork, T23 W440, Ireland

www.tpassist.com

To my loved ones, past and present,

who have been the real in my heart,

the space for my growth,

the honour in my life,

and the journey that has shaped me.

This book is dedicated to you, my guiding stars.

Chapter 1 – Hiding

1

"Where is your money?" Dukk asked as he turned in his seat to look at two of his crew.

The rest of Dukk's crew had left the cockpit shortly after coming out of the traverse. The A.I. driven process that moved a space craft from the orbit of a planet in one system to the orbit of a planet in another, light years away.

The view out of the windshield was of a featureless planet.

Sitting on the right side of the row of four seats behind Dukk, was Annee, a short, but strong and muscular woman in her late twenties. She had a sharp tongue and a cheeky grin. Her brown complexion with cool undertones, gave her a certain poise and style.

Annee was the backbone of his crew. She was the chief mate. Her skill in managing the day-to-day operations was second to none. She was more politically savvy than him, a useful skill in keeping everyone happy.

Dukk had known Annee for several years. She was his confidant. She had taught him plenty as he had her.

Sitting directly behind Dukk was Luna, the rig's apprentice, and long-range weapons expert.

Luna was in her early twenties, of average height, with brown hair and eyes that matched her brown complexion, which had warm, orange-red undertones. She was slim but strong and incredibly agile.

Dukk hadn't known of her skills with weapons, and specifically her sniper rifle, when he took her on as an apprentice nearly four months prior. Her deadly skills had been demonstrated on more than one occasion.

Owing to her interest in weapons, she had spent the last eleven weeks learning the finer details of the weapon systems on the intergalactic space craft they now occupied. A craft they affectionately referred to as a 'rig', owing to its connection with hauling fresh produce from Earth to all corners of the galaxy.

"What are you talking about?" Annee replied.

"Will they follow us or wait for reinforcements?" Dukk answered.

"They would be dead if they showed up here. The CDL is already recharging and will be ready any moment," Luna said.

"Where is your money, Dukk?" Annee asked having realised Dukk's question wasn't a question.

Dukk smiled.

Annee grinned too.

"My money is on them following us. It is their best option."

"How did you work that out?" Annee asked.

"Ok. So, they don't know what state we are in. We might be dead stick. If they followed and we were seriously damaged, we would be easy pickings for them."

"But we aren't incapacitated."

"No, but, Ann, they don't know that."

"Why not wait. If we can't attack, they would still be better off with waiting for reinforcements."

"Not necessarily. We might be able to repair."

"But they must know they will be dead if we are in a position to fire on them."

"That will still be the case either way. If we are capable, which we are, they are dead if they follow. However, if they wait for reinforcements, one of the vessels will have to traverse first. It would be very unlikely that the reinforcements would want to do that. That is especially true since they will know the remaining arrow failed in its mission. No, the reinforcements will insist that the remaining arrow goes first. The logic being that when we fire on the first vessel, we will show up on radar, and the reinforcement will then have its target. Job done."

"So, the remaining arrow is taken out either way."

"Yes, if we are able to fire on them."

"And that is why their best chance is following now, in the hope that we are unable to fire and before we can repair."

"Exactly."

"So why haven't we seen them yet?"

"While it wouldn't have taken them long to realise that we didn't have time to traverse to another system, they still need to find the right planet. This system has six planets. Granted there are only two of comparable size."

"We have a contact," Luna shouted. "Something just came out of traverse. Not far."

"Glad I didn't take that bet," Annee blurted.

"Identification?" Dukk shouted as he spun back around to his console.

"None. But the traverse signature matches that of an arrow," Luna replied.

"Permission to fire!"

The rig shook as the cannon fired. The space in front of them lit up. The hit had caused a huge explosion.

"Got'em!" Luna shouted.

"Shit! You must have hit a reactor!" Annee exclaimed.

"Initiating evasive manoeuvres," Dukk added. "I am going to see if I can get above the debris field."

"Brace for hard burn!" he then added into the rig wide comms.

The words were now echoing, in the heads of all those on board. This seamless form of communication was enabled via implants just behind each ear. As well as interpersonal communications, the rulers used the implants to monitor their activities. Dukk and the others had recently been introduced to further technology that allowed them to mask their conversations.

When the rig's main engines engaged, Dukk and those in the cockpit were pushed back into their seats.

"I leave the cockpit for a few minutes and you lot go about smashing things up again!" Marr said as she landed into her seat on Dukk's right.

Dukk laughed, then added, "I see you are feeling better."

"Yep. 'Morning sickness,' as Tieanna calls it, is so much worse just coming out of the traverse. The cocktail hit to put you out really knocks you about. So, what's next?"

"Good question. I think we need to review our plan."

Dukk then opened the comms to the rest of the crew.

"Circle up in five. Crew mess," he said.

"Shouldn't we stay here and watch for others?" Luna asked.

"No, I think we have a window to take stock," Dukk replied. "Ann, let's move the conn to the console in the crew mess. Do you want to head in there now and activate it. I will pass the conn over when I see it active."

"Yep," Annee replied as she left her seat.

Dukk smiled as he looked over at Marr, the rig's co-pilot, and his companion.

They had just discovered that Marr was pregnant with twins. A situation that would need further exploration. This was because until the same moment only thirty minutes ago, they both had thought they'd been sterilized like most at the age of ten.

4

Marr was two years his junior. She was of average height and medium build. She was toned and strong. She had fair complexion, with a tint of olive. Her hair was dark brown, and her eyes were light blue.

Marr had started out as the rig's inexperienced co-pilot. It was at the same time as Luna. Dukk wouldn't have typically considered her for his crew. She had tremendous technical qualifications and planet side pilot certificates, but no space time. At the time, he had been looking for a strong co-pilot who could already handle the demands of space. However, he was given no choice by the contracting agent. He was now glad of that.

As Dukk looked at her now, he observed her attractiveness. It was subtle. It was in the way her eyes smiled before her mouth.

Marr looked over at Dukk.

His smile melted her heart every time. The smile was warm, with a touch of seriousness. It was in the way the corners of his mouth curved to meet his petrol hazel eyes. Eyes that looked brown against his hair. She recalled the butterflies were there from the very moment they met.

He looked all his thirty-three years. His wide shoulders and big chest combined with his average height, gave him a stocky look. But she knew from the time together, that he was all muscle.

She pondered the things they had just learnt about his past and how it must be playing on his mind. Finding out who his father was. Finding out that the elite family heir he had recently befriended and worked for, was in fact his younger half-brother. And that by being older he was next in line to inherit their grandfather's fortune.

"We need to talk," Marr said once Luna had followed Annee.

"We do," Dukk replied as he stood up.

Marr stood up too.

Dukk reached over and drew her to him.

They kissed gently.

"But now, we'd better join the others," Dukk said when he pulled back from the kiss.

Marr nodded and smiled.

2

Five minutes later, Dukk was sitting at the head of a fourteen-seater table.

Sitting on his right was Marr. Luna was next to her. Annee was on his left.

On Luna's right was Bognath, the rig's head of security.

Bognath was a minder by profession and first travelled with the crew as a passenger. He then took a temporary role to help with security. Events since had put him on a more permanent footing.

During the time as a passenger, he had struck up a relationship with Luna that had strengthened over time.

Bognath's complexion was warm brown with orange-red undertones. He was slightly taller than average, had short black hair and brown eyes. In his mid-twenties, his look was tough and hard. A look that went well with his chosen profession.

Next to Bognath, was Mentor, the rig's generalist, and medical officer.

Mentor hid his forty-nine years well. He was tall, muscular and of dark brown complexion, with cool undertones. He had dark brown eyes and short black hair with wisps of grey.

Mentor had joined Dukk's crew with Marr and Luna. He was taken on as a generalist, owing to his experience with all aspects of keeping inter-galactic rigs moving. He also had medical qualifications. These skills had been put to good use.

In addition to being a resistance leader and Marr's advisor for the past thirteen years, Mentor had a chequered past as a covert operator. Some of which was still coming to light. The least of which was his involvement in Dukk's upbringing and the relationship with Dukk's mother.

On the right of Mentor was Tieanna, Dukk's mother.

Three hours ago, he and her had been reunited after nearly thirty years.

Tieanna was the childhood friend of Mentor's and his companion from when Dukk was four.

Her long hair was light brown with wisps of silver. She had fair complexion and she had dark brown hazel eyes.

On Dukk's left, next to Annee was Suzzona, the rig's chef and Annee's companion.

Suzzona was also an experienced haulier and a skilled pilot.

A recent addition to the crew, Suzzona had joined the escapades to escape arrest for a side hustle that was coming unstuck.

Suzzona was in her mid-thirties. She was of average height, fit, strong and well proportioned. She had fair complexion and short brown hair. Her brown eyes spoke of strong awareness of the reality of things.

Next to Suzzona, was Bazzer, the rig's chief engineer.

Bazzer was a stout and fit man in his late forties. He had fair complexion, dark green eyes and unkept long red hair that was often secured in a low ponytail.

Bazzer's skill as an engineer kept the space craft's complex array of systems humming.

Dukk had known Bazzer since his first day as an apprentice haulier, fifteen years earlier.

Bazzer had been instrumental in building Dukk's skill and confidence as a haulier. He had helped Dukk get to the position of captain well ahead of what was typical.

On Bazzer's left was Eleettra, the newest addition to the crew.

Eleettra had black hair, pale skin tones and blue eyes. She was in her early forties, and she had the stature of an enforcer.

The official reason for her being on the rig was as personal bodyguard to Tieanna, although Tieanna didn't know or would have wanted it.

Eleettra had been in and out of their lives over the past eleven weeks. Mostly in her role as a minder and security professional. She had also struck up a relationship with Bazzer, although they both kept the details well hidden.

The table they all now occupied, sat in the middle of a long and narrow space. That space had a series of doors running down either side. Between the doors were floor to ceiling interactive screens. Most were currently showing a view of the planet they now orbited. Known as the crew mess, this space was the main accommodation area for the crew.

The doors down either side of the table gave access to six double cabins. Three on each side. The forward cabin on the starboard side was the captain's cabin. It had its own ensuite. The rest of the crew shared two bathrooms situated in the aft section of the crew area.

In the most part, Dukk and Marr shared the captain's cabin now. Although officially Marr still also occupied the next cabin on the starboard side. The last cabin on the starboard side was Mentor's. It wasn't clear where Tieanna would be sleeping. For now, her lockers had been put in the guest suite. The first cabin on the port side was occupied by Annee and Suzzona. Luna and Bognath had the next cabin. Bazzer was in the final cabin on the port side. On the earlier occasion, Eleettra had used the double bunk room on the lower levels. It wasn't clear with her return if she and Bazzer would continue to hide their companionship.

Also at the back of the crew space was a kitchen and utility room. Next to it was an airlock that gave access to the upper hatch. Between the bathrooms and the cabins, on either side, were doors leading to ladder shafts. The open space also had a console and a sofa.

Just forward of the crew area was the guest cabin. A double cabin with its own ensuite and kitchenette. Between that and the cockpit was the upper lounge and g-seats for passengers. The rig was able to support nineteen passengers or extras, in addition to the six core-crew.

Aft of the crew mess was the upper section of the engine compartment. The engine compartment spanned the back third and the full height of the rig.

The rig measured just over sixty metres in length. The body of the craft was nine and a half metres tall and twelve and a half metres wide at its widest point. That was excluding the wings and tail. The tail added some six and a half metres to its height. The wings were thirty metres end to end. When sitting on its jacks, the clearance was near twenty-one metres.

The middle level of the rig housed six five-person transport pods. Which also served as escape pods in emergencies. They were contained in two bays. Three in each. One bay on each side. Each bay had a door that opened over the wing. The middle level also contained a large lounge, a three-bed med bay, two g-suit lockers and the port airlock door.

The lower level had a large gym, a utility room, storage, a small twin bunk cabin with a desk and ensuite, a kitchen and dining space for fourteen, two six-person bunk rooms with their own bathrooms, and further consoles and sofas. It also contained an airlock that served both a passenger ramp and hatch.

The three levels were serviced by a set of stairs towards the front of the rig and three ladder shafts. One towards the front and two on either side just forward of the engine compartment.

The rig's hold sat in the middle of the rig. It spanned the lower level and middle level. The floor of the hold was also a platform that could be lowered to enable loading of large robotic containers.

The engine compartment was accessed via large double doors from the back of the hold space and via smaller doors in each of the aft ladder shafts.

"I guess you've all gathered that we had an encounter with the second arrow," Dukk said to get the conversation started.

"Yes, it was hard to miss," Bazzer joked. "There will be no chance of interrogating them now."

"Did a single blast of the laser cannon really cause that?" Suzzona asked.

"Yep," Luna answered.

"Could that happen to us?"

"Absolutely," Eleettra interjected. "While twenty percent smaller than an interceptor like ours, all things considered, the arrow is the same. A direct hit on one of the three reactors would be catastrophic for us too. This is the downside of having the three TLM series ten reactors in the same space as the three enormously powerful TLM TH8 quad core, twenty-six-gauge hard burner thrusters, and their hard fuel tanks."

"Are we still in danger?" Suzzona asked, ignoring Eleettra's over the top answer.

"No, Suzzona," Dukk answered calmly. "I think we have some breathing space to repair and figure out where we should go next."

"What makes you think that?"

"We had two arrows on our tail after leaving Southern Cross. However, I agree with Mentor's suggestion that their presence in the same system was just coincidence. It was likely that they were part of emergency precautions or leap frogging contingency."

"But they attacked us without provocation!" Suzzona stated.

"Yes, but they could have got that instruction before the traverse."

"That's right," Annee added. "We saw signs of this before we traversed out of Southern Cross. It showed that they were aware that Tieanna had been freed."

"But that means they are still hunting us," Luna countered.

"It does, but only those two arrows showed up. That means the rest of the mammoth ring went somewhere else," Dukk answered.

"How can we be sure of that?"

"They would have appeared instead of the two arrows if this system was their destination. We also know that the ring is always on the move. It rarely stays in a main system for more than twelve hours."

"I guess we would have noticed five massive disc shaped space stations suddenly appearing out of traverse to form a ring around the planet," Bazzer joked.

"Yes, one mammoth is hard to miss, you'd have to be a moron to miss five," Bognath added with a laugh.

"But how does that give us breathing space, Dukk?"

"Suzzona, there were only two arrows. Both were smashed to pieces. There is no relay in any part of this system so they can't have sent any messages. The mammoth ring won't know we are here."

"Could that first arrow have gone for help?"

"We know the CDL hit it," Luna interjected. "The explosion was visible. Granted, it wasn't clear if the reactor got hit."

"It wouldn't make a difference," Eleettra added. "A direct hit with a CDL still rips the guts out of any rig. I can't imagine it was in any shape capable of a traverse. Perhaps they are holding it together, but it won't be going anywhere. And, if they don't have solid propulsion control, they will fall out of orbit and crash into the planet."

"It is unlikely there was anything left of it. The other arrow came after us immediately. They didn't offer any assistance," Annee added.

"They could just not care about each other," Bognath noted.

"None of this really matters with respect to our situation," Dukk said. "Even if they were able to traverse and go for help. It will be at best another eight hours before they traverse and then another nine before they get back. This gives us breathing space."

"Dukk is right," Marr said confidently.

The confidence of the statement drew the attention of them all.

Even Dukk looked intrigued.

Marr was still in conflict over what she alone knew about what had happened. She felt it best to share some of it to appease the conflict.

"I might be able to shed some light on this," she said after a further moment of reflection.

They all waited.

"Bartiamos was right about what he suspected was in the octet in the centre of mammoth one."

"How do you know this?" Dukk asked in a tone that had a touch of concern.

"While you were getting Tieanna out of the cell block on the left side of the octet, I found another way into the right side. I guess Bartiamos' crew lacked my technical skills to get around the DNA enabled mantrap."

Marr did her best to hide the half-truth of the last statement. Dukk saw through it. But he said nothing.

"Not the time," he said to himself.

Tieanna wasn't convinced either.

"This is surprising," she blurted.

After a moment of looking at Marr, she continued.

"The Venefica are very protective of their inner sanctum. Access is for Venefican blood lines only. Only those of Venefican blood lines can access the lounge space. Not the staff or sentinels. It is a panic room of sorts, should the mammoth get compromised. Of note, is that the apartment on the right side of the octet is only for Magnum Reginae and her daughter. I have heard that the apartment on mammoth one has a computer system from which the security of the mammoth ring is managed. It is for this reason that no-one else is

12

allowed in there. Dukk could enter the lounge on the left because he has my blood. Venefican blood. But you found another way in."

"I did," Marr said bluntly working even harder to hide the lie and an increasing sense of dread.

"The queen and her daughter. Blood lines?" Marr reflected to herself.

"What did you find in there, Marr?" Luna asked with enthusiasm, also having sense Marr's discomfort.

"The luxury apartment looked recently used. There is also a data centre, as Tieanna suggests."

"What kind of data centre?"

"I suspect it is storage for video-based monitoring."

"How do you know that?"

"Because of this," Marr answered.

4

Marr pulled a palm size disc from her pocket and held it up for all to see.

"What is it?" Suzzona asked.

"My best guess is that it is a receiver and projector. It doesn't seem to have much storage. It has a buffer, that it appears to write over. I think it's designed to be in direct contact with the network to access the recordings stored in the data centre."

"Where did you get it?"

"I stole it from the data centre."

"What!" Dukk blurted.

Luna laughed.

"What's funny?" Dukk asked having only slightly regained his emotions. "You find it funny that Marr went messing about with that data centre that we suspected had a booby-trapped dark matter containment unit."

"No, that concerns me too. I was laughing at your reaction. Your emotions are off the chart."

Dukk blushed. He had to admit she was right. Something had changed in him since learning he was to be a father.

"What does it project?" Mentor asked in a calm tone to help bring some focus to the discussion.

"I will show you," Marr answered.

Marr then placed the disc on the table in front of her. A projection appeared in the air above it. The image was a fuzzy projection of light. A message was blinking in the middle of the fuzz. It read, 'Waiting for connection!'.

"It doesn't look that useful," Suzzona said in jest.

"I think it is because there is no relay at this location. We have no connection to the outside world. When I first accidently activated it, I saw Craig and Emeelie. The next time I saw the inside of an arrow. Then I saw the inside of the octet apartment."

"What do you mean when you say that 'you saw'?" Luna asked.

"It is like I was looking at a scene through the eyes of another."

"Like you were in their head, looking out?"

"Yes. I heard voices too."

"When was this?" Dukk asked.

"The first scene was when I was in the octet. Then just before Craig and Emeelie joined us. The final scene was just before we traversed after Craig and Emeelie left."

"Was the last time when you were delayed getting to the cockpit."

"Yes."

"Do you think you were looking through the eyes of the same person?"

"Yes."

14

"Any ideas who?"

"Yes, I think it was the queen."

"You've been snooping on the Venefica Magnum Reginae. The queen of the Veneficans?" Suzzona blurted.

"I believe so," Marr answered.

Silence filled the room as they all stared at the fuzzy blinking message.

Eleettra broke the silence.

"Marr, you said it has a buffer. Is there a way to see what is currently stored?"

"Good idea. Let me see," Marr answered as she reached into the projection.

After a moment, the image changed.

"Looks like you are right, Eleettra. This is where the buffer starts. This is the view through the door into the data centre. You can see two cradles. I took this disc from there. The other cradle was empty. The first voice I think is the queen. The second voice, I think belongs to her daughter. Let's play it forward."

The projection played. The image stayed basically the same. A voice filled the room.

"She has been in here! Look the second disc is gone now too. Look at the attempts to cover her tracks."

"But how? There are no signs of anyone attacking us or breaking in?" said the second voice.

"She probably got help from Bartiamos' dim-witted repair crews. Nothing we can do about that. We need to keep him onside for now! Anyway, the how is not important at this moment."

"Why?"

"Because she has just made a huge mistake. Taking that second disc out of here is the opportunity that we've been waiting for. It is time to get rid of her and those discs."

"But without the discs, we can't access this data centre. We will still be locked out of our funds, the weapons systems on these mammoths, and the incubation databases."

"If the discs stop connecting to the network, the locks on this door will automatically reset. We'll have access again. We won't need the discs."

"But the reset waits for six months after it receives the last signal."

"We have made do for over thirty years. We can wait another six months. It must be done. She is somewhere here now. In orbit on one of the craft up here."

"If she is here, we can get the mammoth ring back to earth!"

"Unless we can get into this data centre, we can't be assured that the defences won't fire on the ring."

"What if it was a lie?"

"We've been through this before. We can't take the chance that she was lying when she said Earth defences would attack the mammoth ring if it ever came near it. No, we need to get into the data centre and take back control of the citadels. This needs to be done before we bring the mammoth ring anywhere close to Earth. She must go! We must take her out now!"

"We can't just have our arrows and interceptors fire missiles at them all."

"No, we can't. Not with Craig's flotilla up here. That would surely put us at war with the Atesoughton family. We can't afford a war with them. They are our biggest contributor."

"What do we do?"

"Here is what I see. Craig would be foolish to be directly involved in this. Clearly, he is complicit in enticing the mammoth ring here with that bogus meeting. He had his reasons. But he knows that entering our mammoth and interfering directly to retrieve that woman, would be no different than firing a missile. No! Others are supporting her.

16

She got help like before. Perhaps they are part of his flotilla. On one of the arrows or interceptors. The flotilla mobilised the moment we reached orbit this morning. That was nearly nine hours ago. However, the flotilla will use normal routes, so it won't traverse for another three hours. The scoundrels that are helping her will go somewhere unmonitored. They will traverse soon. Perhaps any moment."

"We don't have much time."

"No, we don't. But our scouts and leapfrog arrows are still counting down. The first wave will traverse any moment. We'll message the captains. If they see a single arrow or interceptor when they arrive in the unmonitored system, they are to fire. No quarter."

"What if we are wrong?"

"No one will know."

"What if they manage to get missiles away too and take out our arrows? How will we know it is done?"

"Let's mobilise further scouts to check. Now put your mask back on. You remind me of her."

The projection returned to the fuzzy message that suggested the device was waiting for a connection.

"Wow!" Luna blurted.

"Wow indeed," Annee added.

5

Dukk was stunned. He wasn't sure what to say. He had more questions than answers. Most he knew weren't for this open forum. Marr was watching him. She was of similar mind.

"As well as generating many more questions, this confirms our suspicions," Mentor said in a calm voice. "We also know that we won't see any further arrows for the next eight hours. Not before three-thirty a.m. And we are orbiting a planet that is away from where they'll be.

17

It is unlikely they will come here, but we should prepare for that. I suggest we defer further analysis for the time being."

"Agreed," Bazzer concurred. "First, we must stabilize the rig. I want to get suited up and take the drones out to inspect the hull. We know that first blast caused a rupture. I want to make sure there isn't any damage to the heat shields before we attempt a deorbit."

Dukk was glad of the shift in direction. He nodded a silent thank you to both Bazzer and Mentor.

"So where do we go after the rig is stable?" Suzzona asked.

"Back to the system where you rescued me," Tieanna said quietly.

"Back into the jaws of the enemy?"

"The mammoth ring doesn't return to the same place for months. It is the one place we know they won't be."

"So, we return to Southern Cross?" Luna suggested.

"What about scouts and other craft that weren't in traverse count down?" Annee asked.

"They will have gone with the mammoths or will have traversed by the time we get back there," Dukk answered.

"What do we do when we get there?" Suzzona asked.

"Any repairs we can't do out here," Bazzer answered.

"And after that? What is our course?"

"Craig suggests we make for Earth," Eleettra said.

"Why would we go to Earth?" Tieanna asked.

"To keep you safe."

"That is absurd! There is too much to accomplish to be worried about being safe."

"What then?"

"We do something useful."

"I've heard that before," Dukk said as he looked over at Mentor.

Mentor smiled.

"Tieanna, what do you suggest?" Marr asked.

"How long was I locked up for?"

"It must have been about twelve weeks."

"Seriously. Wow. Let's have a look."

Tieanna interacted with her wrist wraps and then flicked an image towards the table projector.

A complex mind map appeared in the air before them. Some of the mind map nodes were red in colour.

"This is my master map of the trafficking rings. It includes anomalies in mercenary activities. We need to figure out where the next accumulation of girls might be. We go there and rescue them."

"Wow!" Mentor blurted. "That puts my efforts to shame."

"Yes, my network of students has been very useful for collecting data."

"Students of your training academies within elite households. Like where Emeelie went?" Luna asked.

"Yes, exactly like where Emeelie went. Except they are not my training academies. They are run independently. I may have unwittingly created the template that they followed. But I am not involved in their running. Mind you, the students do see me as some sort of guru."

Tieanna said the last part of the sentence with a chuckle.

"Let me update the timeframes," Tieanna said as she interacted with the map once more.

The image changed. The colour of the nodes changed. A few of the red nodes change to a grey colour. A few nodes went orange, and one node went red.

"There! That is the next possible party!" Tieanna exclaimed.

"Where is that?" Annee asked as she stood up to take a closer look at the map.

After a moment Annee stood back.

"It is a moon near planet Abrolhos in HDK85."

"That's it," Tieanna blurted. "They call it the Abrolhos Island Resort. It is a small resort, like New Katoomba in the Atesoughton cluster. So, that is our destination."

Dukk looked around at his crew. The expressions were mostly that of confusion. Some direction was needed.

"Here is what I suggest. We inspect the rig. Then we load up the DMD and make for Southern Cross. We'll run stealth so that any new arrows don't notice us during the countdown. In Southern Cross we will complete any further repairs before making a track towards HDK85. That will take us at least three days. We'll have plenty of time to explore all this new information and flesh out our plans. How does that sound?"

Dukk's suggestion was met with nods.

Chapter 2 – Introspection

1

"Well, time for the E.V.A.," Bazzer stated as he stood up. "Who else is up for a spacewalk?"

"Before we split, I want to revisit the watch roster," Dukk interjected. "We must be more cautious. And the crew size has grown since the current watch roster was put in place."

"Do you have a new approach in mind?" Annee asked.

"No, I had only got as far as thinking the old approach was oriented around hauling. There was more predictability. The timing of traverses and the like."

"We still need to cover all hours during a passage."

"Yes. And I still think four-hour watches on twelve-hour rotation and three teams. But we need to be able to react fast. That means flight and weapons skills on all watches."

"You, Mentor and Suzzona, have the most experience at the helm. So, you three need to be split across the teams."

"Yes. And Luna is primary on weapons. Marr has been mirroring Luna's learning. Mentor also has knowledge there. They also need to be split across the three teams."

"Can you do both, Mentor?" Annee asked.

"No, that wouldn't be practical."

"I am weapons trained on interceptors and arrows," Eleettra added.

"I put dibs on Luna. No offence Eleettra," Suzzona blurted.

"None taken."

"So, that would be Dukk and Marr; Suzzona and Luna; and Mentor and Eleettra? Does that work?" Annee summarised.

"That works for me," Dukk answered.

There were nods from Marr, Suzzona, Luna, Mentor and Eleettra.

"Does that make me redundant?" Bazzer asked with a laugh.

"No, you'd better keep an eye on Eleettra," Annee said with a chuckle.

She then winked at Eleettra.

"Just like you will keep an eye on Suzzona!" Bazzer said with a laugh.

"That's fine by me," Eleettra said cheekily.

"And me," Suzzona added.

"If Bognath lines up with us too, that leaves Dukk and Marr a little light handed," Annee added.

"Up until this moment, we've managed just fine as a pair," Marr said with a grin.

"You have indeed," Luna noted.

She then added, "Besides, you are now a team of four!"

That comment got a laugh from everyone.

"Will you be up to it?" Annee asked in a more serious tone.

That got everyone's attention.

"Now that you are pregnant?" she added.

"Yes, Annee," Tieanna answered calmly as she turned to look at Marr. "You are going into the second trimester. For the next twelve weeks the bump will be mostly unnoticeable to most. After that, it might start getting in the way."

"You mean when she is," Luna said as she made a movement with her hands to suggest she had a big and bulging stomach.

"Yes."

"Will I still be able to be on this rig?" Marr asked.

"That is something that will need to be reviewed closer to the time."

"Oh."

"Who goes on which watch time?" Mentor asked to move the conversation on.

Annee sat forward.

"I suggest that Dukk and Marr keep the six a.m. until ten a.m. and six p.m. until ten p.m., as it is the best watch hours, and they have the smallest team."

"Yep, I agree," Dukk said.

"I'm good with the graveyard if Mentor and Eleettra don't have any issue," Bazzer stated.

Neither objected.

"Great, so that puts the rest of us on the middle watch from ten a.m. to two p.m. and ten p.m. to two a.m.," Annee summarised.

Dukk nodded.

"So, Bazzer, we part ways at last. It will be odd not pranking you during the watches and beating you in wall ball during our downtime," Luna said with a giggle.

"Rubbish!" Bazzer interjected. "I let you win."

Luna laughed harder.

"Perhaps you'll find time to play against each other in the cross overs," Eleettra suggested.

"What about a new competition, like the one you had on the Dinatha?" Suzzona said.

"Great idea," Bazzer replied.

"How would it work?" Luna asked.

"What about a round robin of doubles? The hold is plenty big enough," said Suzzona.

"Who would be on the teams?"

"We could draw them from a hat."

"Who's in?" Luna asked.

A positive response was gotten from all but Mentor and Tieanna. They gracefully declined the invitation.

A few moments later Annee revealed a random list of pairs in the air in the middle of the table.

Laughter broke out on seeing the list.

The loudest laugh came from Bazzer and Luna. They were paired together.

The other pairs were Marr and Annee, Dukk and Suzzona, and Bognath and Eleettra.

With the point scoring process and match sequence agreed, Bazzer stood and addressed the group.

"Now can I go for a walk?" he asked.

"Yep, and I'll manage the airlocks and drones from the console here," Dukk said as he nodded and stood up.

"I'll come," Bognath added.

"Great, let's go. We will let you know when we are ready so you can kill the DMD," Bazzer said as he headed for the door at the front of the crew mess.

"Tieanna, are you hungry?" Suzzona asked as she stood up.

"Yes, I am."

"I know that Dukk and Marr haven't eaten since breakfast. I have some beef lasagne ready for them. Would you like some of that too?"

"Absolutely. Let me help you with it."

At the console, Dukk organised a series of panels in the air. They showed various video feeds from the internal and external cameras.

"We might still see some activity before we traverse," Mentor said from his seat at the table.

"Yes," Dukk answered. "We'll keep the stealth running and stay out of sight. If anything shows up. I suggest we avoid them. They will only see our signature as we traverse. By then it will be too late. We will be in the wind."

"Good. Also, we are going to need a cover story for Southern Cross."

"Yes, we will. Any ideas?"

"No, not yet."

"I have an idea," Eleettra said from the table where she was still sitting.

They turned and looked over.

"Craig is always on the lookout for local art and crafts to decorate his many properties. We could claim we have returned to pick up something he saw."

"Like that he changed his mind and sent us back?" Marr commented.

"Yes."

"How would it work?"

"When we get there, we go shopping. While doing so, we drop hints to staff. We also mention it to anyone we encounter in bars. We make it sound like we are all very important for getting the honour of returning on the errand. If we sound arrogant and self-important when we say it, it will be ignored mostly. But it might be enough to start a rumour and that will deflect any attention."

"Won't it come unstuck if it gets back to Craig and Emeelie?"

"I will message Emeelie when we are in contact with a relay. She will hold up the story on her side so that it checks out if anyone goes poking."

"That sounds like a great idea."

"Yes, it does," Mentor commented. "It might even work for our return to Abrolhos and then eventually Earth. We could say the items we buy are for a villa on Earth."

"Perfect. Great idea, Eleettra," Dukk added.

Eleettra smiled.

2

"How is this possible?" Marr asked as she poked at the plate of lasagne in front of her.

Marr, Tieanna, Mentor and Dukk were sitting at the table. The rest of the crew were elsewhere.

"Do you mean the pregnancy?" Tieanna responded.

"Yes."

"Mentor?"

"You were selected to help move forward with the resistance plans."

"Is this the grander plans that I was to ask Teacher about?"

"Yes, the part that I know of."

"There is more."

"That is my suspicion."

"So, what exactly is the part that you know?"

"That you and Dukk would have a child together."

"Was that your mission?"

"Yes, part of it."

"Who gave you that mission?"

"Teacher."

"What do you mean by 'part of it'?"

"I was tasked to help create the right conditions for that to happen."

"Right conditions?"

"Put you two in the same space at the right time, so that you would come together under the right circumstances."

"What do you mean by that?"

"So that it wasn't just a chance meeting, but one that came after a period of building a relationship. So that the child would be conceived in a union of love. So that the child would be cherished as a miracle and not rejected or despised."

Marr and Dukk both blushed.

"So, you all being here on the rig was never about the assassination of Craig's father, I mean our father?" Dukk asked to deflect his emotions.

"No, it wasn't," Mentor replied.

"Or shutting down the trafficking?"

"Not directly."

"How much of it was orchestrated?"

"Pretty much all of it."

"More than just the attack on the Bluilda?"

"Yes. Rachelle getting retirement early. The beef contract. Larinette getting the offer for second in command on the Plinthat. Wallace's actions. It all was carefully planned."

"And how about how Thumpol treated me. His desire to have me killed so he could get my rig?"

"No, that was him. He saw an opportunity."

Dukk felt embarrassed. He pushed the feelings aside as best as he could.

"There have been a few close calls," he blurted when the emotions spiked again.

"It can't have been that well planned," he added.

"Well, ok, so there were a few curve balls. But such is the nature of chaos."

This news, on top of what he had learnt earlier, was making Dukk angry. He felt used. He wanted to shout. He turned to look at Marr. She was looking disappointed also. But her expression showed something else. Something that she wasn't sharing. His instinct told him to let it go, for now.

"But what about the sterilisation during the test?" Dukk asked after a moment of further reflection.

"I intervened in your sterilisation. I gather someone intervened in Marr's."

"But how?" Marr interjected as she sat up. She immediately checked herself. Her emotions were all over the place.

Mentor sat forward and spoke in a gentle manner.

He said, "For women the sterilisation isn't what you would expect. Yes, a concoction of meds is administered at the age of ten during the test. But the potency is varied. For labourers, the mix is strong. It is semi-permanent. It causes metabolic changes in the fluid around the eggs. That prevents the sperm from getting into them. For hostesses the mix is less. It reduces the chances of pregnancy but doesn't eliminate it. In all cases with additional meds the process can be reversed. I guess the medical protocol designers, realised the risk to humanity if not managed properly."

"So, I had a weak mix."

"Yes, or none."

Marr let that sit for a moment.

"Is it the same for men," Dukk asked.

"No, men undergo vasectomies," Mentor answered.

"That is why you were in the medical room when I took the test?"

"Yes, and to plant your name as Tieanna had wished."

"I don't understand. I had slits on either side of my testicles as per the other boys. I was sore too!"

"I took over the procedure. I made the slits to make it appear that the sterilisation took place. But I didn't cut the vas deferens. I didn't complete the vasectomy."

"But you said that you were in the medical room during the test to prevent a great travesty."

"Yes, the travesty of not having children. A wonderful gift that is denied to most under the Rule of Twelve."

Silence fell.

"What happens now?" Marr asked after a few moments of reflection.

"What do you want to have happen?" Tieanna asked.

Marr and Dukk looked at each other.

They smiled and a tear formed.

They knew the answer.

"We become a family," Dukk said emotionally.

Marr nodded.

"This is wonderful. Now we have a new mission," Tieanna said with a little emotion.

They turned to look at her.

Tieanna then looked at Marr.

"We must ensure you and your babies are nourished. Eat!"

They all laughed.

"We're ready," came a squawk on the comms. It was Bazzer.

"You'd better finish that before I turn off the DMD," Dukk said to Marr.

"I don't really feel like it. Perhaps I'll try something when we finish watch," Marr answered.

Dukk nodded as he stood and went over to the console.

The port airlock video feed showed Bazzer and Bognath in their helmets and propulsion packs. Two medium size drones were sitting on the floor of the airlock.

"Shutting down the DMD. Brace for zero-g," Dukk broadcasted to his crew.

Moments later his body felt lighter. The dishes on the table started to lift into the air.

Dukk clicked his boots into the floor to keep himself secure.

"Opening port door," Dukk then announced into the comms of Bazzer and Bognath.

With the door open, Dukk activated the drones and watched them lift off the floor and dash out the doorway.

Bazzer and Bognath weren't far behind them.

The external video feeds showed the drones zooming over the hull in a crisscross pattern. Bazzer and Bognath could be seen heading towards the underbelly to inspect the rupture.

"Something is bothering me," Marr uttered idly as she watched Dukk monitor the console.

He turned around. Mentor and Tieanna also returned their gaze back to Marr.

"Our focus is on stopping the trafficking. What about the incubators?"

"What about them, Marr?" Tieanna asked in a gentle tone.

"That they are a lie. That they are a cover for the abuse of young women. Our population doesn't come from labs as we are taught. It comes from elite men impregnating hostesses. And in addition to being done without the hostess's awareness of their fertile state, they are murdered after the birth. Some don't even give birth. They are murdered once it is discovered that they are pregnant. All done under the guise of preventing overpopulation of the planet for the greater good."

By the time she'd finished speaking, Marr was red in the face. Her tone had got louder as she spoke. By the end, she was almost shouting.

Mentor sighed.

Tieanna blushed.

Dukk sat forward. He kicked himself. He had forgotten about that. He had got caught up in finding Tieanna.

Marr checked her emotions. She counted to ten in her head. She inhaled and exhaled deeply to regain control.

The normal noises of the rig filled the room as everyone sat quietly processing Marr's outburst.

Mentor was the first to speak again. He spoke slowly. The tone of his voice had a hint of sadness.

"When I first heard of this truth, I got very angry. I wanted to shout it to the world. I wanted to use my level seven privilege to broadcast the truth."

"Why didn't you?" Marr asked as she sat forward.

"Because I knew it wouldn't change anything. I'd simply reveal myself and be disappeared. All that I'd worked for would be lost. Nothing would change."

"How so?"

"The indoctrination of the masses is strong. So is the ability to communicate any narrative the elites choose. A story would have been spun and most would have hardly paid any attention to anything I tried to share."

"That's fair, but what happened to that anger?"

"I channelled it to where I could make a difference."

"Stopping the trafficking?"

"Yes."

"But things are different now, we have this rig. We have connections. What is stopping us doing something about it now?"

"Teacher."

"What about her?"

"She reassured me that she is working on it and will act when the time is right."

"So, we are back to Teacher's grander plans. Which we know little."

Mentor nodded.

"Mentor, there is something else I don't understand," Marr said after a further moment of reflection.

"What is that?"

"You said that you knew little of the Veneficans. And yet, Tieanna is one. How is that possible?"

"That is my fault," Tieanna blurted. "I hid it all from him. I was embarrassed by it."

Marr sat back again. She quietened her mind. She realised this news would require reflection. She needed to talk to Dukk alone. Especially given what she had overheard before traversing out of Southern Cross and what had really happened in the octet.

Dukk watched her now. There was something else in her expression. Something further to explore when they were alone.

Twenty minutes later, the drones, Bazzer and Bognath were back in the airlock. The inspection was complete.

"How are we looking?" Dukk asked on the comms, as he interacted with the airlock controls.

Bazzer looked up at the ceiling. He knew Dukk would be watching them.

"The heat shields look fine. I think they will hold up during de-orbit. I'll go over the drone data in a little more detail just to be sure. You can load the DMD and get us underway again."

"Great," Dukk answered.

"You ready?" Dukk asked as he turned to look at Marr.

She was sitting on the couch behind him.

She nodded as she took a few deep breaths.

Dukk activated the DMD. A tingle ran through them as the A.I. made the connection with the dark matter and started the countdown to the traverse.

Marr took a few more deep breaths. The DMD start up wasn't as bad as coming out of the traverse, but it still turned her stomach. She held it together.

"The DMD is suggesting the traverse will happen at eight fifty-five a.m.," Dukk said after a moment.

"Excellent," a voice said from the direction of the table.

It was Annee. She was in her g-suit and looked refreshed. Suzzona was with her. She was also suited up.

"If you want to end your watch now, Suzzona and I can cover things. You two must be exhausted."

"Annee, that would be wonderful," Marr replied as she stood up.

"Yes, it would, Ann. Thank you," Dukk added.

They were indeed exhausted. After a quick shower they crashed into bed and were asleep instantly.

3

With the recent events, Marr and Dukk had decided to forgo their usual exercise routine ahead of watch. They opted for a little more sleep. They set an alarm for five forty to give themselves enough time to shower and get into their g-suits.

"How are you feeling?" Dukk asked as he and Marr did their g-suit crosscheck.

"The rest and shower really helped, and now I am hungry."

"Let's stay in the crew mess and have some breakfast."

"Good plan."

In the crew mess, Marr and Dukk found Mentor on his own at the console. The flight plan was visible. It showed the DMD countdown. Three hours remained until the traverse to Southern Cross.

"Anything to report," Dukk asked as he approached.

Seeing Mentor reminded Dukk of the anger that he felt when he realised that he had been the subject of an elaborate plan. He decided now wasn't the time to confront it.

"Nope. It is all quiet."

"The arrow? The scout?"

"Yes. A craft showed up near four thirty. We assumed it was the arrow. It stayed for an hour and then left. We think it was scanning the debris. We tracked its arrival point and trajectory. And we made sure we kept out of sight."

"Was it using stealth?"

"Yep. It showed up on arrival out of traverse and just before leaving again."

"But it didn't see us."

"It didn't behave as such."

"Where do you think it is now?"

"Perhaps visiting other planets and moons in this system."

"That sounds reasonable. Will it return?"

"Maybe."

"Do you want to get some rest. We can take it from here."

"Yep, that would be great."

"Bazzer and Eleettra?"

"They are in the cockpit running weapon usage simulations."

"Marr, if you want to hang here, I'll go and let them know we have the conn."

"Perfect," Marr replied.

Dukk made his way through the passenger seating area and opened the cockpit door.

"Nope, that'll just puncture one of our reactors," Bazzer could be heard saying.

He and Eleettra were sitting in the two seats on the left, in the second row.

"How is it going?" Dukk asked.

"Not good," Eleettra replied as she looked around.

"How so?"

"We are running offensive simulations where there are multiple assailants. Bazzer is trying to work out how we reduce the chances of being blown up. So many of the evasive manoeuvres just result in a less than ideal outcome."

"Oh."

"Avoidance still feels like the best strategy," Bazzer added.

"Food for thought."

"Yes, it is."

"Mentor tells me that we had a visitor."

"Yep. An hour of watching and waiting. Then it left. By your presence, I take it that you are on and have the conn?"

"Yes, Bazzer. You and Eleettra are at your leisure again."

"Great! Time for some exercise," Bazzer said as he flicked away the panels.

Ten minutes later, Marr and Dukk were together and alone again. They were sitting at the table in the crew mess having some breakfast.

"Can I ask you something?" Dukk said between mouthfuls.

"Sure."

"Last night when we were talking with Mentor and Tieanna. I was annoyed over the planning that has taken place to bring us together. When I looked at you, you appeared calm. Like it wasn't a surprise."

Marr nodded and smiled. She was happy that they had this level of connection.

"Why?" he asked.

"I overhead them talking just before Craig and Emeelie arrived."

"When you went down to tell them that we were about to do a hatch-to-hatch docking manoeuvre?"

"Yes."

"What did you overhear?"

"Tieanna was learning from Mentor that the resistance has implemented a fantasy she had made up when she was a teenager."

"What was the fantasy?"

"Her fantasy drew on a Mesopotamian origin story. It was where Marduk defeats Tiamat and her warlord, Kingu, using Imhullu, the wind weapon. She fantasised that Marduk could be reformed by joining the best of the masculine with the best of the feminine. That union would then defeat evil and bring back balance. It drew on the foreshadowing already established in the labels used by the resistance for the five citadels. She theorised that you'd just need to interrupt the sterilisation process for a key and well-placed man and woman. You would then name them and then let the mythology carry it forward."

"You and I, and this rig?"

"That is what it would appear."

"So, your name, Marr, and my name, Dukk, make Marduk?"

"I guess."

"What was meant by the foreshadowing?"

"The five citadels are named Kuedia, Inquis, Norline, Genda and Utopiam. These names were used in mockery by those defeated during the war. The labels were later adopted by the overlords. Clearly, they didn't get the connection. If you take the first letter from each of those titles, it spells Kingu. The name of Tiamat's warlord that is defeated by Marduk using Imhullu, the wind weapon."

35

Dukk laughed.

"This is preposterous," he added.

"Yes, it is nuts," Marr laughed. "And it gets more interesting when you look deeper at the origin story."

"How?"

"So, some depictions suggest Marduk defeats Tiamat and creates the world from her body."

"I am missing something. I see our names and this rig. I also see the citadels in this. But I don't see Tiamat."

"I might have a line on that. So, during the war, the last cities to fall before the overlords escaped to the citadels, were given code names by the rebels. The code names were Tangoalfa, Indiasierra, Alfadelta, Mikelima, Alfaecho and Tangoecho."

"And that spells Tiamat."

"Exactly."

"So, to fulfil Tieanna's fantasy, you and I, and this rig will bring down the citadels and those that held those last cities."

"I guess."

Dukk laughed even harder.

Marr smiled.

4

"There is more, isn't there," Dukk stated after a moment of further reflection.

"Yes."

"What?"

"Tieanna only told that fantasy to one other. Years ago."

"Who?"

"She didn't say. But they did talk about Teacher."

"Tieanna doesn't know Teacher."

"Yes, that is what we understand."

"So?"

36

"Mentor mentioned that Teacher shared the Marduk story with him and other resistance leaders. She also gave him the instructions to intervene in your sterilisation and to bring us together."

"Yes, we know this from him. What is new?"

"They had a brief discussion about Teacher. They discussed the possibility that Teacher is the person that Tieanna shared her fantasy with. They talked about Teacher's looks and age. Tieanna said the age fits but not the looks."

"I am still missing something."

"Yes, you are."

Marr reached into a pocket and pulled out the disc from the octet.

She looked at it with a cautious expression.

Dukk looked at the disc and then at Marr.

"You held something back when you shared the story last night!" Dukk blurted on realising what he was seeing in her expression.

"Yes."

"What did you hold back? What really happened in the octet?" he asked.

"Just after you went in through the left door, I had to take cover from some sentinels. I accidently activated the entrance door panel and fell into the mantrap."

"And you didn't die."

"Clearly."

"That is how you got in. The mantrap rumours are rubbish. They aren't DNA controlled after all."

"No. Well, I think they may still be."

"Why?"

"You have Tieanna's DNA, and she is Venefican. That makes you of Venefican descent too. Your DNA is the way you got through the mantrap. Teacher must have known you were of Venefican descent. Her instructions specifically mentioned that only you must enter the octet."

"Yes, she must have known Tieanna was of Venefican descent."

"How could have she? She hasn't met Tieanna."

"I am even more confused."

"I think the mantrap does work by analysing DNA in your breath as suspected. The oxygen was removed three times and then the doors opened."

"Doors? Only the door on the left opened for me. Did you say doors?"

"Yes, the door on the right opened too."

"What did you do?"

"Well, I was curious. I had seen you enter the left door, so I went right."

"But you were back in the corridor outside the mantrap when Tieanna and I came through."

"Yes. I got your message and bolted. I was just back through as you entered the mantrap."

"Someone has been messing with your path as with mine. Your mother must have been Venefican too. Just like Tieanna. Perhaps she is out there somewhere also."

"Maybe."

"That doesn't explain why the right door didn't open for you too."

"True. Anyway, that's not what's caused me to pause."

"What is it then?"

"Remember in the projection we saw Magnum Reginae looking through the portal window in the door of the data centre."

"Yep."

"She was looking through the window because she couldn't get in. But I did."

"What do you mean?"

"The data centre door was locked. It had a hand panel and I touched it. It took my blood and then the door opened."

"Oh. Shit!"

"Yes."

"Why is your blood able to open that door and not theirs? Someone must have put your DNA into the lock."

"Yes, that is what it would appear. And I think I know who."

"Who?"

"There was a note."

"A note?"

"Yes. The data centre was dusty. It was as if no one had been there in many years. There was an old note on a dusty desk. You couldn't see it from the window in the door."

"What was on the note?"

"It was addressed to a loved one. A child, perhaps. It said something about that child would know what to do if the author was dead, but otherwise the child needed to hide their tracks and run."

"Was it signed?"

"Yes. It was signed 'Love, Helenal'."

"The same name Tieanna mentioned. The person that saved her, and me for that matter."

"I gather."

After a moment, Dukk spoke again.

"Is Helenal the person Tieanna shared the Marduk fantasy story with?"

"Maybe."

"Is the note addressed to you?"

"I am not sure."

"It sounds likely if your blood unlocked the door. It also explains why the right door in the mantrap opened for you. So, Helenal got in there years ago. Wrote the note and then locked the door with your DNA. I guess the mantrap too."

"Perhaps."

"Helenal must be Venefican too."

"I guess."

"Was she the one that took the other disc?"

39

"That is possible."

"So, she can see what the queen sees too. Just like the image we saw."

"Yes, if Helenal has the other disc, she would know things that would be unreasonable to know."

"Just like Teacher."

"Yes."

"I want to show you the replay again," Marr said when she had finished her breakfast.

"Why?"

"I want your view on something."

"Okay."

With the replay complete, Marr and Dukk sat back in their seats.

"Tell me what you got from this?" Marr asked.

"It explains why we were attacked. There might be further scouts. They appear powerless to use the weapons systems on the mammoths. They are also unable to access their wealth. There is something about incubation databases. Tieanna got help with the rescue and they think that she entered the apartment and took the second disc."

"What about you?"

"They didn't mention me."

"Yes, so perhaps they don't know about you."

"Interesting."

"What did you notice about the tone the queen used when referring to others?"

"For most of the dialogue the queen uses 'her' and 'she'. The tone was that of contempt. Then she said 'that woman' in a different tone. It was dismissive."

"Yes. I think she is talking about Tieanna at that point. Otherwise, she is talking about someone else."

"Helenal?"

"I think so."

"That would line up with the note."

"Yes, it would."

"So, the queen thought Helenal entered the octet?"

"Yes, that is what I think."

"We need to share this with Mentor and Tieanna."

"We do."

5

An alarm interrupted Marr and Dukk's reflection.

Dukk launched himself towards the console.

Marr wasn't far behind.

"Something has just exited traverse. It is now orbiting the planet," Dukk said after reading the alert.

"What is it?" Marr asked.

"I can't tell for certain. It is on the other side of the planet. The traverse signature is fuzzy and there is no transponder signal yet. It could be the arrow returning. Or some pirates. Let's move to the cockpit. We'll get a better view."

"Go! I'll transfer the conn when you get there."

Dukk spun around and headed for the crew mess door.

He dashed through the passenger seating area and entered the cockpit.

The view was still that of the featureless rocky planet.

Dukk headed towards the flight controls at the front of the cockpit. The flight controls consisted of two identical consoles. Each console had a vertical wrap around screen that sat just below the windshield, and a horizontal screen that sat just above the knees. Both screens were interactive and fully customisable. From here one could control every aspect of the rig. Joysticks sat on either side of the seats. And each seat had its own holographical projector. In the centre console and in the ceiling above the two seats, were further interactive screens with gauges, switches, and indicators for critical system components.

Once seated at the controls on the left, Dukk reached his hands towards the horizontal screen above his knees. It came to life.

Marr joined him a moment later. She sat into her seat on the right.

Dukk interacted with the controls. A series of external camera feeds appeared on the screens before them. He also overlaid the various radar capabilities. He then projected a representation of the planet on the central projector.

"Let's see the predicted trajectory based on the traverse exit point," Dukk said as the image changed in the air between them.

A bright red line appeared around the holographical representation of the planet.

"And now to overlay our trajectory," he added as a blue line appeared in the air.

They looked at the results.

"Unless they alter course dramatically, they won't come anywhere near us," Marr observed.

"Perfect. And to alter course significantly they will need a prolonged burst of thrusters. That will be detectable, and we can respond accordingly. There is still no transponder. Best we stay clear and not find out who they are."

"Two and a half hours until we traverse. It is going to be a long watch."

"If it stays that long. Anyway, the company is good," Dukk said with a smile as he looked at Marr through the projection.

Marr smiled as she looked back at him.

Silence filled the space. It was like unseen forces had put them together at this moment. They had to wait. They had to watch. Their immediate path was now out of their control again. That sense echoed in their minds.

"What will happen?" Dukk said without thinking.

"Do you mean when the babies are born?" Marr answered instinctively.

"Yes."

"We raise them."

"Do you know how to do that?"

"No, but we've been learning."

"We?"

"Yes, you and I."

"How?"

"The visit to the surface of Newterratwo. The time with Stephen and Meredith and their families. Seeing children of all ages being raised by families and whole communities. And not in sterile parentless dorms like us. On Newterratwo, we experienced what it was like to be a family. We heard of their joys and their challenges."

"I guess. But is hearing stories the same as doing it for real?"

"No, but it is better than nothing."

"True."

"There is also instinct. It is strong with both of us from what I've gathered."

"What do you mean?"

"During the visit to Newterratwo, I was hugely interested in spending time with the expecting mothers. I had initially put it down to my interest in the new and the novel. But I think it is something else now that I realised that I was pregnant already during the visit. I was aware of changes in my body but didn't understand them. My instinct told me to show interest. There was an innate need to understand it."

"I had no interest in learning about birthing or raising children. I was more interested in the workings of the mobile habitat and mining operations."

"Yes, that makes sense because the babies aren't growing inside you."

They both laughed.

"So how was I learning?" Dukk said after a moment of checking the guessed location of the other space craft.

"You were learning by experiencing it. Being around children of all ages. You even told me about the stories you heard of some of the issues they face as parents."

"True. I had forgotten about that."

"We also have Tieanna with us. She has delivered many babies. It was her job before she left Earth when you were four."

"Yes, that is true. And she raised Craig."

"Absolutely, and she did a pretty good job from what we have seen."

"I guess we have time to learn more."

"Yep, six months."

"A lifetime compared to recent events."

They both laughed again.

Marr then pushed herself out of her seat.

"And we have each other," she said as she landed in Dukk's lap.

"We do," Dukk answered as he drew her to him.

An alarm on the consoles interrupted their moment.

Marr turned her head and Dukk leaned over to see what had caused the alarm.

"It is a traverse entry notification," Dukk said on inspecting the logs.

"I guess our visitors didn't think it was worth hanging around," Marr suggested.

"Yes, perhaps they were just rechecking."

"Does that mean we can get back to normal watch routines?"

"Yep, and that means one of us needs to do a walk around."

"I'll go, I need to stretch my legs," Marr said as she leant back in for another kiss.

Chapter 3 – Disclosure

1

Marr pushed herself to standing and made her way to the back of the cockpit.

Instead of taking the door on her right to return to the passenger seating area, she opened the door on her left. Within was the top of the forward ladder shaft. She dropped down to the level below and exited the ladder shaft. Before her was a landing that served two flights of stairs. The aft flight went up and the forward flight of stairs went down. To her left was the door to the port airlock.

She turned right and opened the first door on her left. Within were three beds. The med bay. All quiet. She then opened the door at the end of the corridor. It led to a room with spare g-suits and E.V.A. propulsion and bio system backpacks. Nothing happening in there either.

From there she took the final door on the starboard side of the corridor. It led to the starboard transport pod bay. The bay was long and narrow. Three five-person transport pods were parked nose to end. A large door at the forward end of the space was clearly the opening for launching the pods. She walked down the set of pods and checked they were secure. She then returned to the main corridor.

Crossing over to the port side, she entered the first door after the stairs. That door led to a large lounge with a big screen. All quiet.

She then briefly checked the port utility room with spare g-suits and E.V.A. backpacks.

After that she entered the port transport pod bay. This time, after checking that the three pods were secure, she entered a door at the aft end of the bay. It led into a ladder shaft. She checked the two, spare g-suits before dropping down to the lower level.

The bottom of the ladder shaft had three doors. One forward, one aft and one on the inner side of the small space. She opened the inner door and stuck her head in so she could view the hold. The lights came on. It was empty. The large doors to the forward storage hold and large doors to the engine room were all closed. She pulled back and took the aft door.

That door gave her access to the engine room. She looked up at the massive outer casings of the thruster burners that filled the upper regions. Below them were the three reactors. The generators for the DMD sat vertically in the middle of the room. They ran all the way to the ceiling.

Every time she entered this space alone, she was reminded of the first time she saw a rig engine room. It was on her first day as a haulier, nearly four months ago. Dukk was showing her around. The attraction between them was clear even back then. The butterfly feeling washed over her now as she remembered watching him as they stood just at the engine room door. They stood there while they eavesdropped on Bazzer boasting to Luna about the capabilities of the rig. The boasting was then repeated five weeks later just after they lost the Dinatha and secured this rig.

She stood for a moment. Bazzer's words echoed in her mind.

"Wow, three TLM series ten reactors. Did you know, that, series ten reactors are slightly smaller than the Dinatha's, but more powerful. Having three makes slow running more efficient," Bazzer had said.

"Are those engines all dual mode?" Luna had asked.

"Should be. Let's have a closer look?" Bazzer had said as he looked at the console. "Propulsion is delivered via three TLM TH8 quad core, twenty-six-gauge hard burner thrusters. Once more, they are slightly smaller than the Dinatha's, but they deliver much greater thrust. This bird is going to move fast when we need it to."

"Vertical lift?"

46

"Looks like four vertical, eleven-gauge dual mode burner thrusters."

"What about directional control?"

"Eight five-gauge dual mode thrusters. Like the Dinatha, just more modern, more powerful, and more efficient. Hey, look at those power readings. We clearly have loads of batteries. I haven't seen them yet. Did you come across them?"

"Yep, some are in the wing sections and also up there along the ceiling."

"Oh, cool. Now, what else do we have here! Well, well!"

"What?"

"That is an unlocked industrial printer!"

"By unlocked, you mean we can print parts that are restricted by the overlords, like computational units?"

"Not only computational units, but with the right materials, weapons and ammunition."

"That can't be allowed!"

"Nope. It isn't. We'd be disappeared at once if the observers ever found one of these on our rig!"

"Interesting times!"

"Yes, it is. Imagine having one of these on the Dinatha. We'd have been able to fix the heat shield locks the moment they broke, not have to pay over the odds for citadel approved computational parts. We would have had the old bird singing an even sweeter tune!"

"Are you going to continue comparing everything to the Dinatha?"

"Probably for a bit. Well, at least for the next five years."

Marr smiled as she recalled them all half laughing at Bazzer's poignant comment.

Marr pushed the memories aside and headed to the half-height doors in the side wall of the room. She used a panel on the wall and the doors swung open. She ducked down to look inside. She was looking at the inside of the port wing. Within were an array of tanks, casings and tube-like structures that were part of the weapon systems.

Nothing caught her eye, so she closed the doors and then repeated the process on the starboard side.

From there Marr left the engine room via the door to the starboard ladder shaft. She passed through the space at the bottom of the ladder shaft to the back of the starboard six-person squad bunk room bathroom. She then passed through the bunk room and into the lower kitchen and dining space beyond. She then crossed over to the port side and checked the bunk room on that side. It all looked quiet. Finally, she stuck her head into the gym with its multiple treadmills, exercise bikes and other various pieces of training equipment. Empty. Everyone was clearly still in their beds.

Before returning upstairs, Marr checked the forward airlock with its integrated ramp and underside hatch. It was all in order.

Once back on the upper level, Marr ducked into the crew mess. The dishes from breakfast were still on the table. She took them to the kitchen at the back of the mess and put them into the dishwasher.

2

Marr looked up. Someone was approaching.

Marr was at the console in the crew mess. She and Dukk had moved the conn there after Marr's first walk-around. Dukk was doing the same now.

It wasn't Dukk. It was Tieanna.

Marr turned in her seat. Tieanna came over and sat on the sofa.

They smiled at each other. It was the first moment they had been alone together.

It felt awkward.

"How are you feeling?" Tieanna asked after a moment of silence between them.

"Much better than last night."

"That is good."

"Did you rest?"

"Yes, thank you, I did. The bed in the guest room is far more comfortable than the prison cell bunk I've endured for the past twelve weeks."

"I bet it was. How did you manage being alone for all that time?"

"It wasn't easy, but I've been through worse."

"Do you mean the time after the initiation when you were sixteen?"

"Yes."

"You seem rather jovial about it all. Even when you told the story, I sensed it was hard, but there wasn't anger."

"I have learnt how to get past the anger and resentment."

"But you still went ahead with the retribution."

"By that do you mean the assassination?"

"Yes."

"I may have got past the anger and resentment, but I never forgave him."

"That sounds to be at odds."

"Forgiveness is the best choice, in most cases. However, there are times when turning your back, or even striking them down, might be the better response. Even when someone comes looking for your forgiveness."

"That sounds a little harsh."

"To forgive there needs to be an apology. An acceptance of wrongdoing. An acceptance of culpability. Let me explain that with an example. Let's say Kim decides the Earth is flat and shares this belief with Jordan without giving any real explanation. Jordan adopts this belief without question. Then Riley comes along and tells Jordan that the earth is not flat. Jordan berates Riley for sharing a contrary view. Jordan suggests that Riley is an ignorant idiot. Jordan accuses Riley of being a conspiracy theorist. Jorden then tells others, and they do the same. Riley is ostracised and suffers for this contrary view. Then Kim uncovers something new and comes to the believe that the Earth is not flat. Kim then shares this new view with Jordan. This puts Jordan in a difficult place. Jordan decides an apology is in order and goes to Riley. Jordan says sorry for causing all the pain. Should Riley accept the apology or not?"

"Of course, why not?"

"The question I would be asking here is what has Jordan learnt from this experience? If Jordan can't answer that question promptly and articulate clearly that the mistake was in trusting Kim without question, then Jordan hasn't learnt anything. If there isn't this understanding, Jordan's apology is false. It has no substance. It doesn't deserve acceptance. It doesn't deserve forgiveness. If we want to apologise for mistakes, we must be ready to acknowledge where we failed. We must be willing to openly acknowledge where we failed in ourselves and what we learnt from it. Without that, it is not an apology. It is just virtue signalling. So, if someone wants to make amends with me for their mistake, I ask them what they have learnt and what they will do differently next time. If their answer isn't sufficient, I consider their apology is false. In this case forgiveness isn't the right approach."

"So, you didn't get an adequate answer from Craig's father?"

"No, I didn't."

"What about Magnum Reginae and her daughter. They imprisoned you for three months."

"I have no feelings for them either way at this stage. I am yet to understand if they have remorse for it."

"Remorse?" Dukk asked having just entered the crew mess from the aft starboard ladder shaft.

"Magnum Reginae," Tieanna answered.

"For locking you up?" Dukk asked as he sat on the sofa next to Tieanna.

"Yes."

"What exactly happened?"

"With my abduction?"

Dukk nodded.

"The truth is that I don't know how or why, I was imprisoned on the mammoth. Clearly, I know they were looking for me thirty odd years ago. But I was certain that I was well off their radar."

"But you were in Mayfield the day of the assassination?"

"Yes, unfortunately. I was returning from a meeting with some of the students of other training academies. I got wind of Craig going to the resort at Mayfield. So, I diverted to Mayfield to meet him. I arrived the day before the ring arrived. I went to my usual suite in the resort and had an early night. When I woke the next morning, the ring was in orbit. I skipped breakfast and headed to the port. I didn't want to be in the resort if the Venefica were going to be there."

"You made it back to the port?"

"Yes, I got back to my arrow. Then I got a message from Septemo looking for help to jump the landing queue. I had to go back out into the port to speak to some contacts. I didn't want the request on normal channels. It took time to find someone that I could trust."

"This was the morning we arrived at orbit at Mayfield with the second shipment of beef. The day of the assassination. Mentor made one call to the surface. That was to you."

Tieanna nodded.

"What happened then?"

"The port was awash with Veneficans, their entourage and sentinels. It was tricky staying out of their way. I got stopped a few times and used my Atesoughton family credentials to avoid any questions. With the request made with a trusted port worker, I returned to my arrow."

3

"How did you end up on mammoth one?" Dukk asked.

"I don't know. It gets weird," Tieanna replied as she sat back on the sofa.

"What do you mean?"

"I figured Craig would turn around when he saw the mammoth ring. I also didn't want to be there when the assassination went down.

However, normal departures were on hold because of the Veneficans. I told my crew we were to stay put and wait for an opportunity to leave. To bide my time, I sat up in the cockpit. I had a clear view of the comings and goings. We had arrived when the port was near empty, so we got a bay near the entrance to the hyperloop station. Over the course of the evening, some strange things happened."

"What things?"

"Well, three things. Near nine p.m., I saw one of the security people loaned to Craig's father. He drove past and stopped near an old cruiser. A cruiser capable of moving a dozen or so. I feared my plan to get the girls to safety was falling apart. So, when he left, I headed out into the port to see if I could find out what was going on. I went over to the cruiser and spoke to one of the pilots. I told him who I was, and he laughed. He said I wasn't invited to the party and to mind my own business. That was frustrating as my plans to get the girls to safety relied on them being in the penthouse. The staff there were going to help me. So, I headed back towards my arrow to see what else I could do. Then a message came into my comms. It was odd. I knew something was very wrong. So, I ducked into a corner, and I sent a message to Septemo."

"This is the message where you said it was a hydra and you'd only cut of one of the heads?"

"Yes, that message."

"You also said 'they know'?"

"Yes."

"What did you mean by that?"

"That was the weird part. The odd message I got before I sent the message to Septemo."

"What did it say?"

"It said '"They know, they are coming! You must not say anything to them. Not anything about anything.'"

"Who was it from?"

"It was anonymous."

52

"But you believed its authenticity sufficiently to add it to your message to Mentor?"

"Yes. It was strange, but it felt authentic."

"In your message you also said 'They are coming for him. Let go of me. Don't look for me. Keep him safe.'"

"I did."

"What did you mean by that?"

"I thought the odd message was about you. I thought they must know about you."

"Who are they?"

"I had no idea at the time, but I guess now it was referring to the Veneficans."

"What happened after you sent the message?"

"I woke up in the cell in the mammoth ring."

"Did someone get the jump on you in the port?"

"I guess so."

"When you left to speak with the cruiser pilot, did you tell your crew where you were going?"

"No, I didn't. I just left quietly. I doubt they even knew I had gone."

"That was careless."

"Yes, it was."

"A moment ago, you said that there were three weird things. The first was seeing the security detail. The second was the odd message. What was the third?" Marr asked having sat quietly listening to all of this.

Tieanna looked over at Marr.

"I thought I saw her. Well, kind of."

"Saw who?"

"Helenal."

"When?"

"Twice actually. The first time was when a cart drove past the front of the arrow just before six p.m. She was in a skiing outfit driving the cart. Then later, as I ventured out to investigate the cruiser, I thought I saw her with a group of Veneficans in the back of another cart. They were unmistakable, in their white full-face masks, and their blood red, hooded cloaks. She knocked her mask off, and I got a glimpse of her as she went to put the mask back on."

"What do you mean by when you said, 'kind of'?"

"I didn't get a clear view. It was more of a general shape. Her manner. I couldn't see much of her face. It was odd. It was like I was seeing her all those years ago. Which makes no sense because she would be old now."

Tieanna finished the statement and looked deeply at Marr.

"What?" Marr asked having sensed Tieanna's gaze had changed in its intensity.

"You also remind me of her."

Marr felt uncomfortable again. Just as she had when Craig stared at her the previous evening. It was when he was talking about his meeting with Magnum Reginae and her daughter.

Dukk noticed the discomfort.

"What happened when you woke up in the cell?" he asked to deflect the attention from Marr.

"What do you mean?"

"Were you hurt?"

"No, I was fine. I had a headache, but I was unhurt. I was there in the cell on the bed, with them staring at me. Talking and making me even more worried about you."

"Them?"

"There were two Veneficans, in their masks, standing in the doorway. They were looking at me. Before leaving, one said, 'This is the opportunity we were waiting for. This daughter slipped from our grip before he was born. Sure, she is not pretty like she was when she was sixteen, but it is her. Very cunning to hide under our very noses within an elite family. Anyway, this will surely bring him to us.'."

"Was it Magnum Reginae and her daughter?"

"I am not sure."

"Wait! They didn't mention Dukk by name!" Marr stated.

"No, but who else would they be talking about?"

"Did they ever refer to you by name?"

"No, they didn't speak to me directly. In fact, no one spoke to me at all after that. I remained in the cell until Dukk appeared. Food and water were passed through a panel in the door."

"Are you sure that is exactly what they said?"

"It was the last words I heard for weeks. I am certain that is what I heard."

"Perhaps your detainment was always about Craig?"

"What do you mean?"

"They wanted him to participate in their induction ceremony. Perhaps they were going to use you as a bargaining chip. Perhaps Craig's father simply pointed you out as Craig's nanny. The same nanny who was preventing them from getting at him."

"But they recognised me from when I was younger. They knew I was Venefican."

"That doesn't mean they knew about Dukk. If they lost track of you when you were sixteen, they might have not known you fell pregnant."

"I had never thought of that."

4

"Can I ask you about something else?" Marr asked after further reflection.

"Of course," Tieanna answered.

"I'd like to know more about the Veneficans."

"What would you like to know?"

"Would you start at the beginning and share everything you know?"

Tieanna nodded and smiled.

"Their leader calls herself Venefica Magnum Reginae. Some refer to her as Magnum Reginae. Most call her the queen. There number is always exactly sixty-one. Magnum Reginae and sixty Venefica. And there are several hundred helpers. Younger women that do their bidding. The Filia. They also employ men, and they go everywhere with a load of sentinels. They advise and they meddle. They mostly live between the mammoths and the citadels back on Earth. The Filia are the Venefica's daughters and granddaughters. When a Venefica dies, their place is taken by their direct descendant. Their daughter. The Filia. The identity of their own daughter isn't known to the Venefica. It is kept secret. Only the queen is privy to this information. This tradition also applies to the queen. So, the queen's daughter, the Regina, is the next in line to be Magnum Reginae."

"They have daughters and then they don't ever see them?"

"That is partially correct. The daughters are raised in incubation centres. Just like me. When they are sixteen, the initiation ceremony is conducted. They are impregnated. When the child is born, the Filia is taken into service of the Veneficans. They serve and wait for the day when it is their turn to become a Venefican. So, a Venefica might cross paths with their daughter or granddaughters. They may even work with them. But they never know it."

"That sounds cruel."

"No more so than most. Take you for example. You don't know who your mother or father are."

"I guess."

Marr took a moment to process that.

"I've heard the term 'New Puritans' used when referring to them. What do you know of that?" she then asked.

"Rumours really. The Veneficans origins are unclear. However, around the time of the reset, some members of the movement that formed the Veneficans, were also labelled New Puritans. Some assume they are one and the same."

"Weren't the New Puritans a much older movement that saw themselves as moral inquisitors. The ones who should decide what is right or wrong. What is good or evil. What one should be able to say or not say, think or not think. That type of thing."

"Yes, that is my understanding."

"Do the Veneficans see themselves as moral inquisitors?"

"Most definitely."

Dukk was watching this. He was also thinking about it.

"If the girls are impregnated at sixteen, Venefica will have multiple generations alive by the time they die. Perhaps a daughter and up to four further descendants if they make it past ninety-six?" Dukk stated.

"Yes, that is correct," Tieanna answered.

"So, the queen must have multiple descendants too."

"Not quite. The queen and her descendants don't undergo the same tradition as the Venefica. There is no initiation ceremony. They are paired more carefully and generally have a daughter in their early thirties."

"That still means three generations."

"Yes."

"How old is the current queen?" Marr blurted.

"Some suggest she is in her early sixties," Tieanna answered.

"Has she been queen long?"

"For about thirty years."

"What do you mean by 'about'?"

"It isn't clear what happened to the old queen and the current queen's mother, for that matter."

"What do you mean?"

"So, when the current queen was in her early thirties, and just after giving birth, the old queen, her grandmother, died. It would have been assumed that the current queen's mother would have taken the grandmother's place. However, that didn't happen. A few years later the current queen appeared as queen. Some say she murdered her mother."

"Odd!"

"Yes, it is, isn't it."

After a further moment of silence, Tieanna stood up.

"If that is all the questions for now, I want to stretch my legs. I understand there is a gym on the lower level."

"Yes, there is," Dukk answered as he watched her leave.

When Tieanna was gone, Dukk turned to look at Marr. She was in contemplation.

"What is it?" Dukk asked.

"Helenal again," she answered.

"Yes, it is odd."

"And we know from the projection that the queen and her daughter have been locked out of the data centre and the mammoth weapons, for thirty years. The same timeframe."

"True."

"Helenal is involved somehow."

"Yes, it sounds like it."

"Is she responsible for the death of the current queen's mother?"

Dukk sat back. Marr's question had caught him off guard.

"How do you suppose that?" he asked eventually.

"She was there in the octet, long ago. Perhaps she used the would-be queen to re-program the system. To plant my DNA. To lock it. And then she killed her. Perhaps she is an assassin too."

"If we suspect Helenal is Teacher, you have to ask yourself if Teacher is capable of all that."

"It was thirty years ago. A lot can happen in that time. People can change."

"I suppose."

"I need to think about this all some more."

"Me too," Dukk said with a smile.

5

"Are you ready?" Dukk asked as he looked over at Marr.

"As I will ever be," she replied.

The crew were seated behind them in the cockpit. Tieanna, Bognath, Suzzona and Eleettra were in their seats in the passenger area. The traverse countdown was showing five minutes. They were in g-suits and helmets. And they were plugged into the med lines.

"People let's do this," Dukk said into the crew comms.

"Let's do this by the book. We don't know what or who may be waiting for us when we reach Southern Cross," he added.

"Right you are, captain," Luna replied cheerfully.

"Finger near the trigger, Luna, not on it. We are still moving under the Atesoughton family colours. We don't want to start a war by taking out another family's cruiser."

"Copy, captain. Near trigger. Not on it."

"Bazzer, systems?"

"Reactors are humming. Integrity at one hundred percent. Biosystems good. All green," Bazzer replied into the comms.

"Copy. Mentor, vitals?"

"All stable. Calibration is at ninety eight percent," Mentor replied.

"Copy. External comms, scanners, Ann?"

"Still nothing since that craft left two hours ago. We are out here alone," Annee replied.

"Copy. Stealth tech, weapons and defences, Luna?"

"Waiting for your signal to bring down the stealth. Weapons fully loaded and on standby."

"Copy. Marr, flight control?"

"All set, captain."

"Check-in."

"Ready," was the response from all in quick succession.

"Ready too. Deep and full breaths everyone. We are committed. Three minutes. Load up those in the back," Dukk said firmly.

"Juice running. Heart rates dropping," Mentor replied.

They all waited. A minute later Mentor added, "All stable."

"I am taking back med control," Dukk said as he interacted with his console. He then watched the countdown.

"Thirty seconds," he announced.

"Twenty seconds."

"Ten seconds. Kill the stealth. Running the juice. See you on the other side," Dukk said as he hit the button. Seconds later, the cocktail hit his blood stream. His consciousness faded.

Moments later Dukk came around. The sickly feeling swelled. It was a combination of nausea, shortness of breath and dizziness. Suggesting it was unpleasant would be a gross understatement. He fought back. He focused on his breathing. He counted to ten, three times. His awareness came back. He was through the worst of it.

Racing below them was Southern Cross, a planet of size similar to that of Earth. And like most habitable planets orbiting a red dwarf sun, it was tidal locked. They had arrived on the side away from the sun. It was dark. A red glow coloured the rim of the planet as the sun came into view.

"Status," he croaked into the crew comms.

"Back," croaked Luna.

The rest of the crew weren't far behind with their check-in statements.

Even Marr was on top of it. The eight hours sleep had helped. She had come a long way since her first traverse four months ago. She had been concerned that the morning sickness would have her gagging again like that first time. But she managed to bring herself through the side effects of the g-juice hit.

"Excellent. Med control back with you, Mentor. Vitals?"

"All stabilising, captain."

"Systems, Bazzer?"

"All green," came the reply.

"How are the skies looking, Ann?"

"It looks like the usual array of G5 rigs and the odd cruiser. Looks like the usual morning traffic."

"No hostiles?"

"Nope. Doesn't look like it."

"Great news. Marr, do you want to put in the landing request?"

"Yep, on it."

"Great. Let's run up the DMD so I can load a bogus entry. We might as well have some comfort as we wait."

"Done," Bazzer replied.

Dukk loaded the details. A tingle ran through them as the A.I. reached into the dark matter and engaged the neural pathways that were threaded through the belly of the rig. Their limbs got heavy again as the gravitational effects of the DMD's activities came into play.

Dukk opened the broadcast to the others.

"Welcome back to Southern Cross. We have made a request for landing. If it was like two days ago, we'll be waiting for about three hours. I'll get back to you once we have landing permission."

"Breakfast anyone?" Suzzona announced.

"Absolutely," Bazzer replied. "What is on the menu?"

"Well, now that I know we are going back to Southern Cross, I can restock. I had just found a dependable black-market supplier when we had to leave in a hurry yesterday. So, it is eggs, back rasher bacon, tomatoes, and mushrooms."

"Count me in," Luna replied.

"That reminds me," Dukk said. "Can you each let me know if you are low in EU credits linked to your fake digital IDs? We are still under Craig's expenses so I can give you each a further allowance. However, I don't want to go above your savings cap as the observers will take it from you. Let me know if you are low."

"Roger, captain," Luna replied.

"Now you've reminded me," Annee added. "Our typical cover while in port is always two on watch. The watch groups with four can decide between them who does which of the two four-hour rotations. This means we'll only be on once in twenty-four hours. That is all except Dukk and Marr. Does anyone want to volunteer to cover them and take the extra rotation?"

"We'll be fine," Marr interjected. "Besides, I could do with more rest."

"Tieanna will need to stay put for obvious reasons," Mentor added. "So, I'll stay with her and can cover any times you want to take a little longer."

"That would be good, thanks Mentor," Dukk replied.

Chapter 4 – Framing

1

"Now we get to see what this yoke is up to," Marr said after the others had left the cockpit.

"What are you talking about?" Dukk asked as he watched her interacting with the console.

"I set up some tracing before the traverse. I want to see what the disc did once we came in contact with a relay. There look."

Marr was pointing to a busy screen of words and numbers.

"What am I looking at?"

"This is a packet trace. It occurred to me that the disc might have other features, in addition to sharing a video feed of what the queen sees. I was concerned it might be sending as well as receiving."

"Oh."

"Yes. Oh indeed. So, I started a trace this morning. I discovered that the disc is active all the time. Even when it wasn't projecting an image. It was sending packets via the rig's communication network. Before the traverse, it was only looking for an outside link. Now it is connecting."

"This is gobbledygook to me. What do you see?"

"The disc made a connection to the relay and then sent a typical handshake request."

"Handshake with what?"

"That is odd," Marr said having just ignored Dukk's question.

"What?"

"The handshake request packet has something else in it. I've seen this before."

"Where?"

"On Earth. In the early days of my training. I studied communication protocols. I studied how to intercept messages and decode them. It helped us know what the observers were up to. From time to time, I would see odd content within messages. No one knew what it was. It was passed off as a legacy protocol that was since superseded."

"Perhaps you were seeing the other disc in use?"

"Maybe."

"Can you decode it?"

"Maybe now that I have a reference point."

Marr flicked open another couple of panels. Her hands moved at lightning speed across the controls. Words and letters spewed into the air. Dukk lost track of what she was doing.

"Ok, found something," she stated, eventually.

"What?"

"The disc and the relay have been exchanging information. I can't decode the details, but from extracting patterns it looks like a command associated with a transponder ID. Perhaps the disc is trying to find the mammoth ring. There is some other information in the packet. It is where you would expect caller ID information."

"What does that mean?"

"It could be nothing more than the disc ID."

"Could it be sending details about its location."

"Even if it did, it won't be a problem."

"Why?"

"If the queen wasn't able to locate the other disc, then she doesn't have access to the information the disc is sharing."

"So even if this disc is sharing its location, the queen can't use it to find us."

"That is what I imagine. Oh, that is interesting," Marr stated after a closer inspection of the data.

"What is?"

"There is a coded extender bit in the transponder packet."

"It could be piggybacking."

"What do you know of this?"

"I have heard rumours that in the past the relays could use rigs moving through a system to carry messages for them."

"In a covert manner?"

"Yes, that is my understanding."

"But you've never seen it happening."

"Until now."

"If I am thinking about this right, using the piggyback capability, messages could be moved between systems without relays, so long as rigs were moving about and engaging with transponders?"

"Yes, that is how I understand it works."

"What now?"

"Let's see what happens when we start the projection."

Marr pulled the disc out of a pocket and placed it on the centre console between them. A projection appeared in the air above it. The image was a fuzzy projection of light. A message was blinking in the middle of the fuzz. The message said, 'Searching for source!'.

Marr then returned to the packet trace.

"Anything new?" Dukk asked.

"Nope. Just the same stream as before."

At that moment, the disc emitted a loud beep.

A new message appeared. It said, 'Low battery!'.

"Oh, that might be a problem," Dukk observed.

"Yes, sitting in a cradle for thirty years doesn't do much for prolonging battery life."

"How do we charge it?"

Marr picked up the disc. She turned it over and inspected the base. She looked at the part of the disc that she had seen sitting in the cradle.

"I've not seen a shape like this. It wouldn't fit into our wrist wrap cradles or any others that I know of."

"We will have to make a new cradle to charge it."

"We'd need to know the amp and voltage needs. Get that wrong and we might damage it."

"We'd better get some advice."

Dukk opened his comms. He sent a connection request to Bazzer, who accepted it.

"What's up, captain?"

"Got a sec?"

"Sure. Breakfast won't be ready for another few minutes."

"Cockpit."

"On my way."

Moments later Bazzer opened the cockpit door.

"What's going on?" he said as he came over to them. "Having a lovers tiff and need my companionship advice?"

"No! No thank you," Dukk said with a laugh.

"What then?"

"The disc needs charging," Marr answered.

"Let me have a look at it."

Bazzer took the disc from Marr. He turned it around a few times and then laughed.

"What?" Marr asked.

"This is old. I haven't seen connections like these in ages."

"Can we make a charger?"

"We don't need to. We already have one. Look."

Bazzer then reached over Dukk to where he was charging his wrist wraps. Bazzer lifted the wrist wraps out of their cradles. He then pushed the cradle to the left and it popped out of the console. Beneath it was another cradle.

"This disc uses an old-style charger. It was superseded. These consoles are still based on generation three specifications. Rather than completely replacing the chargers, adapters were used."

Bazzer then dropped the disc into the exposed cradle.

When the disc hit the cradle, something unexpected happened. Not only did the disc start to recharge, but Dukk's console changed. A series of new panels appeared. Each flickered with greyed-out information. Overlaid on the information was a blinking message. The message read, 'Waiting for connection!'.

"Holy cow! What is this?" Dukk exclaimed.

"That is for you to figure out. My breakfast might be getting cold," Bazzer answered as he turned and left.

Marr got up. She came over to Dukk and sat in his lap so she could get a better view. She then reached over and started interacting with the panels.

"Look," she said after a moment. "This panel looks like mammoth controls. See there are five numbered forms with buttons and place holders for labels and information."

"Yep," Dukk answered.

"And this is some sort of database. A map of connections. I wonder what the nodes are representing. Oh. Wait! Here is another panel with five numbered forms. This might be for status of the mammoths."

"Nope. Look at the symbol at the top."

"Oh. It looks like a citadel."

"Yes. See the image has the three levels, each representing one of the three rings. You have the outer ring, with its seventy-foot-high walls and huge doors for rigs to enter. Then you have the middle ring with the vast green houses, incubation dorms, warehouses, and factories. And the final level, represents the inner circle of the citadel with its fine buildings, huge stretches of greenery and towers."

"The image even has shapes that represent the worker accommodation embedded in the walls to deter attackers."

"These controls might be what the queen was talking about when she said the Earth defences would fire on the mammoth ring. Perhaps this provides some sort of link to the defence systems within the citadels."

"Really? What would Veneficans be doing with access to citadel defence systems. Surely that would compromise their ability to defend themselves."

"Yes, I guess it would. Odd."

"What else have we," Marr said as she moved things about to expose the final panel.

2

The final panel had sixty-one numbered buttons. One button sat above five groups of twelve buttons. In addition to the number, a date was written on the button.

Marr reached in and clicked one of the buttons in a group of twelve.

A popup panel appeared.

The popup panel had a table with seven rows. The first-row label matched the number of the button Marr had pressed. The other row labels were numbered one to six. The columns had a date, an icon, a series of toggle buttons and a menu button. The toggle buttons were all labelled the same for each row. The labels read, 'Live', '1H', '4H', '24H', '48H'. Some of the rows had a blank date and missing status icon. The buttons for these rows were disabled.

"What is this?" Marr asked.

"I think the dates are birth dates. They are roughly sixteen years apart. If these five rows represent people, they range in age from fourteen to seventy-eight. The icon is some sort of connection status. It looks like a no connection symbol."

"The buttons perhaps control what the projection shows. Who's eyes we see through."

"There are sixty-one on the first page and then up to seven on these popup panels."

"Magnum Reginae, the Veneficans on the first page and their daughters on the popup."

"Wow. Of course."

"What of the other buttons. These with a number and the letter 'H'?"

"If 'Live' selects for what is happening right now, perhaps the other buttons are shorthand for the last hour, the last four hours and so on."

"Perhaps a summary or highlight of activities?"

"Maybe."

Marr went to press a button.

"Wait," Dukk said.

"What?"

"Let's find the queen first. Surely her button should be toggled."

Marr closed the pop-up. She then clicked the button above the groups of twelve.

A popup opened. It had a format similar to the first popup. Except there were only four rows.

All rows had a date in the second column.

The first row and the third row had no status icon. The buttons on these rows were disabled.

The second row and fourth row were populated. The status icon was showing the disconnected symbol they had seen on the previous popup. The buttons were enabled.

"That first date would make the queen ninety-five years old," Dukk observed.

"Look at the 'Live' button. It is toggled in row two. The date is sixty-three years ago," Marr added.

"That doesn't make sense. If it controls what projection the disc provides, for the queen, I would have thought that it should be toggled on the first row."

"It should. Also, I didn't think the voice was that of a ninety-five-year-old. More of a sixty-year-old like the date on the second row."

"Odd. Look at the dates on row three and four. They are the same. Thirty-one years ago."

"Twins?"

"Or clones."

"What are you talking about?"

"We know cloning was used in the past. Why not more recently?"

"Oh shit!"

"What?"

"Dukk! That is my birthday!"

"What is the big deal? Lots of people share the same day of the month."

"No, it is actually the date of my birth," Marr said as she turned to look at Dukk.

"Oh!"

Marr and Dukk stared at each other.

"I am a twin! And the queen is my mother!" Marr blurted.

"Your mother? You are a twin? Are you crazy?"

"I am pregnant with twins. Twins run in my blood line."

"This is conjecture. What if this all has nothing to do with you?"

"Getting through the mantrap. And then into the data centre where I stole this disc. Then the way Craig and Tieanna both stared at me when they talked about Magnum Reginae and her daughter, and Helenal. They mentioned familiarity. Then Tieanna said she thought she saw Helenal that evening in Mayfield. It was near six p.m. It was when we came back from skiing. She saw me, not Helenal. This isn't just conjecture."

"Wait, what has Helenal got to do with it?"

"Can't you see? We are pretty sure the eyes we have been using are that of the queen. The 'Live' button is toggled on the second row, not the first row, because there is someone else. The queen's mother is still listed here. Perhaps she is alive. Tieanna said Helenal is in her mid-nineties."

"Are you saying that Helenal is the queen's mother. Wait! That would make Helenal your grandmother. Oh shit! And that would make Helenal the Magnum Reginae. And what if Teacher is Helenal. That means Teacher is the queen not the one parading and claiming the title. Wait! Teacher is your grandmother. This is nuts."

70

Marr went quiet.

"Look, let's not jump to conclusions," Dukk said after a moment of reflection. "And besides, Teacher looks nothing like you. You have fair complexion, and hers is brown. And, you don't have the same eyes."

"Yes, the skin tone thing doesn't work. But I could have my father's eyes."

"We need to talk to Teacher!"

"Yes. We need to talk to someone who doesn't want to be found."

"We need more information."

Marr turned back to the panels.

After a moment she reached in and toggled the '1H' button on the second row.

A message appeared. It read, 'Request sent'.

"And more information we shall have," Marr said quietly.

"Do you two want something to eat?" came a squawk on their comms. It was Suzzona.

"We'd better keep this to ourselves for now. Until we figure out what is going on," Marr said.

"Ok. Hungry?"

"Not really. But it might be sensible to step away from this thing for a bit."

"Good idea. Let's move the conn to the crew mess."

3

A little over three hours later they were all back in their seats, suited up and with helmets on. They were preparing to deorbit. They had just shut down the DMD. They were weightless again.

During breakfast they had all come up to speed with what had happened to Tieanna. Marr and Dukk had left out what they had discovered about the disc. After hearing Suzzona's plans to spend some of their crypto to get fresh produce from the black market, it was decided to extend their stay a little and have some downtime. Bazzer had also made the point that doing the repairs properly would be easier if they weren't rushed.

Marr and Dukk hadn't spoken again of the disc. They had put it aside for the time being and focused on finishing their watch and spending time in the gym.

"Everyone ready?" Dukk said into the comms as he did his final deorbit checks.

"Absolutely," Luna answered.

"Bazzer?"

"Yep, I checked everything three times. The reactors are hot, the shield indicators are in the green and engines are primed. All systems go."

"Good. We will be fast and heavy for this approach. Traffic report, Ann?"

"The skies are all but empty. We are the last in the queue."

"Copy. Vitals?"

"All stable," Mentor replied.

"Copy. Flight control, Marr?"

"External comms is now with Ann. Bazzer will keep an eye on rig integrity. Nav is with you as usual. And I am ready to watch the thrust and pitch indicators."

"Excellent. Approaching deorbit point. Standby."

After a moment, Dukk opened the broadcast channel to all on board.

"Here we go. Hold tight."

He then authorised the descent sequence on the autopilot. This started with the thrusters pivoting the rig one hundred and eighty degrees.

The rig shook and groaned. Even Dukk felt his stomach turn. The necessary maneuver and the resulting g-force pushed their g-suits to their limits. He looked over at Marr. She was focused. Clearly working hard to keep the morning sickness at bay.

Next the main engines gave a quick burst. This slowed the rig so it would drop out of orbit. Another burst of the thrusters brought the rig back one hundred and eighty degrees again.

Now a final burst of both tail and bow thrusters pointed the nose into the forty-degree angle needed for re-entry.

The re-entry alerts sounded just before the colour of their view changed to bright red. Then a thunderous noise engulfed them as they entered the atmosphere. They were now committed and at the mercy of their preparation.

Soon the view and the sounds changed. They were in.

It would take them two hours in a controlled descent to reach the space port in the main settlement. Like most on tidal locked planets, the space port was built into the side of a mountain separate to the settlement. The rig would decelerate gradually as it approached the mountain. Then for the last stretch, the rig would pitch up and use its main engines to come to a complete stop. It would then use thrusters to set down on a pad on the side of the mountain. Hanger doors would then open and rig thrusters would be engaged once more to move the rig inside the mountain.

"Check-in," Dukk announced on the crew comms after authorising the descent plan in the autopilot.

"Systems still all green," Bazzer replied. "Starting exchangers to charge the fuel cells."

"Copy. Vitals, Mentor?"

"All stable."

"Copy. Anything else?"

There was no response.

"Great," Dukk said before opening the broadcast.

"Hello again. We have a two-hour controlled descent. The last fifteen to twenty minutes will be under hard burn. Please be back in your seats by two thirty-five. Out for now."

Dukk then removed his helmet as those behind him did the same and pushed themselves out of their seats.

He turned to Marr as she put her helmet on the side of her seat.

"How are you holding up?" he asked.

"I am fine," she replied as she looked over at him. "Lots to think about. Especially with what we learnt about the disc. But I'm good for now."

Dukk smiled. Marr smiled back.

"I am good to hang here if you want to take a moment."

"You are funny. I know you like your time alone during descent. You don't need to use any of this madness to hide that."

Dukk laughed and shrugged his shoulders.

"But I will take a kiss before I go," she said as she pushed herself up.

4

A little over two hours later, the rig was on the ground.

From the cockpit Dukk could see all the other craft parked in the ellipse shaped hanger.

He scanned them. There were fifteen space craft of size similar to their own.

"Half full and no blood red anywhere in sight. This is good," Dukk reflected to himself.

The seat to his right was empty. Marr had left just after the rig had landed on the pad outside the hanger. The last stages of their approach had knocked her about. Dukk had manoeuvred the rig into the hanger without his co-pilot. Which wasn't a challenge given the many years he had hauled in and out of ports like these.

Dukk opened the comms to the port air traffic control.

"Port control, this is the Imhullu. We are set down. You can raise the air wash barriers. We will lower our ramp and await the security inspection."

"Copy, Imhullu. I have put in a request for ID checks. We have had a busy day, it could be twenty minutes before they reach you," was the reply.

"Copy. Out."

He then turned his head over his left shoulder. He could see Bazzer in the corner of his eye.

"Power us down, my friend, let's get some R and R."

"Powering down," was the reply.

Dukk then turned his head to the right.

"Ann, it could be twenty minutes before the security people arrive to check our IDs and inspect the hold."

"No worries. I'll go down now, lower the ramp, and wait for them."

He then opened the rig broadcast.

"Hello again. We may have to wait for twenty minutes for security to arrive. Then we are free to go about our usual business. As discussed before deorbiting, we will be planet side for just over forty-eight hours. Let's plan to have a pre-launch circle up at six p.m. the day after tomorrow. Enjoy the stay."

Dukk then loaded the checklists and started running through the post landing procedure.

"Hi," Marr said as she plonked back into her seat.

"Are you okay?" Dukk said as he looked up from the checklists.

"Yep. I managed to hold it together. Putting my head down for ten minutes helped counter the g-forces of that final hard burst before we landed on the pad."

"That's good to hear."

"Yes, it is. Tieanna said it will get easier. She also said that reducing medicated aid would be good where I can. It will help the babies build up natural resistance to the conditions. They will be natural flyers."

"Really. What does she mean by natural flyers?"

"I guess she means they won't need as much medication for launch."

"That will be interesting to see."

Marr smiled.

"So, what's the plan?" Marr asked as she activated her console.

"The checklists are nearly done. Once the security checks are complete, we'll be free until six a.m. tomorrow morning. Mentor and Tieanna are going to cover the evening watch."

"We could head into the settlement and get something to eat."

"Yep, we could. Any preferences?"

"Nope, so long as it isn't dubious street food like yesterday."

Dukk laughed.

"Security are here," Annee squawked on the comms.

"Do you want to bring them up?" Dukk answered as he flicked open a video feed.

The video feed showed the under belly of the rig. The ramp had been lowered. The massive jacks gave a clearance of near five metres, so the ramp was impressive as it extended aft from just behind the forward jack.

Annee was standing at the bottom of the ramp looking up at the camera. The security person was standing nearby.

"There is only one official. He says they are short-handed. He wants to check our IDs, down here, at the bottom of the ramp."

"Okay, we'll come down. Do you want to tell the others."

"Yep."

Moments later a chime hit their comms. Annee's voice then echoed in their heads.

"Security have arrived. They will be checking IDs at the bottom of the ramp. Can everyone come down now so we can get this done and dusted."

Dukk nodded to Marr. She got up and led the way out of the cockpit and down the two flights of stairs.

They met the others on the way.

At the bottom of the second flight, they used the forward door to enter the airlock. The ramp was down.

As they used the ramp to drop to the hanger floor, they checked their implants. They made sure they had selected the fake digital IDs they had gotten after the Dinatha blew up.

Annee was waiting for them.

"He wants to start with the captain," she said as they formed a line at the bottom of the ramp.

Dukk stepped forward. The security person lifted his hands towards Dukk.

Dukk's information appeared in the air between them.

"Dellington, you are the captain?" the security person asked on reviewing Dukk's ID.

"Yes, I am," Dukk replied.

"I see on the rig information that you are on contract to the Atesoughton family. Flotilla escort. The flotilla left yesterday. What are you doing back so soon?"

"The boss was doing some shopping. Sent us back to pick up something he saw."

"Ah, yes, playing lackey to the bosses. Odd creatures they are. But I guess, it beats working in the labour camps back on Earth."

"It does," Dukk said in a curious tone.

"What do you have to pick up?"

"Sculptures using indigenous woods," Marr interjected.

Dukk looked over at Marr. He smiled. It was a part of the cover story that he had overlooked. He was glad she hadn't.

Marr grinned back at him.

"Very good, next," the man said as he lowered his arms.

Dukk stepped aside and allowed Marr to move forward.

After Marr was scanned, she came over to joined Dukk. He was standing just back from the ramp looking up at the rig.

"Thanks for rescuing me there," Dukk said quietly.

"Rescuing you?" Marr asked.

"Yes, I hadn't thought about what we might be back here to buy."

"Neither had I."

"But you came up with the indigenous wood sculptures idea so fast."

Marr grinned.

Dukk looked over at her.

"What?" he asked.

Marr laughed.

"You had your eye on those sculptures when we were killing time yesterday. That idea was what you wanted to buy."

"Yes," Marr answered with a giggle.

"Getting notions?" Dukk asked with a laugh.

"Well, you are the heir to the Atesoughton fortune. Besides this rig has loads of credits from the assassination fee and the contracts from Craig. We were already flush with credits before we found out who your father was. Why not spend some of it."

"Good point. Yes, I haven't quite got my head around all of that yet. It makes a change from being in debt and barely making do."

"Yes, that is true for us all."

"So, will we get back upstairs and change so we can go shopping?"

"Absolutely," Marr said with a grin.

5

Thirty minutes later, Marr and Dukk were making their way towards the port's hyperloop station. Having showered and changed into grey staff uniforms, they coordinated in fitted grey shirts, slacks, and matching jackets. For added protection against space port conditions and increased anonymity, they layered up with grey hooded cloaks. These were the uniforms they had been given when they started the charade as an escort vessel in Craig's flotilla.

Moving from the rig to the hyperloop meant walking behind the rig and entering the large service corridors. The corridors ran around the length of the ellipse shaped hanger. They were large so they could accommodate the robotic containers that were typically used in hauling produce. The corridors would bring them to a large open space that served as both storage and the entrance to the hyperloop station.

"I can't imagine it," Dukk said as they walked.

"What can't you imagine?"

"Not working. Not hauling."

"What are you talking about?"

"As you reminded me, I am the heir to the Atesoughton family fortune. Does that mean I would have to adopt their way of life?"

"I would think that you, more than most and going forward, wouldn't have to do anything you don't want."

"From what Craig has told me, there are many aspects to his life that he finds tedious."

"Like what?"

"Endless talk fests with the heads and representatives of other elite families. The process of 'maintaining good relations' as he puts it."

"Oh, I see, yes. Politics."

"Yes, and not just that. He said much of his time was taken up arbitrating mundane matters. Hearing grievances of other family members. Making judgements. Handing out funds. Reprimanding overindulgences. He then complained about negotiating trade deals. Investment analysis. Buying and selling. All the things needed to keep the family fortune growing."

"Perhaps he is being dramatic. He has a team to support him. Emeelie is there for a start. Your grandfather is old but must be doing some of that still."

"I guess."

"It is something Craig and you will need to work out."

"Yes, it is."

"Besides, this will all be a shock to him too. He was all geared up to take over from his grandfather. He was raised to do that. Suddenly, that might be in question."

"That is on my mind too. I wouldn't know where to start."

"Well, we have time to think about it."

"We do. We won't see him for a week or two. At the earliest. It will be wise for him to keep his distance while we have Tieanna with us. At least until we are back on Earth."

"Yes, we know the Veneficans won't be going there anytime soon."

"Hey, wait up," a voice called from behind them. It was Luna. Bognath was with her.

Marr and Dukk stopped, looked back and waited.

"As the head of security, I think it wise we travel in bigger groups," Bognath said when he and Luna reached them.

"You don't feel we can look out for ourselves?" Dukk challenged.

"Perhaps when it was just Dukk the haulier and Marr the keeper. But that is not who you are now," Luna suggested.

"Who are we now?" Marr asked.

"For one, you are crusaders. You have just rattled a big hornet's nest. That will surely have repercussions. Secondly, Dukk is the rightful heir to one of the biggest and most powerful elite families. And finally, Marr, you are carrying the future heirs to that family. If there were targets on your backs before now, they will only get bigger when this kind of news gets out."

"How will it get out?" Dukk asked without thinking.

Marr frowned. The enormity of their predicament hit her.

"Nothing stays hidden for ever," she said. "And when the stakes are high, people do some odd things."

"You are talking about Craig?"

"And Emeelie."

Luna and Bognath nodded.

"So, what does this mean for our plans this afternoon?" Marr asked after further reflection.

"We hangout," Luna answered in a gleeful tone. "Besides, we've hardly seen anything of each other lately."

"I had planned to revisit some of the high-end art shops. And pick out something cool that we can suggest we are buying for Craig."

"Great, let's go."

"Ok then," Marr replied as she turned and headed off again.

Chapter 5 – Dose of reality

1

The entrance to the hyperloop station had a self-service ID gateway. They all checked themselves through and headed for the hyperloop.

The automated transport system was busy, so they kept quiet and enjoyed the short ride through the mountain and into the adjacent valley.

The settlement consisted of medium height buildings, densely packed into the floor of the valley. Smaller and more lavish looking buildings sat on the slopes of the surrounding hills.

Dotted along the hilltops were massive structures supporting large lamps. These shone down, creating the illusion of sunlight. This was a typical feature of settlements on planets in the habitable zone of systems with red dwarf suns.

Also, on the hillsides were massive air purification complexes. They purified the air around the settlement, negating the need for domes and tunnels.

The gang disembarked the hyperloop in the centre of the settlement. They then walked in the direction of the markets.

"How are you?" Luna asked as her and Marr got a little ahead of Dukk and Bognath.

"Fine," Marr answered quickly.

"Seriously? With all that has happened, you answer with 'fine'!"

"How else should I answer?"

"Well, for a start, where are you at with discovering that you are pregnant?"

"Oh, so this is curiosity, not concern."

"A bit," Luna laughed.

Marr smiled and then answered.

"If I am honest, it has been a relief."

"Really? How so?"

"Discovering that I was pregnant gave an answer to feeling out of sorts."

"Aren't you scared?"

"Scared, no. A little apprehensive if anything."

"Like about giving birth?"

"Yes and being a good mother. None of which I have any knowledge of."

"What do you mean by good?"

"Good in the sense that they have what they need to make it in life."

"You are already brilliant at helping others build skills in how to make it in life. Look at me."

"Is that a complement?"

"Of course. You are brilliant. You have taught me so much about how I can make the most of my natural talents. Look at what you did with helping the girls rebuild their lives. Then of course there is the success in rescuing Tieanna."

"Thanks. I guess I have done alright when one looks at things like that."

"Absolutely. One might even go so far as to say that you are unstoppable!"

"Thank you," Marr said as she put an arm around Luna and gave her a gentle squeeze as they walked.

Marr smiled. She needed that lift. She felt even more proud in that Luna had noticed and leaned into what Marr needed.

"Let's have a drink?" Luna said as they came across a small pub.

"Now? We are supposed to be shopping for some sort of art," Marr answered.

"It will fuel our artistic side," Luna said as she opened the door.

"Sure," Marr answered confidently as she followed Luna in.

The small shabby looking place was mostly empty. A publican stood behind a bar opposite the door. To their left, two men were sitting on stools at the bar. There was a table on their right with four at it. Three men and a woman. They hardly looked up as Marr and Luna walked over to the bar, sat on stools, and ordered drinks.

Once the drinks were served, the publican moved out from behind the bar. He nodded towards the two sitting on the left of Marr and Luna. He then headed towards a door at the back of the room. The door had signs for the 'Exit' and 'Restrooms'. The publican opened the door and closed it behind him.

"Cheers," Luna said as she raised her glass and clinked it with Marr's.
Marr lifted her glass, nodded at Luna, and then took a deep swig.
As Marr put the drink down on the bar, she felt a little odd. Then it got worse. Her head started to spin. She felt dizzy. She started to lose control of her muscles.
As her head fell forward on the bar in front of her, a face bounced into her memory. One of the men on her left. A pilot from the repair shuttle. One of the men she had sedated when her and Dukk had raided the mammoth ring.

Marr could see and hear, but she couldn't move.
Luna had collapsed too. Her head had flopped down on her right side. Marr and Luna were now staring at each other. Marr could see utter terror in her eyes.
"Well, well," said a voice. "Now see how it feels getting a load of drugs fed into you."
A man stuck his head between Marr and Luna and smiled.
"But, unlike the drugs you gave to me, the drugs I've used here, will keep you aware of what is happening to you."

The man then laughed. More laughter came from the other side of the room. Marr assumed it was the table of four on their right.

"Let's move them to a table and have some fun."

Marr could hear activity behind her. It sounded like the door was being bolted shut and the blinds adjusted.

2

"What is going on?" Dukk stated.

He and Bognath had fallen behind. Dukk figured that Marr and Luna needed some space to catch-up.

As the men approached the place that they had seen Marr and Luna enter, the windows went dark. The shop banner went off and a closed sign appeared in its place.

Dukk went to open the door.

"Stop. Back door," Bognath said as he turned and dashed towards a side alley.

Dukk ran after him.

Bognath came to a stop at the corner of the building. He cautiously peered around the corner.

He then stood back and whispered.

"There is a man standing in an open doorway. It must be it. Follow my lead."

Bognath then stumbled around the corner.

"It has got to be here somewhere," he slurred.

Dukk took the hint and followed Bognath around the corner with a stagger and a stumble.

Bognath and Dukk made their way down the alleyway, doing their best to imitate drunks.

When they got to the man, Bognath swayed a few times and then looked up at the man.

"Piss off," the man said.

"Weir looken fa da tonto muerto," Bognath slurred as he swayed.

"Tonto muerto! Never heard of it, now get out of here," the man replied.

With that, Bognath half staggered towards the man.

The man tried to push him back, but as Bognath got in close he flicked his head back and headbutted the man, square in the face.

The man stood for a moment in shock before collapsing in a heap.

Bognath jumped over the man, turned, and then dragged him into the doorway.

Dukk followed and closed the door behind them.

Inside was a corridor. They crept down the corridor towards a door at the other end. On either side were doors for restrooms. They opened the door at the end of the corridor, and looked in.

The scene that confronted them was disturbing.

Two men were man handling Marr towards a table.

Luna was collapsed at the bar.

Four others sat around a table laughing at the scene.

"I'll take the table of four," Bognath muttered as he launched away from Dukk.

Dukk didn't hesitate. He launched towards the two men lifting Marr.

In the corner of his eye, Dukk could see Bognath lifting two chairs.

Dukk picked up his speed and opened his arms. As he met the two men lifting Marr, he swung his arms together. His forearms collected the heads of both men and smashed them together. They all collapsed to the floor.

Dukk pulled himself up and dashed over to the bar. He reached in and grabbed the biggest bottle his hands could get a grip on. He swung around towards Marr and the men. The men were pushing themselves up. They were dazed but not out.

Dukk swung the bottle and smashed it against the closest man's head. Still holding the neck of the now broken bottle, Dukk jabbed it towards the face of the other man. He missed. The man swung wildly as Dukk attacked and managed to brush Dukk aside. Dukk went with the motion and stepped over them all. He then swung around, grabbed the man's hair and pulled his head back to expose his neck. He then drove the broken bottle in with all his might. It ran true. The man collapsed.

The first man was still going. He staggered towards Dukk and collected him in a bear hug. Dukk crashed to the floor under the weight of the man. Dukk pumped his fists into the man's back. The man screamed and tried to get up. Dukk kept pounding. Eventually the man pulled back just enough for Dukk to lift his back. He angled his body to get leverage and then slammed his forehead into the middle of the man's face. The man rolled off with his hands covering what was left of his face.

Dukk got to his feet, turned, and slammed his boot into the man's head. The man stopped moving. Dukk then looked over to the table of four and Bognath.

Bognath was just lifting himself off the pile of limp bodies.

He looked over at Dukk.

Dukk nodded his head towards Luna.

He then went to Marr and turned her over.

Marr had heard more noises and then found herself being squashed under the weight of the two men. Her head had landed on her side. She could see other legs and hear fighting. After what felt like an age, she realised someone was turning her over. Her eyes met Dukk. Tears flooded in.

"Marr, can you hear me?" Dukk shouted.

The flow of tears gave him the answer.

"Looks like R-GHB," Bognath shouted.

"Yep, we are going to need help."

Dukk opened his comms. He made a call to Annee.

"Dukk, what's up?" was the reply.

"Marr and Luna have been drugged. We think R-GHB. Bognath and I are in a compromised position. We don't know how long we'll be able to stay here. We are going to need support. Position tracking is on."

"Copy. Give me a sec."

Dukk returned to Marr.

He moved her away from the men and glass and put her into a foetal position. It was the best he could do.

Bognath had done the same with Luna.

"I'm going to check the rest of the building," Bognath said as he headed towards the back.

Dukk went over to the door and checked that it was locked.

Dukk's comms sounded. He answered it.

"Mentor and Bazzer are on their way to you now. I am bringing them into a comms loop."

"Copy. Bring Bognath in too," Dukk replied.

The comms chirped as the group call was enabled.

"Mentor, Bazzer, Bognath are you on?"

"Yep. What is your situation?" Bazzer replied in a manner that suggested that he was running.

"Marr and Luna entered a pub. Looks like something went bad. They are awake but unable to move."

"Hostiles?"

"All accounted for," Bognath said on the group call.

"Is this localised or something else?" Mentor asked. He was also puffing.

"These look like pilots. I would suggest they are Bartiamos' repair crews. They must have recognised Marr. It looks like payback from yesterday," Dukk answered.

"Roger. Hold tight."

3

Fifteen minutes later, there was a loud knock on the back door.

Bognath headed off.

A moment later he returned with Mentor and Bazzer in tow.

Mentor went straight over and knelt next to Marr.

He pulled a device from his bag and wrapped it around Marr's neck. He then went over to Luna and did the same with another device.

The device started to beep as it took blood samples and then administered drugs via the medical line attachment at the top of their spinal cords.

Marr felt her senses return. It wasn't pleasant. With it came a sickly feeling. Then her body convulsed. She vomited on the floor in front of her.

"Let it all out," Mentor said as he held Luna, who was doing the same.

Dukk supported Marr as she reacted to the meds.

When it stopped, she pulled herself up to a sitting position. Dukk helped her shuffle away from the vomit on the floor.

"It happened so fast," Marr said in a strained manner.

"One sip and we went down," she added.

"It is a good thing that Dukk and Bognath weren't far away," Bazzer observed.

"Are you up to walking?" Mentor asked as he removed the med devices from around their necks.

"Absolutely," Luna slurred as she tried to get to her feet.

She stumbled and wobbled.

"I feel drunk," Marr said as she tried to stand.

"Not surprising," Mentor answered. "The cocktail must have been strong to knock you out that fast. That, combined with the meds that you just got, and you are going to be intoxicated for a good while yet."

"Only one drink! You two are losing your touch," Bazzer joked as he poured spirits on the bar and floor to mask their presence.

"Yep, cheap drunks," Luna giggled.

"Let's get out of here," Dukk said as he put his arm around Marr and helped her stand.

Mentor helped him as Bazzer and Bognath helped Luna.

"Back door," Bognath said as they moved off.

When they reached the back door, Bognath stopped.

"Before we leave, have you got something to wake up the publican? I want to have a chat."

Mentor nodded and reached into his bag.

A moment later the man was coming around.

The first thing he saw was Bognath's face.

"Hi, sorry about the broken nose. Now, listen to me. Me and my friends, were never here. The two women had a drink and left. The mess in there, is a bar brawl that went wrong with your regulars. Call it in. But keep us out of it. Have a good look at my face. Because it will be the last face you will ever see, if I hear anything of this or ever see you again. You bring us into this, and I will put your lights out permanently. Understood!"

The publican nodded reluctantly.

Bognath let the man's head drop and followed the others out the door.

"What about our shopping?" Luna slurred as the six of them made their way back towards the hyperloop station.

"That will have to wait," Dukk replied as he continued to support Marr with Mentor's help.

"Perhaps, you lads will have to go instead," Marr giggled.

"Yep, shopping is definitely what is on my mind at this moment," Dukk answered in a sarcastic tone.

"Tomorrow then," Luna said.

"Let's see how you all feel later, before you go making any grand plans," Mentor added.

"I am as fit as a fiddle. This won't bother me."

"Well, you weren't the ones doing the cleaning up in there," Dukk answered as he observed the soreness in his hands and back.

"Need some loving attention?" Marr slurred.

"Yes, I will need lots of loving attention."

"Cut it out you two!" Luna giggled.

A little later, Dukk and Bognath were sitting on beds in the rig's med bay.

Marr and Luna had already been seen and sent to bed to sleep it off.

"That was impressive," Bognath said as Mentor dressed the cuts on Dukk's hands.

"What was?" Dukk answered.

"The efficient manner in which you dispatched the two that had Marr."

"You took those four in the same amount of time."

"Putting down thugs is my line of work. You are a haulier."

"The haulier world isn't just long and quiet hours in the abyss. We run into trouble from time to time."

"Yes, that is obvious. Your style speaks of running into trouble."

"What do you mean by that?"

"It lacks finesse."

"What would you expect from a haulier? Please and thank-yous before you get your head smashed in?"

"No, I guess not," Bognath said with a laugh.

"It did the job," Mentor said. "That is what counts."

Dukk grinned.

"By the way, just before you headbutted the bar owner, you slurred we were looking for the tonto muerto."

"I did," answered Bognath.

"You said it with such confidence. Is it a place you know?"

"No, it isn't a place. It is a phrase in Spanish."

"One of the banned classical languages?"

"Yes."

"What does it mean?"

"Dead fool," Bognath answered with a wide grin.

Dukk laughed so hard he nearly fell off the bed.

4

At first Dukk wasn't sure if he was awake or dreaming. It was the early hours of the next day. He could hear a familiar sound. It was a long time since he had heard something like it. The sound was that of someone sobbing. It was like what he heard as a boy in the dorms of the incubation centres. Sometimes it was others. Sometimes it was himself.

Dukk opened his eyes and looked around. Marr was curled into a ball at the edge of the bed. She was the source of the sobbing.

Dukk moved in the bed. He went to put his arms around her.

She at once turned and snuggled into his chest. He wrapped his arms around her and pulled her close.

While the sobbing abated, Marr was still in a state of shock. The events of the last twelve hours weren't sitting well with her.

Eventually Marr muttered, "Luna said that I was unstoppable."

Dukk sensed her turmoil. He said nothing. He just held her tight.

After a moment, Marr said, "I thought I was more than most."

"What do you think now?" Dukk asked.

"That I am just the same as everyone else."

"What is that?"

"Vulnerable."

She then added, "Without you and Bognath, I would have been hurt badly or even killed."

Dukk said nothing.

After another period of silence, Marr said, "You didn't disagree."

"What do you mean?"

"You think that I am vulnerable?"

"What I think isn't relevant."

"Why?"

"Because this is for you to make peace with."

"You are abandoning me?"

"No, I am holding you. But I can't find the door for you or open it for that matter."

"Shit! That is deep," Marr said with a laugh.

Dukk smiled.

"You've been doing some reading?" Marr said as she pulled herself back to look at Dukk.

"Yep."

"The keys and doors?"

"Yep."

"I had forgotten about that. I'd like to read it again."

"Now?"

"Why not!"

Dukk pulled himself away slightly so he could reach his wrist wraps. He then flicked a panel into the air above them. He opened the hidden archives. He had been studying them since learning of them shortly after losing the Dinatha. After a little searching, a passage appeared in a panel. He then read it aloud.

"Choice is a journey. The choice is to engage or not to engage. That journey is not easy. Your journey is a path through many doors. The doors stand for the changes in who you are and your context. The experience of life happens between each door. The secret is to know which door is next. However, uncovering that secret isn't enough. You now face another challenge. To open the door, you need the key, which you know you already have. You know that everything you ever need is already within arm's reach. It makes sense therefore, that you already have the key. So, you have the key, and you have uncovered the secret to understanding which door. However, for so much of the journey you will find yourself dropping the key as you walk towards each door. You succumb to less-than-ideal behaviours, and you let yourself down. The added challenge then as you look for the key again, is not to lose focus of the door. You lose focus as you pick yourself up and return to the behaviours that serve you. This is the journey of life. You must accept that you will drop plenty more keys, lose focus of plenty more doors, and spend lots of time searching for both again. With acceptance comes engagement with what occurs between each door. Then only can you see the wonderful experience of who you truly are."

"This piece is brilliant. Exactly what I needed," Marr said quietly.

"Will you tell me what happened?" Marr asked after further reflection.

"After you were drugged?"

"Yes."

"What can you remember?"

"Very little. There were noises. I was manhandled and then dropped. Then you were there. Then Mentor was there. Then I was sick. Then it all got very fuzzy. I have a sense that we returned here. Then I was in this bed alone. I started to sob uncontrollably and suddenly you were here again."

"I guess the counter drugs that Mentor administered caused the blackout. You and Luna were very chatty all the way back. It was very amusing."

"Did we make fools of ourselves?"

"A little," Dukk laughed.

"Oh dear. Anyway, I want to know what happened in the bar."

"Bognath and I saw the place go dark. We figured something was wrong and entered from the back. The barman was at the back door.

Bognath did the drunk charade trick and knocked him out. Then we entered the bar and took down all those in there."

"There must be more to it. Who took down who?"

"I took down the two that were manhandling you. Bognath took down the four at the table. There wasn't anyone else."

"Did they drop me when you came at them?"

"Kind of."

"What do you mean?"

"I smacked their heads together. They dropped you as they collided."

"Oh!" Marr laughed. "So, you caused these bruises on my shoulders?"

"Sorry, if I lack the finesse of a trained assassin like you," Dukk joked.

"That's ok," Marr said as she snuggled in tight. "I will forgive you."

"Cheeky!"

"Will there be repercussions?" Marr asked.

"For taking out those pilots?"

"Yes."

"Mentor said he will message Bartiamos. He will smooth things over."

"I gathered from when we met him, that their relationship has been strained in the past."

"Yes, I got that impression too. However, Mentor was confident it would be fine."

"Ok then. And, what about the shopping?"

"I suggest we complete our watch, then go in again, as a group, do just the shopping and take no side excursions."

"Yes, that sounds like the right move."

"What about you? Are you going to be okay going back in?"

"Getting right back on the horse is the right move."

"Have you ridden a horse?"

"No," Marr giggled.

Dukk laughed.

"Our watch starts soon, however since we are in port, we don't need to get up unless we have to open the door."

"Good," Marr said as she drifted back off to sleep.

5

Later in the morning, Marr and Dukk were at the table in the crew mess.

"Why is there nothing there?" Marr said as she looked up.

After some more rest, they had used the gym and then had breakfast. Dukk had just returned from clearing the dishes. The disc sat between them on the table. It was projecting a message. It said, 'No activity'.

"You pressed the '1H' button, right?"

"Yep."

"What else happened when you activated it just now?"

"There was a new message alert. The alert said that a report had been delivered. I opened the report, and this is all it showed."

"Is that time sequence data?" Dukk said as he pointed to some numbers above the message.

"Oh! Of course! Good observation. Twenty-three thirty-five. It is using coordinated universal time. We have been using Utopiam time, which is ten hours ahead of universal time. So, we pressed the button yesterday morning at nine thirty-five. That means it went and retrieved a report for the preceding hour. It was late. So perhaps she was asleep."

"Then, if we insert it into the charging cradle again and select one of the other buttons, we should get a report for a longer time frame."

"Yes, maybe. Let's try."

Marr grabbed the disc and went over to the console in the corner of the crew mess. Dukk followed and sat on the sofa behind her.

With the disc sat into the cradle, the panels appeared again.

Marr quickly found the buttons and pressed the button labelled '48H'.

A message appeared. It read, 'Request sent'.

She then pressed the button labelled 'Live'.

A new message appeared. It read, 'Source acquired. Lag: x3 ~ 120m'.

"What does that mean?" Marr asked as she sat back.

"It looks like a relay delay."

"What do you mean?"

"It must use relays to retrieve the recordings from the mammoth. Relays use modified DMDs to move messages every twenty minutes. The mammoth would have done three traverses since the day before yesterday. The 'x' three represents the number of traverses. You would double that if considering the request needs to get there and back. Twenty multiplied by six is one hundred and twenty. That is the number of minutes."

"So, it will take one hour to start the live stream, then it would be another hour before we start seeing live updates."

"Which means we must wait."

"Yep, that is what it looks like."

"Would the report retrieval take the same amount of time."

"I guess so."

"More waiting."

"Yep."

"What are you waiting for?" Tieanna asked having just entered the crew mess via the forward door.

Marr looked over at Dukk. He shrugged his shoulders.

Marr turned around to face Tieanna.

"The live feed from the disc," Marr said bluntly.

Tieanna looked at her for a moment. She then looked at Dukk before returning to Marr.

"Is this safe?" she said in a gentle manner.

"Yes, so far. We don't think the queen can use it to track us."

"No, Marr, I don't mean safe in that way. I mean, is it safe for you or us to have access to such information. Information like this could be used for all kinds of purposes. It isn't easy to see the true consequences of what we do until much later."

"Oh, I see. Yes, absolute power corrupts absolutely."

"Yes."

"What do you suggest we should do?" Dukk asked having quietened his mind and listened for an answer.

"Great question," Tieanna answered.

"We be clear about why we are doing it and regularly check ourselves against that reason," Marr blurted.

Tieanna smiled.

"So, what is our 'why?'" Dukk asked.

Marr sat back. She knew her reason was to find out who she was. But also, just because she was curious, if she was being honest with herself. At that moment it occurred to her that those weren't great reasons.

Dukk watched Marr as she sat back. He felt he knew her reasons. They weren't good ones.

"We need to know their movements so we can stay clear of them and keep you safe," Dukk lied.

"And when I am safe?" Tieanna asked.

"We don't use the disc anymore," Dukk said in a less than convincing tone.

"Ok then. So, how do I get something to eat if Suzzona isn't around?"

Tieanna then headed off in the direction of the kitchen.

Marr watched Tieanna disappear into the kitchen. She then turned back to Dukk.

99

He grinned.

"What?" she asked.

"We need a better reason."

"We do."

"I feel like a naughty child," she added with a smile.

"Me too," Dukk said with a laugh.

A kerfuffle in the direction of the crew mess door interrupted their moment of connectiveness.

"I don't know. I think we need some clothing rules," Eleettra could be heard saying as her, Bognath, Bazzer and Luna made their way into the room.

"You are just making excuses. Bazzer and I beat you and Bognath fair and square," Luna retorted.

"Marr and Dukk, what do you think?" Eleettra asked as she arrived at the table and noticed them at the console.

"About what?" Marr asked in reply, before gasping.

"That," Eleettra said as she pointed at Luna and Bazzer.

Bazzer and Luna were wearing hot pink outfits. Calling them outfits would be a little on the generous side as there wasn't much fabric involved. Luna was wearing a ridiculously small bikini that barely gave any cover and look to offer very little support for her ample breasts. Bazzer was wearing skin-tight shorts that left little to be desired, and a skin-tight singlet that barely covered his overly muscular upper body. They also had matching wrist and head sweat bands.

"I see you've upped the ante," Dukk said with a laugh.

"Ante?" Eleettra inquired.

"Yes, that is how they dressed for their first wall ball match on the Dinatha."

"Well, I found it very distracting."

"Me too," Bognath laughed.

"So, who is our next victim?" Luna jeered.

"Me and Dukk!" exclaimed Suzzona having heard the noise. She had been in the bathroom.

"And, I'll go one better," she added as she ripped off her top and dropped her pants.

She now stood before them, completely naked.

The room erupted into laughter.

The noise was so loud that no one noticed, Mentor open his cabin door and ask, "Did I miss something?"

Chapter 6 – Retribution

1

Two days later, the rig was in orbit of a featureless planet in the Mimosa 3 system. They were halfway to HDK85, the system where they would find the resort on a moon orbiting planet Abrolhos. It was the possible location of another party.

The remainder of the time in Southern Cross had been uneventful. Other than completing the purchase of some art to honour the charade, they had stayed clear of the settlement. With the repairs complete, they had made for orbit and begun traversing again.

Marr and Dukk had spoken little of the revelations they had uncovered; however, they had continued to check the disc and the reports.

There was little on them. The queen mostly kept to herself. The report showed a few conversations. Most were operational in nature.

The queen had received word that two of her arrows were destroyed in an unmonitored system adjacent to Southern Cross. However, the reports gave little indication of how it had happened or if anyone had survived.

It was clear to Marr and Dukk that the queen didn't know about themselves. She had made plans to visit Bartiamos. It wasn't clear when. She had indicated that she needed more information about Craig's flotilla, and she felt Bartiamos was the only one she could squeeze for intel.

They did uncover one useful piece of information. The queen had given an instruction to alert the Filias. They were to be on the lookout for an Interceptor and a woman matching Tieanna's identification.

It was near eight p.m. The crew were about to have their daily shared meal.

"Everyone is ready to eat," Dukk said as he entered the cockpit.

Marr was sprawled in her seat at the front of the cockpit. She was looking up. On the console projector was a star chart.

"What are you looking at?" Dukk asked as he came over to her.

"The Solar System."

"Where?" Dukk asked as he crouched down next to her so he could look in the same direction.

"There," Marr said as she raised her arm to point.

Marr was pointing at some stars through the upper section of the windshield.

"It looks so small," Marr said in a dreamy tone. "So far away."

"Yes, that is because it is, far away," Dukk said with a chuckle.

Marr sat up.

"Did you know we are one hundred and eight parsecs from Earth. Or just over three hundred and fifty light years. That means the light reaching our eyes at this moment, was seen on Earth in the Victorian era. Steam driven engines were the norm. They didn't have combustion engines, fusion power, computer chips or anything like that. Space travel was still the realm of fantasy."

"Yes, and women weren't even able to vote in most places. Funny, how no-one can vote now."

"Do you know some feel giving women the vote was the start of the demise that created the world we now have?"

"No, I didn't know that."

"Yes, so much has been hidden from view."

Dukk leant in to kiss Marr.

"I love the way your mind works," he said as their lips separated.

Marr smiled.

"Food?"

"I love how your mind works, too," Marr said with a chuckle.

"Lead the way, captain," she added.

"So, what is the plan for our next rescue," Luna asked when she returned from taking dishes to the kitchen.

With the meal over, they all looked at Tieanna.

After a moment she addressed them.

"First, we need to find out where they are keeping the girls. Most parties aren't like Mayfield. In Mayfield they had control over both the accommodation and the red room. In the weeks prior to the gathering, they could accommodate the girls in the same location. Everywhere else, the gatherings are held in resorts that are block booked for the week of the party. The girls are accommodated somewhere else until that week. The accommodation won't be far from the resort. We need to get near enough to the resort to find out who has the booking. We can then track it back to other bookings in the nearby settlement. With some carefully placed bribes we might be able to locate the girls and their minders."

"That sounds like searching for a needle in a haystack," Marr commented.

"My network of students will make light work of it. They will know about all the movements of people within the settlement."

"But you can't be gallivanting around. We know from monitoring of the queen, that her network of helpers, and I guess spies too, are looking for you."

"Yes, that is correct. I will have to stay hidden and connect you all with the network."

With that the conversation moved to lighter matters.

Over the next thirty-six hours, some normality returned to their lives for a time.

"How did you get on?" Dukk asked Luna as she entered the crew mess.

The rig was parked in the hanger of the space port of the main settlement on the planet of Abrolhos.

The crew had gathered to hear what Luna had uncovered.

"Tieanna, your contact was solid. I have some information that I think will be useful. The girls are here in the settlement. An entire floor of rooms in one of the mid-range h-pod hotels has been blocked booked for several weeks. The contact said the same group of mercenaries have been bringing in groups of girls every few weeks. A booking has also been made at the resort on the moon. The same person who booked the h-pod hotel booked the resort."

"For when?"

"The resort booking starts today."

"Any details of who made the booking?"

"Nope."

"So, it sounds like we simply get the girls before they go to the moon!" Dukk suggested.

"If we just grab the girls, we miss an opportunity," Tieanna noted.

"To take out the perpetrators!" Luna blurted.

"Yes."

"What do you suggest?" Marr asked.

"Scorched earth."

"How?"

"We get the girls and make sure they are safe. Then we go into the resort and take out everyone involved."

"What if there are other innocents with the perpetrators?"

"Innocents?"

"Family members who know nothing of this. And staff."

Tieanna stared.

"Could we set a trap?" Dukk suggested. "Bait those who are in the know and therefore reduce the risk of taking out innocents."

"Yes, some sort of triage would been needed to reduce collateral damage," Marr answered. "What do you have in mind?"

"I haven't got that far."

"The perpetrators will want to keep their distance from the movement of the girls," Bognath observed.

"So, if they think the girls have been delivered as planned, will they simply show up for the party?" Luna asked.

"Yes."

"How closely will they watch the movements of the girls?" Marr asked.

"Good question," Bognath answered.

"We'll have to question those transporting the girls."

"I guess."

2

"Which one should we wake up?" Luna said as her, Marr, Mentor and Bognath stood over three limp bodies. They had left a fourth in the corridor.

In addition to information, Tieanna's contact had given them codes to the hotel's rear door. Near midnight, they had used nano drones, gas pellets and darts to knock out the four strong security detail who were guarding the girls.

Mentor, with Bognath's help, lifted one of the men into a chair. They used cable ties to secure him. Mentor then injected a substance into the man's med lines.

Moments later the man looked up. He tried to break free. Mentor back handed the man in the face causing him to slump back into the chair.

"What is the plan?" Marr said as she brought her face right up close to the man's face. The tip of the mask she was wearing pressed against his nose.

"What are you talking about?" the man slurred.

"What is to happen to these girls?"

"We are taking them to the resort on the moon."

"When?"

"Tomorrow?"

"How?"

"A shuttle."

"Then?"

"We bring them to the red room to be inspected."

"And then?"

"We leave and then guard the doors for about forty-eight hours."

"Then?"

"We clean up."

"When does the inspection happen?"

"In the afternoon."

"Tomorrow?"

"Yes."

"Who is in the room for the inspection?"

"Just the clients."

"How many?"

"Four to six."

"Security?"

"Nope. Just us."

"Are they armed."

The man laughed.

"What made you laugh?" Marr asked firmly.

"They are generally naked, so no they aren't armed."

"How does it playout tomorrow?" Marr said after further reflection.

"The girls get up, get into their outfits, put on a cloak and at midday, we head to the port."

"Outfits?"

"Leather bikini costumes."

"What about g-suits and helmets for the launch and traverse to the moon?"

"The shuttle pilots provide them."

"They are on the take too?"

"In a manner. We pay them in crypto."

"How much?"

"One thousand per person travelling."

"Tell me about the shuttle!"

"It is the normal moon shuttle. Goes there and back daily. Brings staff and cargo back and forth."

"You are transporting the girls using a routine shuttle?"

"No. Normally, it leaves here first thing, stays out there for the day and returns in the evening. It has been chartered for a further trip around midday. It will return here just for us."

"Doesn't that raise an alarm with the port authority?"

"It isn't uncommon for them to return during the middle of the day for safety checks, routine maintenance, and training. No-one pays it any attention."

"How many travelling?"

"Us four and twelve girls."

"Are they expecting the exact number?"

"No. The charter contract will have said up to sixteen passengers. Nothing more specific. We don't always have twelve girls. Sometimes things go wrong, and we must go in with less."

"Do you need to check-out of this hotel?"

"No. It is all paid for in advance."

"Do you have any communications with the client?"

"What do you mean?"

"Between now and the inspection?"

"Nope."

"So, the plan has been pre-agreed?"

"Yep."

"How do you know where to go?"

"I've been given instructions."

"Give them to me."

"Top pocket."

Marr reached into the man's top pocket. She extracted a piece of paper. Scribbled on the note were directions. The instructions described how to get from the port to the resort and then to the red room.

"Who gave you this note?"

"They did."

"The clients?"

The man laughed again.

"What!" he then said.

"What is that supposed to mean?"

"Who in the world are you people?"

"Not relevant. Who gave you this note?"

"The organisers of course. Who else?"

"What do you mean?"

"Holy shit. You are having me on!"

Marr stared.

The man sighed.

"Look, clients pay a pretty penny to attend."

"Who to?"

"You seriously don't know!"

Marr stared again.

"It is run from Earth. Out of the hostess training centres. The trainers are the organisers."

"Are there any others organising parties?"

"I've heard that some try. But they get shut down. Wait! Are you the crew that took down that rogue party that was running out of Mayfield. Word is that the crew followed the clients to New Montana and blew their heads off."

Marr did her best to keep a blank expression.

The man continued to grin.

110

"We are going to put you to sleep now. Permanently," Marr said calmly.

"Fine, I'm tired of this shit."

"Explain that!"

"You start out in security. It doesn't make much, but it is okay. Then you hear of a way to make a little extra. You take a chance, and you get sucked in. There is only one way out now."

Marr nodded towards Mentor. Mentor reached into his bag and retrieved a handheld device. He fiddled with the device for a moment before connecting it to each of the men's med lines.

"I still feel a pulse?" Luna stated as she checked the men, a little while later.

"Yes, I only gave them a sedative to induce a coma," Mentor replied. "They will wake up in a few days. The staff in this hotel will find them tomorrow and put them into a med centre. The sedative has a trace of opioid. To the medical staff this will look like partying gone wrong."

"Was that always the plan?"

"No. I changed it."

"Why? This one even expressed a wish to die."

"There are fates worse than death. Besides, what I heard just now, gave me reason to pause. I am intrigued. It might be in our favour for rumours of our escapades to circulate."

"But why alert the organisers?"

"A frightened enemy is more likely to make mistakes."

"They can be more dangerous too."

"True."

"Let's steal their IDs," Marr said as she cut the ties securing the man to the chair. He fell forward.

She then added, "They will be implicated in this. Death might have been more considerate. Anyway, we should get some rest."

3

Several children were playing directly in front of her. They were dashing about, laughing, and pushing and shoving each other. Marr looked on with awe and joy.

Suddenly, one of the children stopped and looked over at her.

"Who are you?" the child said.

Marr was perplexed. Marr thought these children knew her as she knew them.

"Hello!" the child said again. This time the voice had a critical tone. And it wasn't the voice of a child. It was the voice of a teenager. A teenage girl.

Marr snapped herself to attention. She must have drifted off.

Marr had taken the fourth watch. She had set herself up on a chair in the corridor, so she could see the exits and the doors to each of the h-pods.

"The replacement escorts," Marr blurted having regained just enough situational awareness to supply the practiced answer.

The girl before her was scantily clad. She was in her mid-teens. Just like the girls they had rescued in New Montana.

"Are you taking us to the party instead of the others?" the girl said.

"Yes."

"Great! I am so excited," the girl said with glee as she dashed back into the open door behind her.

Marr got to her feet and followed the girl to the open door. Within was a chaotic scene. Food trays, towels and clothes were strewn everywhere. The girl from the corridor was jumping up and down on the bed. Another girl, dressed in the same manner, was jumping on the bed with her.

"This is going to require every inch of our training!" a voice whispered in Marr's ear.

It was Luna.

"Yes, it will," Marr replied as she turned.

Dukk was starting to become a little concerned. They had agreed radio silence. But he was still starting to worry. It was late morning and he thought he would have got some kind if signal by now.

There was movement. He sat up from his seat in the cockpit to get a better view as he looked out into the hanger. He could see a group leaving the hyperloop station. They were heading in his direction. Sixteen of them. All wearing black cloaks. Some were carrying black carryalls.

"They are coming! Turn on the video scrambler," Dukk said into his comms as he jumped up and headed for the door.

"We don't have long," Marr said as she marched up the rig's ramp.

"Bring them up to the lounge," Annee said.

With the girls settled into the seats in the lounge, the gang closed the door and regrouped in the corridor.

"What's next?" Dukk asked bluntly.

"We know where the perpetrators will be and how to take them out," Marr answered.

"Where? When?"

"On the moon. This afternoon. The details will have to wait. For now, we need Annee and Suzzona to come with us. We are going to impersonate the girls. You two, Luna and I. Mentor and Bognath will pretend to be escorting us. This charade will get us into the red room and in front of the perpetrators. We can take them down quickly and efficiently. There shouldn't be any collateral damage."

"Now? What will we do?"

"Get the girls settled. We've simply told them that the party has been moved."

"How are you getting to the moon?"

"The mercenaries had charted a shuttle. It is waiting for us right now."

"When will you be back?" Dukk asked.

"All going well, we will be back on the same shuttle later this evening," Marr replied.

"We should prepare to launch the moment we are back on board," Mentor added.

"Before you go, I want to do our typical welcome and set the tone," Dukk stated.

"Yes, good idea," Annee added.

"Absolutely," Marr responded. "Besides, we need to resupply our weapons. We also need to get into our g-suits and get our helmets."

"How long have we got before you need to be at the shuttle door?" Dukk asked.

"About ten minutes. Ann, will you get all the black cloaks. Getting all of them will be easier than explaining why we need to borrow two of them."

"Will do."

As Marr, the raiding party and Suzzona disappeared up the stairs, Dukk led Annee into the lounge. Tieanna followed. Bazzer and Eleettra stayed in the corridor.

It was loud in the lounge. The girls abruptly stopped talking and looked up at Dukk as he entered.

"When are we going to the party?" a girl blurted as she sat forward.

"Where are our party outfits?" another added.

"I am hungry," said one.

"I need to go to the toilet," was the claim from a fourth.

114

Suddenly the room erupted into noise once more. There were demands and questions.

"Enough!" Dukk shouted as he advanced to the centre of the room.

The noise stopped instantly.

Dukk then looked at the girl who spoke first. He stared her directly in the eyes.

"What is your name?" he asked in a gentle tone.

"Donmenja," she answered in a timid voice.

"Donmenja, welcome. Do you want your questions answered?"

"Yes."

"Good, because that is why we are here. I am going to say my piece. I will then hand over to my chief mate, Annee. She will speak to you. After that, if your questions haven't been answered, you can take turns to ask. Is that okay?"

Donmenja nodded.

4

Dukk started to speak. As he did, he looked at each of the girls individually. He concentrated on looking them directly in the eyes. Which needed more than his usual focus. The girls had discarded their black cloaks, they were scantily clad, and some were topless.

"Welcome all, my name is Dukk, the captain of this rig. As mentioned, this is my chief mate, Annee, and this is our special advisor, Tieanna. You will be introduced to the rest of the crew in due course. While you are on this rig, you are subject to my rules. You are to stay within the designated accommodation area and not try to enter any areas marked otherwise. You fend for and clean up after yourself. The kitchen and service docks will be kept fully stocked. The bathrooms and living spaces will be cleaned when the opportunity arises, so it is in your interest to keep on top of it. There are washers and dryers if you need them. Fighting of any kind will not be tolerated and result in confinement. If there is an emergency, you are to do exactly what you are told by me and my crew."

Dukk paused to let that sink in.

"These rules are non-negotiable. Of course, you have the right to refuse them. If you aren't happy with these rules, you are free to leave and you can find your own way. Anyone want to leave?"

Dukk paused once more. The girls all shook their heads. There was a sense of awe in the room. They were being spoken to in a manner that wasn't familiar to them.

"Excellent. I will now hand you over to Annee to finish the briefing."

"Hello girls," Annee said in a firm but natural tone as she stepped into the centre of the room. "I need to go out, so I will leave you with my colleagues to get you settled. You will be shown to your bunk room, where you will find bedding, clothing, and everything you will need for this passage. You will have to remain on this rig for the day as we have a tight schedule and can't afford any delays. I will be back ahead of launch to conduct a safety briefing. Now, please go with Tieanna to the dorms on the level below. She will orientate you and then get you signed into the rig's systems. I will collect your cloaks as you won't need them while you are on this rig. Please leave them on the seats in here."

Dukk went to the door and held it for Annee. She crossed the corridor and bolted up the stairs. Tieanna was next. Behind her came the girls.

"This way girls," Tieanna called as she headed down the stairs to the lower level. "The gentleman there is Bazzer. He is the rig's engineer. The lady is Eleettra, she will help me get you settled. Keep up."

"What have we got ourselves into this time?" Bazzer asked as he watched Eleettra disappear down the stairs behind the girls.

"A galaxy of trouble is my guess," Dukk answered as he headed for the stairs to the upper level.

"Are you okay?" Dukk asked Marr as he entered their cabin.

"Tired, but yes, I am okay."

"The raid of the h-pod hotel went well then by the looks of it."

"Yes, and we have more troubling information."

"Like what?"

"The hostess training centres on Earth are behind the trafficking," Marr said as she slotted spare magazines into her g-suit pockets.

"I guess that isn't all that surprising at this stage."

"No, it isn't."

Dukk watched Marr in silence as she double checked her equipment.

When done she looked up at him and smiled.

"Come back, won't you," he said quietly.

Marr picked up her helmet then swung her arms around Dukk shoulders.

"Without a doubt," she said as she lent in for a kiss.

Dukk escorted Marr to the lower level. The others weren't far behind.

From the direction of the dorms, they could here Tieanna giving orders.

"On each of your bunks, you will find underwear, an inner layer, slacks, and a top. Get dressed into those now and then take a seat here in the kitchen. We will get some breakfast together while we wait for the captain to return and scan your IDs."

Dukk waited at the bottom of the ramp until he couldn't see Marr and the others any longer. The shuttle was parked at the opposite end of the hanger. He then turned, walked up the ramp and locked the airlock door.

"Is this it? Only six?" the shuttle pilot challenged as he looked at the hooded figures before him.

"Leave it," the co-pilot said.

"Look, I was promised one thousand per head. Six hardly makes it worthwhile."

Mentor stepped forward.

"What's the problem?" he said in an aggressive tone.

"Nothing," the co-pilot said.

"Rubbish, there is a problem," the pilot interjected. "I've already committed that crypto. We were told there would be sixteen passengers. One thousand per head for saying nothing about who we took on board."

"If you stop causing a scene, you'll be getting nothing and we'll make other arrangements," Mentor said firmly.

The pilot stood his ground.

"Besides," Mentor added. "I was expecting to pay my contact, four thousand per head. Sounds like you two have been taken for fools. How about I give that amount to you. You say we didn't show up."

"Done," the co-pilot blurted.

"Great. We will pay you at the end," Mentor said firmly.

"Fine. Now put your med details into that console over there, take your seats and let's get out of here."

Mentor nodded.

"Do you need g-suits, helmets or help connecting the med lines?" the co-pilot asked as she stood back.

"Nope," Mentor replied in a casual tone.

5

Marr focused her thoughts. She cleared her mind. She mapped out the instructions. She visualised their agreed plan. She had briefed the others as they walked to the shuttle. For the rest of the launch, traverse, and landing at the moon resort, they had kept to their own thoughts.

"You can leave now," the co-pilot said from the side door. Beyond was an airbridge.

Marr and the raiding party were sitting in pairs, spread across the five rows of four seats.

Marr unbelted and removed her helmet. She put the helmet on to the seat next to her.

"You can't leave that there!" the co-pilot said as she stood waiting for them to leave.

"We will be with you for the return, later this afternoon," Marr stated as she stood and pulled up the hood of her black cloak.

"We are departing again in just under one hour."

"We'll be back by then."

"Fine, but you need to buy tickets."

"We are not going to buy tickets. I want no record of us being on this shuttle. I will give you an extra ten thousand in crypto," Mentor stated as he joined Marr from his seat in the back.

"You said we'd be paid when we got you here."

"I said that I will pay you at the end. The end of our journey. Our journey ends when we are back in Abrolhos."

"Whatever!"

Bognath led the group out of the port complex. Marr and Luna walked together, behind him. Anuee and Suzzona were next, with Mentor bringing up the rear.

They made their way through the airbridges and tunnels to the resort.

They strolled straight through the reception and took a lift to the third floor. The resort staff ignored them. It felt like it wasn't unusual to see a group of hooded figures moving in such a manner.

As they approached the door to which they understood to be the red room, Marr and Luna got ready. They pulled their arms out of their sleeves, so the cloak hung on their shoulders and concealed their hands. Then they retrieved a silencer from a pocket and screwed it into the handgun. Both then clicked off the safety and checked the location of spare magazines.

As she walked, Marr whispered a reminder to Annee and Suzzona.

"This will be ugly. When it starts, crouch and turn your gaze. If you must look, do it, own it, and then look away. Are we clear."

"Yes," they answered quietly.

The group stopped at the door. Bognath knocked hard three times. He waited for thirty seconds as per the instructions and then pulled open the door. He then held the door for the women and Mentor to enter.

While holding the door, he withdrew a small box from his pocket. As Mentor passed through, Bognath opened the box and held it away from himself. A half dozen nano drones lifted into the air and spread out across the ceiling of the corridor. They now had eyes and ears in the corridor. He closed the door and stepped inside the room.

Marr and the women walked into the centre of the room. Mentor went to the opposite side of the room to Bognath.

At the far end of the room were five men sitting on sofas. They were all naked.

"What is going on!" one man exclaimed as he stood up. "I was assured there would be twelve in this cohort!"

"Change of plan," Marr said as she flicked her arms into the air.

Her cloak flew up. She snatched it with her left hand and tossed it out of the way. Her left hand then came around to join her right hand which was holding the handgun. Luna had mirrored the action.

Annee and Suzzona walked back three paces and crouched down. Mentor turned and dashed towards the other door. Deploying another set of nano-drones and securing it was his role.

Marr and Luna then unloaded a whole magazine each into the mid sections of all five men. All went down. Two were not moving. They were passed out or dead. Three were gagging and choking on their own blood.

Marr and Luna, then walked towards the men. They swapped out the empty magazines as they went.

On reaching the men, Marr pulled a device from a pocket. Luna came over and lifted the hands of one of the gagging men.

Marr then pushed her gun with its silencer hard into the man's left eye socket.

"Open your wrist wraps and unlock all your financial records, both credits and crypto," Marr said quietly but firmly.

"F-you!" the man uttered painfully.

Marr stood back.

Luna twisted his hands and snapped his thumbs back.

The man tried to scream out, choked further and passed out.

They then moved to the second gagging man. He complied. A long beep from the device that Marr was holding, signalled that it had copied the entire contents of the man's records. The third man also complied.

"Two will be enough," Mentor called from his position guarding the other door.

Marr and Luna, then stepped back. They raised their guns in unison and unloaded another magazine each into the heads of the men.

Annee had gone green. Suzzona projectile vomited onto the carpet in front of her.

Marr and Luna, then walked together over to the carryall bag at Bognath's feet.

Each removed the glove from their left hand. Working together and only using their left hand they opened the bag and extracted three medium size plastic bags. Together they opened the first bag. They dropped their guns and magazines into this bag. Then they opened a second bag and dropped the loose gloves into it. From the third bag they extracted a spray bottle and cloth. They then took turns inspecting each other for spots of blood. They used the spray and cloth to clean each other.

Marr then went over to Annee and Suzzona. They were still crouched in the middle of the room.

"Stand up and step away," Marr said calmly.

She then sprayed the carpet and vomit.

Meanwhile, Luna had walked around and collected the spent shells. They too went into the bag with the guns. Then she had taken a vial and snapped it over the bag with the guns. She closed the zipper on the bag. A hissing sound could be heard as the guns were sterilised. She then came over to Marr with the second bag. Marr dropped the cloth into it and the remaining gloves. Luna then snapped a further vial into the bag and placed the whole thing onto the vomit on the carpet. The bag started to hiss and smoke. Then, it simply dissolved into nothing. The vomit and a large section of carpet disappeared too.

With their cloaks back on, they walked back over to Bognath.

"Let's go," Marr said in a dry and emotionless tone.

Mentor and Bognath retrieved their drones as they left.

Nothing was said as they retraced their footsteps, sat back into their seats on the shuttle and were transferred back to Abrolhos.

Chapter 7 – Debriefing

1

"How did you get on with the girls?" Marr said to Dukk as she stepped out of the en suite bathroom.

Dukk was sitting on the bed opposite.

"The girls are wild, but Tieanna has them under control. How did it go on the moon?"

"Clinical."

"No trouble?"

"Nope."

"Ann and Suzzona look shaken."

"Yes, they had to see myself and Luna killing those men. It was messy."

"You sound indifferent about it."

"I am not. I am suffering. I just know it isn't useful to express that grief until clear of danger."

"Can I help?" Dukk said as he stood up.

"Yes, hug me," Marr said as she melted into his arms.

"What is the plan with the girls?" Marr said quietly as she enjoyed the closeness.

"Tieanna wants us to return to Earth straight away."

"Not take the girls on a tour like the first eleven?"

"No, she thinks it will be easier to red pill them back on Earth. She said after assessing them briefly, it would be better to keep them thinking they are still going to a party, for now."

"Ok, so are we preparing for departure?"

"Yep, launch request has been accepted. Bazzer has the resupply complete. We can leave the moment you all are ready."

"Great, and we can debrief the raid once in orbit."

"Perfect. I was about to start preparing the flight plan. Will we do it together?"

"Sure. Do you want to get started while I get dressed?"

"Yep. See you in the cockpit," Dukk said as he broke from the embrace and headed for the cabin door.

Once dressed, Marr opened the cabin door to follow Dukk.

She stepped into the crew mess.

Annee was heading towards her cabin from the direction of the bathroom.

They both stopped and looked at each other.

After a moment, Marr smiled and said, "Are you okay?"

Annee shrugged her shoulders.

"How is Suzzona?"

"Same."

"Can I help in anyway?"

"I am not sure."

"Will you let me know if you come up with something?"

"Yes, I will."

Marr went to turn and leave.

"I have a question," Annee blurted.

Marr stopped and waited.

"How do you do it?"

"Do what?" Marr answered.

"How do you stay so calm when killing people?"

"Mindset and practice."

"What do you mean by mindset?"

"A mindset that includes acceptance of where evil comes from."

"What do you mean?"

"Evil exists, but it doesn't exist outside of us. It exists within us. We're all capable of terrible things. Accepting that, is the key to being able to do what I do."

"What about room for making mistakes?"

"Making mistakes is not the same thing as what happens in the realm of evil. Specifically, the evil that quashes hope. The kind that steals away hope and choice. The type of evil that is conscious. Intentional. There is only one solution for this. The solution is to end it. Clean, clinical. Snuff it out."

"Have you done that before?"

"No, not like this afternoon."

"You've killed others, though?"

"Yes."

"How?"

"Usually from a distance. Or discretely."

"Oh."

After a moment of reflection, Annee continued.

"You mentioned practice just now. What kind of practice?"

"I practice disconnecting my emotions from the necessities of the task at hand."

"How?"

"By practicing the chain of events. Over and over, again."

"Like the clean-up routine?"

"Yes, that and firing weapons."

"Will you teach me?"

"What do you want to learn?"

"Firing a gun."

"Why?"

"I get the feeling things are going to get very real before this is all done. Being competent with a gun might be useful."

"Yes, I will show you what I know."

"Thank you," Annee said with a smile.

"I'd better go help Dukk get ready for launch."

"Yes, and I've got a load of new passengers in need of herding. Will you tell Dukk that we'll be ready for the evacuation drill in about fifteen minutes."

Marr nodded as she turned.

2

Meanwhile Dukk had created the flight plan and projected it to the space in the centre of the cockpit.

"What have we got?" Marr asked as she joined him.

Dukk looked up at Marr. He then followed her gaze back to the projection.

"So, our first leg takes us via HDK216, HDK145, Drafuse 9, Drafuse 7, Drafuse 5 and into the Midway hub at Drafuse 1," Marr stated as she inspected the projection.

"Yep, then Drafuse 3, Tapecue, IK91, IK56, and Innes, brings us back to orbit of Earth."

"Two weeks until we are back on Earth?"

"Yep, that is about the size of it."

"Can we really keep the girls in the dark for two weeks?"

"Good question. We'd better raise that during the debrief after launch."

Marr nodded.

Marr walked through the projection and sat into her seat on the right.

"Ann said she'd have them ready for the evacuation drill in about fifteen minutes," Marr said as she started opening pre-launch checklists.

"She is very optimistic," Dukk laughed. "Has she seen them since she got back from the moon?"

"I don't know," Marr laughed. "Didn't you say Tieanna had them under control."

"I did say that didn't I."

"I guess we will know soon enough."

"We will."

Dukk opened his comms to the crew.

"Circle-up in five. Let's have a quick check-in ahead of launch."

Acknowledgments came back immediately.

Dukk then turned to Marr.

"You up for taking us up today?"

Marr looked up.

"Seriously?" she asked.

"I figured it is about time you started pulling your weight."

Marr laughed.

"Wait! Are you serious that I pilot the launch?"

"Yes. Are you okay with that?"

"Absolutely," Marr answered with a grin.

"Excellent. Let's join the others," Dukk said as he stood up.

With everyone gathered at the table in the crew mess, Dukk flicked the flight plan to the table's holographic projector.

He then addressed his crew.

"Let's keep this brief and operational. We'll debrief today's events once we are in orbit. In summary, we'll be taking the typical trade route back to Earth. Apart from a twenty-four hour stop at Midway, we'll keep moving. Any launch related questions or concerns?"

Dukk's question was met with shaking of heads.

"Great. Bazzer, how are the rig systems?"

"All set, captain."

"Excellent. Ann, housekeeping?"

"Next task on my list is to get our guests ready for the evacuation drill."

"They are already suited up," Tieanna added.

"Perfect. We are ready then," Annee replied.

"Anything else to raise?" Dukk asked.

No one had anything else.

"Great. I'm off to complete the external inspection. I'll close the door on the way back and we'll run the drill."

Five minutes later, Dukk was watching the ramp retract. As it clicked into place, he opened the broadcast to the crew and passengers.

"Good evening, all. Your crew and I will now start making final preparations for departure. And I'd appreciate if you would follow all instructions so we can get underway on time. I am pressurising the cabin and starting the integrity tests. You may find your ears popping during this process. Also, the internal doors will close themselves to accommodate the tests. If you need to move about, please wait for the access panel to show green again. Once underway, it will take us about fifteen minutes to get clear of the settlement. After that, we'll have a seven minute hard burn to reach orbit. I will be back to you with further details of our flight plan once we are in orbit."

Dukk then opened his comms to the crew as he interacted with a console and located the evacuation drill procedure.

"Bazzer, let's go hot."

"Copy," was the reply.

"Marr, you can put in the lift-off request."

"On it," was the reply.

"Ann, I suggest we go with a simplified drill. Just housekeeping and passengers."

"Copy," was the reply.

"Activating now," Dukk said as he hit the button to start the drill sequence.

A high pitch siren rang out followed by a repeating single long tone. The lights turned orange and arrows illuminated in the floor.

Dukk headed for the door to the stairs. He waited there.

After a moment Annee opened the door from the lower level corridor. Behind her came twelve girls. All dressed in g-suits and carrying their helmets.

Annee called out as she led the group up the stairs.

"Remember what we talked about. Straight up to the middle level. Split up and make your way to the furthest transport pod first. Fill the back three seats and leave the two front seats for crew. And remember if you didn't have your suit on when the alarm sounds, come directly to the evacuation point. There is a spare suit for you there."

Mentor and Tieanna made up the tail of the group.

Dukk waited for them to pass. He then crossed into the corridor and use the forward ladder shaft to reach the upper level and cockpit.

3

"We'd better do our cross-check," Dukk said as he entered the cockpit and approached Marr in her seat at the front.

"Absolutely, captain," Marr said as she stood up and reached in for a warm embrace.

"Seriously," Luna said as she entered the cockpit.

"Aren't you supposed to be helping Bazzer run up the reactors? You are still the rig's apprentice!" Dukk challenged.

"I delegated it to Bognath," she said with a wink. "Besides, he said he was happy to stay clear of the passenger area until the girls are seated with helmets on."

"He is a wise man," Dukk answered.

They all laughed.

With the cross-check done, they took their seats.

Marr started preparing her console for launch.

Dukk projected a series of video feeds. Some of the video feeds were of the hanger below, behind and in front of the rig. Other video feeds showed the rig's main corridors, stairs, and transport bays.

The internal camera feeds showed Annee and the others moving about the pods.

Dukk smiled.

"We are going to need to do this drill a few more times, if we are to have any hope of bringing those girls safely through an emergency."

Marr looked over at the chaotic scenes on the projections.

She laughed.

"You know what they used to do in the early days of planet side flight?" Luna asked.

"Tell us," Dukk replied.

"During the pre-flight safety briefing, they would tell the passengers if there was a sudden loss of cabin pressure, they were to put their heads on their knees."

"For safety in the case of a crash landing?"

"No! It was so they could kiss goodbye to their butts," Luna said with a hearty laugh.

Dukk and Marr laughed too.

"Port air traffic control have granted us permission to taxi. They are lowering the air wash barrier," Marr said after listening to a message on her comms.

The external video feeds gave a visual of the barriers being lowered.

"Time to get everyone to their seats," Dukk said as he ended the evacuation drill.

Dukk then opened his comms to his crew.

"We have approval to lift off. Let's get everyone seated. Mentor, I need estimates of how long it will take to get med systems online for our guests."

After a moment, Mentor replied.

"Tieanna has already synchronised their med details. Once seated, we are good to juice them up for launch."

"Excellent news. Bazzer, what is your update?"

"We are on our way up," was the reply.

Dukk watched the internal video feeds, as Tieanna led the girls out of the transport bay and up the stairs to the passenger seating area. Annee and Mentor disappeared in opposite directions. A rig schematic on

Dukk's console showed airlock doors closing as his crew checked everything for launch and made their way to the upper level.

Five minutes later the crew and passengers were in their seats. They all had their helmets on, and the med lines were connected.

Dukk then enabled the crew comms again.

"Check-in please. Passengers and vitals, Mentor?"

"All hooked up and stable. Med lines are primed," Mentor answered.

"Engines, integrity and biosystems?"

"The reactors are humming. The burners are priming. The coolers are on. Integrity is at one hundred percent. All systems are green," Bazzer replied.

"Stealth tech, weapons and defences?" Dukk asked.

"Diagnostics are clear," Luna replied.

"External comms, scanners, Ann?"

"It is quiet this evening. We are the only departure," Annee replied.

"Sound. Marr, are you ready?"

"Yep, all set."

"Anything else, anyone?" Dukk asked as he turned and looked back. He was met with smiling faces.

"Excellent. Co-pilot, the controls are yours," Dukk said as he moved his gaze from the others back to Marr.

"Roger, Captain. Passing port control comms back to you. Hold tight everyone."

"Way to go, Marr," Luna squealed.

Marr nudged the joysticks. The rig trembled as the vertical thrusters engaged to lift the rig gently off the hanger floor and towards the taxi strip. Marr navigated the rig out of the hanger and set it down on the pad in the mountain side.

"Abrolhos air traffic control, this is the Imhullu. Requesting launch permission," Dukk said into his comms.

A moment later, Dukk got the signal. He then opened his comms to Marr as he nodded at her.

"We have a green light."

Marr interacted with the autopilot. The vibrations and noise increased as the thrusters and then the main engines engaged. The rig lifted away from the pad and then moved into the reddish darkness beyond. After fifteen minutes of gradual lift, the hard burners engaged. The rig nose turned skywards and shot towards the upper atmosphere.

4

Three days later, the crew were gathering for their evening meal together.

The rig had recently arrived out of traverse into Drafuse 5. In the morning, they would be traversing to Drafuse 1 and the location of the Midway hub space station.

The past three days, since leaving Abrolhos, had been straight forward in some ways and not in others.

It had been straight forward in that the crew went about running the rig as they would normally do. They maintained the systems that kept them alive as well as giving attention to their mental and physical wellbeing.

It hadn't been straight forward in the sense that their twelve guests were very demanding. They hadn't taken well to the delay and news that they were going back to Earth. Tieanna had done a reasonable job of keeping them in check, but it did need help from the others. That left little room for exploring the grander plans and bigger picture.

Dukk and Mentor were already sitting together at one end of the crew mess table.

"I have been trying to get my head around what really happened," Dukk stated. "It is hard as there is so much information in the hidden archives. I am confused about many things."

"What is an example?" Mentor asked.

"I read that EOs, and observers gained complete control by automating most jobs. They removed the need for humans to keep things working. A.I. based machines did everything. Mass strikes or solidarity had no effect. Another aspect was the introduction of a centralised and controllable form of credit, the EU. The overlords gain complete control over what everyone did or didn't buy, even what was accumulated. Save more than two months of earnings typical for your designation, and the excess is taken away. Even retirement is just an agreement to be sponsored by the citadel in return for the years of service. That comes with lots of restrictions. Failure to comply and you'd starve. Self-censoring and obedience are necessary for survival. Some of the original plans don't make sense against the world we now live in."

"Like what?"

"Okay, so first, apart from traversing, A.I. does little else. Humans perform most tasks again. I realise that the A.I. went rogue when it discovered how to traverse, but we caged it and harnessed its power. Why did we then revert other tasks, like food production and transportation. Why didn't we simply continue to use A.I., but in a cage. Also, surely, if they watched everything and controlled how we accumulated credit and spend it, they would have seen the introduction of crypto."

"It is interesting that you raised both aspects at the same time."

"Why?"

"Because the answer is connected."

"Which is?"

"Elites."

"What about them?"

"While they were aligned at the beginning, it didn't last. Such is the nature of power. Over time they became unaligned. When they started to jostle for position again, they needed wriggle room. The wriggle room is where corruption plays a part. They needed spies and the ability to undermine each other to get ahead."

133

"How does this relate to A.I. and crypto?"

"Humans were inserted back into the process because humans are corruptible. Machines are not. If an elite needed something to break or move in a certain direction, they simply made it worthwhile for the human in the process to succumb to their will."

"And the crypto is the grease that oils that corruption."

"Exactly."

"It is why they tolerate it. Even use it themselves."

"Yep. But not only that. They made it. It was made to replace physical currency. Paper and coin. It was originally called Bitcoin. The term crypto was used to hide its origins."

"Why then, is it dangerous to use? Especially on Earth, where you'd be disappeared if you use it."

"That is to keep its use limited to those moving in elite circles, not those on the ground in crucial roles producing fine foods and wines."

"Hauliers have been using it for as long as I can remember."

"Yes, but only away from Earth and only on the black market. Only in places where elites play."

"But what stops an elite corrupting those on Earth in fine food production to get ahead."

"Something has been keeping them at bay."

"You don't know."

"No. It was never clear to me. It feels as if the citadels are protected in some way. The elites can do what they like everywhere else, but the citadels are treated differently. My best guess is that some sort of moratorium is in place so that the fine foods and wines keep coming. I didn't go lifting too many rocks for fear of finding a snake."

"Look at this," Annee blurted as she emerged from her cabin.

She walked over to the table and enabled the holographic projector.

An image of a man appeared in the air above the table.

"What is it?" Suzzona asked having just put down a large casserole dish into the centre of the table.

"It is a message from Grant, the head of the Hintaught family. I was browsing the broadcast news channels."

Marr came over from her seat at the console near the crew mess table. The others turned to watch as Annee enabled the playback.

"I am here to share with you some disturbing news. Three days ago, two members of the Hintaught family, two members of the Artrudwab family and one member of the Ferrearmas family, were gunned down in cold blood. This unprovoked attack is thought to be the work of a group of rogue mercenaries. It comes after a similar attack in New Montana, eleven weeks ago. And an attempt on the life of the Venefica Magnum Reginae, last week. It is thought that this violent and uncivilised group is determined to undermine the peace, security and stability that has prevailed for over one hundred and fifty years. The group is thought to be associated with an interceptor called the Ukendt, which went missing just prior to the attack in New Montana. I am here to ask other family leaders to join me in backing efforts to track down these miscreants and restore peace and security. The Veneficans have kindly offered to lead that search effort. I have put my fleets and financial resources at their disposal. I ask that we all get behind them."

"Oh shit!" Luna exclaimed as the broadcast ended.

The crew slumped into seats around the table. The mood was sobering.

"They know about us?" Suzzona said from the head of the table.

"I guess so," Annee added solemnly.

"No," Mentor said.

They all turned to look at Mentor.

"No. They don't know about us," he added as he continued to stare at the paused playback.

"How so?" Annee asked.

"They are still using the Ukendt name. They don't know about us or that we have the Ukendt under a new name. This is fishing."

"But they have connected the events in New Montana with the events in Abrolhos."

"Yes, but if they knew about us, they would have used our new rig name."

"But they also connected us to the raid on the mammoth ring."

"With a false narrative."

"So?"

"It is a game. They are teasing for more information. They don't have the truth."

"What do we do with this then?"

"I don't know."

"I might be able to help with that," Marr said quietly.

They all turned to her.

"I've continued to retrieve summary reports of the queen's activities. It is mostly dull so I fast forward. I've also got a little behind. I went to catch up just before the last traverse. There was a report from yesterday. I nearly skipped over an interaction between the queen and her daughter. I caught a bit of it. I haven't been back to it yet, but from what I caught, I think it might shed some light."

Chapter 8 – Making way

1

"From the message data, I gather the recording was taken from the private apartment of mammoth two," Marr said as she interacted with the disc.

After a moment, an image of a masked and hooded figure appeared in the air above the disc.

"What do you want?" said a voice.

"I have information," the masked and hooded figure replied.

"What about?"

"The killing on the moon resort near Abrolhos."

"Let's hear it. And hurry up, I am tired."

"The five clients weren't killed by the mercenaries who were moving the girls. Those mercenaries were found drugged up in their h-pod while the shuttle was still on the moon. It couldn't have been them. Also, large sums of credit were found in their personal wallets. It was transferred after the shuttle returned. It looks like a setup."

"Any sign of the girls?"

"No. Nothing yet."

"What of the shuttle pilots?"

"They aren't forthcoming with information."

"Resort staff?"

"Nothing new. Just that, six hooded figures went up to the room. They left thirty minutes later."

"Port staff in Abrolhos."

"They aren't being very helpful."

"This is so frustrating. Our Filia aren't up to the job."

"Pity the Ukendt team are still unreachable."

"Yes, it is."

"They could clean this up."

"Maybe."

"They did a good job of cleaning up loose ends after Craig Atesoughton the Second tried to get in on our business."

"Good job? How can you say that?"

"The cruiser he was using to bring girls from Earth. That got taken out successfully in Layton 16. Also bringing those two observers to the resort to create leverage, and then framing the assassination on one of them. It allowed them to get their own observer on the G5 rig, to plant the bomb that took it out. It tied up that loose end nicely."

"Yes, they did pivot well to frame the observer when they found Craig dead."

"And don't forget that framing the observer helped surface the level seven defector. The accomplice."

"Thosmas?"

"Yes, in retrieving the framed observer from the lock-up in Mayfield. We now know a potential source of some of the leaks back on Earth."

"True."

"Can you pause for a minute," Tieanna interrupted.

Marr reached over to the disc and paused the playback.

Everyone turned to look at Tieanna.

She had turned green. She looked like she was going to be sick.

Dukk gathered his thoughts. He had been right and wrong.

Marr was at the same realization.

"The Veneficans are behind the trafficking!" Annee blurted.

"I've been a fool," Tieanna muttered.

"We've all been played," Mentor added.

"At least we now know who got in the way," Luna added in a sympathetic tone.

"And who was behind taking out the Dinatha," Bazzer added.

"On the bright side, we have inadvertently taken out their wet works crew," Bognath stated.

"There is more, will we continue?" Marr said on realising idle pondering wasn't going to get them anywhere.

"Yes, we should hear what else they have to share," Dukk replied.

Tieanna nodded.

Marr interacted with the disc. As the voices started again, the eyes of the queen were still roughly on her daughter.

"Any news on the whereabouts of Thosmas?"

"Nope. The traitor has disappeared into thin air."

"Yes, probably using fake IDs. Any news of Craig's girls. The ones that we sent to New Montana?"

"No. Still nothing. Without Filia in the Atesoughton cluster, information is near on impossible to obtain."

"Yes, and that is why we needed the Ukendt team. The old man pays us a handsome fee to keep our distance, but we are therefore blind."

"Do you think the grandson will continue to pay us to keep our Filia out of their settlements?"

"Unlikely. Without Filia installed as carers and nannies to indoctrinate, the grandson is beyond our reach. And with the old man's age and the assassination of his son, it is even more important that we find Helenal and those discs. Once we have control of the EU credits again, we won't need to appease the families. We won't have to beg. We can resume our plans in full."

"That's interesting," said the queen's daughter.

"What?"

"What if the Ukendt crew are behind the killing of our clients?"

"Oh! Of course! The Ukendt crew has found a new pay master. They got a better offer. That makes sense. They must have faked their disappearance at the same time as they destroyed that G5 rig and its crew. And they nabbed the girls, both in Abrolhos and New Montana.

Perhaps they killed the clients because they didn't agree to the new arrangement!"

"But how did they find out about Abrolhos? The Ukendt crew were operating in the vicinity of the Atesoughton cluster. It is on the opposite side of the galaxy."

"Those men in New Montana knew of it. They were weak and stupid. No doubt they squealed before they were dispatched."

"Who is the new pay master?"

After a moment of silence, they both shouted, "Thosmas."

"Of course!" the queen said in a reflective tone. "Thosmas is playing us! For sure. This rogue is coming after our operations."

"But why interfere with our operations? There are plenty of girls. There are plenty of family members looking for this service."

"Maybe the cretin didn't plan to. Maybe when we signalled that we were putting a halt to Craig's operation, Thosmas saw a new opportunity. Perhaps the observer had Craig killed and then infiltrated our mercenaries. And then goes about cleaning up. Freeing that observer in Mayfield was cleaning up. With the help of the Ukendt crew, Thosmas then went to New Montana, killed the uncooperative clients, and took the girls."

"But why our girls and clients? Why not just operate independently?"

"The bounty?"

"What bounty?"

"The bounty someone put on the observer's head. Two million credits."

"I don't understand what that has got to do with it."

"Perhaps the bounty forced the observer's hand! The bounty meant the observer no longer had access to citadels and girls. Thosmas needs a new supply of girls to provide the service. And that's why the observer is targeting our operation."

"Is this really something to worry about?"

"Absolutely!"

"But a few dead clients and twenty-four missing girls, won't even make a dent on our operation and revenue streams. And just because they know of one red room, doesn't mean they know of all the others."

"No, but damp leads to rot. That could bring the entire house down. We have worked too hard to build the infrastructure and network. And we can't tolerate this questioning of our authority."

"What about Helenal?"

"What about her?"

"Is the observer and the Ukendt crew helping her, too? Southern Cross isn't far from Abrolhos."

"Yes, perhaps. Any sign of that other woman?"

"No, she hasn't shown up in port records. She must be evading the checks and ID gateways."

"Yes, more fake IDs."

"It is a pity Bartiamos hasn't been forthcoming."

"Yes, claiming that the scanners in the relays were down for maintenance when we were in Southern Cross is a dangerous game to be playing. Claiming he couldn't tell us which interceptors had a change in headcount is nonsense. When we have our funds and control over the weapon systems in these mammoths again, he will be the first to pay."

"What can we do?"

"We pull rank where we still have influence. We get involved directly."

"How?"

"Tell our head of operations it is time for some scrubbing."

"I don't understand what that means."

"She will. Now be gone."

And, with that, the recording finished.

"Oh shit!" Luna exclaimed.

"Mentor, you were right," Dukk said quietly as they all stared at the end of the playback.

"Somewhat," Mentor acknowledged.

"Let me get this straight," Luna interjected. "The queen and her people are running multiple trafficking rings. They built the red rooms. They take the girls from Earth and put them in harm's way. They take money from elite family members. And they were behind the sabotage, the attempt on our lives. All of it!"

"We missed the real target when we had the ring in Southern Cross," Annee reflected.

"The queen?"

"Yes, and her daughter."

"Even with the mammoth ring's weapons being out of their control, with all those arrows and interceptors, we wouldn't have got near them."

"Don't forget the sentinels," Bognath added.

"What do we do?" Annee asked after a few moments of silence.

"We clarify what we think they don't know, and work with that," Mentor replied.

"What don't they know?"

"They don't know we know about all their red rooms via my network of students," Tieanna added.

"Or that we killed the Ukendt crew," Luna said.

"Or that we have the Ukendt," Annee said.

"Or that we can see into the queen's activities," Suzzona stated.

"Or who raised the bounties."

"Or who we really are," Marr said.

Silence gripped the room again.

"They don't know our true aims," Dukk said quietly after a few moments of reflection.

Everyone turned to look at him.

"They are chasing a false threat," he added.

"Yes, Dukk, and that might be the most crucial piece of information," Mentor noted.

"Perhaps we should encourage that delusion," Marr suggested.

"How?" Annee asked.

"Dukk, do we still have the original Ukendt databases?"

"Yes, Marr. They will have been backed up before I installed our own databases."

"Perhaps we can reverse engineer their digital IDs."

"And put them back on the map," Luna said with glee.

"Yes, exactly, Luna."

"How would that be done?" Annee asked.

"If we have their digital IDs, we can use them within our implants. We can go about the hubs and settlements as if we are the old Ukendt crew."

"But won't everyone be looking for them now."

"We'd just use their IDs occasionally to move through a gateway. She will see it. We can leave a bread crumb trail to keep her misconceptions alive. If we keep our distance, she will never be close enough to us to do anything about it until we are long gone."

"What if the local security people notice?"

"We'll have to run a test. Monitor local security people and see if they react."

"How long before we'd be ready to run a test?" Dukk asked.

"Hacking the IDs won't take long. I could do it now ahead of the morning traverse. We could run a test at the Midway hub tomorrow afternoon."

"Great, that is our next step."

"Will that work? Aren't they mobilising resources to find the old Ukendt crew? What will that look like?" Annee asked.

"Extra hassle at ports," Bazzer answered.

"What do you mean?"

"More sentinels about the place. More stringent inspections on arrival."

"You've seen something like this before?"

"Years ago."

"Is this going to be a problem, especially if they are looking for you, Tieanna? The extra makeup and fake ID have worked thus far. Not to mention your network of students tampering with port logs. It has kept your actual face out of port records, and us for that matter. But aren't sentinels more capable? What if we run into them?"

"We'll have to run extra interference," Marr interjected.

"How?"

"The sentinels are transhuman. Their sight and sound are augmented. Just like ID gateways. Those systems can be hacked. We can make sure they aren't able to record our faces."

"What do you think she meant by scrubbing?" Bazzer asked.

"Securing their operations," Bognath replied.

"How?" Annee asked.

"Eliminating possible information leaks."

"Or setting a trap," Mentor noted.

Mentor's comment got their attention again.

"What can we do about that?" Annee asked.

"Take more precautions."

"Like what?"

"Perhaps we should go dark."

"The girls," Marr commented.

"Yes."

"You don't think bribing the port staff will not be enough to keep the girls hidden as we pass through the hub?"

"No. Not now."

"Are we able to get back to Earth without a refuelling stop?" Annee asked.

"Yes, plenty if we run without stealth," Dukk answered.

"And with stealth?"

"I am guessing that it would be touch and go. Using unmonitored systems would cut down the time in orbit. That would give us some extra margin. But we'd be running blind again. No updates from broadcasts or the disc. Either way, I'd have to do the calculations against an updated flight plan. Are we willing to take the risk of moving through unmonitored systems?"

No one responded.

"Do we have a choice?" Tieanna asked.

Still, no one said anything. The silence was the answer.

"What will we tell the girls?" Annee asked.

"I will handle it," Tieanna answered.

After a further moment of silence, Dukk said, "Well, if no one has anything else to share, I think I'd better get the flight plan updated so I can feed the DMD a new destination for our next traverse."

There weren't any more comments.

"Okay then. Marr, let's move the conn into the cockpit to make the adjustments."

"Will do, you go ahead. I'll send it when you are there."

3

"What does it look like?" Marr said as she entered the cockpit.

Dukk was sitting in his seat. A star chart was being projected into the air before him.

"I have found a path via DX5H, TGH5, IK32, IK15 and IK56," Dukk replied as he read the labels that were dotted along a red line. The final dot was labelled 'Sol.'

"Fuel?" Marr asked as she took her seat next to Dukk.

"It looks okay. Tight, but doable. We'd better hope the base south of Utopiam has plenty of supplies or we won't get off the ground again."

"Time frame?"

"Just under two and a half days to reach orbit of Earth."

"That saves us thirty-six hours if you take into account the absence of the twenty-four-hour layover in Midway."

"Yes, but I think we should include an intermediary inspection at IK32. That adds back twelve hours. Taking the unmonitored track will save us twenty-four hours."

"So, not that much difference. It still puts us back on Earth, seven weeks since we dropped off the first group of girls and the observers."

"Yep. Do you think they will be back at the base?" Dukk said as he gave the DMD the coordinates for DX5H.

"Some will," Marr replied. "Others may decide to go deeper into the wild."

"Any bets on who will be there?"

"Nope. I guess I hadn't thought much about who would have made that choice."

"It must be a frightening place for them."

"Having to make the choice?"

"Yes."

"I am not sure about that. It is an easy choice to make once we let go of certainty."

"Letting go of certainty makes choices easier?"

"Yes, the world we exist in promotes certainty of safety. However, certainty is an unattainable goal. Certainty is only achieved in the absence of choice. The absence of choice means you have no freedom. So absolute certainty equates to no freedom. By believing in the certainty of the safety provided by the Rule of Twelve, we give up autonomy. We give away the ability to choose. We trade choice for safety. The deprogramming process helps let go of certainty. Once that happens, making choices is easier."

146

"I have lost you. What do you mean when you say, 'certainty is only achieved in the absence of choice'?"

"Certainty is the state of being definite or having no doubt about something. That implies an absence of workable alternative possibilities. It implies an absence of alternative paths or options. If there are no alternatives, you have no choices to make. Therefore, certainty doesn't have a need for making choices. Or, put another way, certainty exists only in the absence of choice."

"So, by letting go of certainty we have to acknowledge the possibility of alternatives."

"Exactly."

"But how does that make choice making easier?"

"Acknowledging the possibility forces us to explore them. We are forced to consider one possibility over another and therefore the trade-offs that comparison implies. The ability to consider trade-offs makes making choices easier."

"By having a willingness to explore risks and benefits?"

"Precisely."

"Is this about taking responsibility for making one's own choices?"

"Yes, but it is also about flourishing."

"Flourishing?" Dukk said in a curious tone.

"Yes, the state of growing vigorously. The concept of thriving."

"I get what flourishing is, but how does this relate to choices and certainty?"

"For flourishing to occur at an individual, community, and societal level, you must create the conditions for hope. Without hope, there is no flourishing."

"Why does flourishing require hope?"

"Flourishing is growth. Growth is the learning that takes place in going from one state to another state. The learning comes from the delta. The learning comes from the choices made against the outcome realised. Without certainty we must take a leap of faith at times. We must hope for the best as we step into the jungle. So, hope is a crucial component of growth. And therefore, hope is a necessity of flourishing."

"You have lost me again."

"As already explained, to have certainty, you need to have every variable and assumption fully explored and exhausted. You must remove all ambiguity in terms of the path you must take, your community must take, or all of society must take. Only then will you have certainty that it is the right path. If you have certainty, you have no choices to make. You have no risks to take. You don't need to apply a degree of hope that the choice you make is the right one. To have certainty you must remove all other options. You must remove all other choices. Or you must allow them to be removed for you. There is no need to hope that your choice is right. If there are no choices, there is no hope, if there is no hope there is no flourishing. Flourishing only happens when there is uncertainty."

"Wow, that is a lot to take in. I might need to sleep on it," Dukk concluded with a laugh.

Marr smiled.

4

The next morning, Marr and Dukk were back in the cockpit. The rest of the evening had unfolded as per usual. As had the traverse into DX5H. With the rig in slow running and the DMD given the instructions for the next traverse, the crew had got back into their morning routine. Marr and Dukk were still on watch and had gone back into the cockpit to check on an alert.

"What does it look like?" Dukk asked having reached the cockpit a little after Marr.

"Nothing, I think. Turning up the sensitivity of the passive proximity scanners might be overkill."

"If we are being hunted, we want to know if anything else is out there using stealth."

"Yes, I agree with that, but having to visually check all feeds might not be enough to stop an all-out attack."

"No, it won't. But we've proven we can respond well to that. Visual checks are to head off someone creeping up on us and getting on board."

"We did ok on the Dinatha, when we had no stealth or weapons."

"Do you mean when we used the DMD bounce?"

"Yes, your and Bazzer's skills in resuscitating everyone was all we needed."

"But we have a bigger crew now and more passengers. Getting to everyone in time might not be possible."

"So, we check the feeds."

"And do some orbit estimations."

"Divide and conquer?" Marr asked.

"Absolutely."

"What is your preference?"

"None."

"Fine, I'll do the orbit estimations and you check the feeds."

"Perfect."

Marr interacted with her console and an image appeared in the air before her. It showed the planet they were orbiting. The projection also showed their position and the path they were following.

She then copied the details from the alert and instructed the navigation system to project all potential orbit paths, based on the location of what ever had triggered the alert. Blue circles appeared in the projection.

She then looked over at Dukk. He was interacting with several video feeds.

"Anything?" she asked.

"Nope. Nothing showing up using various spectrum filters. You?"

"Nope. If that was a thruster firing on a vessel using stealth it isn't going to be anywhere near us anytime soon. The signature wasn't enough to cause a speed change. It could have only been a small orbit adjustment. Like what our thrusters do every couple of hours to avoid dropping out of orbit and crashing into the planet."

"Great. So, we can discount it as a rock or space debris colliding."

"And that means it is time to go back to our normal routine."

"Is it your turn or mine for a walk around?"

"I can't remember," Marr laughed.

"Are you restless?"

"Nope. But I am tired."

"Ok, I'm off. You relax," Dukk said as he leaned over for a kiss.

With the cockpit to herself, Marr extracted the disc from a pocket and sat it into the charging station.

The configuration panels appeared on the console.

She checked the reports. There was nothing on them.

She then explored the final panels again.

She went into the first sub panel with the four rows. The sub panel that she felt included her record.

She mindlessly started clicking the toggle buttons on the third row. The row she figured was her own. The buttons still didn't respond. She then clicked the menu button at the end of the row. A further sub panel appeared.

Marr gasped.

"Why haven't I been in here?" she said aloud.

The panel had a toggle button, a table, and two further toggle buttons.

The label on the top toggle button read 'Inherit permissions: OFF'.

The labels on the table rows included, 'General', 'Flight Controls', 'Mantrap', 'Common Area', 'Apartment', 'Server Room', 'Weapons control'.

The labels on the table columns were '1','2','3','4','5'.

The cells had toggle buttons. The labels on the cell toggle buttons all read, 'Full'.

The first of the two toggle buttons below the table read, 'EUs Override: ON'.

The second toggle button read, 'Incubation database reveal: ON'.

Marr closed the panel and then clicked the menu button against the fourth row. The same sub panel appeared. However, the first toggle button here read, 'Inherit permissions: ON'. The table was blurred. As were the two toggle buttons below the table.

Marr backed out again and clicked the menu button against the second row. The row she knew was for the queen. In this sub panel the label on the top toggle read 'Inherit permissions: OFF'. The table was enabled like the first sub panel, however the labels in the cells were different. The 'Server Room' and 'Weapons Control' rows for all columns had the label of 'None'. The other column cells had the label of 'Access Only'. The toggle buttons below the table read, 'EUs Override: OFF' and 'Incubation database reveal: OFF'.

Marr closed the sub panel and went into the menu of the first row. It looked like the details for the fourth sub panel.

"Oh shit," Marr said aloud.

"What is going on?" came a voice from the cockpit door.

It was Luna.

"I just discovered why I could get into the mantrap and server room," Marr said absently.

"What are you talking about?" Luna asked as she plonked down in to Dukk's seat.

Marr smiled as she looked over.

5

"Wait! You think you are the queen's daughter?" Luna asked.

Marr had just finished sharing the details of the disc and her adventure into the data centre within mammoth one.

"Yes," Marr replied.

"Who else have you shared this with?"

151

"Only Dukk."

"What does he think?"

"He isn't convinced. He thinks there could be other explanations."

"I tend to agree with him. So, Mentor and Tieanna know nothing of this?"

"Not to my knowledge. I haven't spoken to them about it."

"That might be for the best. At least until you talk with Teacher."

"I think so."

"So, the EU credits!" Luna said to shift the focus of the conversation.

"What about them?" Marr replied.

"You must have some sort of override."

"I guess."

"How do we verify it?"

"I don't know," Marr answered.

"Verify what?" Dukk asked as he appeared from the door to the forward ladder shaft.

"I think I have the ability to control all the funds in the citadels."

"And perhaps, the galaxy," Luna added.

"What are you talking about?" Dukk asked as he walked over, turned, and leant against the forward console.

"EU credits," Luna answered. "Marr thinks she has permission to control or manipulate the flow of credits."

"Oh. That could be useful."

"It could, if we can work out how to do it," Marr noted.

"Emeelie said something about this when she was showing me how to access the videos they took from Mayfield. There was some sort of DNA sampling device on the desk in the study in Emerald Valley. She said family members use them to access their EU credit shadow accounts."

"Shadow accounts?"

"Yes, she said unlike for most of us, the spending habits of elites isn't tracked or visible to observers. They have other places where they keep their wealth. They can transfer what they need to visible accounts if they are interacting with us unprivileged."

"Perhaps observers have access, too?"

"We should ask Mentor, or even Tieanna."

"Yep, that would be a good idea."

That afternoon, Marr went looking for a quiet moment with Mentor. She found him, with Tieanna, in the cockpit. They were on watch. They were repeating the alert orbit estimations as she and Dukk had done during their watch.

"Hello, Marr. Is everything all right?" Tieanna asked as Marr stood in the cockpit.

"Yes, all is good. Though, I have a question that I hope you can help me with."

"What is the question?"

"Are you familiar with EU credit shadow accounts?"

"Yes, the families use them to manage their wealth."

"How do they do that?"

"The interface is like what we have for managing our credit. The system on our wrist wraps. The system that we use to see transactions, check our credit limits, and transfer funds to another. The only difference between what we have, and they have, is that they can choose different accounts. They aren't limited to their primary credit account."

"My credit account interface doesn't have the ability to choose accounts."

"No, the capability in the interface is hidden for most."

"How is it unhidden?"

"You need to use a DNA sampling device when you have the interface open?"

"How does it work?"

"It samples your DNA and verifies it against the Rule of Twelve records. You are then granted more access based on your lineage."

"Elite family lineage?"

"Yes."

"So, if Dukk used the DNA sampling device he would in theory get access to the Atesoughton family accounts?"

"Yes, I guess he would. Although, the system does consider inheritance. I think the oldest living member of the lineage must delegate access."

"What happens if that person dies before delegating access?"

"I don't know. I guess the system must have some sort of override."

"Interesting?"

"What is this about?" Mentor asked having seen between the lines of Marr's questions.

"Emeelie mentioned EU credit shadow accounts to Dukk. I just wanted to know more about them."

"Why?"

"I guess being the older brother, Dukk is in theory in line for inheriting his grandfather's wealth. That might not sit well with Craig and others in the family."

"No, it is something we might need to pay attention to."

"I think it will work out fine," Tieanna added. "Provided everyone keeps talking."

"Yes, keeping the communication channels open will be important," Mentor concurred.

Marr nodded and smiled as she took that in.

"Is there anything else?" Tieanna asked after a moment of shared silence.

Marr looked between Tieanna and Mentor. She didn't know Tieanna well enough to read her. However, she knew Mentor. She knew by Mentor's demeanour that he wasn't convinced. It was clear in his expression that he felt her interest in shadow accounts wasn't just because of Dukk's situation. She had an idea.

"Yes, Tieanna, I have one other question that has been on my mind."

"What is that?"

"The woman that helped you. You said she shared her real name. She asked you not to mention the name 'Helenal' to anyone else, apart from when you shared the full story to us."

"That is correct."

"So, she wasn't going by Helenal when you met her."

"No, she wasn't."

"What name was she using?"

"Moontour was the name she went by."

"Moontour!"

"Yes."

"That sounds familiar. Do you know what the name means?"

"No, dear, I haven't ever given it much thought."

"Ok. I'd better let you get back to keeping us safe from visitors."

Tieanna smiled. Mentor nodded.

Chapter 9 – Unearthing

1

"I have it!" Marr announced as she looked over at Dukk.

Marr and Dukk were in the cockpit. She had been staring at Earth. She still wasn't used to seeing her home planet from space. It held such awe for her.

A little earlier the rig had arrived out of traverse on the last leg on their return. Dukk was interacting with the navigation, radar, and communications systems.

"Have what?" he asked.

"The meaning of Helenal's alias."

"What are you talking about?"

"Two days ago, when I asked Mentor and Tieanna about shadow accounts, I also asked Tieanna about Helenal's fake name. The one she'd been using at the time instead of Helenal."

"What name was she using?"

"Moontour."

"Like a tour of the moon?"

"No!" laughed Marr. "But it is interesting you said that. Because spelling it with 'moon' and 'tour' had thrown me."

"What do you mean?"

"I had assumed the spelling as you suggest and focused on the memory associated with someone using that name. I felt I may have met someone with that name. Just now, while staring at Earth and seeing the continents rushing by, it occurred to me."

"What did?"

"The name isn't familiar because of meeting someone with that name. It is familiar because the name has meaning. But not in our language."

"Which language?"

"One of the old languages used in the Celtic regions before the reset. I even did some searches for 'moontour'. Nothing showed up because while pronounced like that, it isn't spelt that way."

"How is it spelt then?"

"It is spelt M-ú-i-n-t-e-o-i-r."

"That sounds completely different."

"But when spoken with the correct pronunciation it sounds like 'moontour.'"

"And what is the meaning."

"It means 'teacher'!"

"Oh shit."

"Yes. It is all converging to a single point."

"We really need to talk to her."

"We do," Marr said as she pushed the thought out and took stock of what was in the air in front of Dukk.

"Do we have a plan?" she asked.

"Yes, I think so," Dukk replied as he pointed to a spot on the projection of the Earth. "This G5 has been approved for deorbit. I think it will suit our needs."

"When?"

"In about ninety minutes. We are near its trajectory so our minor adjustments should not give up our position and make the use of stealth superfluous. We can break orbit in its wake and get down barely noticed."

"And then how long before we are set down in the caves south of Utopiam?"

"Another two and a half hours after that."

"Six hours after exiting traverse."

"Not bad considering."

"Really?"

"Yes, at busy times, when I was hauling, we could be up here for eighteen hours. Maybe even a whole day."

"Are you exaggerating?"

"A little," Dukk replied with a grin.

At that moment there was a knock on the cockpit door.

Dukk flicked open a video feed. It was Eleettra. He hit the unlock button.

Eleettra marched right to the front of the cockpit and turned to face Dukk.

Dukk looked up and smiled.

"I got a message from Craig on the encrypted channel. It is for you."

"Flick it over to the cockpit projector," Dukk replied.

An image appeared in the air in the centre of the cockpit. The image was the head and shoulders of a man. He had fair complexion, light blue eyes, and dark brown hair. He looked a little younger than Dukk.

Eleettra reached in and enabled the playback.

"Hi Dukk, I gather you didn't get back to the beach house. Wherever you are, I hope you are safe. Dukk, our grandfather wants to meet you. In fact, he wants me to introduce you. How he knows about you is baffling. He just mentioned it out of the blue. Anyway, the sooner the better, as his health is failing. If you want to give me a window of when you'll be back on Earth, I will arrange to be there and host the meeting."

"Is that it?" Marr asked as the image disappeared.

"Yep," Eleettra replied.

"How do I reply?" Dukk asked.

"It must go back via the secure channel. I can record a message and send it to him."

"Tieanna said she wants to spend at least a week on the ground with the girls. Will that be enough?"

"It depends on where he is now."

"Ok, let's tell him we are here now and will wait for his response and see what happens."

"When you are ready," Eleettra said as she held up her wrists.

Dukk stood up and faced Eleettra.

"Ready," he said.

Eleettra nodded.

"Hello, Craig. Yes, we are all safe. We had some other business to attend to first. We don't plan on going to the beach house. However, we are back at Earth and will wait for your message."

Dukk smiled and paused, to signal the end of the message.

Eleettra dropped her wrists.

"To the point," Marr said with a laugh.

"What? What else would I have said?" Dukk asked as he turned to look at her.

"I have no idea how to answer that. The workings of the brains of men, are a total mystery."

Eleettra laughed as she started interacting with her messaging app.

"Done," she said after a moment.

"Great," Dukk said as he took his seat again.

Before turning to leave, Eleettra leant forward to get a better view of Earth racing below them.

"I never get tired of that view," she said.

"Me neither," Marr added.

"Do we have an ETA?"

Marr looked over at Dukk. He nodded.

"About ninety minutes until deorbit," Marr said.

"And on the ground?"

"Just before ten p.m. local time."

"Great. I'll leave you to it," Eleettra said as she turned and headed for the door.

2

Dukk released the joysticks and sat back in his seat. It was the second time he had manually flown the rig into the hidden cave-based hanger at the back of the main resistance base south of Utopiam. This time it had been harder. He felt there was more at stake. It played on his mind.

"Are you okay?" Marr said as she looked at him.

Dukk turned and smiled.

"Yep," he said.

"You look a little more tense than last time when we negotiated our way through the wind farm graveyard, over the shoreline, through the trees and up the valley towards these caves."

"Yes. It feels different this time. It feels like the risks we are taking have a greater weight. There is more to be lost if I mess up."

"Yes, I feel that too," Marr said as her hands came to rest on her abdomen.

"Bazzer, let's power down," Dukk said as he returned his attention to the controls.

"Right you are, captain," was the reply.

"Mentor, how are our guests?"

"Stable. Sleeping soundly."

"How long before they come around?"

"At least two hours."

"Will that be enough time to work out what happens with them next?"

"I hope so. The base should have the capacity to accommodate us for the week to red pill them. But we will need to check. We might have to watch the girls and keep them under a little longer if we hit any snags."

"Suzzona and I can stay put and keep an eye on them," Annee suggested.

"Bognath can help, too," Luna added. "He is working hard to complete his medical training. I am sure he will lend a hand."

"That works," Dukk said to focus everyone's attention. "So, Marr, Mentor, Tieanna and I, head into the base to investigate. Everyone else stays put for now."

"I would like to come," Luna added. "I want to see the first group of girls. If they are back."

"Yes, of course," Dukk replied.

Dukk undid his belt and stood up. He turned to look at his crew.

"Ann, the conn is yours."

Annee nodded as she unbelted.

Fifteen minutes later, Dukk led the group from the bottom of the ramp across the dark hanger floor. With the cave doors closed, and the moonlight no more, the only illumination was coming from the rig's navigation lights.

Dukk was leading them in the direction of doors that he knew were hidden in the cave wall. As they approached the wall, a crack rang out and a bright light filled their view.

"Welcome, captain," a man said from the doorway.

"Hello, Ricardi," Dukk replied.

"Marr, Mentor, Luna," Ricardi added with a nod. He stopped at Tieanna.

"This is Tieanna," Dukk said after following Ricardi's stare. "Tieanna, this is Ricardi, the base leader."

"Hello, Ricardi," Tieanna said in a pleasant tone.

Ricardi didn't move. He just stood staring.

"She is with me," Mentor said to break the tension.

"She looks like you, Dukk," Ricardi said as he moved his gaze back to Dukk.

Dukk smiled.

With that Ricardi shrugged his shoulders and turned.

"Follow me," he said as he headed off down a wide and tall corridor.

Marr suddenly felt extremely nervous. Meeting Teacher was occupying her thoughts. The questions were playing on her more so than any other moment since they broke orbit. It had been fourteen weeks since they had last spoken. And that encounter was brief and confusing. The cryptic message they received seven weeks ago had been mostly understood, but there were many more questions now.

The walls of the corridor were rough, dusty, and cluttered with pipes and cables. It was dimly lit. Their path took them past storage areas and workshops. Most spaces were unoccupied on account of the time of day. Deep within the base they entered the accommodation area. It was more brightly lit and cleaner.

Ricardi took them past a series of doors.

He stopped at one and knocked gently.

"Come in," came a muffled reply.

Ricardi opened the door and gestured for them to enter.

Marr stepped through first. Luna was right on her tail.

The room was a large dorm with twenty-four bunk beds. Only four looked to be occupied.

Four tall, slender, but shapely, teenage girls were sitting on the floor in front of some of the beds. They were dressed in green fatigues and wearing black hiking boots. They wore no makeup, and their long, black, and dark brown hair, was tied back in low ponytails. They were playing cards.

The girls' faces lit up as they recognised Marr.

Marr's heart sunk. But only for a moment. The disappointment of not finding Teacher in this room, was replaced with the joy of seeing the girls.

"Luna, Marr," one exclaimed as they all got to their feet.

"Hello, Lilaho, Kayila, Nabiel and Mella," Marr answered.

"Where are the others?" Luna asked.

"They all decided to go further into the wild," Lilaho answered.

"That wasn't for you?" Marr asked.

"No, Mella and I want to be raiders. We've returned here to continue our training," Nabiel answered.

"And what about you, Lilaho, and you, Kayila?"

"I want to return to space. To do what you do," Lilaho answered with a gulp.

"Me too," Kayila added quickly.

"Will you introduce me?" Tieanna said as she stepped out from behind Marr and Luna.

"Sorry, of course," Marr answered.

With the introductions done, Tieanna addressed the girls.

"I am delighted that some of you have found your way back to this base. I have a special request for you. On our rig are twelve more girls. We rescued them from a fate not unlike your own. However, unlike yourselves, they didn't see the truth of their predicament. They still believe they are privileged and on their way to party with elite family members."

Tieanna paused and looked at the girls.

The girls' expressions changed. They looked disheartened. The reminder of their ordeal was brought back to the foreground.

"What do you need from us?" Nabiel said after a moment of silence.

"I need you to talk to them about what you experienced. I need you to help them see the reality. I need you to share what happened to Zarra."

"That will be hard," Lilaho said softly.

"Yes, my dear, it will be. And you won't be alone. Marr, Luna, I, and the others will be here to help and be with you when you share."

"How will it happen?" Nabiel asked.

"We are going to bring the girls here, to stay in this dorm with you. Over the next week, I will work with you to help bring them in to awareness. Then they will go into the wild, just like your friends."

The girls continued to stare. Their expressions softened a little.

"Is that okay?" Dukk said quietly to Ricardi. They were standing together at the back of the group.

"Of course, it is. The resistance is always welcoming to newcomers. Let me know what you need."

3

Six and a half days later, Dukk was on the treadmill. He looked up as he felt the door open.

Marr came through. He smiled and hit stop.

He stepped off and embraced her. They kissed deeply.

"I've missed this," she said as she pulled back.

"I need a shower," Dukk replied with a nervous laugh.

Marr squeezed him again.

Marr, Luna, Mentor, and Tieanna had spent most of their time, since arriving back on Earth, with the girls, deep within the base. The others had stayed on the rig.

"How is it going?" Dukk asked when they pulled back again.

"Breakthrough. That is why I chanced coming back to see you."

"Breakthrough?"

"Yes. It has been incredibly challenging. Lots of crying. Lots of tantrums. The worst of it happened last night after the story circle. But there was a breakthrough. Things are completely different this morning. The girls are engaging and talking about going into the wild to meet girls like themselves."

"Like themselves?"

"'Free' was the word they used."

Dukk smiled.

"So, what happens now?" Dukk asked after a moment of enjoying looking at Marr.

"Nabiel and Mella will help some of the raiders bring the girls into the wild to meet the others. It is part of what Nabiel and Mella need to do if they are to become raiders. They will then return to the base to continue training."

"When?"

"With the change this morning, there isn't anything in the way. I'd suggest they might be ready to leave tomorrow."

"Lilaho and Kayila?"

"They have their hearts set on coming with us."

"Are they up to it?"

"I think so."

"They will be apprentices."

"They are good with that."

"Any sign of Teacher?"

"Nope."

"Are you disappointed?"

"Yes, but I guess she did say she would see us again near the end. I guess that we still have more to do. It isn't the end yet."

"I guess not."

"So, do you have to go back straightaway?" Dukk said in a slightly provocative tone.

"No, I don't," Marr said with a giggle.

Dukk went to turn towards the door.

"But there is something else?"

"What is it?"

"Another report from the queen."

"What did you learn?"

"Let me show you," Marr replied as she retrieved the disc and enabled the projection of the report.

The familiar masked face appeared in view.

"What?" uttered the queen in a dismissive and impatient tone.

"Head of operations wants to talk to you."

"What about?"

"She is concerned that changing the schedules won't be enough."

"What does she mean?"

"She is worried that the new schedules will become known, and they will attack again."

"Then she should tell them all to take extra precautions."

"Like what?"

"Tell her to tell the clients to put on extra security in the resorts so they don't get themselves shot to pieces. And tell her to put further mercenaries in the port and hotel to protect the assets."

"Will that be enough? The group were efficient."

"Even if we could spare further resources, we don't want to expose ourselves by getting too close to the clients or the assets. No, it is better if we let everyone believe that the hostess training centre managers are behind all of this and not us. Besides, we still have a contingency."

"What is the contingency."

"That isn't for you to know. Now, be gone."

"That puts a spanner in the works," Dukk said as Marr put the disc back in her pocket.

"Yes, we need to rethink our approach."

Dukk's comms sounded. He checked the caller ID. He accepted the call.

"Eleettra, what's up?"

"There is a message from Craig."

"Where are you?"

"In the crew mess."

"On our way up."

"What is it?" Marr asked as Dukk returned his attention to her.

"There is a message from Craig. Eleettra has it in the crew mess."

"Let's go," Marr replied as she leant back in for a final kiss.

"Eleettra, what is in the message?" Dukk asked as he and Marr entered the crew mess.

"Coordinates, approach instructions and a request to share our ETA. Here, I'll share it with you," Eleettra said as she flicked her wrists towards Dukk.

Dukk caught the message. After scanning it, he flicked his wrists at the projector in the ceiling above the crew mess table.

An image of the Earth appeared in the air before them. The image started to spin. The image then zoomed in on the large continent in the southern hemisphere. Two markers appeared on the image. One marker showed their location, and the other showed the location provided in the message.

"We are here on the east coast. The coordinates are on the west coast," Dukk said.

"What is out there?" Marr asked.

"Nothing from what I've seen when we pass over it."

"It must be camouflaged like the beach house south of Citadel Inquis."

"I guess it must be."

"From looking at the location marker, it must be Zuytdorp," Eleettra stated.

"Zuytdorp?" Marr asked.

"It is one of the largest compounds that the family has built on Earth. It is one of Craig senior's favourite places."

"Have you been there?"

"A few times. Though, I never left the hangers. How long will it take to get there?"

"It would take a couple of hours. Three tops," Dukk answered.

"What should I put in the reply?" Eleettra asked.

"Marr, are we certain the girls are ready for us to leave?"

"I'll have to check with Mentor and Tieanna, but I'm ninety nine percent sure that we can leave whenever we want."

"Great! Let's give ourselves a buffer of twenty-four hours to hide our location. Eleettra, will you reply and suggest we can be there tomorrow at midday."

"Will do," Eleettra replied as she turned and headed towards the console in the corner.

Marr turned towards Dukk.

"I guess we will have to postpone our catch-up. I'd better head back into the base and talk to Mentor and Tieanna."

"I guess so," Dukk said in a reluctant tone.

But before Marr could turn, Dukk put his arms around her and drew her in. She accepted the embrace.

"Wait," Marr stated after the kiss. "We can't leave here in daylight. It will expose the location of the cave entrance."

"We'll leave pre-dawn."

"But if the trip is a couple of hours, we'll be there mid-morning."

"We'll take the long way around to cover our tracks. We will turn a three-hour journey into six."

"That works. I'll tell the others."

Dukk smiled and pulled her in for another kiss.

This time, Marr did a better job of letting go and enjoying the moment fully.

4

"Anything yet?" Annee announced as she took her seat in the second row of the cockpit.

"Nope," Marr replied as she reviewed their flight progress towards Zuytdorp.

"What was the instruction again?"

"Simply start our descent and then open channel Z8H when we are within fifteen minutes of set down."

"Anything new from the archives?"

"Nope. All we still know is that this region was known as Zuytdorp on account of a large sailing ship that was wrecked at this location, three hundred years before the reset."

"The vegetation has changed?" Luna added.

"Vegetation?" Annee asked.

"Yes, the mass greening that has occurred globally over the last two hundred years has completely changed the landscape here. When the Zuytdorp sailing ship met its demise, this area was bleak and barren. It isn't like that anymore."

"Ann, will you take over monitoring external channels? I want Marr and myself free to focus on taking evasive action if this isn't what we hope it is." Dukk interrupted.

"Of course," Annee replied.

Dukk opened his comms to his crew.

"Hello again. We are on final approach. Please take your seats and check your belts are secure. Hopefully, this will be smooth sailing. But encountering a few bumps isn't out of the question. Bazzer, systems update please."

"All green. On our way back up now," was the reply.

"Excellent. Lilaho and Kayila, how are you holding up?"

"Very well, thank you, captain," came the reply from Lilaho.

"That's good to hear," Dukk said in a kind tone.

"We have it!" Annee blurted. "It must be my touch. Exact set down instructions have been shared on channel Z8H."

"Great, pass them over to both Marr and I," Dukk answered.

"Sharing the details now."

After a moment of reviewing the instructions, Dukk looked over at Marr and said, "Are you happy with those?"

"Yep, that looks in order."

"Great. Adjusting the autopilot to take the exact location."

Five minutes later, with everyone belted in, the autopilot started the final approach adjustments. The rig groaned as the thrusters worked hard to slow things down but stay airborne. The rig's nose pointed up as the airspeed was no longer enough to maintain lift. The main hard burners carried some of the job of avoiding a hard landing.

Dukk adjusted the video feeds in the cockpit and passenger seating area, so that everyone had a clear view of their approach. In the centre of the video feed was their target. Initially the view simply showed green bush and grass stretching towards the ocean to the west of them. Then the view started to change. The ground was opening. A huge hole appeared. An underground hanger. The autopilot made the necessary adjustments to bring the rig through the hole and set it down gently.

"What now?" Marr asked as she looked up from her console.

"I am not sure," Dukk replied as he stood up to get a better look at the inside of the hanger.

The hanger was large enough for two vessels of their size. It had the typical equipment for repairs and resupply. The number eleven was painted onto a wall. A door in one wall looked large enough for the Imhullu to pass through. The adjacent wall had another door, but it was smaller. Next to it was a set of stairs. The stairs led to a set of doors. Doors that had the appearance of the entrance to a hyperloop.

With the hanger roof closed, fluorescent lights on the walls illuminated the space.

"Dukk, we are being hailed," Annee announced.

"Any signature?" Dukk asked.

"Nope, but it looks legit."

"Let's get the others in here. It might save some time."

"Good idea."

"I'll go," Luna announced as she bounced out of her seat and opened the cockpit door.

"Bognath, Suzzona, Tieanna, Lilaho, and Kayila, do you want to join us," Luna said from the doorway.

"Put it through," Dukk said once the others were gathered at the back of the cockpit or standing in the doorway.

An image of an attractive woman appeared in the air in the middle of the cockpit. She looked to be in her mid-twenties. She had black hair, creamy skin, and light green eyes.

"Welcome, Marr, Dukk and the crew of the Imhullu."

"Hello, Emeelie," Marr replied.

Emeelie smiled.

"I have some requests before you enter," she said kindly.

"Of course," Dukk answered.

"Power down the rig, lock it, and get onto the hyperloop. You won't need to bring anything. Everything that you will need will be provided."

"Weapons?" Luna blurted.

"Please leave them in the rig. The hyperloop won't run if weapons are detected. As you can imagine, Craig senior takes his security very seriously. And these are troubling times."

"Would it be best for someone to stay with the rig?" Annee blurted.

"If you wish, however the hangers here are very secure. It would be typical that only staff stay behind. That won't apply to any of you as you are all seen as guests. Besides, Craig senior wants to meet you all and he doesn't have a lot of patience."

"How much time do we have?"

"Ann, the meeting with Craig senior is schedule for later this afternoon. You have plenty of time to get over to the residential

172

complex and settle in before that time. Staff will meet you at the complex entrance and answer any other questions. To authorise you, I need your digital IDs. Please share them now via this channel. I must go."

"Thanks, Emeelie. Will do," Dukk said just before the transmission ended.

Marr looked over at Dukk.

"That was a little odd. Can we still trust Craig and Emeelie?"

"I don't know," he replied.

"What if it is a trap?" Luna blurted.

"It isn't," Tieanna said from the doorway. "This is standard procedure."

5

With the rig powered down and secured, the party made their way across the hanger floor, up the stairs and into the waiting hyperloop carriage.

The carriage was enclosed. There was no glass or windows like many of the hyperloops they had used in citadels and distance settlements. Dukk went over to look at a safety schematic on the front bulkhead. It described evacuation procedures. There was a map. From the illustrations Dukk deduced that the hyperloop tubes were attached to the wall of a much larger circular tunnel. The tunnel linked the hangers with the settlement in a closed loop. Evacuation points indicated there were stairs to the surface. The map suggested there were fifteen hangers. Dukk contemplated the scale of the complex if it supported that many hangers of the size of the one, they had just landed in.

An alarm sounded to indicate that the hyperloop carriage was about to move. Dukk turned and jumped into a seat next to Marr.

Dukk grinned nervously as he looked ahead.

"Apprehensive about meeting your grandfather?" Marr asked.

"Yep, and Craig. How can you tell?" Dukk replied as the hyperloop accelerated and pushed them back into their seats.

"You are looking for emergency exits," she said with a giggle.

Dukk chuckled.

Five minutes later the hyperloop carriage came to a stop.

The opening of the doors exposed them to a large circular atrium. They stepped out onto a circular platform that sat in the floor of the atrium. The atrium was at least four storeys high. The ceiling was transparent. Blue sky could be seen beyond. Dukk concluded there must be camouflage on the outer surface as he hadn't seen anything like it on their approach. The wall behind them, as well as the walls to their left and to their right, had the appearance of the inside of a lush rain forest. It wasn't clear from where they stood if it was fake or real vegetation. The wall opposite was a waterfall. It splashed into a pool that covered most of the floor of the atrium. In the middle of the pool was a silver spire. It reached up to the ceiling.

They all looked about in awe.

As the hyperloop doors closed behind them, a triangular canopy appeared at the bottom of the waterfall. The canopy rose, splitting the flow of water, and exposing large double doors. At the same time the silver spire started to move. It started to disappear into the water. As the spire dropped, the top half started to split open. It had the appearance of a flower blossoming. The two halves opened and created a bridge between the double doors and the platform the group stood on.

As the bridge made good, the doors opened. A man, dressed in a black three-piece suit, came through the doors, and walked swiftly across the bridge. He stopped just in front of them. The man looked to be in his late fifties. He was tall with black hair, cut short and parted down the middle. He had a stern look about him.

"Welcome to Zuytdorp. My name is Jeeves, I am the head of house here. Mr Atesoughton, it is an honour to meet you," he said as he bowed his head towards Dukk.

Dukk stumbled. The use of his grandfather's name for himself had thrown him.

"Thank you," Dukk replied cautiously. His voice had a hint of embarrassment.

Jeeves then lifted his head and turned towards Marr.

"My Lady, it is an honour," he said as he nodded his head once more.

Marr nodded and smiled nervously.

Jeeves then lifted his head again, and this time he turned towards Tieanna.

"Tieanna, ma'am, welcome."

"Thank you, Jeeves," Tieanna replied confidently.

Jeeves then nodded to each in the party and welcomed them individually. Each time he addressed them by name.

Thanks, and nods came in return. A general sense of bemusement prevailed.

With the formalities out of the way, Jeeves looked up and addressed them all.

"Mr Atesoughton, My Lady, and your party, if you would allow me to escort you into the main atrium. This way please."

With that, Jeeves turned and headed back across the bridge.

Dukk took Marr's hand and together they followed.

On the other side of the double doors was another even larger circular atrium. It was at least nine storeys high and coned shaped. The top being slightly wider than the bottom. The ceiling was like the space they had just left.

They stood halfway up on a balcony. Each level, above and below, had a balcony that went around the atrium. A series of stairs crisscrossed the space to give access between the levels.

The wall in front was all glass. The ocean was beyond. The sun, high in the sky, was bouncing off the waves. They were dark blue in colour and angry looking. A third of the atrium was below sea level. Waves splashed up against the glass. Large fish could be seen occasionally swimming past the glass wall. The floor of the atrium was a series of large swimming pools.

Staff in grey uniforms were dotted along the balconies. They were looking over at the group. Their faces held pleasant expressions, with a touch of awe and curiousness.

"Holy shit," Luna exclaimed as she came through the doors and onto the balcony.

Her words reflected the reaction in all their minds.

Chapter 10 – Reconnecting

1

With everyone through the doors and gathered on the balcony inside the main atrium, Jeeves turned and spoke to them as a group.

"Your IDs have been activated within the complex. You will know where you have permission based on doors that do and do not open. All parts of the complex are accessed via this atrium. You can see the stairways before you and there are elevator lifts behind you. There are also service stairs, service elevator lifts, secondary passageways, and evacuation tunnels. You shouldn't need to use them.

"Accommodation is on levels six, seven and eight. Levels one, two and nine are where you will find pools, gyms, and various recreational areas. Level four is where you will access the library, the study, and the banqueting halls. Level three has the lounges. We also have medical facilities and related services on levels two and nine. We are currently on level six.

"Emeelie has provided me with pairings and room allocations. Please let me know if I have made any mistakes or if you would like to change anything. Mr Atesoughton and My Lady, you are on level eight. Mentor, Tieanna, you are on the level above, level seven. Everyone else, your accommodation is on this level. Annee, Suzzona, Bazzer and Eleettra, your rooms are to my left. Luna, Bognath, Lilaho, and Kayila, your rooms are to my right.

"Your audience with Craig Atesoughton, the first, is at seven p.m. Please dress formally. Clothing options are within your suites. Let me know if you need anything else.

"You are free to explore the complex and surrounds, however for this afternoon I've been instructed to ask that you stay inside. Any questions?"

"Where will the audience be?" Dukk asked.

"In the south banqueting hall. Members of my staff will be outside each of your rooms from six forty-five to show you the way. It will be out of bounds until that time."

"What if we are hungry or in the need of a drink?" Bazzer asked.

"Your suites have drinks and snacks. There are refreshment docks in all recreational areas. You can access these at all hours. If you can't find what you need, mention it to a member of staff. They will be present in all recreational spaces between seven a.m. and ten p.m. And a presence is maintained in the main corridors at all other times. Breakfast is served in the sunroom on level nine from six a.m. until eleven a.m. Lunch is served from one p.m. until three p.m., also in the sunroom on level nine, and by the main pool on level one. Dinner is served in the north banqueting hall at eight p.m. Room service is always also available."

"Wow," Bazzer answered.

"What if we want to cook something for ourselves?" Suzzona asked.

"Let me know, and I will make it happen," Jeeves answered.

Jeeves paused and looked around.

On deciding the questions had finished, he stepped back and put his hands out in both directions. He nodded his head.

"Shall we?" Marr said to Dukk as she hooked her arm into his.

"We shall," Dukk laughed as they moved towards a staircase that went up.

On the eighth level more staff greeted them. Without speaking the staff nodded and gestured to a double set of doors in the south side of the atrium.

Arm in arm they approached the doors. Unseen scanners detected their IDs and the doors swung open. Within was a wide corridor. As they stepped in, the doors behind them closed and the pair of doors ahead opened. To their left and right were single doors. These single doors stayed closed as they made their way to the open doors at the end of the entrance foyer.

Beyond the second set of doors was a wide and brightly lit space. To their left was a dining table with seating for eight. A large bunch of flowers coloured the scene. Beyond the table was a glass wall. They could see water falling. They guessed that they were behind the waterfall in the entrance atrium. To their right was a lounge area with three large sofas. There was a kitchenette and bar in an alcove to the right of the sofas. In the corner was a single door. On the opposite wall was another set of double doors. Beyond the lounge area, was wall to ceiling glass. The view was of the ocean. The same view from within the atrium.

Dukk and Marr stumbled towards the windows. They stared out, arm in arm, in awe at the view of the ocean.

Eventually, and without a word, they turned towards each other and embraced. They kissed. Nothing needed to be said.

"Will we continue the tour," Marr said gently after the kiss.

Dukk nodded.

Through the door near the kitchenette, they found a study, with a large desk and separate seating area. It also had its own bathroom and its own door back to the entrance foyer. The other door in the entrance foyer led to a service area with doors to stairs and a service lift. Once back in the living space, they crossed over to the other set of double doors. They needed to be opened in the traditional manner.

Beyond was a triangular foyer. There were two further sets of doors. They tried the set to their left. Within was a large room. It had windows like that beyond the dining table. In the middle of the large room sat two cots. There were also other various pieces of baby

179

furniture. The decor was light blue in colour, and it smelt of fresh paint.

"What is this?" Dukk blurted.

"I think it is a nursery!" Marr said with a stumble.

"What is a nursery?"

"I read about them. Before the reset, people had a dedicated room to raise their babies. The elites even had helpers."

"Do you think this is for us?"

"Maybe."

"But how could they know?"

"That is a mystery to me."

A further investigation of the space found a large bathroom, large walk-in wardrobe, storage room and a small room with a single bed, kitchenette, and en suite bathroom.

They then returned to the foyer and tried the other doors. Beyond was a large bedroom. A huge bed sat in the middle. There was also a multi-sofa seating area and a large vanity table set into an alcove. One whole wall was made of glass. The view was the same as in the living space. They also found a large bathroom and a walk-in wardrobe. The wardrobe was fully stocked with clothes in assorted styles. It all felt like what they found in the suite in Emerald Valley.

With the tour done, they collapsed onto the bed. They had some catching up to do.

2

An hour later, Dukk opened his eyes. The nap had refocused his attention. He turned slightly so he could see the view. Marr was snuggled into his chest. His turning also brought her out of sleep.

"Amazing!" Marr said after adjusting her position.

"Yes, it is something else," Dukk answered disingenuously.

Marr turned to look at him. She had noticed the tone.

"What's going on?" she asked in a gentle voice.

Dukk smiled. He looked at her.

"You sensed my distraction."

"Yes."

"Do you have any thoughts on what that is about?"

"The nursery in the other room?"

"Yes."

"No."

"Why would they do that? Why would they put us in a suite with a freshly decorated nursery for two babies?"

"It could be a coincidence?"

Dukk raised his eyebrows.

Marr grinned sheepishly.

With a sigh, he pulled himself out of the embrace and walked over to the window. Marr got out of the bed, too. She then walked over and inserted herself between Dukk and the window. She pulled his arms around her as they looked out at the rolling seas.

"Someone here had to have known about us and the twins. Who told them?" Dukk asked quietly.

"Craig and Emeelie left before we found out," Marr said in response.

"Yes, only those on our rig knew."

"Eleettra?"

"Perhaps. She does have a secure channel to them."

"We could ask her."

"Asking tough questions of Eleettra will erode trust. Besides, she had been adamant that her allegiance is to Tieanna and therefore, by association, us."

"What about Tieanna?"

"She was adamant that she stays hidden. On several occasions, she even made the point that she was looking forward to the day when she could be in contact with Craig again."

"What should we do?"

"I am not sure."

"Perhaps some air will help?" Marr said as she pulled out of the embrace.

Marr had noticed a panel on the wall near the window. She interacted with it and then turned to look out again.

A balcony with guardrails started to assemble itself beyond the windows. When it was done, a section of glass near the edge opened to expose a doorway.

"Cool," Dukk said with a hint of enthusiasm.

"It is, isn't it," Marr replied with a degree of surprise.

"How did you know?"

"I didn't. I just figured I would see what the panel was for."

"Robes?"

"Yes, that might be a good idea. We don't know who else might have discovered these retractable balconies."

A few moments later, Marr and Dukk were on the balcony, standing together, wearing bathrobes. The sun was blinding. The strong wind was masking the sun's heat and intensity. The noise of the wind was drowned out by the noise of the waves. And it was hot.

"Wow! Exhilarating!" Marr shouted.

"Absolutely," Dukk yelled back as he lifted his head and took in the salty air.

After a few moments of enjoying the elements, Dukk turned to Marr.

"We need more information!" he shouted.

"Who?" Marr replied.

"Jeeves!" they shouted at the same time.

"Yes," Dukk added. "He did say to contact him if he got any of the arrangements wrong."

Dukk turned and made his way back inside. He crossed through the living area and back through the entrance foyer. The suite doors opened on his approach. He stepped onto the balcony and looked about. A grey uniformed female staff member was standing near the stairs they had used earlier.

The woman had noticed Dukk's arrival. At once she started walking towards him.

"Can I be of assistance," the woman said on approach.

"Yes, please. We would like to speak with Jeeves."

"Of course. Would you like to speak with him here in your suite?"

"Yes, that would work."

"I will contact him. The chimes will sound in your suite when he is in your entrance foyer. Is there anything else?"

"No thank you."

With that the staff member smiled, then turned and interacted with her comms.

Dukk turned and went back into the suite. He found Marr in the walk-in wardrobe sifting through a stack of t-shirts. She was already wearing one of them, as well as a pair of sweatpants, and running shoes. The colours were earthly and warm. She held up a t-shirt and smiled as he entered the space.

"For you," she said.

Dukk smiled.

He was only just dressed when a gentle chime sounded.

"Jeeves," Dukk said as he headed for the door.

"How may I help you," Jeeves said as Dukk opened the inner doors.

"We have a question about this suite," Dukk answered as he stepped back into the living area to bring Marr into the conversation.

"What is your question?" Jeeves enquired as he stepped into the space and looked around.

"The nursery!" Marr said.

"Ah, yes. Congratulations is in order. Is it not to your liking?"

Dukk and Marr both blushed.

"So, you know then?" Dukk asked bluntly.

183

"Yes, of course. It is my job to know the needs of the guests."

"But how could you know?" Marr asked.

Jeeves looked at Marr for a moment. He then looked at Dukk. He then paused for a moment and then answered.

"Mr Atesoughton informed me."

"Dukk's brother?"

"No, Mr Atesoughton senior."

"But how does he know?"

"It is not my place to enquire how he knows what he knows."

"Any guesses?"

"Sorry, My Lady, speculation would not be proper."

"Please call me Marr."

"Very well, Marr. Thank you. Such a lovely name."

Marr smiled.

"So, he told you about the twins?" Dukk asked.

"Yes."

"That doesn't explain the nursery."

"Mr Atesoughton thought it would be a good idea to make the changes so that you felt welcome here at any time."

"Oh!"

"Is that okay with you?"

"I guess so."

After a moment of silence, Jeeves smiled and said, "Is there anything else?"

"Who else knows?" Marr said bluntly.

"About your news or the nursery?"

"Both."

"I have not shared your news with anyone else. The remodelling is known to two trusted members of my maintenance team. They have not been given any further explanation. And they were instructed to keep it to themselves."

"Cleaning staff?"

"We use automatics for cleaning. Also, I saw to it personally that the suite was ready for you. No one else has been near the suite since it was redecorated."

"Ok then," Marr said in a gentle manner.

"Will there be anything else?"

3

Marr looked at Dukk. He shook his head gently.

"Actually, I have another question," Marr said in a jovial manner.

Jeeves smiled.

"Earlier, you said that there were gyms on levels one, two and nine. Where would be best?"

"What kind of exercise did you have in mind?"

"I would like to do some running, however you requested we stay inside."

"Yes, I did, but if you want to run outside, that can be arranged. Although, at this time of the day, it is very breezy, and the temperature is high, as is usual for this time of year."

"Inside is fine."

"Do you want a personal trainer?"

"No thank you," Marr said with a laugh.

"Right, so then, while all gyms have similar equipment, I would recommend the gym on level nine. It has magnificent views out over the ocean. The gyms on levels one and two are more for classes and weights. They are also below sea level, so the view is like that of inside an aquarium."

"Training gear?"

"Training clothes and shoes are in your wardrobe and also in the change rooms near the gyms and pools."

"Laundry?"

"There are hampers in your suite and all recreational areas. The wardrobes are restocked daily."

"Very convenient."

Jeeves smiled.

After a moment he added, "Will there be anything else?"

"No thank you, Jeeves," Marr replied.

With that Jeeves nodded, turned, and headed back into the entrance foyer. The doors closed behind him.

Marr turned towards Dukk.

"More mysteries," she said.

"Yes, so it would appear my grandfather found out. He also wants us to spend time here."

"That must be expected. I am carrying the next heir."

"Yes, that makes sense. But who is his source?"

"We should ask."

"Yes, that we will."

"Shall we go exploring and have some fun before that?"

"Yes, that is a clever idea. Also, I am hungry."

"Me too."

Marr took Dukk's hand, and they made for the doors. Once back in the atrium, they climbed a set of stairs to the level above. Apart from staff, they didn't find a trace of the others as they explored the pools, gyms, and recreational spaces on the south side of the atrium. They also found the sunroom. Lunch was still being served. After a simple meal of cold meat, cheese, and salad, they continued the tour.

"What is through here?" Dukk said as he opened some doors on the north side of the atrium.

Beyond was a large garage. It had dozens of vehicles of all shapes and sizes.

At the north end there was a ramp that ran up to the ceiling.

As Dukk and Marr wandered around the vehicles, the ceiling above the ramp started to retract. Bright sunlight streamed through the opening.

Dukk and Marr stopped to watch.

A rumble could be heard as the ceiling doors came to rest. The rumble grew to a roar.

Moments later, a four-wheeled vehicle raced down the ramp and came to a skidding stop in the middle of the garage. The vehicle had large tyres, an exposed roll cage and a rear mounted engine. Two people, in open helmets and goggles, were harnessed into the vehicle. They were laughing. The driver of the vehicle revved the engine one last time before shutting it down.

Dust and fumes filled the space. It hid Dukk and Marr from view. The two occupants, a man, and a woman, had extracted themselves from the vehicle before they noticed they weren't alone.

The pair looked over. Dukk and Marr looked back.

"Marr, Dukk!" the woman yelled with enthusiasm.

"Hello, Emeelie. Hello, Craig," Marr replied.

Emeelie rushed over to give them a hug.

"Sorry," she said after the hug, "I am all dusty and buzzing from adrenaline. That dune buggy is so much fun. And I must apologise for my frostiness earlier. Such is keeping to protocols."

"No problem," Marr replied. "It is good to see you. That does look like fun."

"Do you want to come for a spin?"

"Now?"

"Sure, why not?"

"Ok," Marr replied.

Emeelie grabbed a fresh helmet and goggles from a nearby stand and handed them to Marr.

"Come on," she said as she got back into the driver's seat of the dune buggy.

Moments later the noise of the engine was burning their ear drums once again. Emeelie skilfully turned the vehicle around and charged back up the ramp.

Dukk and Craig had said nothing as they watched. When quietness returned, they looked at each other. Each unsure how to start. Then a smile erupted on both faces. Immediately they embraced in a strong and sincere hug.

After the hug, they stepped back and looked at each other again.

"Good to see you, brother!" Dukk said to break the ice.

"It is, brother!" Craig answered.

Craig's tone held a little more caution than what Dukk had experienced in every other occasion.

"So, what happens now?" Dukk asked to keep things moving.

"You take over as head of the family, and I drift into obscurity!" Craig said with a laugh.

His tone had a hint of regret.

"No way! This isn't my life. It is yours. I am a haulier."

"A bloody rich one."

"You seriously think I will step in and take this all from you?"

"It is within your rights."

"Rights or not, it doesn't feel like the best outcome."

"Why?"

"You've prepared for this, your entire life. You deserve this, not me."

"So?"

"Look, I have kept my head down, my whole life. I can't see myself in the limelight, doing politics."

"The rewards come with a cost."

"Keep the rewards!"

Craig looked away. Dukk kept looking at him. Eventually, Craig looked over again.

"So how will it work?"

"Craig, I have no idea. But I am willing to try and figure it out."

"Okay," Craig said in a tone that sounded authentic. "Besides, granddad might have something to say on this."

Dukk smiled nervously. The reminder of meeting his grandfather was suddenly back in front of his mind.

Craig noticed the change. He then nodded over at another dune buggy.

"Want to give it a go?" he said.

Dukk looked over at the vehicle.

"Absolutely," he replied.

Craig took a helmet and goggles and passed them to Dukk. They then went over to the vehicle.

"Is this powered by a vintage engine?" Dukk asked as he took a closer look at the manic looking machine.

"Yes, combustion engines are much more fun and the weight to power ratio is far better than normal engines."

"And louder"

"Absolutely. You really get a sense of what it was like before engine modernisation."

"And it doesn't need charging?"

"Nope, just fuel."

"It doesn't fly?"

"Nope! Contending with the surface is part of the fun. Do you want to drive?"

"Is it hard?"

"Not with the semi-automatic gear box."

"What is that?"

"Jump in," Craig said laughing.

4

"Wow!" Marr said as she removed her goggles.

She and Emeelie were standing on a ridge, ten kilometres north of the complex.

They were looking out at the ocean.

189

The wind was snapping at the large waves colliding with the cliffs below.

The dune buggy was sitting quietly in a clearing, behind them.

"It is so bright," she added.

Emeelie went back to the buggy and retrieved two sets of sunglasses.

"Here," she said as she passed one pair to Marr.

"That's better, thank you," Marr said after donning the glasses.

"Is it always this windy?" Marr asked after a period of silence.

"It is in the afternoons. The mornings and evenings are calmer. In fact, it is something else up on this ridge at night. The sound of the waves against the stillness is an experience to behold. You can truly imagine what it must have been like for those sailors all those years ago."

"But the wreck would have happened during a storm?"

"Yes, that is likely. But after the storm passed, those that survived would have sat on these cliffs or the rocks below, with nothing, contemplating their fate."

Marr smiled. She too was contemplating her fate. She put the thoughts aside.

"Do you come up here often?" Marr asked to distract herself.

"Whenever we are here visiting the old man. Which isn't often these days. Perhaps every other month."

"It is pretty isolated," Marr said as she turned around to look back towards the complex.

"Yep, it is."

"Are there wildlife or wild people about?"

"Wildlife, yes. Emus, kangaroos, dingoes, rabbits, birds and lots of snakes and that kind of thing."

"What about wild people?"

"Not near here. There are reports of small pockets in the south."

"Resistance?"

"We are too far from the citadel to be of any interest to the resistance. It is partly why this place was built here."

"When was that?"

"The family has had a presence here for over a hundred years. This complex was started roughly fifty years ago. It has been updated periodically. The current décor is about ten years old."

"Ten years old and it still feels new. The suite Dukk and I are in is huge. Enough room for the entire crew and then some."

"You have one of the two penthouse suites. Craig and I have the other one."

"What about Craig senior?"

"He changed the services area behind the south banqueting hall. He had a medical facility made for himself. He spends most of his time there and holds all his audiences in the hall."

"Oh, okay. And, the other rooms, on the levels below, are they the same?"

"No. The rooms on the level below have a lounge, bedroom, and study. They don't have the dining space and second bedroom. The rooms on level six have a lounge and bedroom. The spaces within are smaller."

"All the same, it is amazingly comfortable. Even more plush than Emerald Valley."

"Yes, such is the way of things," Emeelie said with a hint of boredom.

Marr senses the lack of interest and changed direction.

"How has it been since we saw you in Southern Cross?" Marr asked as she turned her gaze back towards the ocean.

"Busy," Emeelie replied. Her tone had a touch of yearning.

"Are you still doing the rounds because of the announcement of your primary companionship with Craig?"

"Nope, that is all done. The tensions have taken over as top priority."

"Tensions?"

"Yes, the families are restless. Until recently, fun and frivolity were the main reasons to visit other families or host them. Now it is to prevent trade agreements from unravelling. Or to smooth over relations after small skirmishes."

"Skirmishes?"

"Rumours are circulating that some families are behind the increase in pirate attacks on trade routes."

"Which families?"

"It isn't clear. The Veneficans are also making noises."

"Noises?"

"They are demanding an audience with Craig senior?"

"What for?" Marr asked.

Emeelie turned towards Marr. She lifted her sunglasses. She raised her eyebrows.

Marr noticed the attention and grinned.

"The message from Grant Hintaught?" Marr offered as she continued to look out.

"Yes," Emeelie said as she put the sunglasses back on and returned to looking at the waves.

After a moment, she added, "I gather you didn't come straight back to Earth after Southern Cross?"

"No, we didn't"

"You took a detour to continue Tieanna's crusade?"

Marr grinned but said nothing.

"From the reports, the take down was very professional. It would have taken a crew with specialised skills."

"Is that so," Marr replied.

"It is handy that they think the Ukendt crew are behind it."

"It is."

"Any idea what happened to the Ukendt crew?" Emeelie asked as she turned to look at Marr again.

Marr shrugged her shoulders and kept looking out at the ocean.

"Some things are better unsaid, perhaps," Emeelie said.

Marr smiled.

After a further moment of silence, Emeelie started to fidget.

Marr sensed the irritation.

"Are you ok?" Marr asked as she turned and removed her sunglasses.

Emeelie turned towards Marr. She lifted her sunglasses.

"What did you do with the other girls?" she asked.

"Other girls?" Marr asked in reply.

"There are two with you. There were eleven. I also assume there were others, too. From the detour."

"They are with friends."

"What friends?"

Marr paused.

"Who are you?" Emeelie asked in a firm tone.

"A friend," Marr answered genuinely.

Emeelie rolled her eyes.

"You know what I am asking. You are accompanying one of the galaxy's most notorious assassins. You have the skills of mercenaries. You have attracted the wrath of the Veneficans. Yet, you don't act like ruthless and hedonistic thugs. Who are you really?"

"A haulier that was once a keeper."

Emeelie frowned and turned away.

"What do you want me to say, Emeelie?" Marr pleaded.

"The truth!"

"Are you sure you want the truth?"

"You sound like Tieanna. She said we weren't ready. She just wanted to ask about us and then said she was tired. I think she said that to avoid any further questions. She wouldn't tell us what was going on, or where the other girls were. That is why Craig and I headed out with the dune buggy. To blow off some steam."

"Are you ready to know?"

"How will I know unless you tell me?"

"Can I ask you something?"

"Of course."

"Who is your enemy?"

"What do you mean?"

"Who is between you and what you stand for?"

"I don't know. Other families, I guess."

"Anyone else?"

"The Veneficans."

"Is that all?"

"Yes, why? What is this?"

"So, just those like yourself?" Marr asked, ignoring Emeelie's deflection.

"Yes, of course. Well, I guess. Who else would be in the way?"

Marr said nothing.

After a moment, Emeelie said, "Wait! Are you talking about the resistance?"

Marr paused.

"You are resistance!"

Marr held a blank stare.

"Why would you want to tear this all down?" Emeelie asked blankly.

"Tear what down?"

"The progress being made. The expansion into the galaxy. The riches. The way of life."

"Who has this way of life?"

Emeelie paused. She frowned. She then said, "I get your point."

"Are you going to tear it all down?"

"No."

"Take it for yourselves?"

"No."

"If it isn't that, what is the resistance?"

"It is a game b movement," Marr replied.

"What is game b?"

"Game b is what happens next. If the status quo is game a, then game b is what comes after. The movement is formed on the principles of being self-organising, network-oriented, decentralised, emerging, and oriented towards human flourishing. It looks to build on what works to address what doesn't."

"And what isn't working."

"Equality of opportunity. Most don't have the choice."

"How will things change?"

"That isn't clear."

"So, what are you doing then?"

"Focusing on building and maintaining hope."

"How?"

"By intervening where hope is being stifled or destroyed."

"Like the trafficking."

"Yes."

"So, the other girls are now with the resistance?"

Marr nodded.

With the wind and waves, they hadn't noticed the other dune buggy until it rushed into the clearing. It came to a sliding halt. A cloud of sand and dust engulfed them all.

Dukk and Craig appeared from the cloud as it started to settle.

"Wow! What a view," Dukk said as he came up to Marr and put an arm around her shoulders.

"It is," she replied as she looked back at the view, donning her sunglasses as she did so.

"Nice shades," he said.

Marr grinned.

Craig joined them and stepped over to the very edge of the ridge.

"There," he shouted.

He was pointing towards the ocean.

"That is coin rock," he added.

"What are you talking about?" Dukk shouted back.

"That rock with the waves crashing against it. It is called coin rock," Craig answered as he stepped back from the edge.

"Ok. And?"

"The back of the ship is thought to have broken up on that rock. Silver coins in chests would have sunk to the sea floor. Before the wreck was looted, it was said the sea floor was like a carpet of silver."

"Is there anything left down there now?"

"Only miniscule scraps of metal, thought to be what is left of the anchors or cannons."

"Right."

Craig then turned to Emeelie and Marr.

"Sorry ladies. We took an age to catch up with you. Dukk took a little time to get used to staying out of the bushes."

"You were driving?" Marr asked as she turned to look at Dukk.

Dukk smiled.

"I want to have a go."

"Good idea," Emeelie stated as she turned. "We'll race you back."

"Excellent," Marr replied as she lent in and gave Dukk a kiss.

Emeelie dashed over to their dune buggy and jumped into the driver's seat. She started it and put it into reverse. She spun it around and positioned it behind the other buggy.

"Hey!" Craig shouted. "You are blocking us."

"Yes, just giving us a little time to get oriented," Emeelie replied as she climbed over to the passenger's seat. "Come on, Marr, jump in. I'll give you a run down."

Marr climbed into the driver's seat and got some instructions, as the men stood back and waited.

Then after a few false starts, Marr put her foot down. The buggy's wheels spun, covering Dukk and Craig in a cloud of sand and dust. The buggy then roared out of the clearing in the direction of the complex.

Chapter 11 – Levelling

1

"I am going to need a shower and change of clothes," Marr announced as she put her helmet and goggles back on the rack in the garage.

"Yes, the dust gets in everywhere," Emeelie replied. "There are showers near the pool. Change of clothes too if you don't want to go back to your suite all dusty."

"That is a good idea."

"Have you seen the pools below sea level yet?" Craig asked.

"Nope."

"I was going to shower and change down there. Then use the sauna and take a swim. The pool up here can get quite hot in the afternoons."

"That sounds like a great idea," Dukk said.

"Absolutely, lead the way," Marr added.

Craig led them to some doors beyond the ramp. That gave them access to an elevator lift. The lift took them all the way to level one.

The lift opened to a series of corridors. Craig led the way to a substantial changing room.

The room had lockers, benches, and shower cubicles with three quarter high, smoked glass doors. Craig took them to a side room. It was stocked with casual clothes and swim wear.

After selecting items, they made for the showers.

With bathrobes over their swim wear, they exited the changing rooms via another door. It opened to the floor of the atrium. The wall of glass with the ocean beyond was a sight to see. Even more so than when they entered the atrium, earlier.

The water line was three storeys above them. The ebb and flow of the waves was obvious there. However, at level one it was calmer. Large fish swam in and out of view. Sand and reef were visible against the glass with smaller fish and crustaceans, making their way around.

"Oh wow!" Marr exclaimed as she walked towards the wall of glass, paying little attention to the pools and surrounds.

The others followed.

For a time, they stood together in silence. There were plenty of small fish and the occasional shark and dhufish. The large fish caused them to step back momentarily. But mostly, they stood still.

Eventually Marr turned to look at the rest of the space.

As she did, Craig turned and headed towards some wooden panelled doors near the pools.

"Sauna first, then swim," he said.

"Enjoy, I am going for a swim," was the reply from Emeelie.

"Me two," Marr said.

"Me three," Dukk added.

They had barely moved off when a ruckus caught their attention. It was coming from a set of doors on the south side of the space.

Luna appeared. She was closely followed by Bognath, Bazzer, Eleettra, Lilaho, and Kayila. They were all dressed in gym gear.

"Not a chance!" Bazzer exclaimed as he came into the pool area.

"Look, you chose the competition, now take your defeat like a man," Luna yelled back as they made their way around the pool.

"What's going on?" Marr asked as the groups came together.

"We were finishing in the gym and Bazzer challenged me to a plank competition. He lost."

"You have less weight to hold up," Bazzer said.

"What has that got to do."

Luna stopped abruptly and said, "Oh! Emeelie! Craig! Hi."

"Hello Luna," Emeelie replied. "Eleettra, good to see you again. Hello everyone."

"Hello Emeelie," Eleettra replied. "We have lots to share, I am sure."

"We have. A swim is needed first. How are you settling in?"

"Very well, thank you," Lilaho replied on behalf of the others.

That got a smile from them all.

"And very much looking forward to this evening," Kayila blurted.

Everyone stopped and looked at her.

"This evening?" Emeelie asked in reply.

"Yes, getting dressed up and meeting Mr Atesoughton."

"Well, I am sure he is looking forward to meeting you too."

"And, this time we won't be limited to just black dresses," Kayila continued with excitement.

"Of course! That is right! Our first formal occasion together was overshadowed by Zarra's death."

"It was."

"You have reminded me. Your suites do have a choice of formal wear, however there is a much bigger range in the salon on level two. You can get hair and make-up done there also. And there is a dressmaker, too. There won't be time to make anything new, but you can get adjustments done."

"Excellent. That puts some shape on proceedings after the swim," Bazzer blurted.

"Need a dress adjusted, do you? Or your shirt let out?" Luna barked.

"You will keep, young pup!" was the retort.

With the reunion complete, the newcomers headed for the changing rooms in search of a shower and swimming costumes. Craig went to the sauna and the others went into the pool.

A few hours later, Marr and Dukk were standing in front of the mirror in their suite. She was helping Dukk do his bow tie. He was looking very sharp in a black tuxedo.

Marr had decided on taking a risk with a strapless gown. It was dark blue and had a plunging V neck. It wouldn't have even crossed her mind owing to her full form. However, she was able to have it adjusted to fit perfectly while her hair was getting done. It was a treat she felt slightly guilty about. She got some comfort in that the other women and girls had decided to go a similar path. The time with the other women in the salon had a party atmosphere to it. They completely lost track of time. Marr returned to her suite, with just ten minutes to spare, before they were due to have their audience with Craig senior.

"How are the nerves?" Marr asked as she made final adjustments.

"Better after talking with Craig and the drink in the bar downstairs."

"So that is where you went while us girls got ready."

"Yep, Bazzer, Bognath and Mentor were there too. We even played a few rounds of billiards and still had plenty of time to get up here and get dressed. I was worried that you'd never make it out of the salon."

Marr laughed.

"Shall we?" she asked as she stood back to take in the sight.

"You are absolutely stunning," Dukk said as he enjoyed the view.

2

As they left the bedroom, Dukk paused.

"Are you okay?" Marr asked having sensed the hesitation.

"I am confused about something."

"What?"

"Remember I was telling you that the elites have a sort of DNA sampling device to access their EU credit shadow accounts?"

"Yes, what about it?"

"I had a closer look around while I was waiting. There is one in the study."

"And?"

"Well, I stuck my hand in it."

"What happened?"

"It did nothing."

"What do you mean?"

"Can I show you. It won't take a minute."

"Sure."

Dukk brought Marr to the study. He then found the device and placed his hand on it.

A projection appeared above the desk.

A simple message appeared in the projection. The message read, 'Label missing.' Below the label was a long series of digits.

"That is odd," Dukk said as they stared at the blinking message.

"What is?"

"That isn't what happened last time. Will you try?"

"Me?"

"Sure, what harm?"

"Is it safe?"

"I don't know."

"How does it work?"

"Emeelie said family DNA strands are stored within the mechanism. Hard coded. Strands can then be compared."

"It doesn't have some sort of database?"

"Not for access. Perhaps for assignment of permissions."

Marr paused for a moment. Her gut told her to stay clear. But her curiosity streak and love for technology took over. She put her hand on the device.

Suddenly a new message appeared. It read, 'Tracing initiated.'. Once more, below the label was a long series of digits.

"That is it. That is what I saw earlier," Dukk said with glee.

Marr stumbled back.

"Shit," she exclaimed.

"What?"

"This must be connected to something if it is initiating a trace."

"Connected to what?"

"The account databases I guess."

"Why is that a problem?"

"Because we don't know who else sees the trace."

"Oh!"

"We are about to be late. Let's worry about this later."

"Good idea."

Arm in arm, they made their way back to the atrium. A member of staff met them at the door and escorted them to an elevator lift. The lift took them to level four.

The rest of the crew were there waiting on the balcony outside the south banqueting hall. The styles and colours were varied. Everyone had scrubbed up very well.

Compliments were exchanged as they waited. There was a nervousness in the air.

Just before seven p.m., Craig and Emeelie arrived.

Then exactly on the hour, staff opened the double doors and beckoned them to enter.

Craig and Emeelie entered first. Followed by Dukk and Marr. Then Tieanna. Mentor stood back and entered with the rest of the crew.

The banquet hall was double height. Large painted portraits hung on the walls. The ocean could be seen beyond the full height windows.

A long table sat in the middle of the room. Beyond, and near the window, a solitary man sat in a large chair. The chair was facing slightly away from the window. The man's head was turned. He was looking out at the ocean. Five chairs were positioned next to the man. These chairs were positioned in a row facing the view. Several more chairs were positioned behind them.

Craig led the group past the long table and into the space near the window. He stopped in front of the man.

"Grandfather, I have brought my brother to meet you," Craig said as he came to a stop.

The man turned to look at them. He looked all his ninety-eight years. He had wiry wisps of grey hair, pale complexion, and light blue eyes. He smiled.

"Hello Craig," the man said in a frail and croaky voice.

He then stirred in his seat, "Hello Emeelie, lovely to see you both again so soon. Now help me up so you can introduce me properly."

Craig and Emeelie went to either side of the chair and helped the old man.

Once upright, he brushed off the two as if to suggest they didn't have anything to do with him getting to his feet.

Craig then turned to Dukk and Marr.

"Grandfather, this is Dukk and his companion, Marr."

Dukk stepped forward. Craig senior looked at him intensely for a moment, before lifting his hand.

"Good to meet you, my son."

Dukk reached out and took the old man's hand.

"Good to meet you, sir," Dukk replied, half surprised at himself for the sudden use of formalities.

Craig senior held the hand firmly for a full minute. Nothing was said. He then released the grip and turned to Marr.

"It is an honour to meet you, my lady."

Once more he lifted his hand and gestured towards Marr.

Marr stepped forward and took the old man's hand with both of hers.

She was lost for words. She could hardly understand her own reverence, given this man represented all that she stood against.

Eventually she spoke.

"Thank you, Mr Atesoughton, but the pleasure is all mine."

The old man smiled.

Marr smiled back as best she could. She did her best to hide her surprise. The words had just appeared for her as if deep down she understood what was needed.

"It must be all the training," she thought to herself.

The man then released the grip and looked beyond them both.

3

Dukk and Marr stepped aside.

Tieanna was standing there.

"Hello, Mr Atesoughton," Tieanna said in a slightly teary tone.

"Hello, dear Tieanna," Craig senior croaked and then smiled.

Tieanna stepped over and leant in for a warm hug.

The old man chuckled and did his best to return the hug.

"You haven't lost your spirit, it would appear," he said when Tieanna pulled back from the embrace.

Tieanna smiled.

"How long has it been?" Craig senior asked.

"It has been twenty-nine years since I was last on Earth."

"No, we've seen each other since then."

"Sorry, yes, eleven years ago. Craig's eighteenth birthday."

"Of course. One of the last times I was away from Earth. Will you stay for a time?"

"We will see. I've got work to do."

"Yes, I guess you have," he said as he looked over at Marr.

Tieanna followed Craig senior's glance.

"You know?" she asked when she returned her gaze to the old man.

"Yes," he chuckled.

"Know what?" Craig asked as he watched the exchange.

"That you are about to be an uncle, twice, my dear boy," the old man said with a chuckle.

Craig looked over at Marr and then Dukk.

They both grinned back.

"Twice? Twins?" Craig asked in a quizzical tone.

Dukk nodded.

"Yes, twins," Craig senior said with a giggle.

"How do you know?" Tieanna blurted.

"A little birdy told me."

The old man laughed and started to stumble backwards.

Craig and Emeelie went to stop him from falling back. Craig senior brushed them off again.

He then looked up with a stern expression and said, "Keep them safe. This is a safe place."

Marr looked over at Dukk. He shrugged his shoulders.

Craig senior then looked beyond them.

Emeelie took the hint and continued the introductions. Each time Craig senior acknowledged the crew member directly and shook hands.

Mentor was the last to be introduced.

"Hello Mr Atesoughton," Mentor said as they shook hands.

"Mentor, it is a pleasure to finally meet in person. Your reputation precedes you but does not do you justice. You are quite something in person."

He then turned to look at Dukk and Marr while still holding Mentor's hand.

"And look at all this! Your hard work has paid off. Here. Near the end."

Mentor smiled kindly.

Once more Marr turned to look at Dukk. He looked back. His expression was that of confusion.

On releasing Mentor's hand, Craig senior shuffled back into his chair. Once seated he waved his hands in the general direction of the other chairs.

Everyone took the hint and found seats. Craig, Emeelie, Dukk, Marr and Tieanna took the five seats in front. The others fell in behind.

After a moment of sitting in silence with Craig senior looking at them all, he spoke again.

"You know I envy you lot in many ways. You know, bad asses. Running amok fixing shit. Resisting the terrible things my kind are doing. A solid crew is more than we can ever ask for. Someone to watch your back. Someone to laugh with and cry with. Envy. Yes, envy. Now what do you want to know?"

The question took them all by surprise.

For a moment no one spoke. Then Luna sat up.

"What do you mean by resisting the terrible things?" she asked.

"My dear young maiden, using your sniper rifle to blow up sentinels," Craig senior replied with a chuckle.

"Oh," Luna replied quietly.

After a further moment of silence, the old man spoke again. This time even more slowly.

"I see that I intimidate you all. I am sorry for that. But I know you have questions. This is your chance. Perhaps one of the last. So, ask!"

The last statement had a touch of annoyance in it.

Annee sat forward and spoke.

"Mr Atesoughton, what is your relationship with the Veneficans?"

The old man chuckled, then continued to speak slowly and carefully.

"Good. Finally, something in the right direction. What specifically are you looking to know, young lady?"

"Do you give them credits?"

The old man chuckled again, then took a few deep breaths and spoke.

"Yes, my dear. I've been paying them off for years. Ever since Craig was born."

"Why?"

"It is complicated," Craig senior said in a slightly strained tone.

After a further pause, he continued, "Tieanna wasn't the only one making deals. I too did what was needed to ensure the best outcome."

"What do you mean?"

"The payments keep the Veneficans occupied and away from Earth and us. I did a deal that ensured that both my grandsons would get the best possible care and be protected against interference."

Craig senior paused once more to catch his breath. The group were on edge. They were captivated by his slow and strained words.

"You knew about Dukk?" Tieanna asked in a cautious tone after the silence got too much.

"Yes, I knew," Craig senior answered in a kind tone.

Tieanna looked perplexed.

"Besides," he said after seeing Tieanna was stuck for words.

He then added, "I was given an ultimatum. I was told to get on board or lose everything."

"Who gave you that ultimatum?"

Craig senior smiled. He then answered in a slow, but slightly more vibrant tone.

He said, "Helenal."

"Helenal?" Tieanna asked in reply.

"Yes, it was Helenal's idea."

4

The mention of Helenal's name caused a collective inhale. Marr and Dukk looked at each other and then at Craig. He was looking utterly confused. Tieanna looked a little odd too.

After what felt like an age, Tieanna spoke softly.

"You know her name?"

"Not only that, but I know who she really is," Craig senior replied in a strained tone.

"Who is she?" Marr blurted.

Marr's sudden outburst caused them all to inhale once more.

Eventually Craig senior spoke again as he looked back towards the ocean.

"I am sworn to take that to my grave. She said she will reveal herself at the end."

Silence filled the space.

Eventually Craig senior looked back at the group. He sat up slightly and did his best to project his voice once more.

"These are dangerous times. Your names need to stay hidden."

"Who's names?" Craig asked in reply.

Craig senior took a few breaths then said, "Your brother and his company. Marr and Dukk, especially. The story behind these names isn't for general consumption. Yet. Even these fake aliases you use, must be hidden from view."

"What do you mean?"

"My grandson, your brother can enlighten you."

Craig looked frustrated and turned to Dukk.

But before he could say anything, Craig senior coughed to signalled that he hadn't finished.

They all turned their attention back to the old man.

Eventually he spoke again. His tone was slow and strained. He looked directly at Dukk and Marr.

"You need new names. Names that are suited to your standing. Names that can be announced to the other families. Names that will command respect but keep the truth. What shall you go by?"

Marr and Dukk looked at each other then they turned back to Craig senior.

"I will go by the name of David," Dukk stated clearly.

"And, I will go by Maria," Marr added.

Craig senior nodded and smiled.

After a few moments, Craig senior started to get agitated. He then spoke again. His tone was far frailer now. His words came slowly, but clearly.

"I am getting tired. I wish you well for the dinner, which I won't join you for. Enjoy your time here. Stay for as long as you wish and please return to say goodbye before you leave. But before I rest, I want to speak with my grandsons and their companions, alone."

Silence filled the room again. Mentor was the first to stand. He nodded at Craig senior and made his way towards the door. The others followed suit.

When the doors closed behind them, Craig senior looked back towards the window. After a couple of minutes of silence, he turned back towards Dukk, Marr, Craig and Emeelie.

He spoke slowly and purposefully.

"This is beyond anything I could have imagined when I started to understand what had become of my son. It is more than I could have imagine having two grandsons and two great grandchildren on the way.

"To see you both have grown into fine stoic men. To see you here with your magnificent companions. And to hear that you met and befriended each other, unknowingly is a dream come true.

"It does create a challenge. And I will be honest with you both. I don't have an answer. I don't know how to best set things out. No matter how much I tried, I just couldn't work out how to set things right in my death. I have some things in place which are the best I could produce. But it will be up to the pair of you to make it work."

At the end of the monologue, Craig senior slumped in his chair. He forced a smile. The tone and body language didn't suggest there was anything further to discuss on the subject.

To Dukk, it looked like his grandfather's energy was spent, and their time together had ended. He stood up and went over to him. He bent down before him.

"We will," he said.

He then put his hand gently on the old man's shoulder.

Craig senior nodded. A tear formed in his eye.

The others were out of their seats too. They all came over and bent down as well.

After a moment of looking around at the faces, Craig senior smiled again and said quietly, "I wish I had the energy to join you this evening."

With that they all stood and stepped back. Craig senior turned to look out at the ocean again.

Dukk looked around at the others and nodded his head towards the door. They moved off.

They had barely reached the corner of the table when Craig senior spoke again.

"Maria, keep it safe," he said.

Marr was the first to turn her head. Her new alias wasn't the only thing that got her attention. There was something new in his tone.

Craig senior was looking directly at her.

"You know about the disc?" she blurted.

He nodded.

Her thoughts drifted to the makeshift pouch she had crafted from a knife holster. The pouch was attached to her inner thigh. She could feel the disc against her leg.

"He couldn't know," Marr thought to herself as she stared.

He then spoke softly.

"Keep it on your person. It is too important to fall into the wrong hands."

Marr didn't know what to say.

Craig senior then continued in a barely audible tone.

"These are extremely dangerous times. Your skills are something to be feared. But they might not be enough. You were lucky in Mayfield. You were lucky in Southern Cross. You were lucky in Abrolhos.

Forces are mounting against you. They know about Craig. But not you or David. However, they are learning. Time isn't on our side. But you must prevail. Use all the resources at your disposal."

Marr's mind exploded.

"How could he know all this? What else does he know? What does he mean by 'our side'?" she thought to herself.

5

Marr had to know more. She went back over and knelt before him. The others came back and stood behind Marr.

Craig senior watched them as they approached.

"Will you tell me all that you know?" Marr asked politely.

"That wouldn't take long, but perhaps more time than I have left," was the reply.

Marr smiled. She liked his whit.

"Will you answer more questions?" she asked gently.

"If I can."

Marr paused for a moment. She looked at Craig senior. He looked weary. She knew she needed to be careful. She knew where she needed to go first.

"What do you mean by 'our side'?" she asked.

"Who is your enemy?" he asked in reply.

That caused her to pause. It was the same question she had asked Emeelie, earlier. The things Mentor had shared came to mind. She was still struggling to come to terms with the insignificant role observers played in the scheme of things.

"Families like ourselves share the same enemy," he then added.

"I don't understand."

"The story Tieanna shared about her initiation ceremony isn't the whole truth."

"What do you mean?"

211

"My son was there at the end. He was brought in at the final moment. Drugged and stimulated by others in another room. That doesn't excuse him for his role in it, or what he became after, but he didn't inflict the abuse."

"Who did?"

"The Venefica."

"What!" Marr exclaimed in surprise.

"They beat and rape their own, under blindfold, to create the illusion. Then they insert the man at the final moment to inseminate and propagate the lie."

"The lie that all men are inherently evil?"

Craig senior nodded.

"They do it to create hatred towards men?"

"Yes, and to corrupt and depower the men involved. Their involvement is then used as leverage. The guilt of involvement never goes away."

"Are you speaking from experience?"

"Yes, I am."

"Then why are you supporting them with financial contributions?"

"They control the population. They control the citadels. They control the food production. They control the monetary system. They are too powerful."

"But the queen isn't fully in control. She is blocked from bringing the mammoth ring to Earth. She is blocked from using the weapons."

"The Venefica and Filia are still on the ground. They still have their hands on the levers that matter."

"What about force? You have significant means."

"They still control the sentinels in the citadels. They hold the population as ransom. We must keep our distance. Besides, taking out the regime simply creates a void. A void that might get replaced with something far worse."

Marr sighed. She had read lots of history. She knew he was correct.

"Is there any hope of changing that?" Marr asked after a moment of silence.

"Yes, there is a plan."

"What is it the plan?"

"That is going to be revealed, soon."

"When exactly?"

"At the end."

"Who came up with this plan?"

"The only person that could have any hope of pulling it off."

With the last statement, Craig senior looked back towards the window.

Marr was angry and frustrated. She was getting more questions than answers. She felt it was like talking with Teacher.

After a moment of watching the old man, she reached a decision. She had nothing left to lose.

"Is the queen my mother?" she asked quietly.

Craig senior turned back towards her. He looked at her deeply. As he did, a tear formed in his eye. Marr welled up too.

After what Marr felt was like an age, he spoke softly.

"You already have the answer."

Marr nodded.

"Who is my father?" she then asked in a reluctant tone.

"I don't know. But you already have, on your person, what you need, to find out."

"The disc?"

Craig senior nodded.

"How does the disc work?" Marr blurted.

"You must know more about that than me by this stage."

"Perhaps. But I am still unclear about how the image projection is obtained."

Craig senior looked away and spoke quietly and slowly.

"The comms implants send video and audio feeds to the data centre stored on Mammoth one. The disc accesses the storage."

"All our implants?"

"No, just the Venefica and Filia over the age of sixteen. The implants of the Filia are modified during the initiation ceremony. They just think the modifications are to give them additional IDs and observer cloaking. They know nothing of this spying capability."

"Why?"

Craig senior turned back to look at Marr. He spoke slowly and methodically.

"When a system is built on power and you rule with an iron fist, no-one can be trusted. Especially those around you. The Venefica trust no-one. Not even their own. The disc enables the holder to spy on the Venefica and spy on everyone else via the network of Filia. Nothing in the Galaxy is hidden from the disc holder. It is how they get their seemingly magical power to predict the future. Some would say the information is used to not only predict it but write it."

"Who knows about this capability of the discs?"

"Only the true queen. It is passed to her daughter on her death bed."

"What do you mean by true queen?"

"I think you know the answer to that."

"The current queen is not the true queen."

The old man smiled.

"So, the current queen doesn't know about the monitoring capabilities."

He nodded.

"Do you have the other disc?"

Craig senior laughed. He turned back towards the window.

After a moment, he spoke softly.

"No, I don't have the other disc! A corrupt old fool like me would destroy everything with that much power."

"Power?"

"Yes, power! Seeing what all the Venefica and Filia are doing at any given moment gives the holder an unfair advantage. That brings power. Power to control the narrative and the lives of all. That level of power corrupts the mind beyond repair."

"But you know who does have the other disc."

Craig senior smiled.

His manner made it clear that he wasn't going to share any more on that subject. So, Marr changed direction.

"You have been privy to some information?"

He nodded.

"Have you used that information."

"Where I felt it would be helpful."

Marr reflected on that for a moment. Then it hit her.

"All after the age of sixteen?"

Craig senior nodded.

"So, Tieanna has them."

"Yes."

"Is the holder of the other disc observing Tieanna's movements?"

He nodded.

"And she doesn't know."

Craig senior nodded again.

"She should know!"

"She should."

After a further moment of reflection, Marr blurted, "Is this how you know about the twins and Tieanna's recollection of her initiation ceremony?"

Craig senior smiled.

"Did you tip off Tieanna in Mayfield?"

Craig nodded again.

"What was 'They know' about?"

"The Veneficans had discovered that I had given Tieanna a job. That I had hidden her from them."

"Nothing about Dukk?"

Craig senior nodded in agreement.

He then added, "Maria, promise me this! Do not use the disc to spy on anyone but the false queen. You will learn what you need from her. It will drive you insane to do otherwise. Trust me. Please."

Marr nodded.

Marr noticed his colour changing. He looked totally drained. She smiled.

"Thank you," she said as she stood up.

He nodded as he turned back towards the ocean.

Chapter 12 – New ground

1

"What in the world is going on?" Craig demanded as the doors to the south banqueting hall, closed behind them.

Dukk, Marr and Emeelie stood before him. Beyond was the atrium bathed in orange light from the setting sun.

On the opposite side of the atrium the doors to the north banqueting hall were open. Music and chatter could be heard from within.

The noise from the others disguised the deathly silence that engulfed the four.

Craig then looked at Emeelie.

"You knew! This is why you were odd after the ride in the dune buggy!" he stated angrily.

"Some of it," was the reply.

"Which bit?"

"That they are with the resistance and the rescued girls have been delivered to them."

"That explains the mention of Luna's sniper rifle and Marr's skills. But it doesn't explain the rest!" Craig said in an angry tone.

"I need a drink!" he said as he brushed past.

"Wait!" Dukk said loudly.

Craig stopped and turned back towards them.

"What do you need clarified?" Dukk asked.

"Let's start with, oh, perhaps, is Marr a Venefican and next in line to be queen?"

"I am a twin, so who is next in line, isn't clear," Marr replied.

"Now that I think about it, the resemblance is uncanny. So, the queen is your mother, and her daughter is your twin?"

"That is what I suspect."

"But they don't know about you?"

"That is what I understand."

"And the queen isn't the queen?"

"That is what it would appear."

"Where is the real queen?"

"That isn't clear."

"You don't know?"

"No."

"This is nuts," Craig said as he shook his head and looked towards the ocean and the setting sun.

Silence fell again. Craig then turned back towards Dukk.

"Are you part of the resistance, too?"

"I guess so," Dukk replied. "Well since my rig was blown-up. Before that I was just a haulier."

"How long have you known you were Tieanna's son?"

"Just after that."

"You knew when we were in Emerald Valley?"

"Yes."

"Why didn't you let on?"

"I didn't trust you."

"And now?"

"Yes, of course."

"Can I ask a question?" Marr interjected.

Craig nodded.

"Did you know about the payments to the Veneficans?"

"No," Craig replied.

"The existence of the disc?"

"Nope, this is the first that I have heard of any of it."

"So, we are all learning the truth together."

Craig grinned.

"I guess so," he added.

The mood softened. Smiles appeared on everyone's faces.

Emeelie then spoke.

"Congratulations," she said as she looked at Marr.

Marr smiled even more.

Craig looked at Emeelie, then back at Marr.

"Oh shit, of course! Twins! Yes, congratulations," he then blurted before reaching to hug Dukk and Marr at the same time.

"Thank you, Craig," Marr replied as she unwound herself from the hug.

"But this is a miracle! How did that happen outside the incubation centres?" Craig asked as he stepped back.

"That is a story to be shared over a drink," Dukk replied on Marr's behalf.

Craig smiled. He looked at them all standing there. He then shifted his head to one side.

"I have one more question before we join the others."

They waited.

"Why did you choose those names?" he then asked.

"Names?" Marr asked in reply.

"Maria and David?"

"I can only speak for myself," Dukk blurted. "I have no idea. It just felt right at that very moment."

Craig looked surprised. As did Emeelie.

Marr laughed.

They all turned to look at her.

"Me too," she then answered genuinely.

"Something is afoot," Emeelie observed.

"Perhaps something greater than all of us," Craig added.

Dukk and Marr shrugged their shoulders as they looked at each other and smiled.

219

Dukk then nodded his head towards the doors on the other side of the atrium.

"Yes, and it is my turn to make the drinks," Craig said with a smile.

He then put an arm around Dukk's shoulders and guided the two of them towards the north banqueting hall.

"What does it feel like?" Emeelie asked Marr as they followed their men towards the noise.

"Being pregnant?"

"Yes."

"What kind of detail do you want?"

"The ugly detail?"

"Ok then. So, over the course of the last three months, my breasts have swollen and become tender. I've had nausea and vomiting. Coming out of traverse has been as uncomfortable as the first time. I've been crazy tired. I crave odd foods and have a strong aversion to others. I've had heartburn. And my plumbing is all over the place. On top of that, I've found it harder than usual to manage my emotions."

"Oh. Is that all the time?"

"It comes and goes. This week I've been feeling more like myself. Tieanna says things will get easier. At least for a time now. I am entering the second trimester."

"What happens now?"

"The babies continue to grow."

"When will it be noticeable? When will your belly bulge?"

"I understand that will be part of the third trimester."

"And what about sex?"

"Apart from swings in my mood getting in the way, it is the same."

"Shall we?" Dukk called from the doorway to the north banqueting hall.

Marr and Emeelie had hardly noticed they had stopped walking to have their chat.

"Let's continue this later," Marr said with a smile.

Emeelie nodded as they turned and headed towards Dukk and Craig.

2

Dukk gave up. He rolled over to the edge and flicked his legs off the bed. He had given it his best shot. Two hours of lying awake trying not to disturb Marr was more than he could take.

The rest of his body followed his legs off the bed. With a bathrobe flung over his shoulders, Dukk made his way quietly into the lounge. He went over to the kitchenette and chugged down a glass of water. He then casually inspected the bar fridge.

"Why not," he muttered as he extracted a bottle of beer and headed towards the balcony.

He and Marr had already extended the balcony in the early hours after returning from the dinner. Of which had been thoroughly enjoyable. There had been eating, drinking, dancing, and sharing of stories. It was the wee hours before they made their way back to their rooms.

Dukk stepped out on the balcony. The ocean was calm. The winds of the previous afternoon had abated. It was pre-dawn. The faint light between night and day was creeping its way into the world.

Something caught Dukk's eye as he gazed at the ocean. The balcony on the paired suite on the other side of the complex was extended too. Someone was standing there. A man. He was watching Dukk. It was Craig.

"Cheers," Dukk shouted as he lifted his beer.

"Grab a couple of fresh ones and meet me in the atrium," Craig shouted back.

Dukk returned inside. He collected his tuxedo from the lounge room floor and got dressed. With shoes on, he then grabbed two additional beers from the fridge and headed to the doors of the suite.

Craig was waiting for him. He too was wearing a wrinkled and dishevelled tuxedo. He was holding open a small ice box. Dukk dropped his two extra beers into the box to pair with two others. Craig then closed the box and lifted his own beer to clink it with Dukk's bottle.

"Can't sleep either?" Dukk asked after a slug on the beer.

"Nope. Too much on my mind," was the reply.

"What now?"

"Can I show you something?"

"Sure."

Craig led Dukk down to level five. They entered some service corridors and made their way to the back of the complex.

There they found a large, solid looking door. It unlocked as they approached. Beyond was a large tunnel.

Lights came on as they entered.

Dukk noticed the hyperloop tube attach to the wall above them.

"Is this the tunnel that connects the complex to the hangers?" he asked as they looked up at the two-storey high ceiling.

"It is. This way," Craig answered as he turned right and headed down the tunnel.

"This is big. More than you'd need to move robo-containers around."

"Yes, it is for more than that. Come."

Craig led them to another set of doors on the wall of the tunnel. He interacted with a panel beside the doors. They opened. Beyond was a hyperloop carriage. The carriage was wider and taller than Dukk was accustomed to. The seating area had two levels, accessed via a set of stairs near the door.

"Another hyperloop! Is this freight capable?" Dukk asked as they stepped in and looked around.

"Yes. Each capsule seats eighteen with room for up to fifty robo crates, or a single robo container," Craig answered as he directed Dukk to the seats on the upper level.

"What is it for? And more importantly, where does this one go?"

"You will see. Now strap in, as this moves," Craig said with a smile.

Fifteen minutes later the hyperloop slowed and stopped.

"Where are we?" Dukk asked as he emptied the beer.

"Two hundred kilometres south-east of the complex," Craig answered as he unbelted.

"The end of the line?"

"No, not at all. Not even close. This is one of eight new settlements. Spread over hundreds of kilometres. Connected via a network of hyperloops. Both freight and people capable. All settlements are similar but adapted to the local geography."

Dukk stood up, went down the short stairs and followed Craig out of the carriage.

Before him was a large hall. It had tables and chairs. There were some rooms off to the sides. High windows were capturing some of the pre-dawn light and it was half illuminating the space. The words, "Welcome to Chapman Valley" were printed on a huge banner that was secured to the far wall.

"This is huge. How can it be? I've flown over this area. There is nothing here."

"Integration with the colours of the natural terrain. It isn't visible from eighteen thousand meters. Nothing is allowed lower than that, so it stays hidden. I only learnt of this recently. Jeeves has been showing me about. I've still not seen it all. This is my first time at this location."

"What is this place?"

"It is a processing hall."

"Processing for what?"

"Refugees."

"Refugees?"

"Yes, granddad says it is part of the plan. He says the plans that are in place will create a significant number of people looking for a new home."

"Where from?"

"Here and other systems."

"War?"

"Perhaps. But it might be something else. Let's find somewhere to talk."

With the ice box in hand, Craig led Dukk across the processing hall and through double doors at the opposite end.

The doors took them outside.

Dawn was well underway. There were still some shadows, but it was clear what was in front of them.

It was a roadway. It was earth coloured but clearly man made.

Dukk stepped onto the road and then turned around slowly. They were in a valley. Buildings dotted the floor and sides of the valley. The processing hall behind them was half buried in the side of a hill.

Dukk turned his attention back to the collection of buildings that dotted the roadside and stretched into the distance in all directions. The buildings were surrounded by trees and bushes.

They wandered down the road.

"What is all this?" Dukk asked as he waved his hands at the buildings around them.

"Stores, workshops, services. That type of thing."

"Workshops? Services?"

"Woodwork. Metal work. Mills. Butchers. Bakers. Medical clinics. All manner of services for building and supporting a community."

"What are those?" Dukk said pointing to a collection of buildings off in the distance to their right.

"Housing. Three-to-five-bedroom housing units, set out in groups of three to five. Mini complexes if you like. Each on its own couple of acres. The number of these groups of housing units in each settlement is between five and six hundred. Jeeves calls them multi-generational habitats."

Dukk reflected on what he had seen on the surface in Newterratwo. The concept was similar, except there, the habitats were housed within massive mobile machines.

3

"Where are we headed?" Dukk asked as Craig led them up a flight of stairs on the side of a three-storey high building.

"Somewhere with a view," was the answer.

At the top there was a viewing platform with three hundred- and sixty-degrees views and a chest height guard rail.

Craig put the ice box down on the platform. He opened it and extracted two bottles of beer. After passing one to Dukk, he climbed up and sat on the rail.

Dukk joined him.

"Who made all of this?" Dukk asked after taking a drag on the bottle.

"Our grandfather's people. Skilled labourers."

"It must have taken a good bit of time. And credit."

"Yes, Jeeves tells me the project started twenty years ago. There are other groups of settlements. This group is one of seven. The others are throughout the globe."

"All built by our grandfather?"

"That is what it looks like."

"How is this all powered?"

"The usual. Just like the main complex at Zuytdorp. Dual hybrid solid fuel reactors. With two layers of redundancy across all components. Jeeves suggests that it is important that each settlement is energy independent."

"Why?"

"To reduce the influence one settlement has over another."

"What is that?" Dukk asked as he pointed towards a collection of fenced yards in the distance.

"A mustering station."

"There are cattle here too?"

"Yes, some trial farming is already underway."

"That requires people."

"Yes, each site has a skeleton community of farmers and trades people. They are keeping an eye on things."

"What about wild people?" Dukk asked after a moment of contemplation.

"What about them?"

"This lot might not be visible from the sky, but it is hard to miss if you were wandering past. Are there any around?"

"Yes, absolutely."

"You've met them?"

"No, but the construction workers and those maintaining the place, talk of sightings. They mostly keep their distance."

"So, you haven't run into any problems?"

"Not really, from what I've heard. There were some minor problems in the early stages of construction. I guess we are interfering with their roaming. But when they understand what is being done here, they don't get in the way. I've even heard they are making use of some of the housing units on the fringes of the settlements. They kind of come and go."

"That makes sense if they are nomadic."

"True."

"Why are the settlements spread out?" Dukk asked.

"Jeeves said it has something to do with autonomy. Localised governance."

"That sounds like the kind of thing Marr has been telling me about. It is what the resistance is working towards."

"Tieanna too."

"What is your understanding of it?"

"Centralised governance suffers from bloating and the consequences of corruption have greater impact. The entire system will suffer at the hands of those that get seduced by power. A decentralised system of government isn't perfect, but the problems and corruption tend to be dispersed with it. As a whole entity, it is more resilient. Bad bits tend to wither and die themselves."

"What about economies of scale and the advantages that come with it?" Dukk asked casually.

"Like what?"

"Fending off enemies."

"Good point."

"Speaking of enemies, what about defences here?"

"Like Zuytdorp and all our settlements, we have automated ground to air missiles to deter air traffic. Fly too close to the settlement and you'll meet a fiery end. It is only a precaution as we control the airspace above anywhere that we have settlements or complexes."

"And, what about local security?"

"What do you mean?"

"Entering and leaving the community."

"There is none for now. There isn't anything stopping anyone leaving or arriving. The hyperloop provides a link but it isn't a barrier to movement. It will need maintenance, sure, but it will be available for people to use. To come and go as they please. Jeeves suggests communities will decide amongst themselves and perhaps establish agreements with each other to keep the infrastructure working."

"So, they can choose to restrict movement if they want?"

"Yes, that is what I understand."

"What about space ports? Are the below ground hangers at Zuytdorp the only way in and out for rigs?"

"No, there is a proper space port east of here. It is built a little like the space port at New Montana."

"They have landing pits?"

"Yep."

"They must be visible from the sky?"

"They are below ground. The one here is built within an old open pit mine. They have ceiling doors like those at Zuytdorp."

"And the hangers?"

"Yes, the hangers are all below ground too."

"But the pits still support launch under full power?"

"Yes, the ventilation and exhaust systems in the pits are very impressive. They make use of the disused and extensive mind shafts."

"And there are automated low loaders there?"

"Yep, everything is in place."

"All this, just for refugees?"

"No, I gather from Jeeves that granddad expects this region to be a significant producer of real food."

"And compete with the citadels?"

"Yep."

"Why would you want to do that? What would be the point of it."

"To regain control, or at the very least, regain autonomy."

"Our grandfather mentioned this when he was talking to Marr. Will you tell me more about that?"

"We have no real say in the production of real food. It is controlled by the Filia stationed within the citadels. They say which families get the shipment contracts. The sentinels stationed in the citadels prevent anyone saying otherwise."

"But don't you still have access to the citadels?"

"Yes, and the sentinels keep their distance so long as we don't make any trouble and stay in our villas in the inner ring. It is the reason most families invest heavily in housing complexes outside the citadels. We have more freedom out here."

Dukk gave that last piece some thought then looked at Craig.

"So, the Venefican's run the show?" Dukk asked cautiously. He was still confused about it.

"Yep."

"But the queen doesn't have control over the weapons on the mammoth ring. They can't bring the ring near Earth. How do they have so much power?"

"Fear, I guess. The knowledge you've recently gleaned via the disc isn't common. Most think they are still able to wreak havoc if they wish. We hide our activities here on Earth for fear they will find out and show up with the mammoth ring."

"But our grandfather has significant military power too. The biggest collection of fleets in the galaxy. How do the Venefican's get away with it?"

"They hold the real food production and population creation over us. They use it like a hostage. They are pointing the gun and have their finger on the trigger. We make a wrong move, and we all lose."

"It is a stand off!"

"Yep."

"So, all this is at the risk of incurring their wrath?"

"Yep, nothing will change while the gun is in their hands."

"By that do you mean the sentinels in the citadels."

"Yes."

4

"I am now confused about our history," Dukk stated.

"Who's history?"

"Earth."

"How far back are we talking about?"

"The establishment of the citadels. How true is the resistance story from what you understand?"

"Do you mean the story about the reset and utopian dreamers installing their brainwashed followers into political, governmental, educational, and commercial systems?"

"Yes, that story."

"It is pretty close to the truth, from what I know."

"But that doesn't make sense for where you are now."

"What do you mean?"

"The utopians established the citadels and took control of everything. Most became enslaved and a few got to live a life of luxury, excess and privilege."

"By 'a few', do you mean families like ours?"

"Yes."

"That was certainly the idea, but it didn't pan out that way."

"What do you mean by that?"

"So, I understand families like ours were effectively in control of everything. They had a lot of power. However, the population growth and technology evolution made it harder to wield that power. Our ancestors ran the risk of being overrun and sent to the guillotine, be it a metaphorical one, like the royals of the imperial age or rulers of numerous ages prior. So, the families formed a cabal and aligned with the most progressive. They propped up the progressives. In turn the progressives helped re-establish the controls needed to manage the population. The aim was to usher in a fascist system of control. This included security and money but also food and other necessities. The idea was to return to a feudal system where most were trapped in near poverty. Our ancestors even built the citadels. It was anticipated that the masses would push back from the genocide being carried out. The aim of that was to dramatically reduce the population to a controllable level. Unfortunately, it all backfired. Our forebearers gave the utopians too much power. They took it and used it against families like ours. They let us be space explorers, but Earth was theirs."

"How did the utopians do it?"

"Well, it was the sentinels. The humanoids. Our ancestors knew about them. They funded the research and construction. They knew they needed a good army. A strong and willing army was needed if they were to enslave the people and defend the citadels. But they knew little of the details. They knew nothing of the sentinel control systems. They lacked the understanding of how things really worked. They outsourced everything. Such is the nature of rent seeking.

"When things got to the final blows and the inevitable shift came to move to the citadels, the utopians simply turned the system on. They took control of Earth's population management and food production. The population control wasn't of concern, but food was. Well, not all food. The families weren't concerned with the rehydratable food, just the real stuff. The unfortunate nature of evolution being that our bodies are suited to Earth and the fruit it bears. Rehydratable foods are synthetic. They just don't work without massive quantities of supplements, which eventually have a cost to our health."

"Wait. Didn't the citadels also play a crucial role in our survival. After the war, the Earth was largely inhabitable."

"That is a lie. There was no mass use of destructive weapons. Be they chemical, biological, or whatever."

"But what about the masses that died? The pandemics and all that?"

"Yes, the population was nearly wiped out. But not because of weapons or actual disease."

"How then?"

"Incompetence and stupidity."

"What do you mean?"

"The pandemics and other global dangers were fiction. The dangers were fabricated and propagated using psychological operations. The discovery of the viruses. The treatment protocols. The vaccines and cures. Climate change and counter measures. None of it was real."

"How did so many people die then?

"Fear causes people to do odd things, including breaking the systems they need for survival."

"If the systems were broken, going to the citadels must have been about our survival? Surely?"

"Well ok, the citadels did provide an easy option but look at the real food production now. It is all done in the areas surrounding the citadels. No, it was about control. The 'Earth is inhabitable' narrative was to push the remaining populations into the citadels. It was aimed at leaving most of the Earth available for the families to redevelop for themselves."

"What about wild people?"

"Some were awake to what was going on."

"Ok, but the plan to control everything backfired?"

"Yes, the new puritans turned on us. The families do have a degree of autonomy, but no real power. None with respect to that which is really needed."

"Wait! You said new puritans?"

"Yes, utopians were new puritans."

"New puritans became the Veneficans. So, the Veneficans are the utopians?"

"Kind of."

"What do you mean?"

"In the beginning, those who controlled the citadels consisted of men and women. But over time, the men were murdered or enslaved."

"Leaving just the women, the Veneficans?"

"Exactly."

Dukk pondered that for a moment before realising he was unclear about something Craig said.

"Before when you mentioned refugees, what did you mean?"

"From what I can glean from my grandfather, there are already plenty of refugees out there. There are those who have stayed away from Earth for too long. Their access to their citadel of origin will have been cancelled. There are also those that have basically been abandoned at mining or research stations. At locations on the various planets that we've been working our way through over the last one hundred and fifty years. There are communities there which are just scraping by and would love to come back to Earth."

"All of them?"

"No. Granted, there are those there, of course, who don't want to return and are quite happy where they are. But many do."

"So, you're saying that there are people out there in the galaxy that would be happy to come back and live here in these settlements?

"That is what I understand, yes."

"I don't know. It looks like the life of a labourer in a citadel."

"It won't be."

"Why?"

"Ownership."

"What do you mean?"

"The new arrivals will own the land."

"Own?"

"Yes, settlements will have a land register. It will be used to track titles and claims."

"These buildings look significant. It must have cost something to construct them. Will they have to pay for it?"

"Granddad suggests yes, they will. He said it will be paid in crypto."

"Will refugees have sufficient crypto?"

"Granddad said it will be clearer at the right time. For now, refugees will be given a title on their property on an IOU basis."

"This is an interesting angle."

"In what way?"

"I've been learning that ownership changes how one behaves in relationship to property they own. For the better."

"Yes, that is my understanding too."

"But, if the Veneficans are watching and have their hands on the guns, how will the refugees get here?"

"Granddad said there needs to be a way to move people under the radar. Somebody needs to visit these communities and spread the word that there is a viable alternative to the citadels. But it needs to come from the right place."

"What do you mean?"

"It must come from a place of trust. From somewhere admirable."

"By that you mean not from elite family members?" Dukk said with a chuckle.

Craig laughed and then said, "yes, not from a family member. It would just be seen as part of the same system."

"Who then?"

Craig said nothing.

"From a hero of sorts, perhaps?" Dukk said after further reflection.

"Yes, like from a group of rogues sticking it to the elites."

Dukk laughed, and then after a pause, said, "Us?"

"Why not?"

Dukk laughed again. He then noticed Craig was grinning but not laughing.

"So how would it work?"

"Cloak and mirrors," Craig answered.

"What do you mean?"

"With our father dead, and grandfather on his deathbed, the heir apparent needs to become more present. And that includes the recently discovered next in line, David. He and his new companion need to be introduced. The families are not going to be happy if the richest and most powerful family is hiding their heir."

"I have no interest in spending all my time meeting the heads of families."

"No, you wouldn't need to spend all your time, just a small portion of it. And the movement of your fleet would give you cover. It would cloak you as you go about spreading the news about this alternative here on Earth at these settlements. The fleet may even be useful in moving refugees under the radar."

"This is nuts!"

Craig smiled again.

"Wait!", Dukk blurted. "What do you mean by movement of my fleet?"

"Granddad will insist that you now move with protection. You might get away with the minimum like I do and move relatively fast. But I wouldn't be surprised if he orders a fleet to go with you."

"If your flotilla comprises of two cruisers, two interceptors and four arrows, what makes up a fleet?"

"What have you been doing all these years moving through the galaxy?"

"Keeping my head down," Dukk said with a laugh.

"An escort fleet accompanying one or more super-cruisers typically has a dozen or so interceptors and, double that number of arrows, and one or two destroyers. Plus, support craft."

"Yes, now that you mention it, I guess I was aware of fleets moving through but never gave the exact configuration much thought."

"Well, now you will have to."

"So, I am supposed to sit pretty in a cruiser and have a bunch of arrows and interceptors with me everywhere I go?"

"That is what David and Maria will need to appear to be doing."

"Oh, I see. The Imhullu with its crew of mercenaries is going to join David and Maria's flotilla as an escort craft?"

Craig nodded and grinned.

Dukk shook his head. He was starting to get a sense of what being part of a family meant. It was just swapping one cage for another.

"Didn't you recently have the family mammoth upgraded?" Dukk asked after a further moment of silence.

"Yes, the upgrades confused me until I learnt of granddad's settlements and the plan for the refugees."

"In what ways?"

"As well as weapons and technology, the upgrades included repurposing of several storage areas into bunk accommodation. I'd initially thought it was for transporting troops. But now I see it wasn't for that at all."

"Refugees."

"Yes, that is what I understand."

The sun was now pushing above the horizon. Dukk yawned as he watched the colour change.

"Bedtime?" Craig asked as he too caught a yawn.

"Good idea," was Dukk's reply.

Thirty minutes later, Dukk quietly crawled into the bed beside Marr. On sensing his return, she moved herself into his arms.

"Where have you been?" she muttered.

"To visit a new world," was the reply.

"That's nice," Marr answered as she drifted back off to sleep.

5

Later in the morning, Marr was entering the foyer of their suite. She was heading upstairs in search of some breakfast and then perhaps some exercise. She had left Dukk snoring loudly. The bedroom had stunk of stale beer. She looked forward to hearing later where he had disappeared to.

In the foyer there was an envelope sitting on a corner table. Marr paused for a moment as she hadn't noticed the table before. It was clearly put there for the purpose of holding the envelope. She picked up the envelope and opened it. Within was a simple note. The note read, 'Marr, I have a message from Teacher. I will be in the library for the morning. Mentor.'

Marr put the note back in the envelope and placed it back on the table. She then made her way swiftly to level four.

Marr found Mentor sitting alone in the library. He was sitting in a corner reading. He looked up as Marr approached, smiled, and put the book down on the coffee table in front of him.

"I got your note," Marr said as she took a seat opposite.

"Yes, let me play the message for you," Mentor replied as he interacted with his wrist wraps.

A projection appeared in the air above the coffee table.

The image was of an elderly woman. She had dark brown complexion and haunting black eyes. Her wild grey hair was drawn back exposing two disfigured ears and scars that ran down the side of her neck. She wore her hair this way as if to ensure everyone saw the scars as a mark of pride.

Mentor started the play back.

"Welcome back, my dear girl and congratulations," Teacher said in a voice that was broken and strained.

After a pause to catch her breath, she continued.

"I understand some of the pieces of the puzzle are coming together. I am sure you have many new questions. Answers must wait, once more. They will come."

She paused again briefly, before concluding.

"Mentor has been given further instructions. Work with him and I will see you all soon."

"Is that it?" Marr blurted as the image dissolved.

"Yes and no. I also got written instructions."

"What are they."

"Basically, I was given the details on how to help bring your new identities to life."

"What do you mean?"

"Unlike Dellington and Maldana, the fake identities we purchased in Maple Tower, the identities for David and Maria can't be within the system."

"System?"

"The ID system we all use. The Veneficans have access to it. Teacher suggests that while it will take resources and time, they will be able to see it is fake."

"Oh. What is the alternative?"

"Bartiamos."

"What has the master ship builder got to do with this?"

"Now I understand the real reason Teacher insisted you visit the surface at Newterratwo."

"Which is?"

"A narrative is to be created around that planet. If David and Maria started out on Newterratwo they won't be in the system."

"But we are in the system. We have implants and spinal med lines."

"Yes, she thought of that too. I can replace your implants with newer ones. I can make some surgical adjustments to your med lines attachments. It will look like they were installed more recently than at the age of twelve as most."

"Is that a big procedure?"

"No and a local anaesthetic will be sufficient. I looked into it earlier when I replaced Tieanna's implants. The medical facilities here are second to none."

"So, she has normal ones now?"

"Yes, no more snooping on her."

Marr laughed, then said, "I made a promise to Craig senior to only snoop on the queen."

"Yes, I concur with that advice."

"What about the backstory?" Marr then asked.

"That isn't clear yet. Teacher said that Bartiamos has the details."

"Wait! Won't this expose Bartiamos? Doesn't he want to keep the details of his operation hidden?" Marr asked after further reflection.

"Yes, that is my understanding. I am not sure how it will work. The message just says Bartiamos will help. She suggested that he owes her."

"So, what happens now?"

"We need to visit him."

"When?"

"Soon."

"Why soon?"

"Firstly, because Craig senior isn't well and hasn't got long. But also because there is something else."

"What?"

"DNA testing."

"What do you mean?"

"Tieanna and I spoke with Craig senior this morning. The elite family leaders won't just accept our word that Dukk is the next heir. They will want proof."

"DNA is the proof?"

"Yes."

"How will it be done?"

"A committee will need to witness the DNA sampling. Both of Craig senior and Dukk. They will then witness the process of comparing Dukk's DNA to Craig senior's DNA. That will ensure authenticity. It is standard procedure. Craig has already been done. With the announcement of David, they will demand the same."

"Committee?"

"Yes, a Venefican representative and one representative for each family."

"They all need to be there?"

"Yes."

"Clearly there is no trust amongst them."

"No, there appears not."

"Will both Dukk and Craig senior need to be present?"

"I understand they already have a sample for Craig senior. They will just need Dukk's DNA."

"So, we visit Bartiamos to get an agreed backstory. Then the announcement is made. Then this committee does the DNA sampling. And the sooner the better."

"Yep, that is what I understand."

"I guess we'd better get back to the rig and on our way."

Mentor nodded.

"Can I ask you something about your time as a level seven observer?" Marr asked after a moment of further reflection.

"I am still one, be it in exile."

Marr rolled her eyes at Mentor's attempt at a joke.

"What do you want to know?"

"Three months ago, you told us that there were no EOs and observers above your level. You said that the elites called the shots. That doesn't appear to be the case."

"No, I was wrong about that. It was one of the topics discussed with Craig senior this morning."

"What was the outcome?"

"It is clear the Veneficans call the shots. They have the real power in this galaxy."

"How did you get it wrong? Who did you get your orders from? Who did you report to?"

"Our orders came via the same A.I. generated EO avatars you would see in the citadels giving broadcasts. We would interact with them just like any video call. We had just assumed the elites were behind the artificially generated projections."

Chapter 13 – Power

1

Dukk opened his eyes. It was dark.

"A dream. It must have been a dream," he muttered as he tried to fathom where he was. He tried to digest the pre-dawn excursion with Craig.

He swung himself out of bed. Marr was gone.

He checked the time. Mid-afternoon.

"Maybe it wasn't a dream," he said quietly.

With a bathrobe flung over his shoulders, he opened the bedroom doors.

The brightness of the light from the lounge nearly knocked him over.

The lounge blinds were open. The balcony was extended. The afternoon sun was filling every corner of the room. And the door to the study was ajar.

Dukk pulled the bathrobe into place and tied the belt. Then he walked across the lounge and pushed open the study door.

Marr was sitting at the desk. She was slouched back in the large chair staring out the windows beyond the desk.

"Hi," Dukk said as he stood in the doorway.

Marr smiled, pulled herself out of the chair and came over to him.

When she reached him, she pushed open the bathrobe and inserted herself within.

Arm in arm they kissed.

"You need to brush your teeth," she said as she pulled back a little.

Dukk shrugged his shoulders and smiled.

"Looks like someone raided the fridge in the early morning and went on an adventure," she said as she turned them in the doorway so they could look at the lounge.

She drew their attention to a pile of clothes in the middle of the lounge. A pair of shoes were there too. And the carpet had spots of red dirt.

"So, it wasn't a dream," Dukk said with a laugh.

"I have lots to share," he then added.

"Me too," Marr said as she squeezed harder and enjoyed the warmth of his body.

"First, I need a shower and then something to eat."

"You go shower and I'll organise the food. Any preferences?"

"Something light," Dukk replied as he pulled back from the embrace.

"Will I be able to go back to rehydrated protein extracts, after all this real food we've been having lately," Dukk muttered as he made for the bedroom.

Marr used the internal door from the study to enter the suite foyer. She then opened the suite doors. A staff member was standing on the balcony as always.

"Can I help you?" she asked on seeing Marr.

"Can I get food brought up to the room?" Marr asked in reply.

"Of course. What would you like?"

"Something light."

"Sweet or savoury?"

"Savoury."

"A meat and cheese platter?"

"Perfect."

"Anything else with it?"

"No thank you."

"No problem. The chimes will sound in your suite when the food arrives. It shouldn't take more than fifteen minutes. Is there anything else?"

"No, that is it. But, when it arrives, will you just leave it on a table in the foyer?"

"Of course."

"Thank you."

Marr returned to the suite and made her way to the bedroom.

She then slipped off her clothes and headed towards the bathroom and the sound of the shower running.

2

"Show me," Dukk said as he wiped his mouth.

Stories had been shared after the shower and as Dukk had enjoyed the meat and cheese platter. The last piece of news focused on why Marr had been staring out the window when Dukk had got up. She had been reviewing the disc and the recordings from the last forty-eight hours.

"The disc is in the study," Marr said as she got up from the table.

Moments later they were in the study.

Marr sat at the desk.

Dukk dragged another chair over and sat beside her.

Marr interacted with the disc and the projection appeared in the air above it.

The scene was typical. In view was a masked figure as seen through the eyes of the queen. The masked figure was presumed to be the queen's daughter and Marr's twin sister. She spoke first as the playback started.

"There is some news from Southern Cross."

"What is it?"

"The Filia have been keeping an eye on those two pilots from the shuttle. The shuttle that was involved in the raid of mammoth one."

"What did they find out from the pilots?"

"Nothing."

"How is this news?"

"One of the pilots is dead."

"What happened?"

"There was some kind of pub brawl. The publican said he went out the back for a short time. When he came back in, six of his patrons were dead. The pilot was one of them."

"How is this of interest?"

"The informant was near the bar at the time. She said she saw two women go in. A short while later, two men went round the back. A little later again, two further men arrived. They too went round to the back. Not long after, the two women and those four men appeared from the back. They headed back towards the Hyperloop. The publican didn't mention any of that. The publican just said the two women came in, got a drink, and left."

"Why would he lie?"

"I guess he is hiding something."

"What was on the comms recordings?"

"Nothing on the pilot's comms. As you know, Bartiamos restricts access to those. There isn't much on the comms recording from the others. It's too muffled. There are definite sounds of a fight, but there isn't any indication of involvement of the other men."

"Do we have any identification?"

"No, no facials. The IDs were not picked up either. They must be using some kind of cloaking mechanism."

"If they went directly back towards the Hyperloop, perhaps they were going to the port?"

"Yes, the Filia thought that too. They checked. There was a lot of movement through the ID gateway. Nothing unusual. And the video footage was down at the time."

"It seems to be happening a bit too much lately. We need to correlate occurrences of video being out. Find out which rigs were around at the time. Look at Abrolhos too. Pity we have no access to Mayfield or New Montana. We find a correlation and we find them. Perhaps they got the rig renamed."

"Actually, we thought of that and had a look."
"What did you find?"
"Clearly someone is scrambling. However, we ran into a problem with correlating."
"Tell me."
"One of the Atesoughton fleets was around at the same time. It made it difficult to narrow down the correlation."
"Which fleet?"
"Delta."
"Couldn't be!"
"As you know, we only know of its presence because the crews are harder to bed than most. We struggle to get the pillow talk. But port records show several craft, including interceptors, arrows and G6s, present at the same time as the scrambler was used in Abrolhos and Southern Cross. The crafts were registered to the Atesoughtons or on commission to them."
"This means nothing. You are trying my patience. What makes you certain it is Delta?"
"We cross checked records of their other fleets. There are signs that the home fleets, the Western fleet, and the Eastern fleet, are in their cluster. The Southern fleet is travelling the main trade route to Earth. It passed through Kaytom 6, two days ago. Alpha fleet is still at or near Earth, as it has been for several years and since the old man last left. Beta fleet is back at Venus, having been shadowing Craig the Third's flotilla as usual, and was already on its way back to Earth, during the attack on Abrolhos. So, the other presence must be Delta."
The queen laughed.
"What is funny?"

"I'd forgotten that that young pup thinks he is free to go about as he pleases, with his little flotilla, while the old man keeps a close eye on him using an entire fleet."

"Oh, yes, and we found something else."

"What?"

"We thought it was odd that Delta was about, given they are more likely to be found shadowing the trade routes."

"And?"

"We looked into our records for details of Delta fleet's movements in recent times."

"What did you find? And where is it now?"

"Indications are that it is back in the Solar System. Likely orbiting Venus. It went there after Abrolhos. It was near Southern Cross when we got attacked. It came there via Abrolhos. Prior to that it was in the Solar System. And before that it was in the Asimov cluster. The trail gets fuzzy before that, but we think it may have crossed over from the Atesoughton cluster via the outer edges. Our spies tell us that it was near New Katoomba and before that, New Montana. The timeframe matches the murder of those three men and disappearance of the girls."

"Maybe the old man was simply providing further cover for his grandson?"

"Perhaps. But it does get stranger."

"How?"

"Delta fleet visited Newterratwo twice, over the course of four weeks. After the first visit it went the long way back to Earth. Then it returned more directly. After that, the movements of Delta fleet matched that of Beta fleet. That was until we were attacked in Southern Cross. Delta and Beta fleets then went separate ways until Delta returned to the Solar System a week ago. It might be connected to these attacks."

"That is an interesting idea, but what is the obvious answer?" the queen asked.

"I am confused."

"The obvious answer is protection."

"Protection?"

"Yes, the purpose of Beta fleet is to protect the old man's heir. What if there is someone else worth protecting?"

"It would take two fleets."

"Exactly."

"Oh, that reminds me," the daughter said with a tremble.

"What is it?" the queen demanded.

"Something odd."

"Spit it out girl."

"A tracing request has been flagged. It is from an EU credit shadow account authorisation."

"Why is this of interest to me?"

"The flag related to missing data."

"I am losing my patience! Explain yourself."

"A failed trace request was intercepted by our Filia. The error said, 'Label missing.'."

"So?"

"That usually indicates missing data. It could also indicate the data is obscured. Hidden. Perhaps tampered with."

"I know what it means, silly girl. Did you check the tree?"

"Yes. The male branch on the first trace suggests the requestor is a direct heir to Craig Atesoughton."

"He is young to have an heir."

"No, it relates to Craig senior. The old man."

"Interesting. So, perhaps there is another valuable target that the old man wants protected. And the female branch?"

"The data is missing. But we found something."

"What?"

"We reversed engineered the sequence."

"And?"

"It isn't from the typical lines. It is of the restricted lines. Like the Veneficans."

"Nonsense. We are tracing our lines separate to the central database. We know the precise details of all our descendants."

"But only the last thirty years. It could be older. Perhaps Helenal's tampering?"

"Nonsense. It is the other thing."

"What other thing?"

"Abominations born in abandoned settlements. Not Earth born. Dirty blood."

"Oh."

"You said 'first'?"

"Yes, a second failed request was intercepted. A little after the first."

"Branches?"

"No data. Perhaps it is more of Helenal's meddling?"

"Enough of this tampering theory. You are paranoid. Do we know where the requests were made?"

"Kind of."

"What do you mean?"

"The trace came from a connector to the Atesoughton family database. We have no visibility within their network. It could have originated from anywhere within the Atesoughton infrastructure."

The daughter said nothing but moved nervously.

"What else?" the queen asked.

"We found another correlation."

"Which is?"

"The bounty on Thosmas."

"Did you find out who raised it yet?"

"No."

"What then?"

"Several other bounties were raised at the same time."

"And?"

"It is the crew from that G5 rig the Ukendt was meant to have destroyed."

"Thosmas' bounty was raised after that. The G5 rig crew might have survived instead of the Ukendt crew! Shit!"

"What?"

The queen sighed, then said, "It means we have a foe that we don't know. At least two. And the proximity of the failed requests suggests they are known to each other."

"At least it confirms the Atesoughtons are connected to our recent woes. Even more reason to destroy those discs and get into the data centre. Perhaps this also can be used to explain Thosmas' behaviour and the disappearance of the Ukendt crew?"

"No! We have missed something vitally important."

"What?

"Find out what you can on the G5 rig crew. I need to think. Be gone."

When the playback finished, Dukk got up, walked over to the window, and looked out at the rolling swell.

Marr got up and came over to him. She inserted herself in his arms. They looked out together.

"What do you think?" She asked.

"Looks like our days of freewheeling it through the galaxy are numbered."

Marr laughed.

"Yes, that is one way to put it," she added.

Dukk smiled before saying, "We'd better get the crew together. Time to bring everyone up to speed and plan our next move."

"Yes, it is."

Dukk's mind drifted. Something wasn't adding up. Distant memories started to appear. It was as if past events were suddenly aware of each other. New connections were being made. Dukk closed his eyes. He did his best to make sense of it.

Suddenly, Marr straightened up and turned in Dukk's arms.

"That DNA scanner has a charging port on it," she said as she pulled away.

She grabbed the disc from where she'd placed it on the desk and put it into the charging cradle.

"Wait, weren't you worried about the trace?" Dukk asked as he watched her.

"Yes, but now we know they can't really get anything of use from it," she answered as she sat into the desk chair.

She then put her hand in the DNA sampling device, as she had done the previous evening.

A message appeared in the air over the desk, it read, 'Label missing.' However, unlike before when Dukk tried the second time, the label had an edit icon next to it.

"Oh, that's interesting," Dukk said as he sat down next to her again.

4

Marr interacted with the edit icon. The label was now editable.

"If this is my identity within the EU credit database, what name should I give it?"

"I would suggest your new name. The new alias we're going to be introduced with."

"Yes, that feels right to me, too."

Marr interacted with the edit box and entered, 'Maria'.

The system accepted the change. A new menu panel appeared in its place. The menu had three buttons. The first button had an icon of a tree. The second button had a currency symbol as it's icon. The final button had a search icon on it. In the top corner of the panel, there was a silhouette of a person with the label of 'Maria' beneath it.

"What is all of this?" Dukk asked.

"It means my sister is right about the meddling."

Marr clicked the silhouette.

A new panel appeared. Within were settings for display options. There was a button with the icon of a tree and a button with the icon of the currency symbol.

Marr clicked the tree button.

A new panel appeared. It contained a family tree. In the centre was a silhouette labelled, 'Maria'. There appeared to be other nodes in the tree, but it was all blurred. Hovering within the blur was a button. It simply read, 'Reveal'.

Marr clicked it.

A line now appeared to the right of 'Maria'. The line linked to another silhouette. The label on that was 'Cieloi'. Then two lines grew out of the top of 'Maria'. Two further silhouettes appeared. The first was labelled 'Michael Ferrearmas'. The second was labelled, 'Charmeli'. Two lines then appeared above 'Charmeli'. Two further silhouettes. One of them was labelled, 'Helenal'.

Marr and Dukk failed to notice the rest of the family tree as it was populated. Their attention was on the confirmation of what they had suspected.

Marr sat back in the chair and stared.

Dukk turned and looked at Marr. He waited to see how she would react.

"My father is Michael Ferrearmas," Marr said quietly after a few moments of silence.

"Yes, that is what it appears."

"Do you know who he is?"

"Yes, he is the next in line for the Ferrearmas family. He is in his mid to late sixties from what I understand."

"The family name is familiar."

"I think I know why."

"Why?"

"One of the men you killed in Abrolhos was from the Ferrearmas family."

"Oh."

Marr clicked the silhouette for Michael. A new tree appeared. One of the lines on the same level as Michael was dimmed. Beneath the silhouette was a date range. The birth and death dates. The death date was two weeks prior.

Marr frowned.

"This means nothing," Dukk said quietly.

"Or it could mean I shot my father's brother?"

"Does this knowledge change anything?"

"No, I guess not."

Marr then reversed out of Michael's tree. They then looked further at Marr's lineage. The men were all from elite families. Atesoughton was the only family name absent from the list. They also decided they were looking at the line of earlier queens, starting with her mother, Charmeli, then Helenal, Charloa, Doarena, Hilda and finally Lorenta. There were no records beyond Lorenta. They assumed she must have been the first queen. Her birth year was minus six, indicating she was a child at the time of the reset. She would have been in her sixties when the citadels were established. They concluded the timeframe made sense.

With the family tree exploration complete, Marr navigated to the currency symbol against her profile silhouette.

"What is all this?" Marr asked as they stared at rows of numbers.

"It is a list of credit and crypto accounts," Dukk answered. "The left column looks like an account number. The icons in the middle column show the type. The right column is the current balance."

"Are you sure? The current balances are astronomically high."

Marr clicked the account number for one of the rows. Another panel appeared. It showed dated transactions.

"These are recent transactions. Look at the descriptions. It looks like some kind of operating account."

"Do you recognise the transaction codes?" Marr asked.

"Yes, they look like rig identifiers. I recognise the codes from my own rig account statements."

"Big groups of them. Like a fleet was refuelled."

"Yes, those look like refuelling amounts. But the balance is several hundred million. And this is one of the smaller numbers. If they are accounts, we are looking at trillions. It would suggest means that are beyond comprehension."

"Are we looking at one of the Venefican's accounts used for refuelling their fleet?"

"More than that."

"What do you mean?"

"Those controls at the top of the list. They are for managing payments. For sending credit to other accounts."

"So?"

"They are enabled."

"Yes, they are."

Marr closed the panel and opened another account. They found more of the same. Lots of transactions involving large sums of credit. In every case, the controls for transferring funds were enabled.

"I think we need to get a reference point," Marr said as she sat back.

"What do you mean?"

Marr closed the screens.

"Let's try your ID."

"Oh, of course."

Dukk leaned over and put his hand in the DNA sampling device.

A message appeared in the air over the desk, it read, 'Label missing'. It was just as the evening before. And there was no edit icon next to it.

"I guess I am not as special as you," Dukk said in jest.

"That's intriguing. Let's try something."

Marr made a note of the series of digits below the label. Then, she put her hand on the DNA sampling device.

When the menu appeared, she clicked the search icon. She then entered the series of digits she noted from Dukk's attempt.

The search results produced a new screen. There was a message. It read, 'Label missing'. And this time there was an edit icon next to the message.

Marr clicked the edit icon and entered, 'David'.

"Now, try again," Marr said as she sat back.

Dukk repeated the process. This time, a new message appeared. This message read, 'Digital ID mismatch'.

5

"Oh, I forgot," Marr blurted.

"Forgot what?"

"I have a new digital ID for you. Jeeves gave it to me this morning. He gave me mine too. They are our real IDs."

"Real IDs?"

"Yes, the ones associated with our DNA. Elites have them. It gives them the ability to bypass ID gateways and all sorts. You need it to access this system because the system samples your DNA."

With the new digital ID applied to Dukk's implants, he tried the DNA sampling device again. This time it worked and the options and panels that appeared, were like what Marr had experienced. There was one difference. All the controls for transferring were disabled.

"I guess that is permissions related," Marr observed as they looked at one of the accounts.

"Yes, or perhaps it is the override," Dukk said in reply.

"Let's try something else," Marr said as she made a note of the account number.

Marr then gained access via her DNA once more. She then put the account number into the search. The account appeared with the same details they had seen moments before under Dukk's access.

"Oh, shit," Dukk exclaimed.

"Yes, the transfer controls are enabled. The override isn't just for accounts linked to my family lineage. It is everywhere."

"This is what the queen and her daughter meant by having control again."

"I guess it is."

"That's interesting," Dukk said as he sat forward.

"What are you looking at?"

"Show more of the account history."

Marr scrolled the panel and older transactions appeared.

"This account is being cleared. Lots of credit leaving. Nothing coming back in."

"It is. Let's have a look at your family's other accounts."

Dukk accessed his details again. Together they looked at other accounts and balances.

"Yes," Marr said after a time.

She then added, "Over the last ten years, your grandfather's been on a big spending spree. Your family has very little credit left. Seems to be plenty of crypto, but little credit. Where's the money been going?"

"Well, perhaps it has been the materials and labour required to build the settlements here on Earth. It has drained everything."

"It is almost as if he knows what is coming."

"It is."

Before moving on, they visited Dukk's family and confirmed what they already knew. That being, that Dukk's father was Craig Atesoughton the second, and his mother was Tieanna.

With the exploration complete, Marr stood up and then moved around the desk. She avoided looking at Dukk as she walked over to the window.

In silence, she gazed at the rolling seas.

Then after a few minutes, she spoke in a soft tone.

"Do you know what this means?"

Dukk stayed quiet and smiled. He sensed Marr was going to answer her own question.

"It means that combined, you and I are the most powerful individuals in the Galaxy. We can do whatever we want. We have the means to influence everything. We can see what others are doing, what's going on via the Veneficans' own network. We can control the flow of money. We can decide where it goes, where it doesn't go. We can hold people to ransom. We can build an army. We could be like gods."

Marr trembled as she said the last sentence.

Dukk paused. He watched her. He contemplated. He gave the moment space.

After a couple of minutes, Marr turned and stared at Dukk.

Dukk felt she was now ready for a response.

"Yes, Marr, it does look that way. But what do you want? What do you want to do with this power?"

"I don't want this type of power. It feels too much. It feels scary. I don't know what to do with that. This is awful. Nothing could have prepared me for this feeling."

"I feel that too. It certainly is a little bit overwhelming."

"A little bit?" Marr asked in a sceptical tone.

"Alright, very overwhelming."

Marr turned around and looked out of the window again.

Her emotions were all over the place. She was coming to terms with the new information. It brought to the fore her confusion of what it all meant to her.

Here she was looking at a recording through the eyes of her mother looking at her sister in a mask. Neither of whom she had ever met. And all indications were that they sat at the top of the darkness. A darkness that she had been taught to fight against since she was a child.

Though she tried, she just couldn't feel anger towards them. She was feeling something else.

Dukk got up and went over to her. He put his arms around her and together they watched the ocean in silence.

Marr focused her mind. She released the fear. She allowed her mind to empty. Then another thought appeared. She turned in Dukk's arms and looked at him.

"With these types of resources and this type of access, we could just disappear. Find our own little spot. A little paradise somewhere in the Galaxy. Have the twins. Keep our heads down. Have a quiet life."

"That's an interesting thought."

After a moment, he added, "I guess we need to think about what's important to us."

"Yeah, what's important. That's a good thought. Great question."

"What's important to you?"

"My head is spinning. I can't find an answer. What do we do?" Marr asked as she hugged him.

Dukk paused. He cleared his mind. The answer appeared.

"Nothing. I think doing nothing different is our best course."

"We wait, and see?" Marr suggested as she lifted her head again so she could look at him.

"Yes. Allow things to unfold."

"The creed?"

"Yes. Focus on that which is real in the heart. Create the space so that the process can emerge. Honour that which serves you well. Engage in the journey as it unfolds."

Chapter 14 – Pivoting

1

Later that evening Dukk had gathered the crew for a debrief. Craig and Emeelie were there. Jeeves was also present to represent Craig senior.

Everyone was up to speed on the new aliases, the DNA testing, the need to visit Bartiamos for the back story, and Craig seniors' new settlements. Dukk and Marr had left out the news relating to what they had discovered via the DNA sampling device and what they had uncovered about the family fleets.

"So, anyone got any thoughts on how we move forward?" Dukk asked.

"We mustn't lose focus of the mission to shut down the trafficking," Tieanna blurted as she sat forward.

"Yes, absolutely," Annee said in support.

"How will we do that if the schedules have changed?" Marr asked.

"Easy," Tieanna replied.

She smiled before adding, "Now that we know who is operating the trafficking, and how the parties are run, it wasn't hard to find the new schedule. My network of students simply looked at block bookings at h-pod hotels in settlements that had nearby resorts. Unfortunately, we also discovered there was a lot more going on than we'd previously thought. Also, the locations are spread out. And hard to get to. Like New Katoomba in the Atesoughton cluster. It will be impossible to intervene in them all. But we still should try."

"Where and when is the next most viable location," Annee asked.

"Buout Keya, in two weeks," Tieanna answered.

"Where is that?"

"It is a moon orbiting New Kowloon. A planet in the K-ARP system, in the APR cluster," Craig answered.

"Who is out there?"

"The Sung Yee family."

"It is not in the same direction as Newterratwo," Bazzer observed.

"So? Do we just abandon these girls?" Annee blurted.

"What if we head to Newterratwo, then onto New Kowloon?" Dukk suggested calmly.

"Do we have time?" Annee asked.

"If we went direct, it would take a week from here to reach Newterratwo. That would still give us a week to get to New Kowloon. It might require some big traverses, but I don't see why not."

"And what about the extra security in the resort, and at the main settlement's port and hotel?" Marr asked.

The last few words of her sentence were delivered with a stutter. It had just dawned on her that she hadn't given it a moment's thought since she learnt of it.

"We've been thinking about that," piped Luna.

"Who are 'we'?" Marr asked.

"Bognath, Ann, Suzzona and I."

"What did you come up with?"

"What if we never go into the port or the hotel? Or the resort?"

Marr sat back and smiled. She could see where Luna was going.

Luna noticed Marr's body language and grinned.

"How do we rescue the girls and take out the perpetrators if we don't go into the hotel, the port or the resort?" Dukk asked, having lacked Marr's knowledge of the finer details of covert operations.

"What if we take the girls off the shuttle, on the way to the resort?"

"Any attempt to get near the shuttle would obviously raise an alarm," Dukk added.

260

"And we don't want that. We'd attract all sorts of unwanted attention," Luna answered in a jovial tone.

"I am confused," Dukk said. "How do we take them off the shuttle without going near it?"

"We get onto the shuttle before the security and the girls are boarded. When it is just the pilots."

"How would that work?"

"We hang out in orbit at New Kowloon and wait for the shuttle to make its way back for the midday pick up. We stay in stealth. We jump them as they are preparing to deorbit. We get on board. We then secure the pilots and land the shuttle ourselves. We wait in the port for the minders and girls. During launch we adjust the g-juice mix to take out the minders. We then dock and get the girls off the shuttle."

"And the perpetrators? How do you propose getting past the extra security while minimising collateral damage?"

"Drones!"

"Drones?"

"Yes, we use drones to access the red room and terminate those disgusting animals."

"You'd have to be close enough to fly them."

"Yes, if we were in the port on the shuttle."

"Let me get this straight. We commandeer the shuttle on its way back to New Kowloon. We let the girls and minders come on board as normal. Then, we take the girls off when the shuttle reaches orbit, then continue to the moon. We then land the shuttle at the moon resort's port. After that we deploy the drones from the shuttle, to do the rest."

"Yep."

"What happens after that? How do you get back to the Imhullu?"

"We launch after the drone strike. You traverse to the moon and pick us up. You stay on the dark side, of course, to stay hidden if anyone on New Kowloon is looking. We leave the shuttle in orbit at the moon. Eventually the pilots and minders will wake up. By then we'll be long gone."

"You've got it all figured out," Dukk said with a laugh.

Luna smiled.

"Wait! Who is flying the shuttle?" Dukk asked after a moment of reflection.

"Me," Suzzona blurted. "I've flown them before. Did it for a time to make a little extra credit."

"Are you sure you are up to it? What if the minders figure it out?"

"Bognath will come with me."

"And, with his newly acquired medical training he can spike the g-juice?"

"Exactly."

Dukk thought about that, for a moment, then turned to Marr.

She took the hint. She looked for flaws. After a moment, she saw two.

"Bognath doesn't have the physique of a pilot. Also, what if the minders already know the shuttle pilots?"

"That's the genius of the plan," Luna answered.

"How so?"

"Well, we use the heighten security concerns to our advantage. We say the crew change is to provide additional security for the transfer to the moon. As we uncovered in Abrolhos, the minders operate on a need-to-know basis, so it will be hard for them to question anything new."

"And what about jumping the shuttle on its way back to the main settlement?"

"I've seen how it is done," Bognath said quietly. "It was when we secured the Imhullu just before the Dinatha was taken out."

"And I've done plenty of E.V.A. It is second nature to me," Suzzona said.

"I can lend a hand too," Mentor added.

2

"Right, then, we have a plan for the raids. What's next?" Dukk asked to focus everyone's attention.

"What about spreading the word about the refugee settlements back here on Earth," Suzzona asked. She had been quite interested in the idea the moment she had heard it.

"Yes, we need to do that, too," Craig said.

"How would we do it?" Dukk asked.

"You wouldn't just rush in. That is for sure," Suzzona added.

"What do you mean?" Lilaho asked.

"Even if we aren't associated, or seem to be associated, with one of the families, they are still not going to trust us or want to listen to us. Why would they?"

"What would help with that?" Dukk asked.

"You would have to have something to offer them. A peace offering of some sort."

"Perhaps credit or crypto?" Lilaho suggested in a quiet tone.

"Unlikely, as they have their own forms of currency."

"What would they be interested in, then?" Dukk asked.

"Medicines, vitamins. Anything that they can't get from their own planet, like real food," Bognath suggested.

"We could bring some," Lilaho said, having gained a little more confidence.

"Won't that feel a bit patronising, like a bribe?" Suzzona replied.

"What about Robin Hood?"

Everyone stopped and looked at Lilaho.

"You know," she said with a slight stumble. "Like the Robin Hood Raiders. Steal from the rich and give to the poor. That kind of thing."

Dukk laughed. He then said, "Yes, that could work. We could fill a container with medicine, vitamins, some real food. And drop it in and go under the banner of the Robin Hood Raiders. At the same time, we could say there is a new option for them if they want to take it."

Everyone joined in with giggles and a little clapping.

"So, what do we need to do that?" Dukk asked when the giggles dropped off.

"We just need to get containers full of stuff," Craig replied. "We've got ample. We can organise that from here or from one of the many other locations on Earth and elsewhere."

"Could we get one on board the Imhullu right now?" Annee asked. Craig nodded.

"How long would it take to organise that?" Dukk asked.

"Jeeves?" Craig deflected.

"From what I know, just off hand, we could probably get half a dozen containers organised in a week or so. We have the stores here in this location."

"How long to organise the first one?"

"A day, I guess."

"We take one with us and have the others follow?" Annee suggested.

"It sounds like we have a plan for spreading the word. What else?" Dukk asked to keep some momentum.

"We need to make the announcement and then get the DNA testing done," Craig said in reply to the question.

"And we need the backstory sorted out," Mentor said.

"Yes, good points," Dukk answered. "How long after the announcement would the DNA testing take place?"

"It depends on where it is done," Craig answered.

He then added, "It would have to be a safe and neutral location. Somewhere that all the families are happy to send a representative to."

"Like where?"

"I'd think Bartiamos' is the only place that would be acceptable to everyone."

"Newterratwo isn't central, but it can be reached within seven to ten days from main settlements."

Craig nodded.

"It would appear that all roads lead to Bartiamos now and not Rome," Luna blurted.

The others looked over with curious expressions.

Luna grinned.

"Ok," Dukk said in a firm tone to get everyone's attention again.

He then added, "We go to Newterratwo to get the back story, make the announcement, do the raid, and then do the DNA testing seven to ten days later."

At that moment, Jeeves coughed. It got everyone's attention.

3

"Sir, may I make an observation?" Jeeves asked in a polite but stilted tone. He looked directly at Dukk.

Dukk nodded.

"You will now have to factor in that you will be moving with a fleet. Your grandfather will insist on it."

Craig laughed and shrugged his shoulders as if to say, "I told you so."

"They won't be accompanying us to Buout Keya. That wouldn't make sense," Marr blurted.

"It will attract too much attention," Bognath added.

"Is there a solution?" Dukk asked.

"The fleet will need a reason to be there," Emeelie suggested.

"Like what?"

"I guess we could continue the trade agreement tour."

Dukk nodded. After a pause he continued.

"Jeeves, I want to know about the fleets."

Dukk's tone was casual. He did his best to hide his actual motives.

"What do you want to know?" asked Jeeves in reply.

"Please help me understand how the fleets move. In all my time hauling, while I've come across fragments of them from time to time, I've never really seen an entire fleet."

"Our fleets or in general? The strategies used by the families vary."

"Let's start with ours."

"We change ours around occasionally just to stay secure. We move along trade routes, mostly. However, we don't use the planets that have relays on them. The fleets are big enough that they can operate their own form of relays by using arrows and interceptors to leapfrog and stay behind. Fleets also regularly send support craft to the planets that have a relay, to pick up and broadcast messages."

"That explains why we don't really see fleets as a whole."

"Yes, although you will notice their presence if you observe hubs and planetary ports, because of course, parts of the fleet dock from time to time to collect supplies and so forth."

"So, if one wasn't paying attention, you'd hardly notice their presence, even if a large fleet was orbiting a nearby planet?"

"Yes, that's correct."

"What about their configuration, location and assignments."

"That's a lot of information."

"Do your best, please, I want to know."

"Ok. So, the Eastern and Western fleets are similar in size. They each have two carriers, five destroyers and a raft of support craft, including interceptors, arrows and G6s. These two fleets are based in the cluster and their assignment is to protect it."

"What are G6s?" Luna blurted.

"A G6 is a supply rig. Like a G5, but the hold space only supports one robo-container as it is fitted with fixed tanks for transporting fuels."

"And a carrier?"

"A carrier is a heavily armed support craft. Like a fortified hub that can traverse."

"Like a mammoth?"

"Yes, but one-third of the size and without the comforts. It is used to repair, refuel, and resupply the fleet. It can traverse with a dozen or so smaller craft in its hold, making it ideal for helping move the fleet through the system without the need to visit hubs."

"And a destroyer?"

"A smaller and more agile version of the carrier, but with better weapons and with less storage capacity. It can also go planet side if needed. Though, they rarely do as it takes a considerable amount of hard fuel to get them back into orbit."

Jeeves paused in case Luna had further questions. He then looked back at Dukk. Dukk had an expression of anticipation. Jeeves read the expression as a request to continue.

"The Southern fleet is of similar configuration to the Eastern and Western fleets, but with only one carrier and three destroyers. Its role is to help protect the main trade routes. It is currently on this side of Kaytom Beach."

Jeeves sat back in his seat as if to signal that he had answered the question.

Dukk sat forward. He kept his expression neutral. He knew there was more.

Dukk smiled and then asked, "And the others?"

"Others?" Jeeves answered innocently.

"Alpha, Beta and Delta?"

"Oh, yes, of course," Jeeves replied sheepishly.

He then added, "They are of similar configuration to the Southern fleet and are currently located here in the solar system."

"Are they really?" Craig asked in a surprised tone.

Jeeves nodded. His expression was slightly less composed than they had seen thus far. There was a touch of unease in it.

"And their purpose?" Dukk asked as he sat back in his seat.

"Protection," Jeeves answered bluntly.

"Of whom?" Dukk said in a tone that had a hint of authority.

"The purpose of Alpha fleet is to protect the head of the family, Craig senior."

"Beta?"

"Beta fleet has been assigned to protect Craig."

"Me!" Craig blurted.

"Yes, your grandfather felt that it was necessary. It shadows the movement of your flotilla."

"Since when?"

"It has had this purpose since you were eighteen and able to move freely."

"Did you know this?" Craig asked as he looked firstly at Emeelie, then Tieanna and finally at Eleettra.

They all shook their heads.

Craig sighed in defeat.

Dukk sat forward. He wasn't finished.

4

"And Delta?" Dukk asked in a quiet but firm tone.

"You," Jeeves answered in a dry tone that had a hint of guilt.

Dukk nodded.

"What! Since when?" Craig blurted.

Jeeves wriggled in his seat slightly. He was clearly now feeling uncomfortable.

"Since forever," Dukk answered, having read between the lines.

"What do you mean?" Craig asked.

"Isn't that right, Jeeves?" Dukk asked in answer to Craig's question.

"Yes, sir, Delta fleet has shadowed your movements since you first started hauling."

"What!" exclaimed Annee, having been the first to verbalise the shock that the others shared.

"You knew?" she then asked as she looked at Dukk.

"Not until this afternoon, but hearing it was like the dots being joined up in my mind. The dots being a familiar looking rig that was always present in a hub or citadel port. Or similar patterns on scanners when traversing trade routes."

"What about you, Bazzer, did you know?" Annee blurted.

"I suspected we were being followed," Bazzer answered. "But I always assumed Mentor was behind it."

"Mentor?" Annee asked.

"Nope. This is all news to me," Mentor answered.

Annee shook her head and sat back in her seat.

"Jeeves, how did they track me all those years?" Dukk asked.

"As you know, you hauliers share your flight plans with port authorities and with system relays. With the right connections, especially with those who make and maintain the relays, it isn't hard to track a rig. I understand it got a little more challenging when the Dinatha was destroyed. Delta fleet had to deploy scouts to neighbouring systems and planets. But they caught up with you eventually as you returned to Mayfield."

Dukk nodded as he realised that he already knew that.

He then asked, "Did they know why they were tracking me?"

"No, Dukk, they didn't and still don't. Even I only became aware of this truth very recently."

"The queen knows about Beta and suspects something about Delta too," Marr added.

That comment got everyone's attention. They now looked at Marr. Even Jeeves looked a little taken aback.

"What does she know?" Mentor asked.

"She knows where they are. Beta fleet doesn't hide its movements. Delta does. The Veneficans deduce the fleet's movements through a process of elimination."

"I'll need to have a word with the Delta fleet commander," Jeeves muttered.

"We can use this to our advantage," Mentor stated.

The others looked at him. They stayed silent.

"We have both Beta and Delta move in the directions we need them to. They can operate as support and cover but also as a decoy."

"Craig senior won't like either of his grandsons moving freely, unprotected," Jeeves stated as he sat forward.

"Especially, now that Marr is carrying his future heirs," he added.

"He won't need to worry. If we coordinate it well, and secretly, none of us will ever be far from either Beta or Delta."

As Mentor finished speaking, he sat deeper into his chair and turned to look at Dukk.

Jeeves sat back. He looked pensive.

Silence filled the room again.

Dukk's mind was racing. The way Mentor was looking at him was odd. A thought struck him. He sensed an opportunity had been presented.

He sat forward, looked directly at Jeeves, and spoke in an authoritative tone.

"I am going to take control. I will direct the fleets. Both Beta and Delta. Make it happen."

Jeeves was visibly startled by Dukk's tone. For a moment he said nothing. Then he stumbled some words.

"This is not something I can arrange. You will have to raise it with your grandfather."

"How do I organise an audience?"

"I can do it first thing. He should see you tomorrow."

"And the first of the containers with supplies, will it be ready in twenty-four hours?"

"If that is what you desire."

"It is."

Jeeves nodded. He looked shaken.

Dukk sat back in his seat and looked around.

Jeeves wasn't the only one who was in shock at Dukk's demeanour.

Most showed the signs, or at the very least, confusion. All except, Marr, Mentor, Annee and Bazzer. They smiled.

Dukk sat forward again.

"Alright, unless something significant changes, the plan is to link up with the fleets and travel in the direction of Newterratwo.

"We'll find a suitable place on the way to start our Robin Hood activities. We will visit Bartiamos to get the backstory. We then announce my existence to the families and invite them to witness the DNA testing.

"Meanwhile, we visit Buout Keya. With that sorted, we return to Newterratwo for the DNA testing. With that done, we continue both the raids and Robin Hood activities under the cover of a grand tour to meet the other heads of families. Let's aim for launch at midday, the day after tomorrow."

"A midday launch will be visible," Annee stated.

"It would be typical for launches from here to be visible, especially if escorting," Eleettra countered.

"Of course, I forgot. We still have a legitimate reason to be here."

"Besides," Dukk said in a less authoritative tone. "I think the time for hiding in the shadows is at an end. It is time to step up."

Dukk stood up. He was tired and felt he wouldn't be alone in thinking it was time for rest.

"So, we'd better make the most of our time tomorrow," Craig said as he stood up too.

"What do you suggest?" Luna inquired as she stood.

"Surfing."

"Out there?" Suzzona asked as she pointed at the rolling seas.

"No, there is a new settlement in the southern corner. It only takes twenty-five minutes on the hyperloop. The settlement is called Margaret River. Years gone by; it was a renowned surfing spot. World famous. Amazing surf, big swell sometimes too. But there's a few different breaks we can explore."

"Count me in," Luna stated.

Marr had hardly noticed the conversation about surfing. She was observing her own feelings and emotions. Seeing Dukk command the room had touched her. She was seeing him in a new light. She liked the feeling.

5

The next thirty-six hours passed without much further elaboration. The current thinking was rehashed multiple times as the crew enjoyed downtime on the beach and back at the complex.

Everyone was on board with what was proposed. The only addition was that Dukk had clarified his crew roles. Owing to her existing network of contacts, he had assigned Eleettra to family liaison. She would be responsible for maintaining communications with the family and ensuring they aligned their plans with any cross-family commitments. Lilaho and Kayila would join Dukk and Marr's watch roster. Typically, apprentices would start with learning the rig's systems. However, Dukk felt it was too soon for them to be apprentices. Instead, he decided that they would join the rotation with the least crew members. That was his and Marr's.

Dukk had also held a conversation with his grandfather. Dukk got no resistance to his desire to direct the two fleets. The only stipulation being that the fleets continue to be nearby.

In addition, Dukk and Craig had agreed they would effectively travel together with the fleets. Craig's flotilla would travel in full view, without Craig or Emeelie, via typical trade routes as it always did. In doing so it would provide cover for all their activities. They had also agreed a strategy for when they were spreading the word about the settlements or shutting down a party and retrieving a group of girls. The fleet would traverse to the target system but arrive at a non-typical planet. One without a relay. The Imhullu would then traverse to the target planet unaccompanied. The fleet would drop scouts into orbit of that planet to keep an eye on things. Thus, the fleet was never far and could respond quickly if needed. And finally, to conduct the meetings with the other heads of the families, they would simply re-join Craig's flotilla as it arrived in orbit of the target planet.

Dukk and Marr had enjoyed time together but steered clear of discussing any of the bigger questions.

"Those crates must contain the supplies, replacement uniforms and garb we'll have to wear for official events," Annee said aloud.

"And that must be the robo container with the Robin Hood offering," Bazzer added.

She, Bazzer and Dukk were standing in the doorway of the hyperloop station. They were looking down at the Imhullu. Several crates and a robo container sat next to it on the hanger floor.

They had arrived at the rig before the others to commence launch preparation.

The others were making the most of their last moments in luxury. Craig senior had also been difficult to find time with, so a group were with him now to say goodbye. Marr was in the site's medical wing with Tieanna. They were doing a final check-up. Tieanna wanted to take full advantage of the facilities and staff before they returned to the rigours of space.

Dukk liked to get to the rig first. It had only been a couple of days, but it still felt like a lifetime since he was on the rig.

Dukk had shown Annee and Bazzer the alternative way out of the complex. The way that Craig had shown him. The path through the back of the service corridors that led to the wide tunnel. The wide tunnel where he and Craig had accessed the second Hyperloop to visit the settlements. From there, they used a stairway to climb up to a door. The door put them into the Hyperloop entrance they had used to access the welcoming atrium. Going this way avoided any delays and unwanted attention.

Dukk paused and looked down at the rig. Annee moved slightly at his side. She was sensing his distraction. Dukk turned to her and nodded before descending the stairs to the hanger floor.

Dukk led the trio to the underbelly of the rig. He then interacted with a panel mounted on the side of the huge five-metre-high forward jack.

A crack echoed in the hanger as the seal was broken on the ramp doors. They stood back as it unfolded towards the floor. The ramp was impressive once extended. Standing beneath the rig they all were reminded of how immensely big the rig was.

With the ramp extended, Dukk headed up the stairs. When he got to the top, he interacted with a console to lower the hold platform. He ducked halfway down the ramp to watch the platform as it made its way to the hanger floor.

Bazzer pushed past Dukk. His destination was the engine room.

Annee had already detached the wireless leads from the side of each of the robotic crates and stacked the devices together.

When the platform reached the hanger floor, Annee pressed the big green buttons on the wireless leads. With the leads in hand, she stepped onto the platform.

In unison, the four robotic crates organised themselves in pairs before following Annee onto the platform.

"I got this from here," she called as she stepped off the platform and headed towards the ramp.

Dukk nodded, turned, and headed back into the rig. His mind was tugging at him as he climbed the stairs to the upper level and the cockpit. It wasn't the rig, the launch preparation or yearning for space again. It was something else.

He did his best to focus on what he stood for, what was important, who he held dear and what was beyond the metals, plastics, and textiles that he knew so well. He tested those thoughts against the distraction.

As he reached the upper level, the answer hit him. He stopped at the door to the cockpit and recalled the other half of the conversation with his grandfather.

"How long have you known about me?"

"I gather you have discovered that answer for yourself."

"You knew about Tieanna's initiation and your son's role in it?"

"Yes, I did."

"And, you knew she had a son and that she got help to hide me?"

"That is correct."

"Yet you had me grow up as most and remain oblivious to my true identity."

"I did."

"Why?"

"I was told to keep my distance and allow you to experience life as an unprivileged."

"Who told you to do that?"

"The plan's architect."

"Who is the architect?"

"I suspect you already know. That is all I will say on that matter, at this time."

"Okay, but why was it important for me to grow up as unprivileged?"

"I don't know for certain, but I have my suspicions."

"Which are?"

"It will serve you better than being raised as privileged."

"How will it serve me?"

"It will serve you in what you must do going forward."

"To lead the family?"

"No," he answered with a laugh.

"What then?"

"Everything."

"What do you mean by 'everything'?"

"I can't say anymore. And perhaps I have said too much. It will be clear at the end."

The unsatisfactory way in which the conversation had ended played on Dukk's mind again.

On entering the cockpit, the first thing that got his attention was his helmet. It was sitting on its stand next to his seat. Quietly waiting to be useful again.

He smiled. He let the distraction wash over him. He had work to do. It was time to be useful again.

Chapter 15 – Acceleration

1

Dukk enabled the crew comms. It was just before midday. Everyone was on board and the rig was locked down and set for launch. Orange lights were flashing in the walls of the hanger.

"Check-in please. Passengers and vitals, Mentor?"

"Med lines primed. All stable," Mentor answered.

"Engines, integrity and biosystems?"

"Reactors are hot. The burners are priming. The coolers are engaged. Integrity is at one hundred percent. All systems are green," Bazzer replied.

"Luna, weapons?"

"Green. Standing by."

"External comms, scanners, Ann?"

"Typical noise from the port controls in the citadels. They are directing the usual deorbit and launch traffic. All clear."

"Marr, update?"

"No change. Launch control have us at plus twenty seconds. Still third to launch. Just behind the cruiser and ahead of the two tail arrows."

"I have T-minus ninety-five seconds."

"Check."

"Anything else, anyone?" Dukk asked as he looked up through the windshield.

The hanger doors were opening. Blinding sunlight burst through.

There was silence on the comms.

"Green light?" Dukk asked as he looked across at Marr.

"Confirmed," Marr said without taking her eyes off the instrumentation.

Dukk brought his gaze back to his console.

"Engaging autopilot on sixty. Sixty-four. Sixty-three. Sixty-two. Sixty-one. Engaging."

For a moment there was silence. Then there was a tremble as the thrusters spun up and started to take the weight from the jacks. The rig shook a little as it rose gently away from the hanger floor. The rig then hovered for a few moments just below the opening. There were more noises and then clunks as the jacks were retracted. Then with a shutter the thrusters engaged further. The rig moved up through the opening and rose into the air.

Dukk looked to his right. The cruiser was rising too. Further up he could see the lead arrow. The rig started to pivot on its axis while still climbing. The view changed from the ocean to the bush lands stretching into the distance. Then the main engines engaged. The rig started to move forward. It rose and arced around to line up behind the cruiser. Then in a convoy, the five craft crossed over the shoreline north of the complex, picked up speed and moved out over the ocean. Forty seconds later the rig's nose came up and the hard burn was initiated. The crew were pushed back into their seats as the rig blasted its way towards lower orbit.

Dukk closed his eyes. He focused his mind away from the crushing weight of his body being flung into the heavens. His thoughts wandered. He pictured the Earth disappearing behind him and the vastness of space ahead. A new sense formed in his imagination. The sense that he was leaving something tangible and real. Ahead was vagueness. Sure, there was possibility but there was also dread of the unknown. Images flashed into his consciousness of all that he had known. Each image faded into a mess of ambiguity.

Marr sunk back into her seat. She too focused her mind away from the physical stress, the vibrations and the noise. She pictured herself enclosed in warm arms. Safe arms. She explored the feeling. She visualised her babies with her in those arms. All safe and secure. The image swirled.

Dukk only opened his eyes as the noise abated. The curvature of the Earth now filled his view. With the silence came weightlessness. He shifted his gaze towards Marr. Even with the helmets he could still see her face clearly. Her eyes were still closed. He waited and watched as she observed the change, tilted her head in his direction and opened her eyes. Their eyes met. Smiles erupted. They were away again.

2

Dukk waited a full minute before re-engaging the comms.
    "Check-in, please. Vitals?"
    "All stable," replied Mentor.
    "Systems. Integrity?"
    "Integrity at one hundred percent. Biosystems in the green. No alerts," replied Bazzer.
    "Flight control?"
    "Logs clear," Marr answered.
    "Excellent. Bazzer, bring the DMD online so we have a little comfort as we coordinate the exact traverse times."
    "On it," was the reply.

The familiar shiver ran through them as the DMD reached into the space between space.
    Dukk interacted with the controls. Moments later he spoke.
    "Welcome to orbit, once more. As planned, we have about twelve hours until we join the fleet orbiting Venus. I will share an update once we have the exact timing agreed. I'd say it is nearly time for lunch. Let's say thirty minutes."

Dukk and Marr removed their helmets as the others behind them, did the same.

Annee stood up.

"Dukk, I'll take the conn in the crew mess when you are done with post-launch checks."

"Roger that," Dukk replied without looking up from his activity at the controls.

"Ann, will you ask Lilaho and Kayila to join us," Marr asked as Annee made for the cockpit door.

"Starting their training immediately?" Annee asked in reply.

"Yep, no point in delaying."

Dukk waited for the rest of the crew to leave the cockpit. He then turned back to Marr.

"How are you?" he asked.

"I am good," she replied with a smile.

"Sickness?"

"Not as bad this time. Tieanna said this next trimester will be a breeze."

Dukk smiled as he looked at Marr's hands. They were resting on her belly.

Moments later, Lilaho and Kayila dropped into the second row behind Dukk.

"What do we have to do?" Lilaho asked as she looked around.

Marr turned to the girls.

"Just observe quietly, and we'll review what occurs to you later today when we are on watch together."

Marr then opened a series of panels ready to receive and decode the message they were expecting.

"Here it is," she said after a moment of further interaction.

"And?" Dukk asked politely as he looked over.

"Flotilla command has us heading to Tau Ceti 5."

"Surprise, surprise."

Marr laughed, and said, "But instead, we'll be taking a different route via Tau Ceti 4."

"Yep. Is the schedule in the message?"

"Yes, the flotilla's lead arrow will traverse in twelve hours and fifteen minutes. We are to start probing the DMD so that we traverse thirty seconds after that."

"Right, we have our target traverse time. Any details on the shell game?

"Yes. Craig and Emeelie will come on board at ten thirty."

"That makes sense. Do you want to open a channel to the fleet's arrow while I load the auto pilot for the rig-to-rig transfer at ten thirty."

"On it. And the traverse countdown to get to Venus?"

"Just checked. It is fifty-five minutes."

"That means that setting the DMD would occur at just after bringing them on board."

"Yep."

"It is going to be busy."

"It will."

"And we'll only just be finished watch at ten p.m."

"Yep, it will be hardly worth handing over the conn until after the traverse at half eleven."

"The arrow is ready to receive our message."

"Great. Send our ETA."

After a moment of silence, Marr looked up and said, "Done."

As Marr spoke, Dukk was already reviewing the rig schematics. He observed that Annee had opened the console in the crew mess.

He initiated the conn transfer. Annee accepted it immediately.

"Lunch," he then said as he stood up.

Later that evening Marr was sitting with Lilaho and Kayila at the console in the crew mess.

"What is that?" Kayila asked as they looked at a star chart.

"The trade route to Newterratwo," Marr answered. "See it starts with Tau Ceti 5, then Tau Ceti 8, Tau Ceti 9, IACA6, IACB2, IACB5, IACB9, IACC4, IACC9, IACD3 and IACE1, before reaching Newterratwo."

"Is that our route?"

"No, we aren't going via the trade route."

"We are going via Tau Ceti 4?"

"We are doing the robin hood thing still, aren't we?

"Yes, we are dropping the container off at Tau Ceti 7."

"Where is that?"

"It is the next system after Tau Ceti 4."

"And what happens after we drop off the container?"

"Let me show you."

After a moment of interacting with the console, a new star chart appeared. Marr then continued.

"After Tau Ceti 7, our route to Newterratwo will take us to IACB10, IACC7, IACC11, IACD1, IACE3 and IACD3."

"Oh. And what exactly, were you and Dukk doing just after the traverse?"

"What do you mean?"

"The back and forth with the DMD instructions."

"We were fiddling with the flight plan so that it appeared we were leaving with the flotilla."

"So, we aren't leaving with the flotilla."

"No."

"We are joining the fleet."

"Exactly."

After a moment of silence, Kayila asked another question.

"What is probing the DMD?"

"We put coordinates into the DMD to get a countdown estimate and do it again if the estimate isn't what we want."

"What do we want?"

"Eleven, thirty-two and thirty seconds."

"Why so precise?"

"When moving with the flotilla we must go at pre-defined intervals. The flotilla commander asked us to traverse thirty seconds after the lead arrow."

"And the lead arrow is traversing at Eleven, thirty-two?"

"Exactly."

Marr paused again to let that sink in and create the space for further questions.

Lilaho was next to fill the silence.

"What is the shell game?"

"Also known as thimblerig, the shell and a pea or the old arm game. It is a gambling game using three identical containers, like cups or shells, and a ball. The aim is to guess which cup has the ball.

"Ok, but what does that have to do with Craig and Emeelie coming on board?"

"When transporting persons of importance, flotillas and fleets do hatch-to-hatch docking in preparation for traverse."

"Why?"

"So, onlookers must guess which cruiser or escort has the prize?" Kayila blurted.

"Precisely," Marr answered.

"What happens when we get to Venus?" Kayila asked without hesitation, then immediately continued, and tried to answer her own question. "We start the DMD countdown to traverse to Tau Ceti 4?"

Marr smiled. She liked that Kayila was paying attention. She also liked that her inhibitions were dissolving. However, Marr made a note to herself to work on the answering one's own questions piece.

"No, we dock with the carrier or a destroyer."

"Why?"

"To save time," Lilaho blurted.

"Exactly, Lilaho. Do you want to explain?"

"Sure. The fleet will get our estimated arrival time via the arrow we communicated with earlier. They will start a DMD countdown to coincide with our arrival time. When we arrive at orbit of Venus, they will be nearly ready to traverse. We dock and then traverse with one of the larger ships."

"Pretty much. Except, they need to factor in time to dock and get connected ready for the traverse."

"After docking, will we take seats within the carrier or destroyer?"

"Not immediately. We will generally be on the Imhullu for traverses. It is safer should we need to make a quick exit after the traverse."

"If we come under attack?"

"Exactly."

"But if the carrier or destroyer runs the traverse, how do we know when to run the juice?"

"Once docked, we connect to the host vessel via an umbilical cord. The host ship will instruct our medical system when to run the juice."

"Oh, wow."

After a further moment of silence, Marr decided to bring things to a close.

"If there isn't anything else, I suggest you might use the remainder of the watch to read through the traverse safety regulations."

Both girls sighed.

As Marr started to get up from the console, Kayila spoke up.

"Marr, can I ask you something?"

"Of course?"

"How did you know Dukk was the one for you?"

Marr smiled, looked away for a moment, then turned back towards Kayila.

"Butterflies."

"You chose a future with one man based on butterflies?"

"Yes, I knew at the butterflies that he was the one for me. However, choosing a future came later."

Marr then winked, stood up and moved away from the console. She headed towards the forward door.

At that moment, Dukk was entering the crew mess via the door of the starboard aft ladder shaft. He crossed the room and followed Marr through the forward door. On the way, he noticed the expressions on the faces of Lilaho and Kayila.

Marr noticed his approach and held the door for him.

"Getting in some practice?" he asked as the door closed behind them.

"What do you mean?"

"Parenting Lilaho and Kayila?"

Marr laughed. She reached in for a kiss.

After the kiss she pulled back.

"Parenting teenagers is something we'll not have to worry about any time soon. From what I am reading, there will be lots to take our attention before that."

Dukk looked on with a quizzical expression.

4

The exit from the traverse put them well clear of most of the fleet. The view as they regained consciousness and conducted the routine post traverse checks, was of a featureless planet racing below them.

"Dukk, we have a message on the secure channel," Annee announced onto the comms.

"What does it say?"

"It contains docking instructions."

"Let's load it up and see what itlooks like."

Moments later, Dukk looked up from the controls.

"We have a fifteen-minute adjustment. A short, hard burn to put us in the vicinity. That will bring us to the fleet. Then we have a pivot and burn to put us on top of the carrier."

Dukk then opened the comms to all those on board.

"Hold tight everyone, we've got about a fifteen-minute adjustment to make. Sit tight while I initiate the initial hard burn. After that you'll have about twelve minutes if you want to get up and about. Let's be back in our seats for the reverse burn and docking procedure."

Fifteen minutes later, the rig was turning after the reverse burn. Most had decided to stay in their seats. Few had experienced coming in to contact with a fleet of this size.

After the initial hard burn, the rig's speed increased across the surface of the planet. Then once in the vicinity of the fleet, the rig pivoted one hundred and eighty degrees. A hard burn was initiated to slow the rig to the speed of the fleet.

Initially the fleet looked like tiny specs. But with the increase in speed, it didn't take long for the conglomeration of craft to fill their view. It was breathtaking. The colossal carrier, the two massive destroyers and the multitude of support vessels.

As with docking in hubs, the rig approached the carrier from the top side. Their target was a set of doors mid-way along the huge craft. Doors big enough to swallow their rig whole. While Dukk was monitoring things, the autopilot was doing all the work.

The rig approached the opening, adjusted orientation, and then floated just above it. Large arms extended up and latched on to secure points in the rig's underbelly. The arms then dragged the rig in.

Orange flashing lights met them as they entered the inside of the carrier's main hanger. The arms were part of a conveyor system that brought them inside as the doors closed above them. The orange lights abated as the doors sealed.

The rig was then moved to a docking space on the side wall of the huge hanger. With the rig secured, a bridge extended from the wall of the hold towards the port airlock door.

The view before them was of a dimly lit space. The shapes of other craft could be just made out in the darkness.

"We have a message from air traffic control. We can extend our bridge," Marr announced.

"Extending our bridge now," Dukk replied on the crew comms.

Moments later, Dukk added, "We have a secure connection. Umbilical cord also attached. Checking for traverse sequence information."

After reviewing the information, Dukk continued.

"We have approximately ten minutes until we traverse. The carrier appears to be already locked down in preparation. I suggest we sit tight. Bazzer, you can power us down."

"On it," was the reply.

Fifteen minutes later, Dukk and his crew had regained consciousness after the traverse.

They peered out of the windshield. Spotlights were being switched on. They could now see an array of arrows, interceptors and G6s docked to the walls of the hanger.

"Dukk, we are being hailed by carrier operations," Annee announced, breaking the silence.

"Put it through."

The image of an operator materialised in the middle of the cockpit.

"Imhullu, welcome to the Davidus Vaderen, the command ship for Delta fleet. Please share your crew and passenger IDs so we can commence clearance protocols. Also, Commander Bryce requests a private audience with your captain. An escort detail will be waiting on the bridge. Please come alone."

With that the call ended and the image disappeared.

Dukk removed his helmet and looked around.

"What do you make of that?" he asked.

"They must have received Jeeves' communication, surely," Marr replied.

"Yes, Jeeves assured me that the fleet commanders would be informed of the new line of command."

Dukk stood up and left the cockpit.

Craig and Emeelie were still seated in the first seats in the passenger seating area.

"How are we looking?" Craig asked as Dukk entered.

"The fleet commander has requested a private audience. Carrier operations also want our IDs. It feels like they don't have any knowledge of who we are."

"That might be true. The request for IDs is standard procedure. Uncleared personnel won't be allowed to leave the rig and won't be able to make use of the host craft's facilities during the passage. We agreed with Jeeves that other than informing them of the change in the chain of command, it would be for us to instruct the commanders. Besides, the commander probably wants to know what is going on. I guess he wants to know why an interceptor from my flotilla is here and why one of his, has been sent in replacement. Also, he might just want to meet the guy he has been protecting all these years."

"Good point. And the IDs? What information shall we share?"

"Share your cover IDs, we have them too," Craig said as he opened his wrist wraps.

5

When the post traverse checks were done, Dukk handed the conn back to Annee. He and Marr then went to their cabin.

"What do you think the fleet commander wants?" Marr asked as she sat on the bed watching Dukk get changed.

288

"No idea," Dukk answered as he got into the grey uniform of elite staffers.

"Is it safe?"

"What do you mean?"

"You are heir to one of the most powerful families in the galaxy. You will have to watch your back!"

"That was the fleet's purpose. They had plenty of opportunity to snuff me out."

"But that was before they knew who you really are."

"Who says they know."

"Good point."

Marr got up from the bed and wrapped her arms around him.

"Come back to me," she said as she snuggled into his chest.

"I will."

With that Dukk broke from the embrace and made for the door.

Marr accompanied him through the rig and to the port-airlock door. She held his hand as the security screen opened.

On the other side of the door was a detail of four uniformed security guards. Each had a holstered gun.

"This way sir," the leader announced firmly on seeing Dukk.

Marr squeezed Dukk's hand gently before letting go. She then stepped back to allow Dukk to move through the door and onto the bridge.

Dukk turned back as he got to the end of the bridge.

Marr was still there.

He mouthed, "I've never left."

She smiled back.

Just beyond the airbridge was a hover cart. It moved off as soon as Dukk and the security detail were seated.

The cart made its way swiftly through a series of narrow corridors to the doors of an elevator lift in the middle of the carrier.

The elevator took them to the carrier bridge.

Six operators sat at consoles near the front of the control room. A man sat in a raised chair in the middle of the room. He had his back to Dukk.

Before the elevator doors had a chance to close, the man raised his hand and made a swishing motion. The four security guards stepped back into the elevator, leaving Dukk standing alone.

The man then stood up, came around the chair and looked at Dukk.

Commander Bryce was a tall man, with blue eyes and pale complexion. He had a buzz cut and was clean shaven. His expression was stern and sobering.

"Captain, this way," he said with a nod.

Dukk followed Bryce through a door at the back of the bridge.

Beyond was a small room with no windows. A console with a chair was embedded into one wall. A table sat in the middle of the space with six chairs.

Bryce closed the door behind them, took a chair at the table facing the door and offered the chair opposite to Dukk.

They both sat.

They stared at each other across the table.

After a minute of silence, Bryce spoke.

"I want answers."

Dukk paused. He tried to read Bryce's expression to get an angle on what was going on. There was nothing.

"And I will give them, if I can," Dukk replied in a cool tone.

Bryce held Dukk's stare for another minute, sat back and began to speak.

"Fifteen years ago, I was given my first fleet command. I was young to be in that position. But I had been led to believe that I was the best of the best. A rising star. Most of my peers weren't surprised that I got a command so young. If I'm honest, I was a little surprised.

"I was then informed that a new fleet was being put together. It was to be used for covert operations. It was to be called Delta Fleet. It appeared too good to be true. And it was.

"My orders came through shortly after I took command. I was shocked. I had to re-read them a dozen times. Do you know what I was ordered to do?"

Dukk said nothing and just stared back with a blank expression.

Bryce continued.

"With an entire fleet at my command, the order was to babysit an apprentice haulier. The instruction was simple and clear. The order was to shadow the haulier everywhere he goes. Be unseen but be within reach to protect him from harm at all costs."

Bryce paused and looked away for a moment before continuing.

"To be fully transparent with you, I resented this command for many years. I even tried to get out of it. Every time I made a request for a transfer, I got knocked back. My superiors eventually agreed to organise an audience with Mr Atesoughton. Not that that made any difference. He just told me I was the best person for the job, and I was doing it with spectacular success. The suggestion of spectacular success confused the hell out of me. All I did was move the fleet up and down trade routes in the shadows, and coordinate scouts with a security detail to be in hubs and ports to keep an eye on you.

"Sure, there were a few close calls. This was especially true of the early years where you found yourself drunk and in the middle of some pub brawl alongside your rig engineer. There was also the odd accident, but you and your crew always came through it without the need for help. But it was mostly very routine. And very dull.

"Over time the resentment faded. It was replaced with indifference. I accepted my fate. For many years that was the way of things. Then something surprising happened. I started to respect you. But that changed yesterday. Now I am angry!"

Bryce paused.

Dukk said nothing.

"Yes, now I am angry. Do you know why?"

Dukk still said nothing.

"Well, I will tell you. Yesterday, I got a new order. A simple order. A request to take orders from another. Fifteen years of following the same order from Mr Atesoughton. And it changes in an instant. Do you know who I am now to take orders from?"

"Yes," Dukk answered confidently.

"Who?"

"You are now to take orders from me."

"Precisely. So, captain, or perhaps I will use your actual name. Dukk, my question is simple. And, think about the answer, because I am tired of being in the dark. I have a mind to extinguish you and your crew and make off with this fleet. I have nothing to lose."

Bryce paused for dramatic effect. The anger was evident in his tone.

Dukk remained silent.

"My question is, 'Who are you?'" Bryce asked in a tone that contained both anger and menace.

Chapter 16 – Expansion

1

Dukk held Bryce's stare.

Dukk reflected. There was a lot to take in. It was dawning on him. His path wasn't just his own. It was the path of many. A path that somebody in the past, potentially Helenal, had put them all on. There was only one way in his mind that this was going to go well. And that involved not lying.

Dukk sat forward.

"I'm the first born to Craig Atesoughton, the second. I am the older brother of Craig Atesoughton, the third. I'm the next in line after Mr Atesoughton. A fact that I only learnt of, three weeks ago."

Bryce sat back in his chair, stunned. After a moment, his face cleared. The threads of the past had clicked into place. It all made sense to him. He then sat forward.

"Well, that explains the message I received before leaving Sol."

He drew his wrists forward and a series of panels opened in the air above the table between them. After some interaction, a video message holder was all that remained in the air.

Bryce then reached into a drawer and retrieved a device like what Dukk and Marr had used in the study in their suite at Zuytdorp. He placed it on the table in front of Dukk.

"I got this sealed message from Mr Atesoughton. The envelope said that only his heir will be able to open it."

Dukk leant forward and placed his right hand on the device.

The video message opened before them. An image appeared. It was the head and shoulders of Craig Atesoughton, the first.

Bryce reached in and started the play back.

"By now, Commander Bryce, you will have met my son's first son. My heir. You know him as Dukk, as will most. He will go by other aliases. The families will know him as David. I trust you will honour this.

Bryce, you have been a loyal servant to the family. In addition to now taking your orders not from me, but my first grandson, you will now take up your true role. You were handpicked years ago. Now it is time for you to step into it.

The following will be made official when you reach Newterratwo and take command of our two mammoths. Yes, in addition to the refurbished, Niels Juel, Bartiamos has constructed us a new mammoth. It shall be commissioned as the Idibura. They will all fall under your stewardship as the commander of the Central Fleet. The central fleet will be made from the amalgamation of Alpha, Beta and Delta fleets. As you know, the commanders of Alpha and Beta fleets are about to retire. I assume you will still see fit to maintain a presence at Earth to fulfil the role of Alpha fleet.

You may want to keep much of this to yourselves for now. And, Bryce, see that both my grandsons are present when you have your next audience with Bartiamos. The reason will be clearer at the time.

Visit me in person when you are next at Earth.

Thank you."

Dukk observed Bryce. He was clearly in a state of shock. A tear had formed in his eye. He shuffled his hands to wipe it away quickly. Then he collected himself and looked over at Dukk.

"Who else knows this?"

"Which part?"

"My new role?"

"No idea. It is the first I have heard of it."

"The new mammoth and amalgamation of the fleets?"

"Same."

"Your true identity?"

"My crew. My brother. My grandfather's inner circle. A few others, perhaps."

"Do other family heads know?"

"Not yet as far as we can determine."

Bryce sat back again. He turned away. He looked blankly at a picture on the wall. It was an image of a blue giant star. He then turned back to Dukk once more. His face softened. A smile came across it. A genuine smile.

"So, what now?"

Duck smiled, and then replied.

"We're going to change the galaxy."

Bryce laughed, and then asked.

"And your orders, what are they?"

"Make a path towards Newterratwo, via Tau Ceti 7, avoiding trade routes," Dukk replied in a direct, but pleasant tone.

"Why Newterratwo?"

"We need help from Bartiamos."

"The other families won't accept a haulier as the next Atesoughton heir. You need a new back story?"

"Precisely."

"And Tau Ceti 7?"

"We are dropping off a container of supplies."

"The outpost? Why?"

Dukk paused.

Bryce sat forward again.

His expression hardened.

"Can I ask you something?" Dukk said as he mirrored the hardened expression.

"What?"

"You said you grew respect for me, rather than indifference. What happened?"

Bryce sat back. His expression softened again.

"It was not long after you got your captaincy. A few close calls and then you just disappeared. We searched the Dinatha wreckage near WXR22 and the nearby planets and systems. Found nothing. Then you showed up again in WZR15. In an interceptor that looked surprisingly like the Ukendt that went missing when the Dinatha was destroyed. Yes, it was one of my arrows that intercepted you. The observer you had on board prevented us from confirming we'd found you again until you landed in Mayfield. Then things got rather exciting, and it got harder to keep tabs on you with the stealth tech. After struggling to keep up with you, I realised you didn't need me or this fleet shadowing you. You not only dodged several very close calls, but you came out on top. Also, you and your crew started showing up in strange places. Joining Craig junior's flotilla. Getting into a mammoth and out again. Making enemies of the Veneficans. While I didn't understand all of it, I could see there was intentionality in whatever you've been up to. It was phenomenal. That is when my indifference turned into respect."

Dukk was overcome with emotion. He did his best to hide it.

Hearing this perspective of what had happened touched his heart. It was confirmation the actions of a few could make a difference.

2

Bryce sat forward again.

"Keeping me in the dark will hinder my ability to fulfil your orders."

"Accepted. I will do my best to enlighten you as needed. But some things will be best not known, for now."

"I can accept that."

"What do you need to know?"

"Tell me about your crew. The three new members you took on after becoming a captain."

"What about them?"

"They are resistance?"

"Yes, they are."

"And is it true, that a master assassin is one of them?"

"Yes, that is true, too."

"You picked up some other crew along the way. The minder and the dock worker from Mayfield. Why?"

"Opportunity and need."

"Does that apply to the others also."

"Pretty much."

"And the passengers you traversed with just now?"

"Craig and Emeelie."

"They are with you?"

"Yep."

"I wasn't notified."

"You are now. Besides, they want to keep a low profile and use aliases whilst here. As do I and my crew."

"Suit yourself. Avoiding the fanfare of having Craig on board is far easier for me. Does Commander Ryien of the Beta fleet know Craig is here?"

"Nope. He will be tracking Craig's flotilla as per normal."

"Will you all be staying with the Davidus Vaderen for the duration of the passage?"

"Pretty much. Apart from Tau Ceti 7."

"What happens then?"

"I want the fleet in orbit of another planet, away from the outpost. You can send a couple of arrows with us, but they are to stay hidden in orbit. I will be taking the Imhullu planet side."

"Craig and Emeelie?"

"They will stay on board here."

"One moment please," Bryce said as he turned his head towards the wall.

"Fleet navigator and CCO, to my office ASAP," was said into his comms.

Bryce then returned his gaze to Dukk.

"What was the purpose of the raid on the Venefican's mammoth?"

"To rescue Tieanna?"

"Your brother's nanny?"

"Yes, and she is also my mother."

"Tieanna and your father?"

Dukk nodded.

"She is on your crew now?"

"She is."

"What role?"

"Medical support."

"Two medical staff on a rig that size?"

"We have our reasons."

At that moment there was a knock on the office door.

"Enter," Bryce called.

Two uniformed men marched over to the desk and stood just left of Dukk. Both did their best to not look at Dukk. It was clear from their body language that they desperately wanted to.

Bryce addressed them.

"Navigator, set fleet traverse for a secondary planet in Tau Ceti 7. Zero delay. Dismissed."

The navigator departed.

Bryce then spoke at the other man.

"Normal surveillance operations for arrival into Tau Ceti 7. Fiver will be orbiting and going planet side. Get there first. The settlement is too small for in-person shadow. Remain in orbit. Stay hidden."

"But!" stumbled the man.

"What?"

"But!" stumbled the man once more. This time he rolled his eyes towards Dukk without moving his head.

"Have I not made myself clear?"

"Umm, yes sir, you have sir," was the response.

"Dismissed!"

The man turned, scurried for the door, and disappeared.

Dukk looked on with a curious expression.

Bryce smiled.

"Fiver is the code name we use for you. I discovered it was your nickname in the incubation centres."

"I see," Dukk replied.

"Like Mr Atesoughton said. I am very good at my job."

"Interesting. So, what was that officer confused about?"

"The chief of covert operations, like all my officers, will now know that the focus of all our efforts, for the last fifteen years, is sitting in my office. He, as the others, will be confused as to why the covert shadowing needs to continue if you are sitting right here."

"Oh."

"What do you suggest I tell them?" he asked in a playful tone.

Dukk gave the question some time to come to rest.

"The truth," he stated calmly.

"Which bits of it?" Bryce asked.

"That I am now giving the orders."

"I don't think that will cut it unless they know your true identity."

"What do you suggest?"

"We tell them a version of the truth."

"Like what?"

"My new orders are to support you in a covert operation of your own."

"I guess that is the truth. Will they accept it?"

"It aligns with what we already suspected. So, I think it will. Besides, Mr Atesoughton already alluded to the fact that you will be known as David to the family. I suggest you do what you can to separate Dukk from David."

"Yes, we've already been working on attire that I will wear as David to hide my features as much as possible."

"Keep your David persona to the heady heights of official family engagements. Also, don't use Dukk. Go about this carrier as Captain Dellington to maintain the pretence of the covert operation."

Dukk nodded, then sat up.

"If there are no other questions for now, I'd best get back to my rig. It is late and my crew will be wondering what happened to me."

"Of course," Bryce answered as he stood.

Dukk stood also.

"Captain Dellington, you will understand that to keep the pretence, I will have to treat you as I do all captains."

"Is that like the way you treated the Fleet Navigator and CCO?"

"Some say that I am old school. I have no problem with that. Do you?"

"No, so long as it is for optics. Otherwise, I want us to show respect and see each other as equals."

Bryce nodded.

3

The process of getting from the bridge to the rig was far less intimidating. There was no security detail, or hover cart.

One of the crew from the bridge had acted as a guide. She was chatty and informative. She pointed out various parts of the carrier as they made their way back to the hanger that housed the Imhullu.

Getting about the carrier wasn't the same as getting about a hub. For Dukk, it felt more like the mobile habitat on Newterratwo. There were some similarities. The air was still stale, but the corridors were narrow and unclad. Everything was functional. No attention was given to aesthetics. The near-zero gravity was different as well. It was more like the rig. On hubs, the emulation of gravity was created by multiple DMDs. Their gravity fields overlapped slightly. This resulted in variations in intensity as one moved about.

Marr was at the port door when it opened for Dukk. He had made the usual request for those on watch to let him in. Marr had been sitting in the upstairs lounge waiting. She intercepted Annee and went down instead. Annee returned to the console in the crew mess and alerted everyone else. No-one had managed to get some rest while Dukk was away.

Dukk smiled on seeing Marr. They hugged.

"Well?" she said before he could even get through the door.

"It's all good," Dukk replied. "Better than good. Let's go upstairs. I am sure the others will be wanting news too."

Thirty minutes later, everyone was up to speed on the conversation that had been had with Commander Bryce.

"Does any of this change the robin hood plan?" Luna asked to shift the conversation.

"Nope, but let's go over it again in more detail now," Dukk answered.

He then interacted with his wrist wraps and a star chart appeared over the crew mess table.

"In about nine hours the fleet will traverse to an outer planet in Tau Ceti 7. We will say a temporary goodbye to Craig and Emeelie, undock and then traverse to the outpost planet. We will deorbit, make some friends, drop off the container and return to orbit. We will then traverse back to the fleet, dock and continue towards Newterratwo."

"How much time will we have on the ground?" Bognath asked.

"I'd like to keep it to under three hours. The fleet will traverse close to nine hours after arriving at the outer planet in Tau Ceti 7. The manoeuvring and local traversing will take about five hours. Let's give an hour grace. That leaves three hours on the ground."

"Not a lot of time to make friends," Emeelie said quietly.

"No, but it is what it is."

"What about getting safely down? Will we be challenged?" Luna asked.

"Yes, potentially. This is something we will have to manage. This outpost is an abandoned mining operation. It will be very basic. Any rigs arriving would be typically carrying supplies they have ordered. They will be suspicious and cautious of unscheduled visits. Though it is unlikely that they will have working defences, they will typically have a working EMP to deter pirates."

"Have you been in this situation before?"

"Yes, on the odd occasion when someone got the order wrong."

"How does it go down?"

"They will typically allow us to land but have the EMP primed to use if we aren't who we say we are."

"But that could go bad for us. We aren't exactly a harmless G5."

"Yes, it is why as we touch down, I want the nano-drones deployed to find the controller for the EMP's power source. We want to take control of it just in case they don't find us friendly."

"Will that be enough?" Bognath asked.

"No, we will need to think about security and what happens after we land. Marr?"

Marr sat forward.

"Luna, Bognath and Eleettra, I want you three to secure the rig and surrounds. Sniper rifle from upper hatch and two guarding the ramp and hold platform. Mentor, you will accompany myself and Dukk for the meet and greet."

"Why you three?" Luna asked.

"Dukk is the captain, he has to be the one meeting their community leaders," Annee interjected.

"Absolutely, and I am not letting him out of my sight on a strange planet," Marr added.

Chuckles erupted around the table.

Dukk sat forward.

"That puts you, Ann, in charge of the rig, with Suzzona in the cockpit ready to get active if needed. Bazzer, you keep the rig humming and help with lowering the platform at the appropriate time."

Annee, Bazzer and Suzzona nodded.

"What about us?" Kayila chirped.

"You'll sit tight in the rig to watch and learn," Marr said in a firm tone.

"I gather that goes for me too," Tieanna added.

Dukk nodded and stood up.

"If there aren't any further questions, it is late, and we have a busy time ahead."

"What about exploring the carrier?" Lilaho asked.

"After this drop off there will be nearly two and a half days of traversing before we reach Newterratwo. Plenty of time for exploring," Dukk replied as he yawned.

4

"State your reason!" was the reply from the outpost operator.

Marr rolled her eyes at Dukk. She then opened her comms again. She was also broadcasting to the crew.

Racing below was the surface of a rocky planet, tinted purple from the red dwarf sun it was tidal locked to.

"We have a shipment of medical supplies," Marr said to the operator.

"We haven't ordered anything like that," the operator stated.

"We still plan to deliver it."

"Not our problem. Landing request denied."

The communications link went dead.

"What now?" Marr asked Dukk on the crew comms.

Dukk interacted with the controls. He initiated another request with the outpost.

It was five minutes before it was accepted.

"What!" was the opening statement.

"My name is Dukk, I am captain of this rig, the Imhullu. We're going to drop these supplies off whether you like it or not. We could drop them from the air and have them smashed to pieces or we can set them down properly. Your choice. I'll give you five minutes to decide."

Dukk disconnected.

He looked over at Marr. She grinned and shrugged her shoulders.

"Are you serious?" asked Luna on the comms.

"Hardly," Bazzer added.

"We are being hailed from the surface," Annee interrupted. "It is a video call."

"Put it through," Dukk said.

"Obscure mode?"

"No, let them see us."

A moment later the image of a woman appeared in the air at the front of the cockpit.

She looked to be in her fifties. Her complexion was pale and sickly looking. She was wearing an old fashion space helmet. The visor was up. She appeared to be sitting in some sort of control room. A wall of equipment could be seen behind her. It looked old and long since used for anything.

"Hello, who am I talking to?" Dukk announced firmly.

"Did you say your name was Captain Dukk?" was the response.

"Yes, I did."

"And your rig is called the Imhullu?"

"Yes," Dukk replied with a little less confidence than a moment earlier.

"Is your co-pilot called Marr?"

"What is this about?" Marr interrupted.

"Are you Marr?"

Marr didn't respond.

"You are Mar-duk with the Imhullu, the wind weapon, delivering supplies we didn't order!" the woman stated.

Dukk was now speechless also.

"That is correct," Mentor interrupted in a confident tone.

The woman smiled and nodded. She then continued.

"Sending you the coordinates of our landing pad. Proceed at your leisure."

The call disconnected.

"Message received with the coordinates," Marr announced.

"Load them up," Dukk said solemnly as he struggled to make sense of what had happened.

"Done."

"Prepare for deorbit," Dukk announced on the comms as he engaged the autopilot.

The crew sat in silence as the rig dropped out of orbit.

When the noise abated, Luna opened the crew comms.

"Is it just me or was that exchange a little weird."

"It could be a trap," Annee replied.

"It isn't," Mentor added.

"Why not?"

"She used Marduk and Imhullu from the Mesopotamian origin story. She thinks we are fulfilling a prophecy."

"What are you talking about?"

"Old stories creep into these abandoned and forgotten settlements. It helps them accept their fate. This prophecy was given to resistance leaders like me. We get about. We look for support in other systems should the need ever arise. While I haven't, others may have shared the prophecy. The prophecy may have been re-ignited by us being listed on the bounty board twelve weeks ago. Being isolated out here, people will anchor their hopes on whatever helps."

"What is the prophecy?"

With the story shared, silence returned to the comms as the rig shook and groaned on its speedy approach towards the settlement's landing pad.

With the post set down check-lists complete, Luna brought the topic at hand back to the fore.

"I don't get it!" she said into the crew comms.

As she spoke, she moved to the front of the cockpit to look out at the scene beyond the rig's windshield.

There wasn't much to see. The landing pad was a large flat space with navigation lights embedded into the concrete. They weren't all functioning. Some were flickering. A light could be seen five hundred metres away in the side of a hill.

"What don't you get?" Marr asked as she also looked out.

"Prophecy or no prophecy, this doesn't feel right."

"Mentor, can you add anything to this? Do they know about Dukk and I?"

Mentor replied, "I couldn't be sure. But I doubt it."

"Well," Dukk interrupted, "whatever this is all about, I suggest we hold the thought. We need to get on with the plan. We've got a job to do here. Marr, you are up."

"Yea of course. Ann?"

"Opening upper hatch and deploying drones. We'll have pictures at any moment," was the reply from Annee.

"The energy controllers are your target."

"Yep, and I'll let you know if there is anything odd."

"Luna, Bognath and Eleettra, get into position."

"Copy," was the response from Luna and Eleettra.

"The air looks shit, we are going to need surface suits," was the response from Bognath.

"Yep, let's all get downstairs," Marr replied as she made her way for the door.

"Ann, the conn is yours," Dukk said as he followed the others out of the cockpit.

He nodded at Suzzona as she entered to take his seat at the controls.

On coming into the passenger seating area, Dukk ran into Tieanna.

"I want to join you," she said quietly from her position in the middle of the aisle.

"Are you sure that is a good idea?"

"Absolutely. I want to see firsthand how crazy this whole idea of mine has become."

Dukk paused.

Tieanna then spoke again.

"Yes, I know Marr overheard me telling Mentor about it. I am pretty sure she told you."

Dukk nodded.

5

Thirty minutes later, Dukk, Marr, Mentor and Tieanna, were standing in a dimly lit room. It was some sort of storage space. It was embedded into the side of a hill adjacent to the landing pad. They had walked to it and entered via an airlock.

Their escort removed her helmet as she secured the door behind them.

Dukk checked his equipment for air quality and then signalled to the others to remove their helmets.

A group of outpost inhabitants stood before them. Dukk counted a dozen. They were dressed in well-worn surface suits. Each had a helmet in their arms.

Behind the group were four carts. Beyond was the entrance to a tunnel.

A member of the group stepped forward. He was pale and frail looking. His hair was grey and unkept.

"My name is Feldo, I am the leader of this community."

"Hello, Feldo, I am Dukk, this is my co-pilot, Marr."

Before Dukk could continue, the group let out a gasp. They bowed their heads.

Dukk didn't know what to do.

Marr was finding it all a bit awkward as well.

After a moment, those gathered looked up again.

Dukk figured he could continue.

"This is Tieanna, and."

Once more, before Dukk could finish, a gasp ran through the outpost inhabitants.

Feldo fell to his knees.

"The follower of the divine is here too," he cried out.

The others also fell to their knees. Tears and sobs could be heard coming from the group.

After a minute, Feldo looked up at Mentor.

"So, you must be Montour, the teacher?"

Mentor raised his eyebrows and did his best to hide his confusion. He then stepped forward and lifted Feldo back to his feet.

"Will you share what you know of us?" he asked Feldo.

"I shall, but not here. Please break bread with us."

Dukk interrupted, "We don't have a lot of time and we have a container of supplies to drop off."

"Our dock workers will help your crew unload the container. Please join us in our habitat."

"How far is it?"

"Not far. Ten minutes in a cart."

Dukk looked at Marr, then Mentor.

Both shrugged their shoulders.

"Ok," Dukk replied.

Feldo turned and pointed towards the first cart. The raggedy group of local inhabitants stepped back to create a path.

Dukk opened his comms as he walked.

"Bazzer, drop the container and help these people get it inside."

"Roger," was the reply.

"Ann, you got eyes?"

"Yes, captain," Annee replied. "We are seeing and hearing everything."

Twenty minutes later, Dukk and the visiting party were seated on cushions on the ground, in an open space, deep within the hillside.

The open space was brightly lit and in the centre of what appeared to be some sort of very large cave. As they approached the centre space in their carts, they saw doorways and windows dotted around the walls. Balconies and stairways linked them.

They had been offered water and rehydrated food portions. They hadn't yet sampled either.

Seated around them were two hundred inhabitants. All looked old, thin, and sickly. Just like Feldo.

During the short journey in the carts, Feldo had explained to Dukk that the outpost community was what remained when the mining and research operations were abandoned forty years prior.

Dukk knew that when that happened, the workers were just left there to make do. They salvaged and did rudimentary mineral gathering. The outputs could be exchanged for provisions.

Dukk also knew that outposts like this that weren't far from Earth, also attracted those who tried to return but were turned away.

"Will you now tell us what you know of us?" Dukk asked as he looked around at those gathered.

"Nothing, other than the leaked teachings," answered Feldo.

Dukk paused. He then looked casually at Mentor, Tieanna and finally Marr. There was no guidance from them.

"Will you share what you know of the teachings?" Dukk then asked in an empathetic manner.

309

Feldo nodded and then spoke loudly so all could hear.

"Montour, the teacher, told the resistance leaders of the vision had by Tieanna, the follower of the divine. In that vision, Marduk, the union of the best of the feminine and the best of the masculine, would come forth with Imhullu, the wind weapon, to defeat evil to bring about balance once more. You are Marr and Dukk, with the Imhullu."

Dukk nodded and did his best to keep his expression neutral, in the hope it would hide his embarrassment.

Marr had been taking this all in. She watched Dukk and his attempt to learn but not offend. She was also battling many voices in her head. The ego was the loudest of those voices. She succeeded in regaining clarity.

"We are and we bring a message," she spoke clearly but with compassion.

Dukk looked over at Marr. She smiled at him. She nodded.

Dukk turned back to Feldo.

"Earth is being repopulated again. Separate to the citadels. All are welcome. None will be turned away."

Dukk spoke with certainty and confidence. His voice was loud and projected.

A murmur ran through the crowd.

"But we aren't welcome there anymore," shouted a voice.

"Things are changing," Dukk replied.

The murmur erupted into cries of joy. Several of the gathered got to their feet and danced.

It was at this moment that Dukk and his contingent, noticed others emerging from the doors in the walls around them. These people were much younger than those already on the floor around them. They still didn't look overly well, but it was clear they weren't old enough to have been left behind when the mining and research operations were abandoned.

After a few minutes, Feldo stood up and raised his arms. Calm returned. He then sat down again.

"When?" he asked.

Dukk looked him in the eye and said, "Soon. Use the supplies we bring to strengthen. We will send others to bring those that wish it. That is all I can share for now."

"So be it," Feldo said in response.

"Now, we must take our leave," Dukk stated as he got to his feet. "There is much work to do."

Feldo nodded and stood up.

Chapter 17 – Rumblings

1

By the time they got back to the rig, the container was unloaded, and the crew were back on board waiting for lift off.

Rejoining the fleet was straight-forward. As was the traverse to IACB10.

Other than an update for Craig and Emeelie on the events that had transpired, little was said until that evening.

After the traverse, the crew had gathered in the crew mess for a meal together. They had chosen to stay on the rig. As being a military vessel, the only food available to them was rehydratable foods.

As the meal progressed, Annee was the first to bring focus back to the events of the day.

"The video feeds from your helmets gave us a good view of the health of those people in the outpost. Some of them won't even survive a traverse, let alone be able to make a life for themselves back on Earth."

Tieanna spoke next.

"Yes, they're not looking well, but what do you mean by make a life for themselves?"

"The settlements that are being built are very basic. The infrastructure there isn't designed to bring in large quantities of foods. Rehydration packs and that type of thing. They're going to have to produce everything they need."

"I think that is intentional," Craig added.

"How so?"

"They're going to have to step up and make it work. If they don't, they won't survive."

"So, we are bringing them from one hellscape and putting them in another?"

"They won't be starting from scratch. There are some provisions already there. There are seed stores and some livestock. There are instructions. There are tools. They can make what they need."

"Weapons?"

"Yes, I guess that's going to happen too."

"What about the medical lines?" blurted Lilaho.

"What about them?" Marr asked in reply.

"Some of the younger inhabitants didn't have them. How will they traverse?"

"There are ways to move people without medical line attachments," Mentor offered.

"How?"

"An old school injection. It can be used to induce a coma. The coma can last for days if needed."

"Why don't we all do that?"

"The hangover. It makes our post traverse sickness feel like a walk in the park."

"Oh."

"Why were the younger people hiding initially?" Kayila asked.

"They have more value," Suzzona blurted in reply.

Everyone turned to look at her. She continued.

"They kept them hidden in case our intentions weren't pure."

"Oh!" was Kayila's reply. Her expression changed as she recalled the events, three months prior in New Montana. Events that had put her in this company.

"I am troubled. Why are they there in the first place?" Lilaho queried in a sombre tone.

"I guess we have the answer to the question of where some of the girls end up," Tieanna replied.

"What do you mean?"

"Perhaps hostesses get dumped in places like these. Pregnant and discarded."

Craig sat back and sighed. He then said, "I now see why grandfather was not overly concerned about how Earth would be repopulated. He must have known."

"How will we get that many people back to Earth?" Kayila asked.

"Not all will want to leave. Others won't be fit enough," Annee answered.

"That still leaves lots more than this or most rigs could carry," Suzzona added.

"Shuttles. Destroyers and carriers have the space," Emeelie said. "They could easily lift large numbers of people from the surface. Destroyers and carriers have capacity in case of emergency."

"Don't forget about the mammoths," Craig added. "The Niels Juel mammoth has been refurbished. We know that much. One could assume the new mammoth, the Idibura, has been fitted for this purpose too."

"It is still going to be a complex endeavour given the multitude of outposts like this one," Suzzona commented.

"Lifting them will be one thing. But not raising too much attention back at earth, will also be a consideration," Bognath noted.

He then added, "How often do you see two mammoths hanging out in orbit around Earth. Let alone see a multitude of shuttles going back and forth to the surface."

"Well, that is a problem for another day," Craig said as he stood, "I am in the need of a drink. Anyone want to have a look to see what the Carrier wet mess has to offer?"

"I'll join you just after ten p.m. Marr and I are on watch until then," Dukk replied.

"Craig, Suzzona and I will join you until we take over the watch from them," Annee said.

"What is the dress code?" Luna asked.

"This is a military vessel," Emeelie replied.

"And?"

"Everyone will be in uniform. No-one would be in casual clothes. Since we are masquerading as staff, we'd better wear our greys."

"That works. I'm in."

A mix of replies followed as the gathering broke up.

A little after their watch finished, Dukk and Marr were making their way through the carrier towards the wet mess.

"What do you make of what happened in the outpost cave?" Marr asked casually.

"What do you mean? Which part? It was all a bit odd."

"This idea that we are some kind of messiahs, or?"

"Or what?"

"Gods."

"I know, right! It makes you wonder. What in the galaxy happened to our species that we got so lost?"

"What do you mean by that?" Mark asked in reply.

"The story is ludicrous and absurd. How can people find themselves so taken by such nonsense? How can they adopt it as their one purpose for living?"

"I guess if they have nothing else to pin their hopes to. Nothing higher than themselves and their circumstances to aim at."

"Sure, but how does one get there?"

"When things are so bad, so brutal that we can't go on, we look for something, anything. Something that will provide salvation."

"Even if that might make things worse or is completely irrational?"

"Absolutely. Under the right conditions we let go of our autonomy and trade it for security and safety. We thrust our faith into something unfathomable, unreal, and beyond anything rational. It is understandable, then that those at the outpost would want something that gives them a sense of a way out. And now that they have found it, they will cling to it."

"And they are clinging to the story that puts us in the frame as gods."

"Yep," Marr said with a laugh as the absurdness of it all dawned on her.

She then added, "How does one behave if one is to be a god? How do we play our part?"

"No idea."

"Perhaps with caution."

"Well, I think we deserve a drink."

"For celebration or commiseration?"

"Bit of both," Dukk answered as he opened and held the wet mess door for her.

2

The wet mess was a large space with a basic bar at the far end, dozens of tables in the middle, and several booths lining the walls. It was busy. It was noisy.

Marr and Dukk spotted their crew crowded around a couple of tables near the bar.

As they walked towards them, the talking stopped. Heads turned. By the time they reached the others, an eery silence filled the space.

"Shit, lads," Luna muttered as she looked up from her drink, "Looks like we are famous after all."

"What?" Marr replied.

"I'd thought we'd be the talk of the town. There was the odd glance but until you two arrived everyone largely ignored us."

"Drinking in peace was working for me," Bazzer added.

Craig nodded his head at Dukk. He'd been sitting against the wall. The nature of his gesture suggested to Dukk that he should turn around.

Dukk pivoted.

A medium size, burly man stood there looking at him. He had the appearance of someone in their sixties and his expression was not pleasant.

Beside him was a younger man. His expression was that of curiosity.

"Hello", Dukk said in a pleasant tone.

The young man said, "Are you that captain from the interceptor that joined us at Venus?"

"I am. Dellington is the name. Good to meet you."

Dukk put out his hand.

"Rubbish," uttered the burly man in a disgruntled tone.

"Excuse me?" Dukk responded as he turned to look at the older man.

They stared at each other.

"You are Dukk," the man said slowly with a clear hint of disgust.

He then added, "You're that scumbag haulier that we've been following around the galaxy for fifteen years. You're the reason we barely get to take any time off, barely see a hub and are barely planet side."

Dukk didn't flinch. He held the man's stare.

Dukk then said slowly and purposefully, "What's your point?"

The man stepped forward and raised himself up.

"I don't see why I have to drink in the same place as you. Piss off," he said.

Dukk stepped forward. He too raised himself up. Their faces were now inches apart.

"I don't want to piss off," Dukk replied in an aggressive tone.

With Dukk's counter, several other carrier personnel were on their feet. Men and women. None looking happy.

Behind him, Dukk heard the movement of chairs as his crew got to their feet, too.

At that moment, a voice rang out from the direction of the door.

"Commander on deck!"

The carrier personnel were all instantly on their feet and standing to attention.

The crowd separated as a tall figure approached from the direction of the door.

"Captain Dellington, do we have a problem!" Bryce stated as he stepped up to Dukk.

"Just making friends, Commander," Dukk replied with a cheeky grin.

Bryce stared at Dukk. His expression held not a hint of how he had received Dukk's reply.

After a full minute, Bryce half turned and stepped back.

Bryce then nodded at the officer who had accompanied him into the room.

A pipe call rang out in all comms. The series of short sounds was followed by an announcement.

"Prepare to be addressed by Commander Bryce."

After a moment Bryce started to speak. His voice echoed in the room as it was broadcast to all on board.

"As you all know, we have guests amongst us. Some of you have speculated as to the identity of said guests. You may think you know the truth, but you do not. Nor shall you know it for now. Furthermore, we treat all guests with respect and courtesy, no matter what we think of them or their intentions. The repercussions will be swift and severe for anyone showing them any degree of animosity. At ease."

With that the carrier personnel returned to their chairs. The chatter, laughter and clinking of glasses resumed. The burly man stepped away without even so much as a glance in their direction.

Bryce turned to Dukk once more.

His expression was still blank.

After another full minute, he turned and made for the door.

Dukk watched him leave before turning to his crew. They were all still standing.

Dukk shrugged his shoulders, then looked at Marr, and nodded towards the bar.

The conversation at the crew table also resumed.

"Where were we?" Luna announced as she took her seat.

"You were about to explain why psychological safety is a trojan horse," Emeelie answered.

"Ah, yes," Luna answered in a sheepish tone.

She then added loudly for Marr's benefit, "Perhaps Marr would do a better job of explaining it."

Marr laughed and turned back towards the table.

"The usual?" Dukk asked as she turned.

Marr nodded with a wink as she put her hands on the back of Luna's chair and started to speak.

"Emeelie, what if I have a room with a single door and I put you in it. The door isn't locked, and you can leave at any time. The room represents a life experience. Now what if I dropped a lion into the room. What would happen?"

"All things being equal, eventually the lion would get hungry and want to eat me."

"What are your options?"

"Obviously I would leave via the door, immediately," Emeelie answered.

The others laughed.

"Sure, and every other time a lion is dropped into the room you are in, you'd leave too?"

"Yes," Emeelie said with a hint of hesitation.

"What if there was a possibility that a lion might be dropped into every room, from that moment on. How would your experience of life pan out?"

"Dreadful. Limited. I wouldn't be able to stay or even enter any room."

"Right. You'd spend your time running out of every room and miss every potential experience."

"Ok."

"What if I put a chain on the lion and anchor it to the wall?"

"That would work. I would be able to enter the room again."

"Right. So, the lion would need to be chained down for every room you may enter."

"Great."

"This is the trojan horse."

"How?"

"If I am controlling the lion with chains, I am controlling you."

"What! How?"

"I can choose to use chains or not. I can determine which room you can enter and which you cannot. Your potential for life experiences is controlled by me. You allow yourself to be the victim."

"Of the lion's hunger?"

"No, my will. You are allowing me to depower you."

"Oh."

"Yes, oh. Your safety becomes dependent on me or somebody else putting chains on every lion."

"Not good."

"No. What else could you do that leaves you empowered, but not eaten."

"I could learn to defend myself against the lion."

"Yes, or even tame it. Put chains on it yourself, so to speak. That way you could go into any room you like, regardless of whether there is a lion in there or not. You'd be safe without anyone else's intervention. You'd stay empowered. You would experience life to its fullest."

"So psychological safety is a trojan horse. It puts my safety in the hands of a third party. It depowers. It turns people into victims."

Marr nodded and smiled.

3

Two and a half days later, the fleet was in Newterratwo. The intervening days had been relatively uneventful. Piggy backing meant less operational activities in running the rig, but otherwise life had a normality to it. The crew had used the time for rest, reflection, and some socialising.

An impressive sight awaited them as they regained consciousness from the final traverse. While via video projections that drew on the carrier's external cameras, they still saw the magnitude of space craft, in various stages of assembly. The projection showed these craft attached to multiple large disc shaped structures, the hubs. Some of the collections of craft were rotating slowly. Other clusters were static. There were huge arrays of airbridges, scaffolding and smaller craft zooming between them all. That was made even more impressive with the addition of the two fleets and Craig's flotilla.

Racing below this mayhem was the curvature of a planet. The view was like what they would see on arriving back at Earth. The light from the yellow dwarf sun, danced off the atmosphere. However, unlike Earth where the cloud systems were varied, all that could be seen here, were huge circular formations. Massive cyclones. With some up to twice the size of others. There was no other formation of clouds. Just these massive circular cloud structures pinned against each other and moving slowly. While officially named Newterratwo, those that called this place home refer to it as The Shipyard.

"Dukk, we have an incoming call from carrier operations," Annee announced, breaking the spell of the view.

"Put it through," Dukk replied.

An image of an operator appeared in the air at the front of the cockpit.

"Captain, disembarking plans are confirmed. You will join a group of arrows and interceptors to hide your movements. The central hub has provided the flight plan. I am sharing it now. You have an audience with the owner. It will take place immediately after docking. Prepare for air bridge retraction and umbilical cord release. The hanger arms will have you moving in less than a minute."

"Copy," Dukk replied as the image dissolved.

"What does it look like?" Dukk asked Marr via his comms.

"Loading it now," was the reply.

After a moment, she continued.

"The flight plan suggests it will take about seventy-five minutes to get around to the central hub. Docking looks like it will be via the main security gateway. So, ninety minutes all up if we factor in getting out of here."

Dukk authorised the plan and then relaxed back into his seat.

His role was more about monitoring as the automated systems in that the carrier and the rig would be doing all the work.

The rest of the crew also relaxed in their seats. They all knew that space travel was largely about waiting and watching.

The rig entered the main hub via the same outer security gateway they had used on their first visit to Newterratwo. That was twelve weeks ago. The gateway was a medium size hanger that appeared to have only one entrance. That being the doors they had entered through. However, once the hanger was pressurised, the opposite wall opened, exposing a much larger hanger. Autonomous self-lifting low loaders brought the rig through to that hanger.

Several hover carts were waiting for them. An escort of armed guards stood nearby. A woman stood out in front of the group. She was looking up at the rig.

"This is far more efficient than previous visits," Luna said in a jovial tone as she peered out of the cockpit windshield.

"That is what it would appear," Dukk replied.

"What is that woman's name again?"

"Vilemia."

"Oh, yes, the personal assistant to Bartiamos."

"I think she'd rather be considered his chief of staff."

"Are you sure we can't come along for the laugh?"

"Nope, we go as planned," Marr interjected. "Me, Dukk, Craig, Emeelie, Mentor, and Tieanna, with Bognath and Eleettra acting as personal bodyguards."

Luna sighed and headed for the cockpit door.

4

The hover carts took them out of the hanger and then into wide corridors. The track to the middle of the hub took them past large windows. The windows showed the planet and other parts of the space craft building operation.

The carts came to a stop outside some large doors. Beyond was a large room. At one end was a large desk. At the other end was a lounge setting. In the middle of the room was a large digital table. In the space above the table, semi-transparent images created the scene they had witnessed on their approach to the hub. One whole side of the room was glass. It overlooked the operation. In the view, were the other disc shaped structures with a multitude of space crafts in various stages of assembly. The planet could be seen racing below.

Vilemia, was the only member of the escort to enter the room with Dukk and the visiting party. Bognath and Eleettra had also been left in the corridor outside the doors.

Standing on the far side of the table looking out of the windows was a man. He looked to be in his sixties. He was tall, bald, heavy set and of dark brown complexion.

324

As the doors closed, the man turned around. He held a blank expression. He looked at those gathered, nodded briefly at Craig, and then spoke.

"Well, isn't this a curious thing!"

"Hello, Bartiamos," Dukk replied as he stepped closer.

It was agreed that Dukk would open and thus make it clear who was the head of the party.

Bartiamos grinned.

He then came over to the table and surveyed the various projections playing in the air above it. He continued to speak as if Dukk's reply wasn't of consequence.

"It is not uncommon for me to get an urgent high priority request for an audience from some head of family or one of their aids. But it is unusual, for said request to be for that of a haulier and his crew. Even if that request did come from a head of family. A request that ordered me to give said haulier utmost respect and to assist him in any way possible. I am told I will only hear the truth."

Bartiamos then lifted his ample arms and waved at the projections.

"Furthermore, I see two fleets here. Who needs an escort of two fleets. And, then there is a further sealed message. A message to me that can only be unsealed by Commander Bryce."

Dukk said nothing.

Bartiamos then looked up. As he continued his monologue, he shifted his gaze to the subject of his words.

"However, it is good to see you Mentor, my old friend. Mr Atesoughton, and Emeelie, welcome. And, Tieanna, it is curious that you are here. I wonder, if perhaps! No. Surely not. Well, were you the subject of the raid on the mammoth ring at Southern Cross? What for, I wonder. Well, I am glad to see you are found again. Even if my suspected involvement in that adventure is generating some flak. I must say I am impressed by your performance, Dukk and Marr. None have succeeded prior. I am curious as to what you did differently. But that is all aside for now as I am more curious as to why am I being addressed by a haulier. Would you like to enlighten me as to what is going on?"

With that Bartiamos looked blankly at Dukk.

Dukk paused. He held the stare. He checked his breathing. He wanted his next statement to hide any lack of confidence that he was now feeling.

"I am the Atesoughton heir apparent."

Vilemia coughed.

Bartiamos trembled slightly before resuming his expressionless stare.

He then simply said, "Explain!"

"The late Craig Atesoughton the second is my father. Craig, here, is my younger brother. I am four years older. My mother kept the secret until she shared it with us, four weeks ago."

"Oh shit," Vilemia uttered.

Bartiamos looked at Vilemia briefly, before returning his gaze to Dukk. He nodded at the same time. The tremble was clear now.

He then looked at Marr.

"And you?" he asked.

Dukk stumbled a little as he followed the shift in gaze.

They were all surprised by the question. It was clear now that Bartiamos had been rattled. The usual air of unflappability was momentarily disrupted as he processed the revelation, displaying a rare glimpse of vulnerability.

Marr collected her thoughts. The question had an intentionality to it. And she was sensing the change in Bartiamos' state. She felt unseen forces were directing her. An answer appeared in her mind. She knew it was right and it was time, however she was struggling to admit the truth to herself, let alone share it. She knew what was needed.

Marr then stepped forward. She was now at Dukk's side.

"I am the Venefican heir apparent," she stated clearly.

Bartiamos now stumbled. Vilemia rushed around the desk and helped him over to the lounge setting.

Once seated, Bartiamos signalled to the others to join him.

With everyone seated on or around the lounge chairs, Bartiamos spoke again.

"Years ago, I made a promise. To whom I can't say. A promise isn't right. It was more like I got an order. Suffice to say I was told that one day, two heirs would reveal themselves to me at the same moment. One for the Atesoughton family and the other for the Veneficans. I was told that their union would bring about a magnificent change. The wrongs that had been done would be undone. But to make it happen, their real identities would need to be hidden for a time. A credible back story would be needed. Everything being done here on the surface is to enable that credible back story."

Most now gasped. Marr sighed. As did Dukk. It was just another piece in the plan. A plan to which they weren't privy to, but to which they now accepted that they were pivotal.

5

"What is the back story?" Dukk asked kindly.

Bartiamos wriggled around to get more comfortable in the lounge chair he had plonked into moments earlier.

"Well before I took over from my father, the operation came under scrutiny. You know by now that my grandfather had done things differently here. He didn't rely on the incubation centres back on Earth for labour. He didn't use them for new people to work the mines and run the operation that his father had built. He went back to old fashion methods of population growth. Anyway, that tradition was continued by my father when he expanded into ship building. I too honoured that tradition when I expanded into ship design. Our success attracted attention. People started asking questions. They wanted to know how we were continuing to grow without drawing labourers from Earth. So, a story was concocted. The story was that illegal incubation centres had been in operation. Centres for hostesses. Centres for family members to come and play. It was close to what others were doing so most turned a blind eye. But the scrutiny continued from one quarter."

"The Veneficans," Tieanna blurted.

Bartiamos nodded and continued.

"Yes, they have spies here and they wanted to control our approach."

"Why?"

"I gather they were putting on pressure elsewhere, on other families, and didn't want anyone seen as favoured or the exception."

"Oh."

"However, then events took over. An accident on one of the outer ship building hubs. Accommodation areas were lost, and people died. Then shortly after, there was another accident. Similar consequences. The mishaps here at the shipyard were widely reported. It created an opportunity for a cover up. A deal was struck. The galaxy was told that the illegal incubation centres were destroyed in the accidents. The Veneficans would then turn a blind eye to what they suspected, and in return we'd service the mammoth ring. The records of the hub accidents were destroyed so the story couldn't be disproven."

"I recall this. I was twenty, moving to a new job as carer for Craig."

Bartiamos nodded and continued.

"It was also the time when your father, Craig and Dukk, was told he could no longer visit here and supervise the orders your grandfather had placed. A job that he had been thrust into, just over four years earlier."

"How does this fit into the back story for Dukk and I?" Marr asked bluntly.

"This is the genius of it. Seeing as no one can disprove the existence of the incubation centres, we can say anything we like about who was born there. This is so long as they are older than twenty-nine."

"Because you have everyone else believe that no further children were born after the centres were destroyed."

"Precisely."

"And the visits of Craig the second fits the years when there was supposedly an incubation centre. Therefore, he could have fathered a child."

Bartiamos smiled.

"So," Dukk interjected. "The backstory is that I was fathered by Craig Atesoughton the second in an incubation centre here. But what happened to me after that?"

"After the accident, you were sent to the surface," Bartiamos replied. "You were raised there, and once old enough, you worked as a labourer on the mining drills. There are already those down there who will collaborate that story. Simple."

"And me?" Marr asked.

"Are you older than twenty-nine?"

"I am."

"Then your story is similar. Any one of the numerous men of the families could be your father. Most come through here at some point. And after the accident, you too, went to the surface. And that is where you both met."

After further reflection, Marr asked, "The promise you made, was it to your father?"

"No," Bartiamos replied.

"But he was around at the time."

"Yes, of course."

After some moments of silence, Emeelie asked, "How does this all then match up to recent times and the heir apparent?"

Bartiamos laughed.

"The backstory would be that the death of Craig Atesoughton the second triggered a disclosure. Hidden records kept secure until his death. It happens all the time."

"And Marr?"

"I was told I didn't need to worry about the Venefican heir. My understanding was that her identity just needs to stay obscured."

Chapter 18 – Trappings

1

Dukk got up from the edge of the lounge he was leaning on. He addressed the group.

"We have the back story. How do we move forward with this? What's next? What do we need to do?"

Bartiamos replied, "Clearly an official announcement will need to come from your grandfather. Announcing you as his grandson. I will leak the story immediately so that when the official announcement is made, it has some credibility amongst the families. They will obviously be looking for a formal DNA test at some point. We probably should do that as soon as possible, given the state of health of your grandfather. I already have an official and verified sample for your grandfather, so the process would just need a sample of yours. It could probably happen within a week. If we move smartly."

"Won't families need to send a representative to witness it?"

"Yes, however the rumours will be enough to mobilise them. They'll come here looking to validate the reports."

"What else is needed?"

"We're going to need some video footage to go with it, both for the rumour and the official announcement. That footage will need to include two settings. First in an official formal family setting. And second, on the surface amongst the habitats and the mining drills. For the formal setting, I suggest it is done with Craig and Emeelie. That will help with credibility."

"How will that work?"

"We capture footage of you moving about on your way to an audience with me, Craig and Emeelie. That would probably do it. We don't want footage of the audience itself; we just want you moving about like it was captured on the sly. We should do that immediately. With that done, then you can get to the surface and get some footage down there."

"They won't need to go to the surface for that footage," Vilemia interjected. "We already have it. You're all in the footage taken for the multi-habitat gathering that took place when you were down there. You were even dressed in their typical clothes. And your hair styles and everything else was very similar."

Dukk looked over at Bartiamos with a concerned expression.

Bartiamos grinned sheepishly.

Mentor was next to speak. He said, "Both Dukk and Marr are known within the galaxy. And on bounty lists in places. That footage will collide with the new backstory. We need them to look different in official family audiences than they do now and did during that surface visit. In official capacity we can hide their actual appearance with makeup and so forth. We have what we need with us on the rig. But there's going to be an anomaly if they are recognised in the new footage or any of the old surface footage."

Vilemia replied, "You'd wear cloaks for the new footage. That would be typical. For the old surface footage, we can pick clips where it's not clear. Use only obscured profiles and that type of thing."

"You'd better 'disappear' any other footage from our archives once you've got what we need," Bartiamos added.

Both Vilemia and Mentor nodded.

Dukk then spoke again, "Even with cloaks we won't want to be seen coming from the Imhullu. That will give us away."

"Absolutely," Bartiamos answered. "You would have to be seen at one of the outer hubs. A hub that had recently docked a surface rocket. We'd get footage of you boarding a shuttle to this hub and moving about here in a cart. That kind of thing."

"How do we get there?"

"Let's schedule the Imhullu for a service at the same outer hub. You can return to your rig and head over there and take up residence in one of the accommodation areas. An area that would be shared by all types of workers, from hauliers, to pilots, to miners to ship builders. Vilemia can ensure the cameras are down when we need them to cloak your activities."

Marr now sat forward and said, "You mentioned that there are those down there who'd collaborate this story."

"Yes. Steven and Meredith. Whom I believe you've already met. It certainly is curious that their habitat was the most convenient for you to see during your visit there three months ago."

"That is curious," Marr answered with a touch of concern in her voice.

At that moment, Vilemia sat up as if she was listening to something on her implants.

"Commander Bryce is here for his audience," she then blurted.

"That reminds me," Dukk said. "Bartiamos, there was something else in the header of the encrypted message. The message you are about to open with the commander. Isn't there?"

"Yes, Dukk. I was instructed to have Craig present, with Captain Dellington accompanying him. I guess that riddle is now solved, too."

"I guess so," Dukk said with a grin.

Bartiamos smiled.

"Well, the rest of us better get going then," Tieanna said as she rose from the middle of one of the longer lounges.

"Yes, I guess we have lots to do," Mentor replied.

Marr looked at Dukk. Her mind was racing once more. How much of this was truly coincidence and not simply planned. Dukk looked back at her. He rolled his eyes as if he had read her thoughts. She smiled and stood up.

333

With the others gone, and Bryce now standing to attention just inside the door, Bartiamos offered them all a drink. Bryce asked for coffee. The brothers agreed. Bartiamos insisted that they all have a shot of vodka. He said that he needed it after what had just transpired. Vilemia served them all from a cabinet that appeared as if by magic from a side wall. Bryce came over to the lounge area to join them.

"To the future," was the toast Bartiamos offered as they drank.

"I guess there is no need for introductions," Bartiamos said as he returned the glass to the tray Vilemia was holding.

Bryce smiled quaintly and then said, "You summonsed me."

"I did, Commander Bryce. I have a message from Mr. Atesoughton. It requires your assistance to open."

Bartiamos flicked a message over to the table. They all gathered around it.

Bryce interacted with the message and the profile of Craig senior appeared.

Bartiamos enabled the play back.

"Bartiamos, it has been too long between drinks. Maybe one day soon, we'll be in the same system once more to resolve that."

There was a pause. Then he continued.

"By now you understand I have two grandsons. Craig, and Dukk, or David, as he will be known formally. David being the older brother makes him the heir apparent for the family. There are things that need to be put in place. I will leave it with yourselves to move forward in that regard. I simply look forward to receiving the words and video I am to broadcast to make it official."

Here the old man paused again briefly to take a few heavy breaths before continuing.

"Bartiamos, Commander Bryce has already been informed of the following. Effective immediately, he will take command of the two mammoths we have for collection. The refurbished Niels Juel, and the newly built, Idibura. These will fall under his stewardship as the commander of the newly formed Central Fleet. The central fleet will be made from the amalgamation of Alpha, Beta and Delta fleets. Furthermore, I command that the Southern Fleet relinquish its role in protecting trade routes and fall back to the cluster. Its support may be needed there as relations with other families deteriorate. I command that the Central Fleet now take responsibility for trade routes. An announcement of this will be triggered on you opening this message. That message will be shared with all officers of the fleets. It will include confirmation of the retirement of Commander Fratel of Alpha Fleet and Commander Ryien of the Beta Fleet. Commander Bryce, I will now leave it in your hands to manage the logistics of all of this."

Craig senior paused for a third time. His appearance looked troubled and teary.

"Now, my boys, my grandsons, it is time for me to step back further from formal responsibilities. I am retiring from directing our military complex. It will now fall to you. In your hands I now trust the security of the family resources. In time you may feel the need to re-negotiate these wishes. For now, to David, I am handing responsibility for the newly formed Central Fleet and therefore protection of Earth based resources and trade routes. I also command that responsibility for Eastern, Western and Southern fleets fall to Craig. This instruction will be shared with all fleet personnel immediately after the official announcement of the discovery of my heir apparent, David."

After another pause, he added, "Furthermore, David, I have just granted you access to our contribution accounts. It is now in your hands. It is for you to decide who we provide financial support to, if at all. By that I know you know what I mean."

With a final sigh, the old man said, "Godspeed" and ended the message.

Dukk looked at his brother. The news had some very interesting connotations. Craig looked back. He was smiling.

"So big brother, the old man has thrown us more curve balls."

"I guess he has," Dukk replied.

Dukk also grinned.

"We have more to toast! Vilemia, pour again," Bartiamos stated.

"Time for celebrating will have to wait, there is much to do," Dukk interjected. "Our immediate priority is writing the copy for the rumour and official messages."

"I can draft those and send them over to you for approval," Vilemia said.

"That would be appreciated, please give them priority."

"Of course. I'll do it as soon as we finish here."

"Commander Bryce, there will be a need to commission the new mammoths and recognise your promotion," Bartiamos added.

"Of course, we'll have to have a formal ceremony and celebration," Craig added.

"I am not one for pomp and ceremony," Bryce said. "I also have lots to do. Re-organising the fleets and bringing the mammoths into the mix will take much effort."

"If it helps appease your concerns, the Niels Juel is ready for delivery. And the Idibura is ready for field testing. Perhaps you could start by taking her for a spin."

Dukk then said, "Bartiamos, you said the DNA testing could be done in a week, if we move smartly. Perhaps we could do some trials in the meantime. I for one would love to see a mammoth underway."

"Yes, that works if we get the rumour circulating today."

"We'd need to do several traverses to field test it properly," Bryce said.

"Perhaps you need a nearby cluster?"

"We'd want a reason if we stray into another family's territory."

"Do we have a reason?" Dukk said in a suggestive tone.

"I still have trade reconciliation visits to make," Craig answered having taken the hint.

"Anywhere near?" Dukk asked.

"Yes, actually. The Sung Yee family. They are headquartered at New Kowloon."

"Does that work, commander?" Dukk asked.

"Yes, that would be workable," Bryce replied.

"Great, let's get to it," Dukk said as he stood back from the table.

"Rain check on the vodka," Craig said with a smile.

Bartiamos nodded.

3

Moments later, Dukk, Craig, Bognath, and Bryce were riding together in an autonomous cart. They were on their way back to the main hanger.

Bognath had waited outside the office instead of returning with the others.

Two further carts accompanied them. One behind and one in front. Bryce had a squad of guards with him.

The news about Bryce's promotion and the newly created central fleet had already reached the officer in charge. There was a short but polite acknowledgement as they exited Bartiamos' office.

"I gather you have some reason to visit New Kowloon like the outpost in Tau Ceti 7?" Bryce enquired casually as they enjoyed the ride.

"Correct," Dukk answered.

"I gather the fleet is to stay in orbit at a nearby uninhabited and unmonitored planet in the K-ARP system."

"Perfect."

"What about Craig's flotilla?"

"It will be with me," Craig answered. "I'll travel ahead of the fleet. I will visit the main settlement on New Kowloon just ahead of the Imhullu."

"What presence, in orbit of New Kowloon, will be tolerated as the escort of the Imhullu?"

Dukk said in reply, "The same as Tau Ceti 7. Just a couple of arrows. They must stay hidden and not interfere with our activities."

"Understood."

"What is the plan for the mammoths?" Craig asked.

"I will manage them into the fleet," Bryce replied.

"I would like more detail, please," Dukk said firmly.

Bryce nodded and then continued.

"I will have Beta fleet accompany the Niels Juel back to Earth. It will be Commander Ryien's final task. Delivery is in the contract, so we don't need to concern ourselves with crew management until it reaches Earth."

"Once there, where will the crew come from?"

"It shouldn't be a problem. I understand from Commander Fratel that, given the monotonous nature of their work in recent years, the Alpha fleet crew will jump at the chance."

"And the Idibura?" Dukk asked.

"Once commissioned, I will draw crew from Beta and Delta fleets. We might be a little understaffed for a time, but its manageable."

"And the field testing? The trip to K-ARP?"

"Me and my team will need to inspect it before we depart for K-ARP."

"How long will that take?"

"It will depend. It is hard to say."

"I need to be in New Kowloon in three and a half days. When can we leave?"

"Still hard to say as I am not familiar with the navigation from here to K-ARP."

"I've looked at it based on how you've been moving the fleet over the last week. All things being equal, it is about two days from here."

"That will be tight. But I can split the fleet. Send a carrier and a destroyer with you and bring the rest with the mammoth when it is ready. It might mean you meet it on the way back."

"So, either way, we depart in thirty-six hours."

"Understood."

"Is there the possibility of a tour of the mammoth?"

"As David, sure. However, it would be highly irregular as Captain Dellington."

"We'll wait until we get back."

Bryce nodded.

Little was said for the remainder of the short journey. Dukk, Craig, and Bognath were dropped near the forward jack of the Imhullu.

"That was interesting," Bognath commented as the three watched the carts disappear in the direction of a row of arrows.

"Anything in particular?" Dukk asked.

"The change in his demeanour. Nothing like that evening in the wet mess on the Davidus Vaderen. It was like he was your subordinate."

Craig laughed.

"What?" Bognath asked.

"Our grandfather just put Dukk in charge of the Central Fleet. With two mammoths, the Central Fleet has more firepower than any other fleet in the galaxy. Including the mammoth ring."

"Oh!"

"I am curious," Lilaho said from behind them.

The men turned around.

Lilaho and Kayila had walked up behind them, unannounced.

"Where did you two come from?" Dukk asked.

"Marr asked us to wait at the ramp for you. We are cleared for undocking. You can seal up the rig as you come on board," Kayila said with a grin.

"You are out here alone?"

"Yes, why?"

Dukk looked towards the ramp. Eleettra was standing there smiling.

"What are you curious about?" Dukk asked Lilaho as he amused himself at the thought of the teenage girls thinking they were waiting on their own.

"Commander Bryce and that fleet," Lilaho answered.

"What about him and it?"

"If he has all that firepower and no-one to stand against him, what is stopping him running off and doing what he likes?"

"Credits," Craig interjected.

"Credits?"

"Yes, the digital currency is centralized. It is managed. He can only spend what he is told to. In an instant we can cut off his ability to supply and fuel his ships or pay the crew. He wouldn't get far, even with extortion. Every financial transaction in the galaxy is centrally managed."

"What about crypto?"

"It isn't generally made available for employees. And, even if they got hold of some, it takes a lot to keep a fleet of that size running."

"I see."

"Do you girls mind if we continue this upstairs as we debrief everyone else?" Dukk said with a smirk.

The girls grinned as they turned and led the way.

4

Twelve hours later, Marr and Dukk were alone. They lay naked in each other's arms in a double bunk of a small room in the accommodation area of the outer hub.

"Do you think we can trust Bartiamos?" Marr asked casually.

"At this point, I think we have to."

"This point?"

"This point in the path that has clearly been set out before us."

"Okay, but he kept footage of us on the surface. Who does that?"

"A video enthusiast."

Marr pinched Dukk to punish him for this meaningless remark.

"Hey!" was the reaction.

"Dukk, we could be in real danger here."

"That is surprising coming from you."

"What makes you say that?"

"You are the warrior. When we met you were fearless."

"That's not entirely true."

"Fair. But is this level of concern warranted?"

"I feel out of control."

"But you have often operated in ambiguity and with only knowledge of your part of the grander plans."

"This feels different."

"How so?"

"It has me questioning the nature of being."

"Remind me of what that is about," Dukk asked as he adjusted his position so he could see Marr's face as she spoke.

"Let's start with what it is not. It isn't sacrificing the present for the past or future. It isn't screaming to high heavens when one stubs a toe. It isn't shouting down a loved one when they upset your flow. It isn't neglecting the garden when you know it needs tending to. It isn't overindulging when the guilt of your action or inaction overwhelms you. No, it is other things. It is allowing a useful thought to swell and bring you to a higher state of consciousness. It is taking the time to understand what the moment is and how it can be engaged in optimally. It is stepping into the path of the punch to shift its trajectory. It is simultaneously putting one's intentions into action while allowing the immediate context to be part of you."

"Okay," Dukk said slowly.

Marr looked at him and thought about the implied question in his response.

"Dependence," she uttered having allowed herself to recognise the dissonance in her thinking.

"What about it?"

"I don't like being dependent on the actions of others to the degree we now are."

"The backstory?"

"Yes, keeping it tight but also the video footage and disabling cameras. Leaking the message. The official announcement. The whole plans speak not only of deception but the willingness of others to participate in that deception. Being dependent on their ability to deceive worries me."

"You like to look after things directly?"

"Yes, that is my preference."

"But we are a team."

"There are more than our team involved at this point."

"When you've run operations in the past, were you always one hundred percent certain of the reliability of your team?"

"No, of course not. There is always margin for error."

"What did you do?"

"Mitigated it."

"So?"

Marr laughed and then said, "I see. I need to mitigate the risks. Now, let me guess your next question."

Dukk smiled.

"What can I do about that?" Marr asked herself.

Dukk smiled again.

Marr's thoughts raced through each part of the plan. She went over the participants and their actions. She questioned her level of concern. She then laughed.

"What is going on?" Dukk asked in a kind tone.

"There are too many failure points to mitigate."

"And?"

"We just need to have fall backs. Contingencies. Mitigation is unrealistic at this point."

"So, what are the contingencies?"

"We need to stay together and be ready to run and take cover if things go to shit. And the Imhullu gives us that capability."

"So, we don't hang out in an accommodation pod away from the Imhullu?"

Marr laughed and said, "No, I guess we don't."

"Well, since the video footage is done, we can go back there as soon as we want. Vilemia said the surveillance equipment will be down for maintenance until the Imhullu departs."

"Good! Let's get out of here," Marr replied as she leant in for a kiss.

5

Four days later, the Imhullu was in orbit of New Kowloon. Stealth mode had been enabled on arrival. Dukk was in the cockpit monitoring the navigation. A projection of the planet and other craft in orbit was being shown in the air above the consoles. The projection also showed the Imhullu's trajectory against that of other craft in orbit. Dukk was making sure they stayed out of visual range. The DMD was waiting for coordinates for the traverse. The rig was already at the right altitude.

Things had proceeded as planned. Craig and Emeelie had gone ahead to the main settlement to have the trade meeting. They then stayed on to socialise and provide themselves with an alibi for the planned moon raid. Emeelie had contacted some of Tieanna's students on the surface and passed an encrypted message back to the Imhullu. Things were in place as they had expected. A group of six girls were to be transported to Buout Keya, the resort on one of the planet's moons. Those girls were now strapped into the seats in the passenger area of the Imhullu.

A few hours earlier, Mentor, Bognath and Suzzona had used the pirate's technique to drop in on the shuttle and commandeer it. Bazzer had piloted the transport pod and returned to the Imhullu. Suzzona and Bognath had then piloted the shuttle to the surface with Mentor along for the ride as a precaution. He had stayed hidden. They had collected the girls and their two minders. The minders were still out

343

cold having had their med feeds modified during launch. The pilots were in a similar state.

The Imhullu had then dropped in on the shuttle when it returned to orbit. Marr and Luna crossed over and the girls were brought on board. Suzzona had then piloted the shuttle and traversed to the moon. The Imhullu would follow soon.

Tieanna, Lilaho and Kayila were at this moment with the girls, helping them get settled for the traverse to the moon. Annee, Eleettra and Bazzer were in the cockpit with Dukk. Eleettra was in the co-pilot seat next to Dukk. She was monitoring long range motion sensors and cameras for anything unusual. A precaution in case they weren't the only ones in orbit using stealth tech. Annee and Bazzer were in their usual seats in the second row.

The only other development of significance was a disc recording that Marr had received. They had all watched a segment of it earlier that day. Things had moved quickly once the shuttle appeared in orbit so there had been little time to debrief the recording's significance. It went as follows:

"The official announcement from the old man was ratified by our spies in Newterratwo. It looks legitimate."

"And was Craig junior there?"

"Yes, whilst no sightings, we did confirm his flotilla and Beta fleet travelled there. We suspect from the numbers that Delta is there too."

"Any details on their identities," asked the queen.

"Not as yet."

"What about confirmation of another child?"

"Without access to the full DNA database we can't confirm it, but the records that our Filia have been taking from the incubators, from the Hostesses and so forth, suggest that the old man's son only had one child. All other pregnancies or completions were terminated."

"What about that woman that we had here?"

"Yes, the records say that her pregnancy was terminated. It didn't complete. It didn't go to full term."

"Let's hope so. Anything else learnt?"

"Yes, it appears the old man's son did spend time there thirty years ago. The story and timeframe match."

"What about the surface activities and the companion of this newly found heir?"

"Only that she was from there too. Both were conceived in the illegal incubators and then raised on the surface. He is thirty-three and she is thirty-one."

"Confirmation?"

"None of our spies can get near the surface. We must take Bartiamos' word for it all."

"So, the bottom line is that we have no trace of this, David. We have no real evidence. Nor anything for this Maria person."

"The DNA test will tell us."

"Only David's father. Not his mother. Nor can we verify Maria's lines as she isn't being tested. Something doesn't feel right. Let's get more of our people over there for the test. More than just the envoy. We need to pry. We need to put pressure on anyone we can. We need more information. Find out who is with them. Who is travelling with them. Who knew of this and for how long."

Cieloi nodded but didn't move.

"What?" demanded the queen.

"There is something else. Another rumour."

"Do tell."

"A prophecy."

"What have you heard?"

"That Marduk with the Imhullu, the wind weapon, will defeat evil and restore balance."

"Yes, that has been circulating for some time now. What is new?"

"An increase in general rumblings."

"Specifics?"

"The mention of Tieanna, the visionary."

"So?"

345

"That name is the name of the woman we had here. The deserter."

"Yes, and why is this relevant?"

"She might be connected to this increased activity."

"Any source patterns?"

"No. Though something seems to have happened on an outpost in Tau Ceti 7."

"Tau Ceti 7?"

"Yes, an abandoned mining settlement."

"When?"

"A week ago. When the Atesoughton fleets moved from Earth to Newterratwo."

"Is it on the path."

"Not directly."

"Send a scout to find out what happened down there."

"We are already quite stretched."

"You said it was indirectly on route to Newterratwo."

"Yes."

"Use the envoy going to witness the DNA sampling. Have them visit Tau Ceti 7 on the way back."

"Ok."

"Now, go away and come back when you have some real news."

Cieloi nodded and turned.

"Wait!" the queen demanded.

Cieloi turned back and waited.

"Any update from head of operations?" the queen asked.

"Yes, she said things are in place. I still don't understand what she is doing."

"It doesn't concern you. Did she say anything else?"

"Just that she made sure they were expendable."

"Good! Now go away."

'They were expendable?' was echoing in Dukk's mind as he sat in the cockpit. He couldn't put his finger on why.

"I want to traverse the moment you have the girls configured in our med system," Dukk said as he looked over his shoulder.

"Just doing the last one. Tieanna can plug the med lines in after that," was the reply from Annee.

"Did you notice anything unusual about those girls?" Bazzer asked in a casual tone.

"Not really," Annee answered.

"They were a little older than usual," Eleettra commented.

"Yes, and they weren't as lively," Bazzer added.

At that moment there was a scream on the crew comms.

It was followed by Tieanna shouting, "I need help."

Dukk flicked open the video feed of the passenger area and enabled two-way audio.

The screaming was coming from Kayila. She was standing in the aisle screaming with her hands on her head.

Tieanna was dragging one of the girls out of her seat. The girl was limp. The other five girls were slumped forward in their seats.

"Help me," Tieanna screamed at Lilaho.

Lilaho was standing there motionless. Clearly in shock.

Dukk launched out of his seat and dashed to the cockpit door.

He flung it open.

Tieanna was now giving CPR to one of the girls.

"I need my med kit," she shouted on seeing Dukk.

Dukk went over to each of the girls. He felt their pulse. Nothing.

"What happened?" Dukk demanded.

Tieanna looked up and said with teary eyes, "They all started convulsing at the same moment. Then slumped forward. No pulse."

Dukk turned back towards the cockpit.

"Helmets on and get seated, we are traversing now!" he said as he dashed through the cockpit door.

"The girls!" Tieanna shouted.

"They are dead. I now know what the queen meant by expendable."

Chapter 19 – Battling

1

"Eleettra, charge the CDL and get ready to fire the rail guns as we come out of traverse. Hand on the trigger. Forward and back," Dukk said as he landed in his seat.

Eleettra already had her helmet on and was busying herself at the controls.

Dukk put his helmet on and sat back in his seat to engage the med lines. He then authorised the DMD. The tingle ran through them all as the DMD engaged and started the traverse count down.

"Twenty-five seconds! Status?" he said into the crew comms.

"All connected, captain," Annee replied.

Dukk then pulled his legs up onto the seat and jammed his boots onto the joysticks.

"Run the juice," he then shouted as he disabled the autopilot and went to manual control.

Annee hit the button. Their consciousness faded.

Moments later the Imhullu was out of traverse and orbiting the moon.

Dukk started to regain consciousness. He felt his feet pushing against the joy sticks. With the autopilot off the rig went into a forward dive.

Alarms sounded. The alarms were indicating that the rig was diving towards the surface.

Another alarm sounded. Incoming missile.

Dukk forced back the traverse sickness. He fought the desire to relax and with a strain pulled his legs free from the joysticks. With his hands, he pulled the joysticks back. The rig responded and immediately started to pull out of the dive.

More alarms. Rig structural strain.

In the comms, Dukk then shouted, "Eleettra, I need you back with us. Fire the rail guns."

Eleettra groaned briefly, fought the traverse sickness and pulled the trigger.

The rig shook as the rail guns fired. The erratic flying coming out of the traverse meant the projectiles were scatted in all directions. The missile ran into those projectiles.

The explosion knocked the rig into a spin.

Two more alarms. One signalled a missile lock. The other indicated the rig's integrity had been compromised.

"Permission to fire at will. Hit anything and everything you can see," Dukk shouted as he fought the added nausea of the spin.

"Missiles away," replied Eleettra as she authorised the program that she and Bazzer had created for such an eventuality.

More noise and shaking occurred as the rig unloaded several missiles.

A massive bang added to the mayhem.

More alarms.

"Engine room breach," Bazzer yelled into their comms.

The rig shook again violently as something else exploded inside the rig.

"Dukk, two more traverse exit signatures," Annee added on the comms.

"Friendly?"

"No. Not Bryce's arrows."

"Eleettra?"

"On it."

The rig shook again as the CDL fired and more missiles were launched.

The space around them was awash with explosions and debris.

The rig was now shaking. Alarms were going off left, right and centre.

"Bazzer, status?" Dukk shouted into the comms.

"Integrity is collapsing. Engine room fire suppressant has initiated. Critical systems are failing. Reactors are going into shut down sequence."

Another loud bang interrupted Bazzer's update.

Dukk frantically flicked through the control panels. The main engines were offline. He then tested the joysticks. The rig responded. He still had thrust control.

"Prepare for crash landing," he shouted as he used the controls to send the rig towards the moon surface.

Moments later the rig slammed into a crater adjacent to the moon resort.

The electronics cut out on impact. There were sounds of ripping and crushing. Then silence.

2

"Guys, get in here," Suzzona blurted on the comms.

She had just completed the docking procedure on landing at the moon resort's space port.

Marr unbelted and was the first into the cockpit.

"What is up?"

"It is all too quiet. The port is empty, and the moon's relay just went down. We have no external comms."

Instinctively, Marr looked up through the top of the windshield.

"Oh shit!" she exclaimed.

Above them was a chaotic scene. Explosions and debris falling. Then she caught sight of a rig plummeting towards the surface. It disappeared into the adjacent valley.

Marr then did her best to look out the sides of the windshield and into the port. The airbridge was starting to extend. Through the small portals in the enclosed tunnels, she caught a flash of blood red. The shine was unmistakable. Venefican sentinels.

"Luna, evasive protocols! Sentinels on the airbridge. Number unknown!" Marr yelled into the comms.

"Scuttle?" was the reply from Luna.

"Any other options?"

"Are we pinned?"

"Yep. Organise it. I'll disable the fire suppressants."

"Roger."

"Mentor, Suzzona and Bognath, get the emergency E.V.A packs. Prepare to evacuate," Marr said as she interacted with a panel on the wall of the cockpit.

"Dukk and the others?" Bognath asked.

"My gut tells me they went down just over the ridge,"

Marr kept looking at the panel to hide her tears. She wanted there to be still hope, but fears of the worst were starting to invade her self-talk.

With the fire suppressants disabled, Marr followed Bognath and Suzzona into the passenger seating area.

Mentor was tending to the pilots and minders.

"What are you doing?" Marr said as she reached him.

"I am waking them up."

"What for?"

"They will need to be conscious to exit."

"They are part of this! Why bother?"

"True, but are we really judge and jury here?"

"You've changed your tune. What will we do with them?"

"Get them out for now."

"They will be witnesses."

"Then we take them with us. We are armed. They are not. Besides, I've also given them a little something to ensure their cooperation. We might as well see what they know."

"Yep, good idea."

At that moment, the co-pilot took a deep inhale and then opened her eyes. She struggled in her bonds and then screamed.

Mentor back handed her.

She slumped back to the floor.

The pilot was now awake, too. She blurted, "What the hell is going on?"

"How about you tell us?" Marr asked in reply.

"Why would I know what you are up to?"

"There are sentinels outside. When the bullets start flying, this is going to go bad for all of us. This is unless you tell us what you know."

The pilot sighed and then started to speak in a defeated tone.

"They arrived this morning. They told everyone that the rogue mercenaries were in the area and probably going to attack the resort. They made the resort staff and guests leave immediately. They told them to go to a moon or another system, but not back to New Kowloon. My co-pilot and I were told we had to proceed as normal as to not raise the alarm."

"That makes sense now," said one of the minders.

"What makes sense?" Marr asked.

"Earlier today we got word of a change of plan. We were told to find alternative girls. Some who were expendable. We nabbed some girls from the local brothels and moved the other girls to another hotel. We gave the expendable girls a cocktail before reaching the shuttle. The cocktail was to react with the launch g-juice. It wasn't to be immediate. It was timed so that the shuttle would land on the moon, and the girls would be delivered before the cocktail had its effect. We thought that it was punishment for the client. It happens when they don't pay up ahead of the party."

"What was the cocktail supposed to do?"

"Kill them."

Marr's emotions peaked. She pulled her knife from her holster and grabbed the minders head in her other hand.

She paused. She checked her amygdala and then let out a big sigh.

She then shook her head.

"You are not worth it. A quick death is too good for you," she said as she stood up and re-sheathed the knife.

Moments later, everyone was standing at the back of the shuttle. Marr and Suzzona were propping up one of the pilots each. Mentor and Bognath had the minders.

"These EVA packs have ninety minutes of air with no propulsion. We won't get far." Suzzona cautioned.

"One challenge at a time. We just need to be out and away from here."

"Which means sitting around and waiting for a rescue."

"I get it, but we won't last long in here with those sentinels, so it's better than nothing."

Luna came dashing towards them from the main door. She had rigged a small bomb to the inside of it. She had also placed further bombs near the cockpit and engine room.

"Let's go," she said as she attached the emergency E.V.A. pack to the front of her suit.

Marr interacted with a panel near the emergency door.

"Radio silence from now on. Secure your boots and hold on," Marr said as they pushed themselves against the bulkhead near the door.

"Ready?" she asked as she looked at her colleagues.

They all nodded.

"Fire it," she said as she looked at Luna.

Luna clicked a control in her glove. At the same moment, Marr fired the locks on the emergency exit door. It disappeared. Simultaneously, an explosion ripped open the main door and punctured the airbridge. The depressurisation happened in both directions, via the main door and via the emergency exit door. It was balanced and not as violent if it had been just one door.

Marr nodded and shoved the pilot away from her. The depressurization sucked the pilot through the emergency door and shot her out of the shuttle. The others did the same. Then Marr released her boots. She too was sucked out of the shuttle.

Luna was last to exit. As Luna was propelled away from the shuttle, she clicked another control in her glove. The main bombs detonated. The explosion caused the shuttle to bounce away from the surface. Flames appeared momentarily and then there was a massive explosion as the reactors went up. The space craft disintegrated as did much of the airbridge. Further explosions could be seen as several sentinels self-detonated. A standard safety feature in case of being overrun.

Marr bounced off the surface several hundred metres away from the port. The rest of them came tumbling in as well.

Marr got herself to a sitting position and looked over at the others. She held her thumb up.

The others sat up and responded in a similar fashion.

They were all breathing.

Marr then got to her feet and pointed in the direction of where she saw the rig crash.

Luna held her hands in the air to indicate she was confused.

With her right hand, Marr pounded her chest over her heart.

Luna nodded. She knew Marr was indicating that her instinct was telling her to go that way.

Meanwhile Mentor and Bognath had rounded up the pilots and remaining minder. The other minder had broken his neck on landing. He was limp. Using their guns, Mentor and Bognath motioned to the three remaining prisoners to follow Marr.

3

Dukk reached over to a panel near his seat. The darkness wasn't an issue as he knew exactly what he would find there. He pulled out a small pack and attached it to the front of his suit. His g-suit inflated slightly. He experienced the sour taste of the temporary air supply. It was working. He then disconnected himself from the med line and unbelted.

Reaching up, again without needing to see what he was doing, he toggled a series of switches. After a long beep, light returned to the panels in the ceiling. A red glow appeared around them. He had successfully re-routed the emergency batteries.

He then pushed himself away from the seat so he could look around. Eleettra was attaching her air pack. As were Annee and Bazzer. There was no sign of blood floating around. A good sign. He then waved in front of each of them and looked for a thumbs up. He got it. That was good too.

Making his way to the back of the cockpit he found the bulkhead was damaged. The cockpit door was crumpled. There was a gaping hole in the ceiling. He put his head through it and looked up. He could see debris falling. Some larger pieces. He made a wish. The wish being that his choice to crash here had got them sufficiently away from the descent path of those larger pieces. A flash caught his eye. It was in the direction of the resort. His heart skipped. He made another wish.

A crackling sound hit Dukk's implants. Then Bazzer's voice. He said, "Testing."

"Receiving," Dukk replied as he pulled his head back into the cockpit.

"I got the backup implant relay working. Not sure how long it will last on emergency batteries."

"Tieanna are you there," Dukk said, ignoring Bazzer's pragmatism.

"Yes, here."

"Lilaho and Kayila?"

"They are ok. We have our air supply working. But I am seeing blood."

"Hang tight, we'll get to you."

"This door is working," Annee added. She was at the door to the forward ladder shaft.

Dukk went over and followed her through the door and into the upper lounge. The top of the ladder shaft was gone as was the door to the lounge and some of the ceiling there. The hole ran towards the crew mess. The door between the lounge and the crew mess was also missing. They made their way around to Tieanna and the girls.

Tieanna, Lilaho and Kayila were all standing looking at a body crushed into the forward bulkhead.

"What have we got?" Dukk asked on the comms.

"Looks like the girl I pulled from her seat got thrown about during the crash. It is her blood that we are seeing."

"That's a relief. Bazzer, how are we looking?"

"Fire suppression appears to be working. All systems got shut down before we crashed. No indication of fire or further rapid unplanned disassembly."

"Good. Pods?"

"I can't get any readings. We'd have to have a look."

"Right. Any parts of this bird still pressurised?"

"I am at the door on the middle level. Door indicators suggest the landing is still pressurised. But this door won't open unless the shaft is pressurized. Which it isn't, with no chance of being. While we still have power, we can use the port airlock door to access the landing."

"Great. Let's try that. We'll have a look at the pods on the way."

Dukk led the group to the hole in the lounge ceiling. They bounced their way through it, onto the top of the rig and looked about.

The tail was gone as was one of the wings. The port pod bay was exposed. No pods were there. Clearly it took a direct hit. The starboard pod bay was crushed by the starboard wing. It had folded on impact.

Dukk frowned.

"Here help me with this," Bazzer said into the comms.

Dukk turned around. Bazzer was holding a tether.

"You take the other end," Bazzer said. "I'll attach it to an exposed beam. We can use it to drop onto the port door."

One-hour later they were all assembled in the lounge on the middle level. The landing on the middle level was indeed still pressurised. As was the lounge, the med bay, and the E.V.A. suit rooms. Dukk and Bazzer had used suits to inspect the remainder of the rig. The lower level was heavily damaged. Some of it was still accessible via the forward ladder shaft. The crew accommodation area was still largely intact but had several holes causing all spaces to depressurise. The engine room was completely inaccessible. That was largely due to the fire suppressant foam. They had lost the main batteries, and the emergency batteries weren't going to hold up for much longer.

Dukk addressed the group.

"As far as I see it, we have very few options. The air in this section won't last much longer. Nor will the heating. We do have sufficient E.V.A. packs for everyone, but we'll only get an hour or so out of them. Our best bet is to suit up and head for the resort. We aren't that far."

"What about the explosion you saw?" Lilaho asked.

"Yes, we have no idea what we will find when we get there."

At that moment two things happened at once. A bright light shone through the window. Having got used to the red emergency lighting, the light nearly blinded them all. Then there was some static on the comms. Followed by Marr's voice.

She simply said, "Dukk!"

4

A little before that, Marr and her party were standing on a ridge in a state of despair. They had travelled in the direction of where Marr thought she saw the rig crash. But they had walked for nearly an hour and found nothing. She looked back in the direction they had come. Her self-talk was telling her that they had missed them.

Suddenly a series of lights came racing towards them.

Marr instinctively crouched. Which wasn't easy owing to the low gravity. She stumbled a little and bounced. The others had similarly awkward responses to the fast-approaching anomaly.

Then a voice blasted in their comms.

"Captain Dellington? Is that you?"

Marr responded, "No, but we are crew."

"Identify!"

"Maldana. Imhullu Co-pilot"

The scouting party raced up and dimmed their lights as they landed on the ridge in a flurry of dust.

Their leader addressed them.

"I am from the Idibura. Commander Bryce sent us to search for survivors."

In focusing all her attention on the grey surface of the moon, Marr hadn't bothered to look up. She did now. Away in the distance, towards the dark side of the moon, a massive circular craft was floating in the luna sky. The under belly was covered in turrets and rail guns. It was painted the Atesoughton blue and had the Atesoughton crest visible in multiple places. Marr could also see a destroyer and some smaller craft.

"How did you find us?" Marr asked.

"We went to the resort first. Ran into a little trouble. A couple of squads are still there searching for any remaining sentinels. With no sign of the Imhullu, we scanned the surface. The only heat signature is just over the ridge ahead of you. If they made it down in one piece it must be them. We are on our way there."

"Can you give us a lift?"

"Of course," the leader said as he stepped around Marr and attached a lanyard.

It took no time to reach the wreck. On Marr's suggestion, the lead scout shone his lights into the window on the port side.

On approach, Marr adjusted her comms to match the Imhullu's emergency relay frequency. She called Dukk's name.

"Marr, you are safe!" Dukk replied.

"Yes."

"I saw an explosion."

"We ran into a little trouble."

"So did we," Dukk said with a laugh. The joy and relief negated any sense of the gravity of their situation.

"Switch back to normal implant channels. Bryce is here with the Idibura. He sent a squad. They have an implants relay on them."

"Will do. The port airlock door is working. See you there."

Marr grinned as the scout backed away from the window and moved towards the port airlock door. The sense of relief was immense. All the memories of their time together raced through her mind as the outer door opened and she and the scout drifted into the airlock. It was in this very airlock that Dukk and her had had their first kiss. When the pressurisation warning lights stopped, she removed her helmet and repeatedly pushed the button to open the inner door. Dukk was there waiting. With the door open, they embraced and kissed deeply.

Two hours later, Dukk was standing on the bridge of the Idibura. His crew with their personal effects had been lifted from the surface. Dukk was the last to arrive back. He had stayed until everyone else was lifted. Once on board the Idibura, Dukk had been immediately escorted to the bridge. On arriving on the bridge, Bryce had cleared the room. Craig was also there. Dukk and Craig had a quick embrace before Bryce interrupted. He pointed Dukk towards a missile targeting console.

"The button is yours to push," Bryce said as they stood next to the controls.

The projection above the console showed the wreckage of the Imhullu on the moon surface.

"Is this the first missile firing for the Idibura?" Dukk asked.

"It is. But if no evidence is to be left behind, the captain must do the honours."

"Right then," Dukk said as he reached towards the fire control.

He stopped and looked back at Bryce.

"What is the Idibura doing here at this moon?" Dukk then asked.

"As instructed by you, we were running tests and staying away from New Kowloon. However, we still had to keep an eye on you, so I had arrows scouting the other planets and moons. On seeing the mayhem here, the arrow traversed immediately to raise the alarm. I brought the Idibura as we were already in orbit of a similar sized moon of another planet. The rest of the fleet was in orbit of that planet so it would have taken longer for them to get here. Imagine my surprise traversing into a battlefield with debris and craft disintegrating all over the place. It certainly gave us the opportunity to see this monster's evasive protocols in action."

"And Craig. What are you doing here?"

"Bryce sent an escort to fetch us. He figured it prudent once we realised there were hostile Veneficans about."

"What about the Sung Yee family?"

"What about them?" Bryce asked.

"We seem to be alone at the moment?"

"They shouldn't bother coming out here. Sure, I suspect they noticed your fire fight. However, like us, the Veneficans must have got permission to be in this system. The Sung Yee family will know to stay out of the Venefican's business."

"You didn't hesitate engaging?"

"Your actions gave me no choice."

"What about more Veneficans?"

"Yes, we'd better not linger here."

"And why were you on the surface searching?" Dukk asked.

"Within the carnage we detected Venefican arrows taking a pounding. We counted four. We saw no sign of you, but figured it stood to reason that you would be involved so we went looking."

"What reason?"

"It is no secret with me that you are on the Venefican's most wanted list."

"Did any Venefican craft make it?"

"The ones that remained, no. Our CDL operators needed some target practice."

"What do you mean by ones that remained?"

"We think one scarpered. The arrows going to get Craig and Emeelie detected a traverse exit in orbit of New Kowloon. It went into stealth immediately. Not long after there was an explosion. No distress signals."

"Scuttled?"

"Or compromised just before the traverse."

"But it was in orbit long enough to send a message?"

"Likely."

"The Sung Yee family will know something is up."

"Possibly."

"More cause to not hang around or leave anything behind."

Bryce nodded.

Dukk turned back towards the missile controls.

As his finger hovered over the button, he reflected to the first rig he had commanded. Nearly four months ago, he had watched that explode too. He took a breath and lowered his finger.

Moments later the projection showed a dust cloud.

Dukk stepped back from the console. He was in a daze. The events of the last few hours were racing through his mind. Other questions were there too. The question of what to do now was the main theme.

Bryce coughed to get Dukk's attention.

Dukk looked over at him.

"Before you go back to your crew, I have something to show you," Bryce said as he turned and made for the door.

5

Bryce interacted with his comms and the command crew filed back into the room.

Bryce then led Dukk and Craig out via the main doors.

They said goodbye to Craig in the large foyer just outside the bridge. He was joining Emeelie in the V.I.P. suite. They would do the traverse from there.

Bryce and Dukk then took a lift to a lower level. From there they used a cart. It took them to a hanger. It wasn't where Dukk had left his crew. This hanger was smaller. A sentry stood at its door. There was no indication that it was even a hanger. Bryce had to provide his biometrics to open the door. The door gave them access to an air bridge that ran along the wall of the hanger. It had windows to see what was in the hanger. The hanger had its own large doors in the ceiling.

Within the hanger were two interceptors. They were painted the Atesoughton blue, had the Atesoughton crest on the tail and a standard Atesoughton six-digit number on the hull. They looked every bit like the typical escort craft Dukk had become accustomed to seeing since travelling with the Atesoughton flotillas and fleets.

Bryce led Dukk to the closest interceptor. He opened the internal security door and led them up to the cockpit.

Everything looked very familiar. It was just like the Imhullu, except this looked brand-new.

Bryce sat at a console and interacted with it. In the air above the console the image of the interceptor appeared. The colour and markings were that of the rig they were in. After Interacting with a few of the controls, the image changed. The image was no longer blue, it was now grey. The typical colour for independent rigs as used by hauliers, contractors, and mercenaries. The same colour as the Imhullu had been. Not only did the colour change, but the markings too. The Atesoughton crest was gone. And written on the side was 'Imhullu.'"

Dukk nearly choked. He then went to the front of the cockpit and looked out the windshield. The nose was grey. He turned and dashed out of the cockpit. He went down to the middle level and through the port door. He dashed along the airbridge so that he could get a proper look at the craft. He looked out the airbridge windows.

"Oh shit," he said aloud as he stared at the rig.

It was as if he was looking at the rig he had just lost.

Bryce strolled up as Dukk tried to fathom what he was looking at.

"The best stealth tech that credit can buy includes a reprogrammable skin," Bryce said casually as he also admired the space craft.

Dukk was still speechless.

Bryce continued.

"The skin and hull markings can be changed on the fly. In an instant you can switch from a legitimate escort craft, to the Imhullu. It doesn't even need to be the same hull markings. You can change the Atesoughton hull ID as you need. It will take the shell game to a whole new level. Furthermore, it will be impossible to guess which interceptor you are in when you are visiting heads of families and so forth."

Dukk looked at Bryce.

"But why use the Imhullu name?" He asked.

"It seems logical to me that you would want to run under that banner but have the capability to instantly change so you can disappear. You also probably want to be able to run decoys. Be in several places at once if needed. That type of thing."

"Decoys?"

"Yes, have one of the others in another location."

"There are more?"

"Yes, Bartiamos said there are eight in total. These two. Two are still in Newterratwo and the other four are on board the Niels Juel, enroute to Earth. He showed me these two when he gave me control of the Idibura. He said your grandfather ordered them. Few know about them. Bartiamos said I would know what to do with them. When I figured out what you have been up to, I knew."

"I don't get it."

"Dukk, if you are going to change the Galaxy, you're going to need to stay alive."

Dukk laughed.

"We have to make way," Bryce then said.

"Of course. Before that, can I ask you something."

Bryce nodded.

"What do you know of what just happened?" Dukk asked.

"You will have to be more specific."

"What exactly did you find here when you arrived?"

"We think there were four craft in orbit, in addition to the Imhullu. Apart from the one that got away, they were all but destroyed. I gather you did most of that. Some fine work, I must say."

"At a cost."

"Yes, but you walked away."

"You said you did some cleaning up."

"There wasn't much left to clean up, to be honest."

"The relay?"

"Looks to have got caught in the crossfire."

"And on the surface?"

"A squad of sentinels."

"Any other personnel?"

"No. But our scouts ran into a series of craft at moons of other planets in the system. One could speculate that they made a quick exit but didn't want to go back to New Kowloon."

"Any other Veneficans in those other locations?"

"No."

"How did you figure out what we've been up to?"

"While you were coordinating the retrieval of your personal effects, I took the liberty of having a little chat with those pilots and the remaining minder. They have been trafficking hostesses. One way party ticket. I put two and two together over what went down in New Montana and Abrolhos. You have been getting in the way and rescuing the hostesses. Admirable."

Dukk let that thought sit.

Bryce then turned towards the door. He interacted with his comms and said, "Show them in."

The door behind them opened. Marr, then Luna and the rest of the crew came through the door. They were all pulling their travel lockers. They also had bags over their shoulders and weapons holstered. Luna had her sniper rifle.

A separate set of double doors slid open further along the airbridge. In the opening were a set of robo-crates. These contained whatever tools, equipment, cookware, linen, and supplies that could be salvaged as they rushed to depart the crash site.

Marr walked straight up to Dukk to embrace him. She paid no attention to what was through the windows.

The others did. Luna was first. She stopped dead, mouth gaping. The others ran into her. There was a bit of jostling and angst as each tried to regain their footing. Each stopped dead once it dawned on them as to what was the hold up.

Dukk laughed at the sight.

Marr's expression changed to curiosity. She was still looking at Dukk.

"What is going on?" she asked.

Dukk smiled and gently turned her via her shoulders so that she could see out the airbridge window.

"You've got to be kidding me!" she stated in astonishment.

"Captain, she is all yours," Bryce said softly next to Dukk.

He then added in a louder and more audible tone, "Your credentials are already configured. I take it that you would be able to load your med records yourself. Please do so right away and take your seats. The umbilical cord is already attached. We will traverse away from here the moment you are plugged in. I can imagine this moon will be quite the focal point very soon."

Dukk nodded and then called out to his crew.

"You heard the commander, let's get on board and plugged in. We still have work to do. I'll debrief you once seated."

Chapter 20 – Stumbling

1

From the moon, the mammoth and its escort craft went to join the rest of the Delta fleet in orbit of an outer planet. Bazzer was the first to speak into the comms as the crew regained consciousness after the traverse.

He said, "I need a drink! And it will be nine hours before the next traverse and two days before we get back to Newterratwo. I figure that gives plenty of time to unpack and get familiar with this new rig."

Dukk spoke next. He said, "A drink is most certainly on the cards. We have lots to talk about and plans to make. Getting some creative juices flowing might be what is needed. However, before that I need a shower. Also, I think this new rig will be safe enough if we lock it and go together. We all deserve a bit of down time. This big bird must have a place or two to get a drink. Does forty-five minutes suit everyone?"

He got words of acknowledgement from them all.

Thirty minutes later, Marr and Dukk collapsed onto the bed. They were panting and their naked bodies were glistening with sweat.

They hadn't wasted a moment after dragging their lockers into the captain's cabin.

"How long have we got?" Marr asked as she lay loosely over Dukk's chest.

"About fifteen minutes, I reckon," Dukk replied.

He then suggested, "Quick shower and throw on a uniform?"

"Yep. I hope the showers in this rig have the cyclone effect we are accustomed to. Without that there would be no chance I'd be ready in that amount of time."

"Let's see," Dukk said with a chuckle and started to lift himself up.

"In a minute," Marr said as she held him in place.

"What's up?" Dukk asked having sensed there was something else pressing.

"What do we do now?" Marr asked.

"With this rig?"

"Yeah."

"And assuming the queen knows a lot more about what is going on?"

"Yes, if she doesn't already know, she will after a quick search of the debris on the moon resort. We have no chance now of getting anywhere near a resort or bunch of trafficked girls. The Robin Hood activities could be at risk too."

"What are the alternatives?"

"I'm back to thinking again, that we should just get out of this. Go somewhere quiet."

"What would that achieve? Do you really want to step away? Disappear?"

Marr paused. She settled her mind and said, "No, I don't. You are right. That's not me at all."

"So, what do we do?"

"We need to find a way to do all that under the radar."

"Absolutely. I guess that's what Bryce meant. Having eight of these rigs. We can move around as normal. Then activate the Imhullu markings to get done what needs doing. We then disappear again shortly after."

"Yeah, OK. I can see how that, combined with the stealth capabilities, could help with Robin Hood activities to spreading the news. But I have my doubts about rescuing girls. We'd find ourselves in constant firefights."

370

"We did alright."

"At what cost? And what are the odds we do alright every time."

"That's fair."

"I am also concerned about bringing large numbers of refugees back to earth. That outpost had hundreds. And that outpost is one of many. The numbers are huge. Even using the mammoths, the ship traffic in and out of orbit will raise alarms, surely."

"Yes, we would need some other reason to have a heavy presence at Earth to handle the volumes we're talking about."

"We need to think differently about how we can achieve the same aims without this level of risk."

"Brainstorming with the crew will help."

"Yes, you are right."

"Good. So can I have that shower now?" Dukk asked with a chuckle.

Marr smiled, then said, "Lead the way" as she rolled off Dukk's chest.

2

Thirty minutes later, Dukk and the crew stepped into the larger of the two wet messes they had identified. They figured if there were others about, the larger space would increase their chances of finding a quiet corner.

While a noisy atmosphere greeted them, silence fell as everyone turned to see who had just come through the door.

In the middle of the room, a man stood up. It was the same burly man who had confronted them on the Davidus Vaderen. His expression was blank. Those around him got to their feet too. The rest of the crowd followed. There was an eerie silence.

Then the burly man's face lit up with a smile. He also started to clap. It was a warm and honest clap. A sign of respect.

Next to him a woman joined in. Then the room erupted. The clapping was deafening.

Marr and Dukk, hand in hand, and the others behind them, stood there dumbfounded.

Then as quickly as it started, the clapping abruptly stopped.

"Commander on deck!" rang out from behind them.

Marr and Dukk turned around. Their crew did the same. They then stepped aside to give Marr and Dukk a full view of the doorway.

Bryce was standing there with a solemn expression.

He looked around once before advancing towards Marr and Dukk.

On reaching them, he looked them in the eyes, before moving into the space between them. They separated to make room.

Marr and Dukk turned as they separated.

The three now stood together facing the crowd.

Bryce then spoke. He asked, "What do you see?"

"Many of the ship's crew," Marr answered.

"I see a bunch of friends. These are some of the people I trust most in this galaxy. I would put my life in their hands. As probably appreciated, rumours move faster than truth. They too put two and two together. I couldn't hide the truth from them any longer."

Bryce then stepped out in front of Marr and Dukk and turned around.

He then bowed his head to one side and said, "Welcome aboard, it is my honour to serve you both."

He then lifted his head and presented his hand. First to Marr and then to Dukk.

They accepted his hand, and they shook.

Bryce then repeated the acknowledgement with each of the Imhullu crew members.

At the end he stepped aside, and said in a loud voice, "Now, let me buy everyone here a drink out of my own pocket. Such is my honour in acknowledgement of what transpired today. At ease."

At that he turned back towards Marr and Dukk

"Vodka?" he asked.

372

Dukk nodded. Marr smiled.

Bryce then turned and headed in the direction of the bar.

With that the burly man walked straight up to Marr and Dukk. He stopped directly in front of them.

Dukk tensed.

Marr took Dukk's hand again. She squeezed it.

Then the man put his hand towards Dukk and spoke, "It will be my honour to serve you both. You have my allegiance."

Dukk smiled and took his hand. They shook.

The man then shook hands with Marr.

Dukk felt his emotions swelling. He kept it together. A thought bubbled into his mind.

"Why? What changed? Is it my lineage?" he asked the man.

The burly man laughed, then said, "No offence to your lineage, but no, sir, it is not that."

"What then?"

"Your actions fill me with hope that there is something better."

"Actions?"

"Intervening in the trafficking. But also bringing hope to those in abandoned settlements."

"You know about that?"

"Yes. We've heard the rumours. And we were monitoring your visit to the outpost in Tau Ceti 7. You are fulfilling the prophecy."

"What do you know of it?"

"Marduk, and the Imhullu, the wind weapon, will defeat evil and bring about balance once more. You are Dukk and ma'am is Marr. Your rig is the Imhullu. You even have in your company, Tieanna, the follower of the divine. The visionary."

Smiles erupted on both the faces of Marr and Dukk.

With that, the man stepped aside and went towards the Imhullu crew.

Behind the burly man was the woman. She too offered her allegiance. Behind her was a queue. Everyone in the room was waiting their turn.

3

An hour later, Dukk was standing with Bryce at the bar once more. Marr and the others were in small groups nearby. Each had a circle of people around them. They were the talk of the town.

"You were a whole lot more standoffish last time," Dukk volunteered.

"Yes," Bryce answered, "That was for the benefit of the rest of the crew that were there at the time. It wasn't just my trusted inner circle as it is today."

"Everyone on this mammoth, is in your trusted inner circle?"

"Yeah. It turns out these newer craft are much easier to manage than the older ones. When I learnt of the capabilities of this monster, I realised that I could crew it with far less than you would expect. Not having a full inventory of arrows, interceptors, and support craft, meant that I could handpick my most trusted people and leave the rest on the Davidus Vaderen."

"So that won't be the case when this is in full service?"

"That's correct. When we are carrying a full load of interceptors and arrows, with the support craft, we'd have pilots and even troops on board. I would certainly have to hold up a certain persona."

"We aren't at any risk, are we?"

"From attack?"

"Yes?"

"Who from?"

"The Sung Yee family?"

"No. Their fleet is miniscule compared to ours. And they spend most of their time protecting the trade routes between here and Earth."

"The mammoth ring?"

"I have scouts coming and going all the time. There is nothing else here or in any neighbouring system."

At that moment there was an alert on Dukk's comms. An incoming call. It was Craig.

"Craig, what's up?" Dukk answered as he turned his head away from Bryce.

"You might want to check the broadcast message from the Sung Yee family."

"Why?"

"You've made the news again."

"Should I be concerned."

"I am not sure. By the way, where are you?"

"We are in the crew mess on level nine. Come join us."

"Is it as frosty as the Davidus Vaderen?"

"Not exactly."

"Emeelie and I will be there in five. Wait until we get there to view the broadcast message."

The call disconnected.

"Anything of concern?" Bryce asked in a casual tone.

"Craig said there is a broadcast message from the Sung Yee family. He said it is worth our attention."

"I'll have it projected."

Five minutes later, Craig and Emeelie were there. The crew had regrouped to welcome them and share what had happened.

Their enthusiastic retelling was interrupted by a projected image on the walls around them.

A banner flashed and got their attention. The banner read, 'Rogue mercenaries taken out in Buout Keya moon resort raid.'

The room fell silent as the broadcast was replayed.

A woman started speaking. The backdrop was New Kowloon with its twin suns.

A label below the woman suggested that she was a spokesperson for the Sung Yee family.

The message read as follows:

"Earlier today, there was an attack on the Buout Keya moon resort. The resort was attacked by the rogue mercenaries who have been trying to undermine the peace, security and stability that has prevailed for over one hundred and fifty years. The unprovoked attack on the Sung Yee family comes in the wake of similar bloody attacks on the Hintaught, Artrudwab and Ferrearmas families. Not to mention the attempt on the life of the Venefica Magnum Reginae. Thankfully, our military, in a joint operation with Venefica Magnum Reginae's personal guard, were able to avert the attack, kill the miscreants and prevent further bloodshed. The space craft used by the rogue mercenaries, the Imhullu, was also destroyed in the operation. If they weren't stopped today; their bloody quest would have gone unchecked and eventually arrived at Earth, the founding place of our civilised way of life. The Sung Yee family are proud to have been instrumental in restoring peace and security to the galaxy."

The end of the broadcast showed a low-quality video clip of the firefight at the moon. The Imhullu appeared briefly before an explosion engulfed it.

Silenced returned to the room momentarily.

The silence was broken by a giggle.

It was Luna.

Others then joined in. Soon the room was awash with laughter.

4

When the mockery had subsided, Dukk and his crew found a table together. Dukk invited Bryce to join them.

"Thoughts?" Dukk prompted to bring focus to the discussion.

"The Sung Yee family are puppets," Suzzona offered.

"And too fond of themselves," Annee said in acknowledgement.

"Definitely."

376

"Does this get in the way of our plans?"

"Annee, no, I think it is quite the contrary," Mentor said.

"How so?"

"They've provided us with a very interesting and useful position. In the message they said that they took down the mercenaries and their rig. They even named it."

"And?"

"But they didn't. We still have the Imhullu."

"A new one."

"But they don't know that."

Luna laughed, and then said, "So we can pop up again and show them that they failed."

"Yes, Luna, but not only that."

"We show them to be incompetent."

"Yes, if we do it right, and get adequate coverage, the whole galaxy will not only know they aren't up to it, but."

"It will support the prophecy!" Kayila interrupted.

They all turned to look at her.

She then added, "Seeing the Imhullu here and there, after today's broadcast, will only give more credibility to the rumours. It will give the prophecy even more life."

That observation caused a moment of pause.

"It could attract more unwanted attention," Emeelie said in a quiet manner.

"It could," Marr agreed.

"And do we really want to be fired on again?" Annee asked.

"It wouldn't need to come to that," Dukk offered.

He then went on to say, "We simply appear in orbit every so often, long enough to show up on the relay and for those in orbit, but not long enough to get ourselves into any difficulty."

"And we have eight of them. Ours, plus the decoys. So, we don't even need to be anywhere near the appearances," Luna added.

"Who would fly the decoys?" Suzzona asked.

"After what you have witnessed here in this wet mess, I'd think finding those willing to participate in this won't be a problem," Bryce offered.

"But what about intervening with the trafficking?" Annee asked.

"Yes, if we just show up here and there, and then leave, how will we achieve anything?" Suzzona asked.

"We won't be able to be involved directly." Marr replied.

"We need another way to stop it," Tieanna suggested.

"Cut the supply," Bognath blurted.

They all turned to look at Bognath.

"Stop the trafficking at source. At the incubation centres on Earth," he added.

"Not plausible. The Veneficans control them," Craig said.

"What about enroute. Take them before they reach the other systems?" Annee suggested.

"It wouldn't be feasible to patrol the many routes for mercenaries carrying girls," Bryce said.

"Earth!" Luna blurted.

Now everyone turned back to Luna.

"What if we stopped the mercenaries as they leave Earth. When they reach orbit. It is out of reach of the Veneficans, and we would only need to be monitoring comings and goings at Earth."

"You'd need to inspect every ship. Like a blockade," Bognath commented.

"You'd need a lot of resources to pull off a blockade," Craig said.

Bryce interjected again, "You have it!"

He then added, "With the central fleet, you have the resources to stop any craft leaving Earth. One mammoth is already on the way there. We can go and join them. It shouldn't take more than a week."

"How will extracting the girls work?" Annee asked.

"What if when we find a mercenary rig with girls, we take the girls to the bases for red pilling as we've already done," Luna replied.

"What about the mercenaries?" Suzzona asked.

Luna paused.

Bognath then said, "We recruit them. Put them to work. They are driven by credits. They work for whoever is paying. Some might not go along with it. We make examples of them."

They all nodded in agreement.

"He would know," Dukk thought to himself.

"Won't a large military presence, in orbit at Earth, cause alarm?" Emeelie asked.

"Yes, it would. The tensions between the families are already at a tipping point," Craig said.

"We'd need a good reason to be there!" Dukk offered.

"Of course!" Marr said loudly. "We do it under the cover of helping resolve the situation with respect to the rogue mercenaries."

"Helping?"

"Yes," Marr said with even more enthusiasm.

She then went on to say, "David Atesoughton, as one of your first acts as heir apparent, you will put the Atesoughton might behind finding a resolution to the situation, once and for all."

"Wouldn't this simply confirm for the queen that the Atesoughton family is involved in the disruption of her activities?" Suzzona asked.

"Yes, but she wouldn't dare admit that publicly. She would have to accept the offer after it is shown the Sung Yee family and the Veneficans have failed today."

That idea needed some processing. Everyone sat quietly considering it.

Dukk then smiled as he connected another dot.

"It serves another purpose," he said.

Marr looked over at him and grinned.

"What is that?" Luna asked having observed the exchange.

"We have the cover to move the refugees!" Marr replied.

"Of course! The blockade with its large presence in orbit gives the cover to receive the incoming refugees. Also, the support craft coming and going gives us the cover to transport them to the surface."

"So, when do we rescue them?" Lilaho asked.

Dukk looked at Lilaho and then at Craig.

"The settlements on Earth are ready, aren't they?" he asked.

Craig nodded.

"Bryce, on the way back to Earth, after the DNA testing, can we go via Tau Ceti 7?"

"Of course," was the reply.

"Do we have the ability to transport several hundred people to Earth?"

"The Idibura has the capacity to bring them. The Davidus Vaderen also."

"And lifting them from the surface?"

"Yes, we have plenty of shuttles for that type of thing."

"Won't the people at the outpost find it strange," Lilaho asked.

On noticing the blank stares, she gulped and added, "On one hand the Atesoughton fleet is being deployed to help address the Imhullu situation. And on the other hand, the Atesoughton fleet arrives there, with the Imhullu, to help rescue them?"

"We offer messaging that subtly encodes our intention," Mentor said quietly.

"How would that work?"

"We use the phrases in the prophecy within the message to the families and the Veneficans. For those not paying attention it will be interpreted as meeting their needs only."

"I am confused."

"The rule of twelve pushes the idea of returning peace and security to the galaxy. We substitute that with the message of defeating evil and bringing about balance once more."

"Oh, I see. That is tricky. So, both the outpost people and the families will believe the Atesoughtons are helping them alone with their situation."

"What about the Veneficans?" Luna prompted.

She then added, "Aren't they sending their envoy to the outpost after the DNA testing?"

"Lifting refugees is one thing, but a direct confrontation with the Veneficans won't support the idea of offering help to find the rogues," Emeelie noted.

Bazzer sat forward and said, "What if they were delayed in Newterratwo. Bartiamos may be able to create the circumstances whereby their escorts or cruisers aren't fit for immediate departure."

Luna laughed, then said, "And then the outpost will be empty when they do get there."

"This is so exciting," Kayila blurted.

She then asked, "Where do we 'pop up'?"

Dukk chuckled, and said, "Next, we traverse to D-ARP, tracking back to Newterratwo via C-ARP1 at the edge of this cluster, before traversing to IACD9 at the edge of the Asimov cluster. Why don't we take a slightly different track. Perhaps take in the hub at IACB5, Utah's Twin. We won't need to dock, just appear in orbit for a bit before traversing away to a moon or outer planet to join the fleet again."

"We don't have time. We are due back for the DNA testing," Marr said.

"We don't need to go. The other Imhullu could go instead," Luna added.

"Why wait?" Bryce interjected.

He then added, "We have several hours before we traverse away from this system. Why not send a decoy back to New Kowloon, right away."

"Will it be safe?" Dukk asked.

"It should be. I still have arrows and interceptors in orbit. They can give support if it comes to it. It will be a good test of both my crew's allegiance to this new endeavour and the capabilities of these new interceptors."

"What's needed to make it happen?"

"Just give the word, and it is done."

With that the conversation turned more jovial. Dukk confirmed the arrangements with Bryce and then the gathering slowly dissipated as tiredness overtook the exuberance.

5

A little over twenty-four hours later, the fleet was in IACD9 and one traverse away from Newterratwo.

Dukk, Marr and the crew were seated around the crew mess table on the new Imhullu. They were waiting for the disc to reconnect. They had the schedules for the arrows returning from a planet that had a relay. One was about to return. When it did, the disc would hopefully receive the updated recording and news on how the queen had reacted to the events in New Kowloon. While in C-ARP1 they had retrieved the report that showed the queen receiving the message from the arrow that had escaped the moon battle. It confirmed she now knew about the Imhullu and the crew aliases. Cieloi had noted that the Imhullu had been present in systems where they had seen other attacks. The queen had given instructions for the Sung Yee family to broadcast the message that Craig brought to their attention in the wet mess. She had also instructed her daughter to have the Sung Yee family fully inspect the moon resort.

"It is receiving," Lilaho announced as the disc came to life.

Marr interacted with the disc and found the report. She started the replay.

"Well, give me some good news," the queen demanded as a masked figure, presumed to be Cieloi, came into view.

"There was nothing there," Cieloi answered.

"What do you mean?"

"The Sung Yee scouts found nothing. The moon resort was destroyed from the falling debris. There were also signs of surface missile hits. All the sentinels were obliterated. There is still no sign of the fourth arrow. It must have exploded and then bounced just after sending the message."

"No other ships?"

"Nope. Just reports of the Atesoughtons doing new ship testing in outer planets of the system."

"Atesoughtons! I knew it."

After a pause, the queen asked, "Anything remain of the Imhullu?"

"No. But, there is something else."

"What?"

"A sighting. It is in the chat rooms."

"A sighting of what?"

"The Imhullu."

"Show me"

The video projection now showed Cieloi projecting an image of New Kowloon. In view was the Imhullu. The decoy.

"When was this?"

"About twenty-two hours ago. Six hours after the battle at the moon."

"Why didn't you bring this to me immediately?"

"I wanted to check the video authenticity first. It took time. It is authentic."

"Incompetence," the queen shouted. "That forth arrow left the moon too early. They didn't wait to confirm the demise. Cowards. If they weren't already dead, I'd have them shot."

Cieloi stood in view. She was silent.

"What! Why are you still here?" the queen demanded.

"We found something on the bounties on that crew and Thosmas."

"What?"

"The bounty authority couldn't be found because the audit trail had been deleted. Only one person can delete the audit trail."

"Helenal!"

"Yes."

"Well, I'll be!"

"What?"

"Maybe we've got it all wrong."

"What are you talking about?"

"Maybe she is carrying out your great grandmother's instructions."

"What instructions?"

"I guess it is time for you to know."

"Know what?"

"Your great grandmother feared we were losing control. She feared the resistance was growing in power and might align with one or two of the families. She felt with their numbers and the family's military power, we might get toppled. So, she devised a plan. She decided to nurture a seed. A seed that was planted many years ago."

"What seed?"

"A fable. A myth that could be used to create the pretence of a new world order to replace the old. Except, of course, as always, we'd still be behind the scenes just under a different guise."

"What myth?"

"You uncovered it only last week."

"Marduk with Imhullu, the wind weapon, will defeat evil and restore balance."

"Exactly."

"I am confused."

"In the late stages of the war there was a fear that our founding members wouldn't be able to overpower the families. They planted a prophecy with the rebels. The stupid fools thought they came up with it themselves. They even gave the remaining functional cities code names that spelt out Tiamat. Then once defeated, they nick-named the citadels after Kingu. Our sisters went with it to ensure the source of the seed was not questioned. Fools!"

"Tiamat? Kingu? I don't get it."

"The prophecy draws on a Mesopotamian origin story. It was where Marduk defeats Tiamat and her warlord, Kingu, using Imhullu, the wind weapon."

"OMG! The five citadels are named Kuedia, Inquis, Norline, Genda and Utopiam. The first letter spells Kingu. The Imhullu is an interceptor. A wind weapon. That is brilliant!"

A dismissive and sighing sound was audible as the view shifted from right to left.

"That's odd," Cieloi said nervously.

"What?"

"The crew of the G5 rig."

"What about them?"

"The name of the captain was Dukk. The co-pilot was Marr."

"So?"

"Reverse them and put them together and you get Marr-Dukk."

"Interesting."

"So, this fable is being brought back to life. I don't understand what you mean by replacing the old with the new. How would it work?"

"A revolution of sorts. Leaders are killed or imprisoned, and a new set of leaders are put in place."

"But aren't we the current leaders?"

"Not as most see it. The idiot plebs think it is the observers and EOs. Which of course it is not. Some may be on to the truth. They will be the ones that should be sacrificed first."

"Who?"

"The observers and those family heads that aren't in our favour."

"Bartiamos?"

"Perhaps."

"This is good news then."

"Maybe."

"What do you mean?"

"It depends on what she is up to. Does she intend to bring us with her when she installs the new leaders."

"Oh."

"We'd better not take any chances."

"What will we do?"

"Seeing as the story already has momentum, we'll find these rogues and put them under our control."

"How will we do that if the Atesoughtons are looking for them, too?"

"Don't be silly. It is very clear now that the Atesoughtons are helping them. No, we need another approach that also calls Helenal's hand."

"Like what?"

After a pause, the queen said, "Let's assume the G5 crew are now on the Imhullu and Dellington and Maldana are bogus aliases. We now have their actual names. Put new bounties on the G5 crew using both original names and their aliases. Two million each for the captain and co-pilot. One million each for the rest."

"Dead or alive?"

"I want Dukk and Marr alive. Dead for the rest. That reminds me. Send a message to the envoy going to witness the DNA testing of David Atesoughton. We must know more about his companion, Maria. Tell our sister that she will be answerable to me unless she finds out who that tramp really is. Now be gone, I need time to think."

"Wow!" Luna stated as the replay ended.

"I've been taken for a ride," Tieanna said in a sober tone.

"So, it is all a lie!" Kayila said in a teary manner.

Lilaho then sat up and in a panicked tone asked, "What else isn't true?"

Annee then sat forward and in a manner only just less panicked than Lilaho asked, "Are we the new leadership. Are we being put forward as the new rulers? Is that really something that we want?"

"Not me, power corrupts and all that!" Suzzona blurted.

"What about Helenal? Can she be trusted anymore? Are we being walked into a trap?" Luna asked. There was a hint of concern in her tone.

"We were marked before, now with those new bounties we are toast!" Bazzer observed solemnly.

"Let's pause and breathe," Marr said to calm the atmosphere.

She was looking at Dukk as she spoke. Dukk was already looking at her. The questions were already on their minds. The concern in their expression gave them solace that they were to face these questions together.

"What does this all mean?" Tieanna said in a dreamy fashion, akin to someone who had just had the rug pulled from beneath them.

"We'd better be vigilant in monitoring what happens ahead of the DNA testing," Mentor stated in a manner that one might have perceived as simply thinking aloud.

Chapter 21 – Validating

1

Two days later, Dukk and Marr were sitting in two large and ornate chairs. The chairs sat on a slightly elevated platform. The platform sat in a long room.

There were others on the platform. On Dukk's right sat Craig. Emeelie sat next to Marr. Behind them stood, Mentor, Tieanna, Luna, Bognath, Annee, Suzzona, Bazzer, Eleettra and four of Craig's security detail. On the floor in front, sat Lilaho and Kayila. All were barely recognisable beneath heavy make-up, wigs, and hoods.

Directly in front of them were several of Bartiamos' medical staff. They all wore white coats and were fussing over equipment on two metal tables.

Beyond the tables, also seated, were the representatives of the Veneficans and families. Each with an entourage of servants and minders. They too were unidentifiable behind heavy make-up, wigs, and hoods.

At the back of the room on an elevated stage, sat Bartiamos and Vilemia.

Along the walls on either side, stood several dozen armed guards. Both Bartiamos and Bryce had supplied these. Bryce was also amongst them.

There was an eeriness to the room. The only sound was that of the medical staff interacting with the equipment on the table. Even the noise of the hub station wasn't audible within this specially designed room.

At once the medical staff stopped working and backed away from the table. One turned and nodded in Bartiamos' direction.

Bartiamos stood and addressed the room.

"The testing is complete. A single representative from each may approach the table to verify the results and collect a copy of the certificate of authenticity."

Bartiamos returned to his seat and waited.

There was silence again. No one moved.

Then a hooded figure with the Venefican contingent stood and approached the table. A brief exchange was had with the lead medical person. Only when the Venefican representative was seated again did the others move. This time there was a certain urgency about it. Each contingent sent forth a member to view the results and collect the digital certificate.

Musing and murmurs rippled through the room as results were reviewed within each group.

With everyone seated again.

Bartiamos stood and boomed his voice over the rumblings.

"What say you? Is this man the heir apparent to the Atesoughton family? Stand now and state your case if you have any reservations!"

Silence returned to the room.

For a full minute nothing happened, then a Venefican stood. She turned slowly to face Bartiamos. While her face wasn't visible behind the white full-face mask, the turn, and the way she held her body had a menacing feel to it.

"Venefica! State your case!" Bartiamos boomed.

"The authenticity of the heir apparent appears to be in order," she said in a commanding and slightly tormenting tone.

"Why then do you address us?"

"The other, who is she?" the Venefican shouted as she turned and pointed at Marr.

With that, four of the Venefican contingent stood. As they did so, their masks and cloaks fell away. Sentinels.

Gasps filled the room.

The guards along the wall stepped forward.

Mentor, Luna, Bognath, Eleettra and Craig's security detail, dashed through the gaps in the chairs to form a barricade. They had their weapons raised.

"Enough!" boomed Bartiamos.

While clearly audible, no one turned to look at him. All eyes were now on the party at the front of the room.

"Venefica!" Dukk stated in a loud and commanding tone, as he stood and pushed Luna and Mentor to the side.

"I am not answerable to you! Nor is my companion," he added in a firm tone.

He then paused to allow that to sink in.

In a softer tone, he then said, "Your animosity isn't warranted. Our paths are for all to see. We are products of the doings of others. We are making our way in the Galaxy as you are."

"Prove it," the Venefican said in a snarl.

Dukk held his position and paused again.

A murmur rang out in the crowd. They were looking beyond Dukk. All eyes were on Marr. She was now standing. She stepped up beside Dukk and took his hand.

Then in a soft and authentic voice, she said, "I shall offer my proof to your queen, and to her alone. Plan for her to come to Earth, as that is where we are now headed. It is our plan to protect Earth and resolve the situation with the rogue mercenaries. Whom, I might add, have repeatedly slipped through your fingers. David is putting significant Atesoughton resources forward for this task."

Marr paused for a moment.

She then said, "Now, take a message to your queen. Tell her, I will prove my authenticity in the same moment as she authenticates herself. We shall for once and for all put an end to the rumours of who is the true queen."

The last sentence was said louder and in an authoritative tone.

Gasps rang out.

The Venefican was visibly shook. Her shoulders dropped.

"Bravo," boomed Bartiamos, fearful of any further escalation.

He then added, "A cheer and a round of applause for David and Maria. Here to defeat evil and bring about balance once more."

The room erupted in to cheering and applause. Everyone was on their feet.

Dukk and Marr stood together, beaming.

The Venefican contingent quietly move towards the exit.

2

"Well, that went exactly as planned," Luna stated with glee.

Dukk, Marr and their crew were standing at the front of the room.

They had just watched the guards escort the remaining family representatives out of the testing room. Bartiamos and his team had also just left.

"Do you think they bought it?" Annee asked.

Tieanna answered, "I think so. Having forewarning of the Veneficans' plans helped get it right. Even Bartiamos' reaction looked very authentic."

"Bartiamos knew of the plan, but he had no part in it," Marr stated.

"Well, he played his part well, even if he didn't know what his part was."

That got a laugh from everyone.

"I am still not convinced it was the right move," Emeelie cautioned. "The posture of that Venefican indicated she was angry. That will get back to the queen."

"We've already been over this at length," Luna answered.

"I know! But is attack, really the best strategy?"

"Do we have a choice?"

"It will be fine," Mentor said quietly from the back of the group.

They all turned to look at him.

He then went on to say, "We already know the queen believes that the Atesoughtons are helping shutdown the trafficking. She knows our names. She even knows Marr and Dukk make Marduk in the prophecy. So, throwing down the gauntlet won't make any difference. Yes, it will increase her anger, but anger can blind her. It opens the door for making mistakes."

"It can also make her more dangerous," Luna blurted.

"Yes, perhaps. And we can take advantage of that."

"How exactly?" Emeelie asked.

"By focusing on being better than our past selves."

"I don't understand."

"Better as a self-reflective measure brings focus to where you are. Not where someone else thinks you should be. This is the idea that you're measuring yourself against your past self. Not anyone or anything else. For those that wish to control us, self-reflective better is a threat. They would rather install themselves as the arbitrators of what better is. It puts them at the top or centre, depending on your perspective. Overly focused on this way of being for others must leak into the psyche of those doing the controlling. This stance leaves them incapable of seeing fault in themselves. Hubris sets in. They are blind to the novel. They have limited ability to foresee the unexpected. We must look for what that is. What better is. We must be even more intentional in what we do going forward."

"Speaking of going forward, what is the latest?" Luna asked having lost Mentor's thread halfway through.

Dukk answered.

"Just before the testing, Bryce confirmed that everything is in place. The shuttles for the lift are on board the Idibura. They are unmarked to help sell our story for being there with an Atesoughton mammoth in orbit. Crews have even been assigned to the shuttles. People Bryce trusts. The fleet is already in traverse count-down. We simply need to return to our rig, get out of this garb and join them. We'll reach orbit of Tau Ceti 7 in three days. From there we accompany the shuttles to the surface and offer the outpost inhabitants the choice. Even if everyone wants to come with us, the lift won't take more than six hours. The Idibura will start traverse count-down immediately on reaching orbit so we should be Earth bound that same day. With only one other system to navigate after that we'll be in orbit of Earth within five days, ready to deliver the refugees to the new settlements."

"You make it sound like a walk in the park," Luna stated.

"Are we sure that Bartiamos can delay the Veneficans from leaving?" Bognath asked.

"He told me just now that it is already done. His repair crews went to the Venefican ships during the testing. They will make it difficult for the Veneficans to leave today or tomorrow," Dukk answered.

"We are going to need to plan out the months ahead," Emeelie noted.

They all looked at her once more.

She then added, "Every representative here tonight, apart from the Veneficans, made a formal request for an audience with David and Maria."

"We've got time," Dukk replied. "Between now and reaching Earth, we can populate the schedule. We'll map it against outposts and do our best to reach them all."

"The families are making demands already in terms of when and where."

"Let's make it clear to them that they are to accommodate our schedule."

"I guess it sets the right tone."

"How will the official visits work?" Annee asked.

"Much like this one, I would think," Marr replied.

"What do you mean?"

"We arrive to the surface with the usual array of arrows and interceptors. Thanks to the new stealth tech, our rig will look like all the other Atesoughton craft. We get changed in the rig after landing, and then emerge for the official audience. We keep it short and then get out of there."

"It will mean we have to carry two squads with us, but the rig has the capacity for it," Dukk added.

"What about their squad commanders? Won't they need the small twin bunk cabin on the lower level?" Annee asked.

"Yes, I think it is time for Lilaho and Kayila to moved up to the crew mess."

"Yes, Marr's cabin is still unused," Luna blurted.

Marr rolled her eyes at Luna.

Luna grinned.

"What about the blockade?" Annee asked.

"Bryce will be managing that. He said that his remit will be best served centrally from Earth. He said it is the best place to coordinate efforts to protect assets on Earth and those moving on the trade routes to the Atesoughton cluster. Seeing as he will be based there, he will oversee the inspections as well."

"Won't we need capacity to carry the refugees?"

"Yes, the Idibura will be used for that purpose. Along with a carrier and multiple destroyers."

"If Bryce is based at Earth, who will command the Idibura and its escorts?"

Dukk grinned.

"You?"

"Us!"

"Shit, I'd better put my learning hat back on," Bazzer blurted.

"Yes, we will all be on a steep learning curve. Now, if there isn't anything more pressing, I am feeling rather uncomfortable and would like to get cleaned up."

"You'd better get used to it, if you are going to meet with all the families."

"Yep, you included, Bazzer," Dukk said with a chuckle.

"I've had my fill of this garb."

"We all had better get used to it! With the bounties we won't be stepping out in any other guise for the next while," Mentor said.

"We are in this together, right?" Dukk asked and then did his best to grin beneath the heavy make-up.

"You are truly hideous," Bazzer replied as he turned for the exit.

3

Three days later, Dukk and Marr were sitting in the cockpit of the Imhullu. They were preparing for lift off. The four hundred people who wished to leave the outpost in Tau Ceti 7 were already on the shuttles and making their way to the Idibura.

Getting to Tau Ceti 7 had been relatively uneventful. As had the updates on the disc. The queen had received the message about what had happened during the DNA testing. But little else was learnt. There had been a lot of yelling and screaming on the recordings but nothing that gave an indication of her next move.

"Do you think every settlement will be as difficult as this one?" Marr asked idly as she interacted with the controls.

"I think this is an exception," Dukk answered.

"How so?"

"We confused them. We spent far too long in that cave chatting. What should have taken less than an hour, took four."

"What would you do differently or better?"

"Nice," Dukk answered with a laugh having recalled Mentor's advice from after the DNA testing.

"Well?"

"Ok," Dukk said as he turned in his seat to face her. "I'd say that we can give them a better life back on Earth. Better than they'd ever have in these abandoned outposts. I would share videos of the new settlements. I would tell them about the land register and localised governance."

"That doesn't sound any different than what we just did."

"I haven't finished."

Marr smiled.

"In addition, I wouldn't be as accommodating. I'd put it out straight. Take it or leave it. Give them very little time to think."

"I don't think that was the issue."

"What was the issue?"

"They told us. They said they didn't trust us. That they'd just be enslaved somewhere else."

"I don't think we can ever solve that. Like Mentor said, the best we can do is create rumours to build credibility. We share the video clip we took of the lift here. The bottom line is that we can't make them come."

"So, we just abandon three hundred people?"

"Are we really going to go over this again?"

"I take offence to that!"

"Look, as you reminded me, we must focus on better. We are embroiled in something. Something significant that we don't truly understand. Yes, the path put before us appears to be helping build hope or at the very least tackles that which gets in the way of it. But we have some fears. We don't really know what Helenal is up to. We haven't confirmed who Teacher is. Even if we strongly suspect she is Helenal. We could just be pawns in a chess game that's been played for aeons and aeons. A game to keep those in power in power and keep the rest of us subdued. But what choice to we have? Do you see any better path?"

"I know. You are right. What we are doing appears to be heading in the right direction."

"Perhaps we come back in six months or a year? When those who have settled on Earth have had an opportunity to share their experiences."

"That worries me even more."

"How so?"

"The other families and the queen will see that. It will alert them to the existence of settlements. That puts the whole project in jeopardy."

"Grandfather is certain that won't be the case."

"You are putting a lot of trust in him."

"I guess I am."

"It also concerns me as to what will happen to those that remain."

"When the queen's envoy arrives?"

"Yes."

"I guess it's a bridge we're going to have to cross when we get to it."

The conjecture was interrupted by a squawk on the comms.

It was Bazzer.

"Captain! We have hot reactors. Priming burners and running coolers. Green on all indicators. On our way up."

"Back to work," Dukk said with a smile as he turned back to the controls.

Marr nodded. She also turned back to her control panel. At the same time, she pushed the anxiety out of her mind. She focused on the job at hand.

4

Three days later, Dukk was in the commander's boardroom of the Idibura. A large room that sat just behind the bridge.

Above the table in the middle of the room was a projection of the massive space craft. Dukk was interacting with the projection. He was familiarising himself with how he might do justice to the role of commander. In view was the schematic of the disc shaped craft with its eight segments. Information labels were hovering above various parts of the craft with its relatively flat underbelly and curved top side. For reference, the projection had several interceptors and arrows floating nearby. That made it easy to see the scale of the craft with its four-storey high rim, ten storey high middle and raised bridge at the hub.

After reaching orbit of Earth, the blockade was established, and the refugees were shuttled to settlements in the northern hemisphere. It was winter there. It was agreed that the cooler conditions would be more like those at the outpost. This would make transition easier.

Bryce had taken on responsibility for the blockade and transport of the refugees, leaving Dukk and his crew free to prepare for their tour.

The blockade had already produced results. In the first twenty-four hours, three mercenary rigs had been stopped. Fifteen girls had been rescued. They were resting on board the Niels Juel. Mentor had planned with resistance leaders south of Utopiam to take them. The plan was to take them there once the refugees were delivered to the settlements.

Marr was sitting at a desk in another part of the room. The air above the desk was filled with the profiles of elite family heads and key players.

Luna, Bognath, Annee and Suzzona had gone to the surface with the refugees. Suzzona was determined to have their own stash of fresh real food, separate to what was generally available on the mammoth. They were seeing what the northern hemisphere settlements had to trade for crypto.

The rest of the crew were in various parts of the mammoth. Mentor and Tieanna were in the communications room monitoring chat rooms for rumours. Bazzer and Eleettra were on the Imhullu doing some maintenance. Lilaho and Kayila were also on the Imhullu. They were using the training simulator.

Craig and Emeelie had gone to visit Craig senior. Dukk decided to stay in orbit. During all the years hauling, he had rarely spent more than a day or two every month on Earth. The two weeks spent on the ground three weeks prior were plenty sufficient for now. Marr had agreed to stay in orbit as well. To be with Dukk but also to reduce the strain on her body during deorbit and launch.

"Dukk, you have to see this," Marr said in a raised tone from her seat at the desk.

"See what?" Dukk asked as he strolled over to her.

"Another recording. It was from yesterday. I must have missed it with all the activities to get the refugees surface bound."

Marr interacted with the disc and started the playback.

Cieloi was talking.

"What will I tell the envoy waiting at Tau Ceti 7?" she asked.

"Tell them to return to the outpost. Kill all those that remain. Make it painful. But before the last die, have them broadcast a story. Have them say the Imhullu rogues enslaved most and left the rest to die."

"This isn't the story that is already being circulated by those that left. They talk of Marduk rescuing them. The story talks of them being taken to a new place where they will prosper."

"Do the usual counter story to say this was misinformation planted by the rogues."

Cieloi turned as if leaving.

"Oh no!" Dukk said in a frantic manner as he interacted with his wrist wraps to access the chat rooms.

Marr paused the recording and looked at Dukk. Her expression was that of fear and despair.

At that moment, Mentor and Tieanna burst into the room.

"We have a problem," Tieanna blurted. "There was an attack on the outpost. It looks like those that remained are all dead."

Dukk shook his head in disbelief as he confirmed this news via the chat rooms.

Marr nodded solemnly.

"Look," she said as she replayed the first part of the recording for Mentor and Tieanna.

Marr let the message continue past the point where Dukk had interrupted it.

"Wait!" the queen said.

Cieloi turned around.

"Any idea yet of what is happening at Earth?"

"At Earth?"

"That woman! Maria. Her threat. The suggestion that the Atesoughtons would be protecting Earth to resolve the situation with the rogue mercenaries."

"What about it?"

"Do we know what that means yet?"

"Oh. Yes, I forgot."

"Silly girl. Tell me!"

"The Atesoughtons' first mammoth, the Niels Juel, arrived in orbit, the day before yesterday."

"What do you mean by 'first'?"

"They have two now. A new one was commissioned just before David's DNA testing. The alpha fleet is there now too. It is no longer based at Venus. It appears to be more than Alpha for that matter. There is an extra carrier and a few more destroyers."

"WHAT! That feels like a blockade! Why didn't you bring this news to me immediately?"

"There has been a lot going on."

The view shook as the queen moved her head from left to right violently.

"Do better!" the queen shouted.

She then added, "It boggles the mind. Perhaps I am missing something. Your great grandmother rarely ventured out of the apartment. Yet, she seemed much more informed just with the information I brought to her. She always said that it would be unbecoming for the queen to have to venture to the bridge and control room herself and mingle with the help."

"Help?" Cieloi asked in an annoyed tone.

"Yes, help. Everyone else. Our sisters. The men. The sentinels. You. All the others whose sole purpose is to hold me on high."

While Cieloi's face wasn't visible behind the mask, the change in her posture suggested agitation.

The queen continued, seemingly unaware of the discomfort caused to Cieloi by her comments.

401

"Step things up on the trade routes. Disrupt the Atesoughtons more than before. Do it at hubs in plain sight. Demand further reparations for our knowledge and advice. Say that these unsettled times demand it. Then make an example of some. Shoot a few of the lowly pilots and that kind of thing if needed."

"Do we really want to anger our biggest contributor?"

"They started it by moving their fleet into orbit of Earth. It is long established that families keep their distance or face our wrath."

"Maybe they know we can't take the ring there?"

"That is absurd. How could they know that!"

Silence fell, but it was clear that the recording wasn't finished. Dukk was getting more agitated. He went to speak. Mentor held up his hand to indicate they should watch the rest of the recording first.

5

Cieloi spoke next as the recording continued. Her tone was soft and had a note of malice.

"Can I ask you something?"

"What?" the queen answered in a suspicious tone.

"Will you tell me how my great grandmother fell out with Helenal? You have always said that it wasn't my time to know. Is it yet?"

"Fine, maybe it is time. Let me think."

After a pause, the queen started to speak slowly and with a hint of melancholy.

"Helenal and gran were always arguing about stuff. But it came to a head about two years before you were born. Helenal was spending her time between Utopiam and Newterratwo. Gran didn't like how friendly she had got with Bartiamos' father. Nor did she like the company she kept in Utopiam. Then after one big blow up, Helenal went at her implants with a knife. Left herself disfigured. She hid it from most with makeup. I never got an answer as to why. It made gran very angry. They barely spoke after that."

"That makes it four years before my great grandmother disappeared?"

"Yes."

"Did you fall out with Helenal at the same time?"

"No, it wasn't then. Well not really."

"What do you mean?"

"We continued to see a lot of each other. Then around the time you were born, things changed. We drifted apart."

"What happened?"

"Gran and Helenal had another big bust up. I think it was something about me. Helenal wanted me to know what it was. Your great grandmother didn't. I asked Helenal about it and she wouldn't tell me what it was about. She just said that she would look after me."

"Will you tell me about my birth again?"

"There isn't much to tell. I was sent to Utopiam once I got pregnant. I stayed there until the birth. There were complications heading into the delivery. I was put out and when I woke you were born. That is all there is."

"What were the complications?"

"Helenal wouldn't tell me."

"Was she there at the birth?"

"Yes, she was the only one there. She was a trained midwife and insisted on doing it all herself. In fact, she was the only person I really saw in relation to the pregnancy. Even for the first two years after your birth, she was the only person who cared for me."

"But you said that you drifted apart around the time of my birth?"

"Yes, she was the only person I saw, but she was distracted and busy all the time. She wasn't the woman I knew before I got pregnant. She had changed."

"Where was my great grandmother?"

"She returned to the mammoth ring just before you were born. She had a galaxy to govern. I never saw her again."

"Will you tell me again what happened to her?"

"All I know is that she was bringing the mammoth ring back to Earth to collect us. On the last traverse before reaching orbit of Earth she just disappeared. I heard that she was returning to the apartment as normal just before the traverse. But there was no sign of her on reaching orbit of Earth."

"And that is when Helenal told you to leave with the mammoth ring and never return?"

"Exactly."

Cieloi nodded a few times, and then turned to leave.

"Wait! You have given me an idea."

There was a pause, then the queen continued, "Land some new rumours. Ensure the rumours are very distant from us. Make sure it can't get back to us. Say the Atesoughtons are helping the rogues to disrupt peace and security. They are plotting to take control of all the other families."

"I can't see the other families buying it. From what I hear, they were very supportive of David and Maria at the DNA testing."

"Who cares what you think. Now go!"

Cieloi turned to leave again.

"Wait," shouted the queen. "I didn't see you taste my soup. It would be no good me dying of poisoning and leaving you to muddle through this difficult time."

"No, that would be no good," Cieloi said sarcastically as she disappeared from the queen's view.

She could then be heard saying in an irritable tone, "It has gone cold, let me get you some more."

"You do that", the queen said in a dismissive manner.

With that, the play back finished.

"This is madness. These people are lunatics. It has got to end. I am going to cut their funding!" Dukk blurted angrily as the disc projection dissolved.

Marr replied, "But we agreed it was best to keep our intentions hidden as much as possible. Cutting it will send a clear message."

Dukk sighed.

He then said, "Yes, you are right. But I don't like the sound of hauliers being targeted and killed."

"Bryce should be informed," Mentor said. "He will have to increase the presence at hubs between here and the cluster. Hopefully, that will disincentivise the Veneficans."

"Let's hope so," Dukk replied.

"What about these new rumours that they are spreading?" Tieanna asked.

"We counter back. We use official channels. We add fuel to it but also sow doubt," Mentor answered.

"How?"

"We say that our fleet intercepted pirates and while not being able to save those on the surface, we managed to offer refuge to those abducted by the pirates."

"Brilliant. That will head off the rumour and put us in an even better light."

"It's going to really piss her off," Marr said quietly.

"We are going to have to accept that everything we do now will increase her anger," Mentor remarked.

"Even more reason to keep on top of what she is up to," Tieanna added.

Marr felt embarrassed. She hadn't been monitoring the reports. She turned away from them and looked at the elite family member profiles again.

Dukk felt it too. He had been distracted by the joy of learning about the mammoth. He stepped around the desk, sat on her chair armrest, and put his arm around her.

"Maybe it is time to start using the disc more comprehensively?" Tieanna suggested.

Marr looked up, and said, "I made a promise not to do that. Craig senior was certain it would drive me insane."

"Maybe the circumstances require it."

"It would be very time consuming to monitor the other Veneficans and their daughters, the Filia. There is over four hundred in all."

"We only need to monitor some of the key players and those on the trade routes," Dukk said.

"It would still take time to find out who that is," Marr replied. "We'd need to view a recording for each and decipher what they were up to."

"Lilaho and Kayila could help," Tieanna said.

"If there was a concern for our sanity, wouldn't the minds of the young be even more at risk?"

"Yes," Mentor added. "Their help would need to be managed with care."

"Do we have a choice?" Tieanna prompted.

"No," Dukk answered. "But we do it with precaution and monitor each other in the process."

"Agreed," Marr said in acknowledgement.

Marr then sat back and returned her gaze to the profiles of the elites.

After a moment of reflection, she said in a dreamy manner, "Will it be enough?"

Dukk said quietly, "Let's hope Bailey's Law still applies. You will inevitably pay the price for your actions."

"Did you find that in the archives?" Marr asked as she turned to look at him.

Dukk smiled.

Chapter 22 – Consolidating

1

Three months later, Dukk, Marr and the crew were sitting in the commander's boardroom of the Idibura.

During the time since starting the tour, nearly fifteen thousand refugees had been delivered to the settlements on Earth. That had involved multiple excursions away from and back to Earth.

The new settlements had mostly been a success. There had been a few failures. The new inhabitants of one community turned on each other. Everything got smashed to bits. Everyone was either killed or left for dead. Another community got overrun by wild people. However, they were the exception. Most of the settlements had got up and running and were already starting to be self-sufficient.

News of the success had travelled. The other families had become increasingly suspicious. Some families had even tried to find the settlements. That hadn't gone well for them. The automated defence systems had done their job efficiently.

Furthermore, the rumours started by the queen had caused concern that the Atesoughtons were trying to take over the food production for themselves. The rumours just added to the family tensions that had already being building independently of Dukk and his crew's activities. Mentor and Tieanna had to spend considerable effort countering these rumours with reassurance that this wasn't the case.

The growing tensions had a silver lining for the tour. It made the meetings with the heads of families short and sweet. The audiences generally involved a gathering in a hall with Dukk, Marr and the others dressed in the same manner as the DNA testing. The conversations were formal, starchy, and short. This suited Dukk and the others fine.

Not having to endure parties or associated activities left them free to visit outposts and bring refugees on board.

Rumours of the new settlements on Earth had also reached the main settlements on other planets. Staff and workers wishing to get out of their current situation had started travelling to the outposts in the hope of being picked up.

In terms of doing further monitoring of the Veneficans, while it took a little bit of time, they had found what they needed. They found the head of operations. Through her they knew where the mammoth ring was and where their disruption activities would be targeted. This information was passed onto Bryce. He was then able to ensure a stronger presence was in place ahead of time. That helped stop the Veneficans from causing harm to innocent hauliers and others working for the Atesoughtons.

There had been an unforeseen benefit of doing the investigations into the other Veneficans. They had found the internal command structure. As well as the head of operations, who had power over the day to day running of the mammoth ring and space-based resources, they found five citadel heads. Monitoring of these five Veneficans enabled Dukk and the others to further influence the activities within the citadels. They not only knew ahead of time where girls were about to be trafficked, but they also knew of other hope squashing activities. Like killings for minor discretions. But also, detection of resistance members. This information was passed to the resistance leaders. As a result, the disappearances had all but stopped. This influenced the mood within the citadels. People were more hopeful and willing to take risks and innovate.

All of this had further enraged the queen. She had taken to doing personal visits to family heads. During which she would look for increased financial support. She also used the meetings to discredit the intentions of the Atesoughtons.

They had also discovered more about Marr's twin sister, Cieloi. They had seen her behaving in a vindictive and cruel manner on several occasions. It was clear that not only did she resent being subordinate to her mother, but she felt the queen was too passive and lenient. It was evident that things would get far worse if Cieloi was queen.

2

"That was touch and go," Annee commented.

Luna responded, "We could have taken them. And the Idibura would have given us cover to get away."

"Thankfully it didn't come to that," Mentor commented. "A firefight with the Artrudwab family's personal guard wouldn't have helped. It would have done us no favours in soothing the growing animosity towards our activities."

"Good then that it is the last of the family meetings," Emeelie added.

"Just as well, as this monster, the carrier and the two destroyers are full to the brim of refugees," Annee noted.

"Back to Earth we go so," Bazzer commented.

"What is the latest from the Venefican's head of operations?" Craig asked.

"It is as we suspected would be the next course after Bartiamos turned them away," Marr answered. "They are heading to the APR cluster and the Sung Yee family to seek safe harbour. Prior to giving that order, she even visited the queen herself again. She requested they move the mammoth to Earth where they control the fuel and supplies. The queen refused as normal."

"What happens if the queen changes her mind?" Suzzona asked.

"That would put us on a war footing," Bognath commented.

"Potentially," Marr replied.

"It wouldn't matter," Craig said. "It will be just their interceptors and arrows to contend with. She can't use the firepower of the mammoth ring."

"That is assuming that Helenal is still with us and not planning something else?" Suzzona blurted.

"Yes, we'd better take precautions," Dukk interjected. "If the queen does move the mammoth ring to Earth, Bryce would have to move a lot more of the central fleet back there as well."

"The APR cluster is about ten days from Earth. Would there be sufficient time?" Annee asked.

"I am not sure. I will share this information with Bryce in our usual briefing. We can discuss it further when we are back there in eight days."

"Speaking of being back there," Craig interjected. "It is time for me and Emeelie to take our leave. Managing the affairs in the Atesoughton cluster has become increasingly difficult from afar."

"When will you leave us?" Dukk asked.

"In a day or two. I've ordered some of the western fleet to make its way towards us. We'll travel back to the cluster with them."

"Don't be strangers," Marr said with a smile.

"Of course not," Emeelie answered.

"Oof," Marr said suddenly.

They all stopped to look at her.

Dukk immediately responded, "A kick again?"

"Yep," Marr answered.

"That reminds me," Tieanna blurted. "You are entering the final trimester. It might be time to be Earth based."

A little while later, Dukk and Marr were alone in their cabin of the Imhullu. They were resting, arm in arm on the bed.

"I'd like us to set up in Margaret River," Marr said idly.

"Why there?"

"It is largely unoccupied. The weather is good. There are beaches and forests."

"There is talk of some of the current group of refugees going there."

"Yes, but not all. There will be still plenty of vacant sites. It would be nice to have one of the multigenerational units north of the river.

In the forest, near the beach. Mentor and Tieanna will likely join us. There will be room nearby for the others too if they like. Though I suspect except for Bazzer and Eleettra, the others will want to keep moving and helping with the Robin hood activities."

"Don't we want to be near the medical facilities at Zuytdorp," Dukk replied.

"Only closer to the time. Besides, it is only twenty-five minutes via the hyperloop. And I don't want to be spending my time underground or in the dry winds at the top of the cliffs."

"Well, that is settled then. Margaret River will be where we will bring our babies into the galaxy."

3

"Dukk, there is a message from Zuytdorp," Marr called from the front door of their unit.

Dukk was on a veranda swing with views of the forest and beach in the distance. He was holding a three-month-old on his knee. She was smiling and giggling at the faces he was making at her.

"Have Craig and Emeelie arrived?" Dukk replied whilst still engaging with the child.

"No, the message is from Jeeves. Your grandfather passed this morning."

"It was only a matter of time. He was very weak when we visited the day before yesterday."

"Yes, all the same, we'd better make our way up there. Jeeves wants us to view the spot on the cliffs near Coin Rock. The place picked out for his burial. Here, you take Ethan with you to tell Mentor and Tieanna. He is dressed and ready to go. He made another total mess of his bodysuit. I will change Ava and get her ready."

Marr passed Ethan to Dukk with one hand and scooped up Ava with the other. She then turned and returned inside.

Dukk smiled at Ethan. The baby smiled back.

411

"Away we go, my little fellow," Dukk sang as he rose with the child in his arms and made his way across the lawn.

Life had taken on a less hectic pace since the decision was made to be Earth based. Six months had passed since.

As planned, Dukk, Marr, Mentor, Tieanna, Bazzer and Eleettra had taken up residence in the settlement at Margaret River.

The rest of the crew had continued to help with the refugees. Craig and Emeelie had spent their time primarily in the Atesoughton cluster. They had all returned to Earth on several occasions to catch-up. And they were all making their way back to Earth having received the news that Craig senior was in his final days.

For those at Margaret River, it had been mostly a blissful time. The birth of Ethan and Ava had caused some turmoil as had the weeks of sleepless nights that followed. Otherwise, it had been a time of long, lazy days. They swam, surfed, walked, rode horses, read, and talked. Mentor and Tieanna had played the role of grandparents very well. They had given Dukk and Marr opportunities to rest and get away for time to themselves. The latter usually involving time in the luxury of Zuytdorp. But on occasion in swags in the woods or on the beach.

They had also engaged with helping build the new community. They helped establish a basic form of local governance and assisted with farming and trades as needed.

The settlements didn't have implant relays. Instead, communications with the outside world were enabled via devices within each housing unit. That slowed things down somewhat too.

As well as learning the ropes as new parents, Dukk and Marr had spent time with Craig senior in Zuytdorp. They had also given assistance as needed with the running of the family's endeavours and the refugee relocation.

Mentor and Tieanna had got involved with establishing a medical facility. Their main activity was helping reverse vasectomies. They had also worked to reverse the meds given to women to prevent eggs from being fertilized. The efforts had started to produce some pregnancies and the hope and joy that went with it for the couples involved.

The situation with the queen and the Veneficans had reached a stand-off. With the end of the trafficking and parties, the Veneficans' means were thinly stretched. The mammoth ring had remained in the ARP cluster and their presence elsewhere, heavily curtailed. So little had been happening, that Marr had taken to largely ignoring the reports. At times, a week or two would go by before Marr would even check the disc for updates.

On arriving at the adjacent housing unit, Dukk went to knock on the wall near the door. He paused and instead peered through the fly screen door into the large open living space beyond.

Mentor and Tieanna were sitting at a table chatting.

"I just noticed something odd about tomorrow's date," Tieanna could be heard saying.

"What is that?" Mentor asked in reply.

"Well, we are now in the year two hundred and two. That means it has been two hundred and two years since the reset."

"Right. And?"

"Tomorrow is the second of February."

"So, the date tomorrow is two, zero two, two, zero two."

"Exactly."

"That is curious."

Dukk knocked. Tieanna and Mentor looked up and both smiled.

Dukk opened the fly screen door and entered.

"Come in," Tieanna said as she rose and went immediately to take Ethan from Dukk's arms. The baby boy smiled and giggled.

"What's up?" Mentor asked.

"Grandfather passed this morning. Jeeves wants us up there to start making arrangements."

"Right. Bazzer and Eleettra?"

"They are already up there. They are doing some maintenance on the Imhullu. Bazzer had a feeling we'd be needing it again soon."

"Fortuitous?"

"Perhaps."

"Any word on the others?"

"Not yet, but they should be here any day now."

4

Later that evening, a gathering of sorts was taking place in the north banqueting hall of Zuytdorp. During the afternoon, Craig, Emeelie and the others had arrived. There was a joyous mood as stories were shared and Ethan and Ava were passed around.

On noticing an alert on his comms, Mentor had withdrawn for a moment.

When he returned his expression was that of apprehension.

Marr noticed and turned to look at him. The others noticed too, and silence fell.

"What is it?" Marr then asked.

"A message from Teacher," Mentor replied.

"What does it say?"

"It simply says, 'Come now. All of you. Ethan and Ava also. Do not delay'."

"Nothing else?"

"Just coordinates."

"Show me," Dukk said as he flicked his wrist wraps at the centre of the table.

An image appeared. It was a map of their immediate area.

Mentor interacted with his wrist wraps and flicked a message towards the middle of the table.

The image spun and zoomed out. In view now was the western half of the continent.

A pin appeared near the eastern edge of the map.

Dukk interacted with the image and zoomed into the dropped pin.

In view were a group of large, red domed rocks.

"The Olgas," Jeeves blurted.

"What is out there?" Dukk asked.

"Nothing from what I understand."

Dukk interacted with the map again. More data appeared. As did detailed satellite imagery.

"It looks to have a no-fly zone," Bazzer observed.

"And those blurred spots on the image there could be surface to air missile batteries," Craig noted.

"The dropped pin is just to the west of the no-fly zone," Annee added.

"Is the Imhullu ready to launch?" Dukk asked.

"Pretty much. Needs fuel but otherwise, good to go," Bazzer replied.

"Right, the party is over. Time to get the travel lockers out again."

"When?" Luna asked.

Dukk looked at Marr.

"We'd need some things for the twins from Margaret River," Marr said.

"At the rig in two hours?" Dukk asked.

Everyone nodded.

5

Four hours later the Imhullu was on final approach.

The crew were all seated. Everyone was in their usual places. Dukk and Marr upfront. Bazzer, Luna, Mentor and Annee in the second row. Tieanna, Bognath, Eleettra, Suzzona, Lilaho, Kayila, Craig and Emeelie were in the passengers' seats. Ethan and Ava were sleeping in capsules strapped into seats next to Tieanna. Jeeves was there too, as were six of Craig's personal security detail.

"There are no qualms about it. That is a no-fly zone. We are getting proximity warnings," Marr said as she interacted with the flight controls.

"So long as we stay this side of it, we should be ok," Dukk said as he checked the autopilot. He had configured it to bring the rig to the coordinates Teacher had supplied.

"Oh shit!" Annee blurted on the comms.

"Ann, what is up?" Dukk asked.

"Orbit scanners just detected the arrival of five massive craft."

"What?" Marr blurted.

"Any details?" Dukk asked.

"It looks like the mammoth ring," Annee replied.

Another sound rang in their comms. It was an emergency alert.

"Dukk, Bryce wants to open a call," Annee then said.

"Put it through.".

Bryce's image appeared in the air above the console.

"Sir," he said.

"Commander," Dukk replied.

"We have a situation."

"The mammoth ring?"

"Affirmative. Requesting permission to take the Central Fleet to DEFCON one?"

"Granted. But fire only if fired on. And as discussed, only use force as needed to dampen tensions."

"Acknowledged. Requesting permission to secure you, Craig, and your clique."

"Denied. Focus on keeping the fleet and our assets secure."

"Acknowledged. Out."

The call dissolved.

"How did we miss that?" Luna blurted.

"No idea. They must have made a few big and risky traverses," Dukk answered.

416

"What do we do?" Marr asked.

Dukk looked at Marr.

"Your call. She is your grandmother. Do you trust her?" he asked in reply.

Marr nodded and said, "Yes, I do."

Twenty minutes later the Imhullu was on the ground. They were all still seated. Dukk was coordinating the post landing shutdown. In the darkness they could see little of their surroundings. To the east the domed rocks reached into the sky. They were barely visible in the moonlight.

"What in the world?" Marr blurted.

"What now?" Dukk asked.

"The no-fly zone just changed. We are now within the protected zone."

"I guess we can't leave then. I do hope you are right about this. Ann, anything?"

"There is a large heat source on the other side of these rocks. About five kilometres away. There is also movement to the northeast of our location. Looks like twelve people are walking towards us. I can see body heat signatures. Nothing else."

"Right, let's go see what this is all about," Dukk said as he stood up.

"Weapons?" Luna asked.

"Yes, I would think so. Conceal them," Marr replied.

On leaving the rig, Dukk and his cohort were met by an armed escort. They were all dressed in green fatigues and wearing black hiking boots.

"What is the story?" Dukk asked as he confronted the leader of the escort.

"Leave your rig. All follow me. Bring your young. We have baby carriers if you need them."

"Do we need provisions?"

"Just a coat if you feel the cold. We have everything else you will be needing."

The leader then looked around at the group and said, "You can carry your weapons if you like but you won't need them, and it is a long walk."

"How long?"

"About ninety minutes?"

"Pace?" Marr asked.

"Medium, ma'am."

"Difficulty?"

"Sinuous with a slight incline, but easy going."

"Breaks?"

"Time is tight, but we can afford a short stop if needed."

"Lead on."

The escort took them into the dim light. From the rig they followed a riverbed and into a narrow gorge. Rock faces loomed overhead on both sides. The sky above was clear. It was awash with stars. They only stopped once to drink some water from a stream that ran down the gorge.

Just shy of ninety minutes later they were at the end of the gorge, looking east. A big open stretch of land was before them. The area was illuminated by a ring of bonfires. From their position they could just make out a large group of people in the middle of the ring. Several dozen.

It was at this point that they heard rumbling. Out of the east came dozens of arrows and interceptors. They swung away to the left and right to avoid the no-fly zone. The blurring they had seen on the satellite image earlier were indeed missile batteries. These dotted the open stretch of land. They were active and rotating as they tracked the craft flying overhead.

Luna unclipped the sight from her sniper rifle and looked around. After a moment she shouted, "Veneficans!"

Dukk and his cohort immediately stood to attention. They all raised their weapons.

Chapter 23 –Terminating

1

On seeing the reaction of Dukk and his cohort, the leader of the escort, turned and said in a calm tone, "Teacher invites you to join her below. Don't worry about the Veneficans. They will land well east of here. They can't get near us but on foot. But keep your weapons raised if you wish. We will not stop you."

The tone and words took them all a little by surprise. There was a kindness and authenticity about it.

Then a voice spoke from the shadows to their right.

"Put them away my dears," the voice said. "You are in no danger here."

They turned. An old woman stood in a gap in the rocks. Two people stood by her side supporting her. Behind her stood several more. Those with the old woman were reddish mahogany in colour. They were naked but for a small piece of cloth at their waist and had white paint on their faces, torso, and limbs.

At the same moment both Luna and Tieanna called out.

Luna shouted, "Teacher!"

Tieanna shouted, "Helenal!"

The old woman chuckled.

Luna and Tieanna then spoke again at the same time.

Luna said, "Your skin colour is lighter."

Tieanna said, "Your skin colour is darker."

The old woman chuckled again before saying, "I stopped dying it when I went into hiding twelve months ago. My skin is simply returning to its original colour."

Marr was teary and speechless. She shuffled a little. That caused Ava to move. The baby was in the sling that Marr had around her torso. Ava's big brown eyes opened. She looked up at her mother and smiled.

Dukk was speechless also. To get a better view of Helenal, Dukk turned. In doing so, the sling carrying Ethan brushed off Marr's back. The baby kicked and wiggled to share his annoyance at his sleep being disturbed.

Marr reached over and took Dukk's hand.

Tieanna then said, "It is you!".

"Yes, my dear child. Now come, show me your grandchildren."

Helenal came across to them. She hugged Tieanna and then turned to Marr and Dukk. She smiled.

"You've done well," Helenal said as she looked at them and then the babies.

Marr and Dukk were still unable to find words.

Helenal then turned towards Mentor. She smiled and nodded.

Mentor smiled back. He too nodded.

Helenal then stood back a little and looked at the group. She smiled as she surveyed them. Then she turned and pointed towards the ring of bonfires.

"Come. We have a little time before they arrive. We will talk down there. What must be done, can't be done in these hills."

Fifteen minutes later they had joined the gathering in the middle of the ring of bonfires. The space was open and wide, but the huge bonfires made it a warm and inviting place. There were rocks and logs for sitting on. These had been arranged to form a sort of amphitheatre. At the focal point of the amphitheatre was a box. There was also food and drink laid out nearby.

The gathering there included resistance leaders and their seconds from across the globe. There were some familiar faces. Robin hood raiders, Trence, Kimince, and several of the girls from the first rescue. Reunions were had swiftly as Helenal made it clear she was going to talk to them all.

Helenal insisted the newcomers join her in the front row of seats. She sat Marr and Dukk on her right and Tieanna and Mentor on her left. Craig and Emeelie sat next to Dukk. The others filed in nearby.

With everyone seated, Helenal stood with the help of Marr and Tieanna. She turned and spoke in a broken and crackled voice.
    "I am old and tired. But I have lots to share, so I have prepared this recording."
    She then sat down again.

It was at this point that the box at the focal point of the amphitheatre started to glow. Then an image appeared in the air above it. The image was five metres high. It was clearly visible to all. The image was that of the head and shoulders of a woman. The woman had the nondescript face that they all knew. It was the face of the citadel broadcasts. The woman looked around and then began to speak. Initially the voice was the familiar harsh tones they had heard many times before. But after the first few words the voice changed. As the voice changed the image also dissolved into another. By the end of the first sentence, they were looking at Helenal speaking to them.

2

Here is what was said.

"Some of what I will share you will know. But much of this story has never been shared with another. This story should answer many of your questions so please be patient and listen."

There was a brief pause before Helenal continued.

"Most of you know me as Teacher and a member of the resistance. That is only half of the truth. The other half is that I am Venefican."

There were a few gasps and the odd murmur. The recording paused to allow quietness to return.

"You may have heard of us, but few know the truth about who we are. You may know that the Venefica are always sixty-one in number with the queen as their leader. The daughters of the Venefica, the Filia, are their dedicated followers and take their place on death. The Veneficans established the citadels, the rule of twelve and are the true tyrants behind the toil you all endure. The Veneficans are the unseen evil that you battle.

Furthermore, much of what you know about us, the Rule of Twelve and related is a lie.

There was never anyone above level seven. Most are at level eleven or twelve. Observers find themselves at level ten, nine, eight or seven until their usefulness wains. They are then mercilessly dispatched to the recycling plants.

There were never any EOs. Just five groups of twelve Venefica allocated to rule over each of the citadels. Everything you see on the broadcast is artificial.

Furthermore, all our messaging and preaching is borrowed or stolen. While it was useful to leverage utopian, cosmic consciousness, and global collective ideals, it was simply borrowed from the psychotic, eugenical, and anti-human thinking that got traction thirty years before the reset.

The association with the utopian dreamers of the past is also nonsense. We took a page from Mao's book, and the treatment of the red guard. After the citadels were established the utopians and progressives, the useful idiots, where amongst the first put through the compost machinery. Most think it was the bodies of the opposition and the non-compliant, that fed those furnaces in the early days. Not at all. We needed workers, people with skills. No, it was the activists and bureaucrats, the useless policy writers, and their ilk, who helped us usher in our regime. When they were no longer useful, they were killed off.

The Venefican label is even a lie. It is stolen from a concept that has its origins in ancient times. You may have heard of a desire to restore the balance by bringing back the power of the Venefica. The Delphi Priestesses. The mixing of ancient medicines. The Mysteries. Bringing on visions and talking with God. We even propagated a lie about restarting the religion with no name, the source of what was known as Christianity prior to the reset.

It was all a lie. My family is no different than any of the other elite families. We have our god complexes. And a desire for ultimate power and control. Perhaps we are different than most because of the self-perceived higher moral standing. Our puritan roots. Perhaps we are also different in that we are all women having killed off or enslaved all the men in our line."

Once more there was a short pause.

"And there is more. My real name is Helenal. I am daughter to Charloa, who is daughter to Doarena, who is daughter to Hilda and finally who is daughter to Lorenta. There were others before that under different guises and Lorenta is not her true name. But all of that is not for this forum.

Lorenta is our founding member. She established the rule of twelve and made sixty of her closest allies the first Venefica. Therefore, she was the first queen. Which, as the oldest surviving member of that line, makes me the true queen. Yes, I am the Venefica Magnum Reginae. Charmeli, my daughter, presumes over this role. She is false and she knows it."

Murmurs moved through the gathering once more. The projection paused for a further moment before continuing.

423

"Let me reassure you now. I have turned my back on the Veneficans and my birthright. Furthermore, I have called you here as I intend confronting my daughter. I intend putting an end to all that has corrupted this world. Let me share more of my story to help bring you comfort."

A further pause was met with utter silence. Many of those gathered had entered a state of shock. Helenal continued.

"The Venefican way is brutal. I was raised to continue that tradition. And I became no less inhumane in my ways. For that I am ashamed.

Part of my training included time spent in disguise among ordinary workers, learning their ways. I spent time in the incubation centres working with Venefica and Filia. I befriended resistance leaders to ensure we continued to control the opposition. I also observed and coached the Filia, the daughters, as they moved from children to adults. I helped with the cruel initiation ceremony each Filia underwent at the age of sixteen.

At the age of fifty-four I came across a remarkable young woman. She was a Filia. Observing her changed everything. She was ten at the time. Living in Utopiam. She was different. Highly intelligent and curious to a degree I had not seen. She loved reading and consumed everything we gave her. It was beautiful to watch, the blossoming of curiosity and creativity. I learnt much about the nature of humanity simply by observing her. Even in that I changed. Then it came time for her initiation. It broke her in a manner that shook me to my core. I couldn't do what was required as part of my training. I decided to intervene. I decided to save the boy she was carrying. This went against the Venefican rule to only have daughters.

Not fulfilling my role brought me into conflict with my mother.

Separate to this, I had been spending time with a dear friend in Newterratwo. Timaios was his name. He was a master ship builder and father to Bartiamos. Timaios built the Venefican mammoths. From him I learnt of secrets. I learnt of the inner workings of the mammoths and how the queen spied on her own, including me. At the age of sixteen Filia have their implants modified. With the help of technology in the mammoth ring, the queen can see and hear what they do. It is controlled by a palm size disc. That spying gives the disc holder visibility of all that which happens throughout the galaxy. For most it appears as if the disc holder can forecast the future.

When I learnt of the spying, I took a knife to my implants. I prevented my mother from further interference in what I was doing. Being beyond her view enabled me to hide the remarkable young woman and save her boy.

That moment in time put us on the path that brings us here today. I saw the opportunity to nurture a story. A prophecy that was seeded by my people, at the time of the reset. It was instilled with the resistance to protect the future should the other families manage to take back control. Yes, the Marduk story was made and planted by the Veneficans. But don't let that discourage you. No matter the origin, it still serves our purpose.

Let me just say this. My path is nothing to be proud of. I was cruel and vicious. I caused pain unnecessarily to others and got joy from it. When I saw first-hand how the induction ceremony broke the beautiful mind of that remarkable young woman, I saw the origins of my own resentment and anger. But it was too late for me. There was no redemption coming or deserved. So, I steered my focus and energy to ending the cycle and finding a better way.

After that, I started putting things in place to bring the prophecy into reality. It wasn't easy. Hiding things from my mother got harder and harder. Then an opportunity presented itself.

My daughter, Charmeli, fell pregnant with twins. That was also forbidden as it confuses the line of inheritance. My mother wanted one of the twins terminated. I refused to allow it and took over the care of my daughter. With the help of Timaios and his friends, I distracted my mother away from Earth. That enabled me to deliver the babies myself. I put one twin in the care of my daughter and had the other baby raised as a normal child, hidden from view. My

425

daughter was left in the dark, too. She didn't know she had twins. I hid it all from her. I couldn't tell her what I had done. I saw too much of my mother in her. She was poisoned. On realising that, I put distance between us. However, my mother suspected something wasn't right. And even with the help of Timaios and his friends, she came looking. When my granddaughters were two years old, my mother made plans to return to earth to confront me.

Fearing my mother would not only discover the twins, but also my plans and the remarkable young woman with her baby boy, I took a drastic step. With Timaios' help I caused a malfunction in the mammoth. He had the prototype of the disc my mother used. It gave me control of the mammoth and other things. My mother found herself ejected into space ahead of a traverse. The mammoth ring arrived back at Earth without her. Her body was never found. The disc disappeared with her.

After that, my daughter took up residence in the mammoth ring. That suited me fine as I needed time to complete the plans. The prototype disc gave me some degree of control over the mammoth ring and the defences here on Earth. So, I banished her and the ring. It served both our purposes that no one else knew that. And that has been such until this day. With my daughter and the ring out of the way, I put both the remarkable young woman and her son somewhere where they could grow and thrive until the time was right. I then changed my appearance, left the citadels, and took up with the resistance. There, I nurtured my plans."

A further pause in the projection was met with continued silence.

"About those plans. I knew I could not remove the Veneficans. The void would simply be filled by another tyrant. No, I knew from all that I had learnt that a new system was needed. A system that many of you are familiar with as you've been building it. The final piece will be revealed soon. At the end.

426

As to the identity of the others in this story. Here under the stars, I am finally reunited with that remarkable woman and her son. As too my granddaughter. As per the plan, that son and my granddaughter have joined to produce heirs. Heirs for both their families. A key piece giving legitimacy to what I have planned.

I will share no more, but all will be answered soon.

We have a little time to break bread together again, for one final time.

I give you Tieanna, Dukk, Marr, Ethan, and Ava. Now come meet them."

With that the image disappeared. Helenal stood, turned around and pointed at Tieanna, then Marr, Dukk and the babies in their arms.

3

During the playback Marr and Dukk held hands. Their emotions ran riot. They squeezed each other's hands at times, synchronously, as Helenal's sharing connected the dots. It was both a difficult and exhilarating period. When it ended, they were in shock. As many questions were raised as were answered. But they had no time to get resolve as the crowd was upon them. They all wanted to shake hands.

A little later, when the crowds had retreated in search of food and drink, Marr and Dukk found themselves sitting alone with Helenal.

Before they sat, some of Helenal's supporters had brought them hooded cloaks and insisted they wear them to fend off the cold. They graciously accepted them and put them on.

"You have more questions," Helenal said quietly as she admired the face of Ava in Marr's arms.

Ethan and Ava were both now awake. They were sucking their fingers and watching with pleasure at the flickering colours caused by the bonfires.

"Yes, I do", Marr answered.

After a moment she asked, "Did you summon your daughter and my sister?"

"Yes, and all the Venefica."

"Are you carrying out your mother's wishes?"

"In a manner."

"You are installing new leaders? New tyrants?"

"No. It will be different."

"How?"

"By giving the people, a new guillotine. By giving them the means to keep the elites in check."

"But how?"

"By empowering the people. Not enough so that they rise and install a new tyrant. Just enough so they will be free to make their own way again."

"The families won't accept that."

"They won't have a choice. They will be crippled financially. They will need to engage with their people to survive."

"I don't understand how you will achieve that."

"You will see."

"When?"

"Soon."

Marr sighed with frustration.

Dukk then spoke.

"Why now?" he asked.

"Your grandfather was instrumental in this plan. He only agreed to cooperate on the basis that he would be gone before the end. That time has come."

"What about my father?"

"What about him?"

"He appears pivotal also?"

"In that he fathered you, yes."

"And his death?"

"It was inevitable. He had a lot of enemies."

"But the timing appears to be important."

"How so?"

"Much of what has happened, occurred because of his death."

"Like?"

"Getting the Imhullu. Tieanna being captured. Meeting Craig. Getting the disc. Our Newterratwo backstory."

"Opportunities that presented themselves. His death just made things easier."

Dukk let that sit.

Marr then spoke again. She realised that she had other questions. Deeper questions.

"Why didn't you visit us? Spend time with your great grandchildren?"

"I was afraid that if I met you and your babies, I might not be able to do what must be done. I might back out. So, I had to force my own hand."

"Who raised me?"

"Me until you were two. Then those in the incubators like everyone else."

"Where did my name come from?"

"It is what I called you from the moment you were born."

"Were you there at the test? Did you intervene in my sterilisation."

"Yes."

"You never had the first disc, it disappeared with your mother."

"That is correct. I have another disc. The prototype. My mother didn't know about it."

"So, for all those years, the queen and my sister were locked out of the data centre on mammoth one because the second disc still sat in that room."

"Exactly."

Marr then asked, "Was I always meant to get the second disc?"

"No."

"But you did reconfigure the mantrap and data centre so that I could get in there?"

"Yes, as a precaution should I die."

"When did you do that?"

"When I made the changes that killed my mother."

"But the note. She would have seen it?"

"I made the changes remotely using the prototype disc. The note was put there after she died."

"You were on the mammoth ring after she died?"

"Yes. Just after and not since. We went to the mammoths when they arrived at Earth. There was mayhem trying to figure out what had happened to her. It was easy to slip in and put the note there."

"Why?"

"As a precaution should you have got discovered before I completed my plans."

"A lot of what we've achieved in the last twelve months has been because we had the disc. We could pre-emptively react. It appears your plans needed our activities. And yet, it was by chance that I got the disc?"

"Yes and no. You were trained in a manner that meant you might ignore my request that only Dukk go rescue Tieanna. While not in the plan, you got it. Which meant I could just go into obscurity and let things play out until the time was right. Besides, there are other ways to get you the information you would have needed."

"You gave Dukk's grandfather the message to tip off Tieanna in Mayfield?"

"I did."

"But she didn't come up with the Marduk story?"

"Yes and No. As you have undoubtedly uncovered, my mother was concerned about losing control. She had me nurture the seed. I did that via Tieanna. Doing that and having her seeing me do that helped keep my mother away from Earth while I raised you."

"She saw your actions via Tieanna's implants?"

"Yes."

"But that meant she would see where Tieanna was and see her raising Dukk?"

"Yes and no. Timaios showed me a way I could loop the feed. Not unlike how your bracelets or modified implants work to block the observers. When I wanted it, Tieanna's actual feed was hidden."

"Why then, did you take your own implants out?"

"I never took my implants out. I simply disabled the recording aspect. The cuts and resulting scars were just for show. I didn't want my mother knowing that I knew a way around that feature of the disc. It was to protect Timaios."

"Bartiamos said the original builders of these capabilities mysteriously disappeared."

"That is a lie spun by Timaios to protect his team and his intimate knowledge of the workings of the mammoth."

At that moment there was a commotion to the east side of the space. There were bright lights and some screams.

"Pull your cloaks around you. Hide your babies and your faces. Then follow me," Helenal commanded as she stood up.

"What is going on?" Dukk demanded as he looked about to see what was causing the commotion.

"It is time for me to make amends. Amends for all the pain and suffering caused by my hand. Both before your birth and since by allowing it to continue. It is time for you to step up, ask and listen. It is time for humanity to find its way again."

With that, two of Helenal's supporters stepped forward and escorted her back to the front of the amphitheatre.

Dukk and Marr stood and pulled the cloaks around them and the babies in their arms. They pulled the hoods over their heads. Then they headed after Helenal. She had gone to stand next to the projection box. She was now alone. Marr and Dukk went to her side to support her.

It was now evident what was happening. Large numbers of Venefican sentinels had entered the space. They were corralling everyone back from the focal point of the amphitheatre.

Before they knew it, Helenal, Marr and Dukk were surrounded. Initially the sentinels rushed forward with their weapons raised. Then as quickly as they arrived, they started to walk backwards. They formed a large circle with Helenal, Marr, Dukk and the babies in the centre. Then a gap opened on one side. A line of Veneficans came marching in. Sixty-two of them. Masked and hooded. Two columns. Two columns of sentinels accompanied them. Two of the masked women came towards the centre, escorted by four sentinels. The remaining Venefica and the additional sentinels formed a circle around them all.

Outside the inner circle there were sounds of scuffles and fighting. Helenal pushed Marr and Dukk behind her, then spoke.
  She said, "My people. Do not resist. Stand down. Trust me."
  Her voice echoed around the amphitheatre. The box at their feet was amplifying her voice.

At that moment one of the masked women in the centre laughed and then shouted, "You are all here! You are fools!"
  Then she screamed, "Sentinels, kill them! Kill them all. And bring me that disc."

To Marr, time appeared to slow. When the sentinels rushed forward the first time, Marr thought she heard Helenal utter, "Order Eight Alpha Echo, Execute!".

Instead of firing their weapons, the sentinels pivoted. Those accompanying the Venefica took one each and brought a large knife

432

to their necks. The four sentinels accompanying the two in the middle, stepped between them and Helenal.

4

"Seize these two and unmask them all," Helenal said in a calm manner.

Once more her voice was amplified for all to hear.

The sentinels holding the Venefica did as instructed as did two of the sentinels in front of Helenal. Their masks were ripped off.

Marr looked on. She was seeing her mother and sister for the first time. They had no make-up. Their faces were sad and furrowed. She saw the resemblance.

"Hello, mother. It has been far too short a time!" Charmeli said with menace.

Her voice was also amplified.

Helenal chuckled. She then replied. Her voice was soft and slow.

"It has, my daughter. Thank you for bringing the sentinels to me. The order I just gave was voice activated. I would have never been able to give it without you bringing them directly to me."

"What order?"

"A failsafe installed long ago. In case of mutiny. The sentinels will now do whatever is needed to protect me. Then once I name my heir, they will immediately kill all Venefica and Filia. They will wipe the slate clean. As we speak, that order is being relayed to all corners of this planet and beyond. Anywhere there is a sentinel. Filia are being apprehended and will soon follow your fate."

"Impossible. How?" Charmeli asked dismissively.

"The order targets the special implants you all have."

"Rubbish!"

"Your hubris is your downfall."

At that moment, Ethan gave a squawk. His hands scratched against the cloak covering his face. He was protesting and wanted to see the shimmering lights again.

"Is that a baby? Who are you hiding behind these cloaks," Charmeli asked.

"Charmeli, not one but two babies. The babies are your grandchildren. They are being held in the arms of your daughter and her companion, the father of your heirs," Helenal said gently.

"What is this nonsense? Who are you? Reveal yourselves!" Charmeli demanded.

"Some know them as Dukk and Marr. You might also know them as David and Maria," Helenal replied.

Marr and Dukk pulled back their hoods.

"Charmeli, may I introduce you to your daughter. Cieloi, may I introduce you to your sister. She is older by twenty minutes."

Charmeli gasped.

"NO! Shoot her," Cieloi shouted at the sentinels in front of them.

The sentinels stood still.

Helenal giggled and then said, "My forsaken granddaughter, Cieloi, I see you do not share your sister's intelligence."

"What is the meaning of this, you old witch?" Charmeli shouted.

"There is truth in that statement, that be for sure. And it is time to make amends."

Helenal then turned to face the crowd. They were still being held back by the sentinels. She said, "It is time to launch the broadcast."

She then turned back to face Marr and Dukk.

A tone rang out in their implants. A sound they were all familiar with ahead of a citadel broadcast. It rang out in every implant, in every person in the citadels and in orbit. Those that were asleep were woken. All others stopped what they were doing. The broadcast was also

434

already in transit. It was moving through the relays to be viewable in every corner of the Galaxy. The broadcast was also on its way to elite complexes. Even those in the new settlements on Earth would soon receive the broadcast via the devices in their housing units.

The box at the focal point of the amphitheatre activated again. The same nondescript face of a woman appeared. Screens in the citadels were now all showing the same image. As before, the woman transformed into Helenal by the end of the first sentence.

Here is what was said.

"My name is Helenal. I am Venefican, I am also part of the resistance, and I am here to set you free. My right to do this will be explained in a video that will be shared via the archives.

As of this moment the rule of twelve is no more. By the end of this broadcast the surveillance and controls will have been permanently disabled. Sentinels will now work for you and not against you. You are now free to organise yourselves.

Temporary governance bodies will take over until you transition to self-elected local representatives. Citadels will now operate independently. You will manage your own production, security, utilities, services, and trade agreements. A selected number of experienced labourers of various designations have just been notified as temporary representatives within this structure. You will have six months to re-organise yourselves and hold local elections.

A separate temporary governance structure has been established to reallocate the intergalactic resources of the Veneficans. It will have twelve months to complete its assignment. The Venefican resources include the sentinels, the mammoth ring, and all accompanying craft. Each temporary citadel governance group must elect three representatives to join others for a monthly gathering of this reallocation governance group. In a moment, I will introduce you to the joint chair of that gathering.

Forbidden material is now accessible to all via the archives.

Observers, your current contribution is no longer required. You are to collect your things from your h-pods and report to the emergency accommodation areas in the ports. You will be processed and assessed for re-integration into labour roles.

The test at the age of ten shall cease immediately as will the current operations of the incubation centres and other population control measures. The workings of which will be made public via the archives. There will be no further killings.

For those under the age of sixteen you shall be withdrawn from the labour rotation immediately and return to schooling. The current school curriculum has just been deleted. Members of the resistance will be making alternatives available.

Management of citadel operations will pass immediately onto senior supervisors.

The EU is no longer legal currency here or anywhere. All accounts have just been deleted. Crypto will remain as the only legal currency. Labourers here on Earth and everywhere else have just received crypto equivalent to five times the earnings for the years of service given since the age of ten. This crypto has been taken from the citadel reserves.

Citadel accommodation pods and retail units are now available for sale through open bidding. Current occupants have the right of first refusal on the final market price.

Citadel farms, orchards, and stocks will also be available for sale. Incumbent keepers have the first right to match the final market price.

The temporary citadel governance bodies shall see that this is done fairly.

Proceeds from the sales of these items will be allocated in this manner. Seventy five percent must go to the borough to which it relates. The remainder to the citadel.

You may have heard rumours of the establishment of new settlements outside the citadels. This is more than a rumour. The Atesoughton family has used much of their means to build them. They are now a viable alternative to citadels. You can now choose where you invest your crypto and what life you want to build for yourself.

For those of you away from Earth. If you wish to return, you may do so. You will be welcome again.

Leases and debt on rigs and other large transportation equipment have just been terminated. Ownership will immediately go to the crews.

This final part of my message goes to elite family members and their staff. You no longer hold any special privileges in the citadels. It is revoked. You are free to govern as you wish your planetary settlements and any complexes here on Earth outside the citadels. The citadel inner circles are now open to all. You have one hour to collect your essentials and leave. The sentinels will ensure you do that. Your properties will be put up for sale by open bid. The temporary citadel governance bodies shall see that this is done fairly. The Venefican mammoth ring now sits in orbit to protect Earth should this be to your disliking.

Finally, I promised to share with you who would chair the temporary governance group to reallocate Venefican resources. I will do that now. But before I do, I will share a further truth with you. Most of you were led to believe that you couldn't have children. You were told that it was too dangerous for humans and humanity. That was a lie. Here with me now, I have proof. Two of your fellow labourers have indeed proven that wrong. Many have heard of these two. They are Marr and Dukk. Their children are Ethan and Ava."

With that the projection changed. It was no longer the artificially created head and shoulders of Helenal, but the actual image of Marr and Dukk with their babies in their arms. The world was now seeing them through Helenal's eyes using the mammoth ring and disc technology.

After a minute, the image faded, and the projection stopped.

The gathering was in silent awe. Those that played small parts in the plan now saw how their pieces fitted together.

Dukk and Marr stood holding hands. They were looking at each other. Tears formed. They lent in and kissed. Then they looked up at Helenal. She smiled. But it wasn't a full smile. There was a sadness there.

"What?" Marr said having noticed the sadness.

Helenal turned around to face Charmeli and Cieloi.

Charmeli was in tears, too. She now looked at Helenal and simply asked, "Why?"

"Why what?" Helenal asked in reply.

"Why are you doing this? What is this all for? What makes you think what you have done is better? What makes you so sure that you have the answers as opposed to what we've been doing for over three hundred and fifty years?"

Helenal smiled, then lifted herself as best she could. She spoke slowly and in a manner that suggested she had dug deep into her last reserves.

"I was raised to think I was a God. When I realised that, I started looking. I asked myself, 'If I was a God, what would I do?' To find the answer I read everything I could find. I learned about the past. I realised that if I was to be a God, I needed to act like one. So, I just pulled out pieces from ancient old stories of how to organise and how to shape society. I found pieces on how to orientate oneself towards a higher order. Then it dawned on me. If you look closer, there isn't a lot of detail in what I just did. I just took away some of the key hurdles. The way forward is going to be heavily reliant on the people themselves. We've already seen this at play in the settlements that the

Atesoughtons have created. Some of them have failed, some failed dismally, but others have succeeded. The only way forward is for the likes of us, to stop thinking we are gods. To start looking towards a higher order and get out of the way of humanity. Let it look after itself."

"Rubbish," Charmeli growled.

She then spat at Helenal.

The spit hit Helenal in the face. As she wiped it away, she said, "We are at the end."

Marr thought about that for a moment. She looked at Ava as she did. An awful thought occurred to her. When Helenal shared her plans, she made no mention of herself.

Marr rushed forward. A sentinel stepped in and held her back.

Dukk also stepped forward to assist Marr. Another sentinel stepped over and prevented him from getting any closer.

"What are you doing?" Marr demanded as she struggled to get free. Which wasn't easy with Ava in one arm.

Helenal smiled and said, "My time is done. I will die soon regardless. I want this. It is my way to make amends for years of evil. I must be the one to clean the slate. I already have blood on my hands. The blood of my sisters will be on me too. With all that gone, you will be able to rebuild."

"No, there must be another way. We need you," Marr said in a teary manner.

"When you two were born, my only insight was that I should devote the rest of my time to bringing the two of you, together. And then destroying my sisterhood. That is all. What happens next is up to you."

Helenal then turned away from Marr. As she did, she said, "Make way" to the sentinels. The two remaining sentinels stepped out of the way.

Marr struggled again. In the struggle, Marr's knife came loose. It fell to the ground.

Helenal then put her arms in the air and shouted, "Sentinels, hear me! Take your blades and strike true. Correct for all the wrongs. End the pain brought upon others. Bring this to an end. End the Veneficans. I name Marr as my heir and relinquish my authority. Fulfil the order."

What happened next, happened very quickly.

Marr shouted, "No," and pushed hard against the sentinel. She managed to free herself but was off balance. She stumbled.

Charmeli was moving before Helenal had finished her command. She snatched up Marr's knife. Just as Helenal finished, Charmeli shouted, "I will prevail!"

Charmeli then swung the knife in an upwards motion slicing through Helenal's throat.

Helenal fell to the ground.

Marr shifted her weight to correct the stumble but then tripped and ended up in a heap on top of Helenal. Ava had come loose and rolled away.

In the circle around them the sentinels, swished their blades through the throats of the Venefica they were holding.

The two remaining sentinels in the centre had stepped forward. They slashed their knives at Charmeli and at Cieloi.

Since Charmeli was already in motion she avoided the attempt on her life. Cieloi was not so lucky. The sentinel's blow was direct and terminal.

The blade in Charmeli's hand was now moving down. Charmeli was driving it towards Marr's back.

Dukk reacted instinctively. He lifted himself up and shoved the sentinel with his feet. He then flicked over, moving Ethan under one arm as his body turned. Once back on his feet he Jumped forward. His momentum carried him towards and over the women. As he flew past, he used his free hand to grab Charmeli's arm and twist it with all his might.

The blade swung around just in time. The butt of the knife hammered into Marr's back.

Charmeli's forward motion brought her directly on top of the blade. It drove through her chest and pierced her heart.

Dukk rolled, put Ethan down and got to his feet. He raced back towards Marr where he violently pulled Charmeli out of the way. He then lifted Marr into his arms.

Tears flooded down their cheeks as they realised that they were ok. Marr then pulled out of the embrace. She reached down for Ava and gave her to Dukk. She then nodded towards Ethan. Dukk went over to lift him.

Marr now bent over Helenal and turned her on to her back. Helenal was already dead. Marr grimaced once, force back the tears, then stood, removed her cloak, and placed it over Helenal's body.

The others now flooded into the space. Annee, Bazzer, Mentor and Luna. Bognath, Suzzona, and Tieanna. Craig, Emeelie, and Eleettra. Trence, Kimince, Jeeves and the girls. And the resistance leaders.

There were hugs and tears. The scene was awash with emotions. Grief and joy. Around them the sentinels had already started dragging the dead Veneficans towards the bonfires.

In the citadels, parties were erupting in bars and on corners. There was confusion too at the sight of sentinels killing the Filia. But also, as the observers and elites struggled to fathom what had just happened.

Eventually Dukk and Marr freed themselves from the group and stepped slightly away. Just outside the amphitheatre they spotted a seat carved in stone. It looked old and slightly out of place.

They walked over to it and sat down.

They embraced and kissed.

Ethan and Ava squirmed between them inside the embrace. With being passed around and with the noise and mayhem, it hadn't taken long before they got anxious and demanded the arms of their parents once more.

Dukk and Marr pulled back from the kiss. They then looked down at the faces of their babies in the arms between them.

"What next?" Marr asked.

"I guess we ask and listen," Dukk answered.

Marr smiled and looked up.

A brightness and warmth washed over them.

The sun was rising. It was the start of a new day.

The End

Continue your awakening at RuleOfTwelve.com.